The Girl Who JUST APPEARED

Jonathan Harvey comes from Liverpool and is a multi-award-winning writer of plays, films, sitcoms and Britain's longest-running drama serial.

Jonathan's theatre work includes the award-winning *Beautiful Thing* (Bush Theatre, Donmar Warehouse, Duke of York's. Winner: John Whiting Award. Nominated: Olivier Award for Best Comedy), *Babies* (Royal Court Theatre. Winner: *Evening Standard* Award for Most Promising Playwright. Winner: George Devine Award) and *Rupert Street Lonely Hearts Club* (English Touring Theatre, Donmar Warehouse, Criterion Theatre. Winner: *Manchester Evening News* Award for Best New Play. Winner: *City Life Magazine* Award for Best New Play). Other plays include *Corrie!* (Lowry Theatre and National Tour. Winner: *Manchester Evening News* Award for Best Special Entertainment), *Canary* (Liverpool Playhouse, Hampstead Theatre and English Touring Theatre), *Hushabye Mountain* (English Touring Theatre, Hampstead Theatre), *Guiding Star* (Everyman Theatre, Royal National Theatre), *Boom Bang a Bang* (Bush Theatre), *Mohair* (Royal Court Theatre Upstairs) and *Wildfire* (Royal Court Theatre Upstairs). Jonathan also co-wrote the musical *Closer to Heaven* with the Pet Shops Boys.

For television Jonathan created and wrote three series of the BAFTA-nominated *Gimme Gimme Gimme* for the BBC, two series of *Beautiful People* (winner: Best Comedy, Banff TV Festival), the double-BAFTA-nominated *Best Friends, Von Trapped!* and *Birthday Girl*.

Jonathan has also written for the shows *Rev* (winner: BAFTA for Best Sitcom), *Shameless*, *The Catherine Tate Show*, *At Home With the Braithwaites*, *Lilies* and *Murder Most Horrid*. To date he has written over a hundred episodes of *Coronation Street*.

Jonathan's film work includes *Beautiful Thing* for Film Four (Outstanding Film, GLAAD Awards, New York; Best Film, London Lesbian and Gay Film Festival; Best Screenplay, Fort Lauderdale Film Festival; *Grand Prix*, Paris Film Festival; Jury Award, San Paolo International Film Festival).

But perhaps most telling of all he also won the Spacehopper Championships at Butlins Pwllheli in 1976.

His novels are *All She Wants*, *The Confusion of Karen Carpenter* and *The Girl Who Just Appeared*.

JONATHAN HARVEY

The Girl Who JUST APPEARED

PAN BOOKS

First published 2014 by Pan Books
an imprint of Pan Macmillan, a division of Macmillan Publishers Limited
Pan Macmillan, 20 New Wharf Road, London N1 9RR
Basingstoke and Oxford
Associated companies throughout the world
www.panmacmillan.com

ISBN 978-1-4472-3846-1

A CIP catalogue record for this book is available from the British Library.

Typeset by Birdy Book Design
Printed and bound by CPI Group (UK) Ltd, Croydon, CR0 4YY

Visit **www.panmacmillan.com** to read more about all our books
and to buy them. You will also find features, author interviews and
news of any author events, and you can sign up for e-newsletters
so that you're always first to hear about our new releases.

For Paul Hunt

ACKNOWLEDGEMENTS

Continued thanks to Wayne Brookes, Camilla Elworthy, Jeremy Trevathan and all at Pan Macmillan who continue to believe in me and publish my books and give me nice dinners. I am incredibly grateful. Also to my agent Gordon Wise for steering me in the right direction. And of course to Michael McCoy and Alec Drysdale for looking after the other side of things.

Thank you to Tim Berners-Lee for inventing the internet. Without it I would have had to go to the library and read books and newspapers to gen up on the issues involved in this book. Nor would I have had the distraction of Facebook or Twitter and the lovely people therein who say things about my books, which is always lovely. Or often rude.

A book is written in isolation but researched in company and to the following people I thank you for letting me pick your brains at various points along the way, or for letting me use your funny anecdotes, or just plain being encouraging and lovely: Jan McVerry, Carmel Morgan, Damon Rochefort, Lee Anderson, Kathy Burke, Emma Clarke, Paris Lees, Annie Wallace, Angela Sinden and Richard Foord. Oh and not forgetting the 4 o'clock Club – put my lights on if I'm not there!

To Alan Toner (Irish Alan) for letting me use his name. Well, he practically forced me . . . And to Jojo Moyes for offering sage advice, over a very nice lunch, about writing dual time-frame novels.

I started playing around with writing Darren's diary many many years ago, before I had written anything else really. I showed these scribblings, done in an exercise book in biro, to my friend Patti Burton who was so encouraging to me before anyone else was. She probably doesn't realize this, or even remember it, but thank you Patti for your belief then and now. And finally I have found something to do with his story!

This book is about a woman searching for her family because she feels she doesn't belong. I'm lucky enough to come from a strong, loving family and I appreciate how rare that can be, so thank you to Maureen, Brian, Tim, Shona and all the Harveys of Liverpool.

And finally to Paul Hunt. The wind beneath my bingo wings. Thank you for, well, everything.

HOLLY

PROLOGUE

1990

This was going to be my Best. Day. Ever. Mummy had brought me to London and we were going to see a matinee performance of *Miss Saigon* at the Theatre Royal, Drury Lane. I loved saying, 'The Theatre Royal, Drury Lane,' and thought that every building or house should be described like this. So, I was in year four at Mattocks Park, but if anyone ever asked me which school I went to, I'd reply, 'Mattocks Park, Alderman Road.' I thought it made me sound like a movie star. And there was usually nothing movie star about my life, living as I did in a boring semi, in a boring cul-de-sac, with boring parents, in a boring market town. I lived in Tring. Tring didn't even sound like a proper place; it sounded like the noise the bell on my bicycle made. Sometimes I pronounced it with a mock French accent to make it sound more exotic. *Tringue.* Or sometimes *Trinje.* Some thought that was pretentious for an eight-year-old, but as Mummy said to the neighbours on more than one occasion, 'She's not exactly a conventional child.'

I knew it wasn't very nice to describe your parents as 'boring', especially when your mum brought you on exciting trips like this one, but this really was the most interesting thing she had ever done *in her life*. And I'm not exaggerating. She used to say I exaggerated all the time. Like the time I told her I'd seen a masked gunman coming into school when actually it was Mr Roberts (the Welsh one, not the Scottish one) in his costume for the Dick Turpin assembly. Or the time I told her Mrs Tipping had given birth to a pussycat called Brandy when actually all she had done was bring her cat into class because she was on her way to the vet's and it was sat in her lap and then it jumped off. Mum just used to reply with a reminder that one of the Ten Commandments was 'Thou shalt not exaggerate.' It was right up there between bearing false witness and coveting your neighbour's ox. But really, Mummy and Daddy were really, *really* boring. And what's more, they were really, *really* old. When I was born, Mummy was forty-two. *Forty-two*. That was old enough to be a granny. I'm surprised the doctors and nurses didn't go, 'My God, woman, what are you doing here? You should be, like, *dead*.' My parents were always the oldest of all the kids' parents at school. So if they came to sports day, or a concert, everyone assumed they were my grandparents. It was really, really embarrassing. Everyone else's mum and dad wore jeans and puffa jackets. Mine wore sensible shoes and grey hair. Yuck.

The other really embarrassing thing was that Mummy was the local church organist. In the week she was a secretary at the nearby college of further education, but come Sunday, she was sat at the Gray & Davison three-keyboard 'monster' (her words, not mine. An organ was an organ was an organ as far as I was concerned) in her red cassock and Persil-white surplice, hands flying. 'Mrs Mills with pipes' my daddy used to call her, though I had no idea what this meant.

And she wasn't just the organist, oh no! She was also the

'musical director'. She had invented this term herself, she claimed, because usually a man being in charge of a choir was called a 'choir master', but the female equivalent would have been 'choir mistress', and – although she wouldn't elaborate on why – she didn't feel that was a very good idea. She was out every Thursday and Friday evening at choir practice, and if there was a wedding on Saturday, she would be out for the afternoon then too. You might think this would have given me a break from her musical-directory ways, but no. And why? Because *I was in her blessed blooming choir*. I know. Mortifying. I hated it. I had to wear the smelly cassock thing too and it itched my neck. And she made me wear pigtails because she felt that was the best look with a cassock. My life was intertwined with hers in a constant round of singing, processioning, cassocking and more singing.

With Thursday to Sunday taken up with churchy things, you might think we got some respite at home Monday to Wednesday. No such luck! Monday and Tuesday were fine, but Wednesday she always had the radio on for a teatime programme called *Choral Evensong*. And she would sit in the living room beating time with a knitting needle, singing along with the hymns. *And she expected me to do the same*. The noise of the organ blasting out of the radio, the only time she would have it on full blast, was like the sound of a thousand people being murdered. And that was no exaggeration.

Monday night was Tring Penguins night, my weekly swimming club, and even there I couldn't escape Mum's churchy ways. When I emerged from the changing rooms to go poolside and join my fellow Penguins, Mummy would shout from the spectators' gallery, 'What locker, Holly?'

And I wasn't allowed to reply with the number of the locker in which I had left my clothes; I had to reply with the equivalent hymn for the number, taken from *Hymns Ancient and Modern*. So if I'd left my stuff in locker number 15, I would have to shout back, '"Before the Ending of the Day"!' Or had I used number 197, it would be, '"The King of Love My Shepherd Is"!' Honestly, the looks I got from the other children when I did this.

And my enforced musical education didn't end there. I had to have piano and cello lessons, and Mrs Baxter who taught me cello smelt of cheese. And I loathed cheese.

So you can understand why I officially hated my life.

Sometimes I would look at my dad while he ate his TV dinner on his stained tray with the beanbag underneath as we watched yet another episode of *Songs of Praise* and I could see the look of vague detachment in his eyes. As if his glasses were watching the programme, to appease Mummy, but behind the glass, his eyes were elsewhere. They were seeing a beach in the South Pacific; they were playing football at Wembley for Tring Athletic – anything other than this, our miserable musical existence. And I felt for, and just like, him. I'd look in the mirror sometimes and see an alien. Like I'd landed from another planet into this weird world I neither liked nor understood. I would visit school friends' houses and wish I lived there instead, with their mess and their spilt ketchup, and their boy band music and their laughter, not a hymn in sight. And my friends would assume that I was really religious, and that my family were, whereas in fact I always suspected Mummy wasn't that fussed about Jesus and the whole God situation. Her love of the church was really just her love of the music. And yes, it glorified God in the extreme and so on, but really she was in it for the pedals.

I was very excited about going to see *Miss Saigon* as I had borrowed the CD from the local library and knew all the words because I had sung along to them non-stop in my bedroom for two weeks, even though I wasn't sure what half of them meant. Plus there was a lady in it called Lea Salonga, which had to be *the* best name in the whole of the universe. Mummy disagreed with me on this – she thought the best name was a crumbly old actress called Googie Withers – but undeterred, I would often practise signing:

love Lea Salonga

in my autograph book for hours. One day I was going to change my name to Holly Salonga and star in *Miss Saigon*, even though Mummy said that wasn't a possibility because I wasn't 'oriental' enough. She had said the same when the local amateur dramatic group were putting on *The King and I* and I wanted to be Tuptim.

My favourite song in the show we were going to see was 'The Heat Is On In Saigon'. I had worked out a whole dance routine to it, using cushions, which I pretended were pom-poms, and lots of high kicks. I was beside myself with excitement that we were finally, finally going to experience it!

But first we were going to do something else incredibly exciting. After taking the train from Tring to London Euston, we were going to have a pre-theatre lunch at . . . McDonald's!!!! I had never been before. We didn't have one in Tring. They had them in Hemel Hempstead and Aylesbury and Leighton Buzzard, but not where we lived. I would get so jealous of other children in my class saying how brilliant their lives were because they'd had a shopping trip to Hemel and gorged on eighty-three Big Macs. I had never had that pleasure.

Till now.

Mummy said I could have whatever I wanted. This was

quite out of character for her – usually she liked to decree what was best for me and what course of action I should take – but today she seemed remarkably 'couldn't-care-less'. She was like a different person. I would have to let her take me to London more often if this was the effect it had on her. She hadn't mentioned church or the choir once. This new her didn't really suit her – she seemed ill at ease, nervous – but *I* really couldn't care less. We were having *fast food*.

I ordered a hamburger, a Filet-O-Fish (my friend Kasey Woodlands had told me they were the tastiest thing *ever*), medium fries and a strawberry milkshake. Mummy plumped for a Big Mac (so I could see one close up), no fries and coffee. With the drinks rattling on the tray, Mummy carried them over to a corner table for two. I looked out of the window onto Leicester Square. It was teeming with people rushing about doing London-y things: families on days out, women with huge shopping bags with fancy names on, coach parties in matching cagoules, a tramp eating a discarded sandwich on a bench with a few pigeons waiting hungrily at his feet. High above on the cinema hoardings were massive adverts for all the latest films: *Ghost*, *Home Alone*. I was almost tempted to ask if we could go and see one of them, but that would have meant forgoing my beloved future namesake, Miss Salonga, so I kept quiet.

Mummy seemed to be working up to saying something. This, too, was out of character for her. As a musical director, she was used to speaking to large groups, and as my mother, she was never backwards in coming forwards about offering her opinion. But something was very different today. It immediately made me feel a bit anxious.

I bit into my Filet-O-Fish. Kasey Woodlands was right: it was like biting into heaven.

But then Mummy spoke.

'You know your cousin Tracey?' she asked in an unfamiliarly tiny voice.

I nodded. Of course I knew my cousin. She was a total swot and wrote thank-you cards to my mummy at Christmas that said things like:

You're my favourite aunty, Aunty Jean. And do you know what else? You light up a room. Like a big, sparkly silver bracelet, catching the light and twinkling so everyone knows it's there.

I couldn't stand her. Plus she called me Alien. To my *face*.

'Well, don't you think she looks like Aunty Beryl?'

Of course she looked like Aunty Beryl. They both had red hair. I had bitten into my hamburger. It was *to die for*.

'I mean, there's no mistaking they're mother and daughter, with that lovely auburn hair of theirs.'

'The boys at school call her Ginger Minge,' I pointed out. I had no idea what this meant.

'Oh, that's nice, dear,' she said.

Which made me think she didn't know what it meant either, because when the boys called her it, she more often than not called them 'gayboys' and then burst into tears.

'We don't look alike, do we, Holly?' She smiled.

No, thank God. I'd much rather have honey-coloured hair than grey, thank you very much. I shook my head, my mouth full of hot fries and strawberry milkshake. They went so well together.

'Well . . . there's a reason for that.'

I stopped chewing. I sat there with my cheeks bulging like a chipmunk. What was she going to say next?

'And the reason for that is . . .'

She looked like she was finding this the most difficult bit to say.

'I haven't got grey hair?' I said through the mixture of strawberry and chips.

'Don't speak with your mouth full, dear. It's not nice. You know it's not nice.'

I nodded and quickly swallowed my food. After which I burped.

She looked furious. 'Holly!' But then she looked like she was trying her hardest to be nice again. 'No, the reason we don't look anything like each other is . . . you're adopted.'

She gave me a broad smile. Then took her first bite of Big Mac.

I froze. I couldn't physically move my arms or legs or any muscles in my face. I held my Filet-O-Fish in mid-air in my left hand and the milkshake carton aloft in my right. I literally couldn't move.

Mummy was making appreciative sounds. 'Well, I can see why you were so keen to come here, Holly. This is rather delicious.'

I looked at my food. And as I moved my eyes, so the feeling in my body returned and I placed the burger and drink on the plastic table. Outside, I was aware of the hustle and bustle, the noise, someone busking with an accordion. The food and drink now seemed like the most unappealing of things. Like I was looking down at a trayful of vomit with horse dung on the side.

'I imagine this has come as somewhat of a shock, dear.'

I wanted to nod, but actually all I kept thinking was, So I'm not going mad after all! No wonder I don't . . . fit in!

And she proceeded to tell me how my real mummy hadn't been clever enough to look after me and was a bit stupid and probably fat and smoked, and so I had been taken away from her when I was a few months old and given to Jean and Ted, who knew all about looking after babies because they had a garden and knew their way around a washing machine. She continued in the vein of how lucky I was that I'd ended up in sunny Tring, in a house with loft insulation, instead of running feral in some Northern backstreet, a world of smog, chimneys and port and lemon.

'What does "feral" mean?' was all I could think to say.

'Wild, dear. You'd probably have had a soiled nappy and not had it changed for days. You were born into a world of . . . black-and-white *Coronation Street*, and now you're . . .' she seemed to be losing confidence with this analogy, '. . . in the sunnier climes of . . . Oh, what was that lovely situation comedy with oojameflip? Julia McKenzie.'

I had no idea.

'*Fresh Fields!*' she shouted, a big grin on her face. 'I do like her jumpsuits,' she added. She did. She actually said that.

And from nowhere I found myself crying. I couldn't stop myself. I was bawling really loudly and the people on the adjoining tables started looking over and I could see Mummy going the colour of a beetroot.

'Try and be quiet, Holly. I know it's a shock, but . . . even so . . .'

She passed me some paper napkins to dry my eyes. I dabbed at them a bit and eventually started to calm down. She obviously thought I was devastated by the news, but actually I wasn't feeling sad that I was different from other children; I was weepy because things were slipping into place, and that suddenly there was a reason for why I had always felt so . . . alien. Gosh, even Tracey had called me it on several occasions. Did she know?

I had known I didn't look anything like my parents. I had known that they were at least ten years older than everyone else in my class's parents. I didn't like the house in Tring and going to church and wearing pigtails. And now I knew why.

These were happy tears. I was crying with relief that I wasn't stupid. Not that Mummy interpreted it as that. She tried to placate me by passing me my strawberry milkshake. I was now intrigued. If she wasn't my real mother, who on earth was?

'What was my real mummy like?' I asked between strawberry slurps.

Her eyes narrowed. 'Let's not talk about her. She's not important.'

Oh. But she was important to me, surely? If she was, like, my *mother*? And maybe I would love her, if I could just meet her. Even if she was fat and smoked and you could see her bra through her blouse and she did common things like wee in the street after going to a pub because she couldn't wait till she got home and she laughed her head off while doing it. But somehow I could sense there was no point telling Mummy that.

Everything in my life felt like it had suddenly changed. This woman before me who had for eight solid years claimed to be my mother, and done a really good job of lying to everyone that she was, had suddenly told me she wasn't. I had abided by her rules the whole of my life and suddenly I thought, Maybe now I don't have to.

'You know, this changes nothing,' she said, taking a slurp of her coffee, then realizing it was still too hot and wincing.

Really? I thought. You think so?

I turned to the people on the next table. They were two ladies, younger than Mummy but still really old. One had her hair scraped up in a pineapple; it was blonde on the ends and black at the roots. Her friend was wearing a lopsided beret. I wondered if they were French. Pineapple Head saw me looking and smiled nervously, no doubt hoping I wasn't going to burst out crying again.

I smiled at her. Then I said, 'I'm adopted.'

She didn't react. She turned her head towards Mummy.

'Holly! Stop showing off!'

'But I am!'

'Holly, stop this!'

The women on the next table started talking in whispers. Mummy put her burger down and announced it was time to leave.

I told her I hadn't finished my Filet-O-Fish. I hardly ever answered back.

She said she didn't care and that she was going to the theatre and whether I wanted to join her was up to me, but she had the tickets, so there.

I grabbed the fish and ate it on the way.

All the way there I kept thinking, I could run away now. I could run away and go wherever I want. She won't be able to stop me. This woman is not my mother; in fact, she has nothing to do with me. I hate her. I've always hated her, and now I know why. *She is not my mother*.

But I wouldn't run away from her. She had the tickets in her handbag.

And. In her defence. She had given me my first McDonald's.

And. She was taking me to see *Miss Saigon*, and it wasn't even my birthday.

In the packed foyer of the Theatre Royal, Drury Lane, I made a beeline for the merchandise stall. Mummy hurried to keep up with me. Possibly relieved I was no longer crying, she linked my arm, something she *never* did, and said quietly, 'Ooh, look at all this, Holly. Isn't it lovely?'

I nodded, and replied quietly, 'I'd like the cast recording.'

This was so unlike me. I would usually have had to beg and cajole and plead, not just announce, 'I would like . . .'

But it worked. Mummy nodded.

'And the souvenir programme.'

Again she nodded.

'And the T-shirt.'

Again success. I didn't ask for anything else as I didn't want to push it.

The woman working on the stall eyed me awkwardly. She looked to Mummy. 'You do know this show is really recommended for sixteen-year-olds and over?'

Mummy paled.

I jumped in. 'I am sixteen!' I insisted. 'I'm a primordial dwarf!'

I'm not sure the woman knew what that meant.

Mummy was a stickler for rules. I would never have been allowed to go and see a 'fifteen' film, but she knew she was in no position to argue today. This was meant to be the best day of my life. In many ways it still was. But she wasn't to know that. She thought she had ruined my life, not improved it. And so she kept smiling at the usherettes, who eyed me with equal suspicion, and muttering, 'I know she doesn't look sixteen, but she is!'

Eventually we took our seats. The show was amazing and incredible and beautiful, and Lea Salonga was everything I wanted her to be and more. I didn't like the woman in the row in front of us who turned round and told me to stop singing along to the songs. And Mum told me (again) to stop showing off when I replied insolently, 'I'm adopted!'

But unfortunately we only stayed for the first half. Mummy made us leave in the interval because there were too many women in it in bikinis.

'Bikinis,' she repeated on the train home, 'and high heels.'

I looked out of the window. So what?

'They were prostitutes, Holly.'

I tutted. But then put on my innocent face. 'What's a "prostitute", Mummy?'

She flustered. I knew full well what a prostitute was: Collette O'Hara who sat on my table for mixed-ability English had told me. 'It's someone who's paid to sleep with someone else.'

'Oh. Sounds a bit boring,' I'd replied.

And again I looked out of the window.

'Mary Magdalene was a prostitute,' she added in hushed tones. As if this was the worst thing in the world.

I didn't care. She had ruined my day, my *life* by making me miss the second act of the show. I was feeling mutinous.

'What, Jesus's girlfriend?'

'She was not his girlfriend! Jesus didn't have a girlfriend!'

'Was he gay like Uncle Peter?'

'*Holly, stop this.*' And then she added, 'Uncle Peter's not gay. He and Colin are just judo partners.'

She looked out of the window, alarmed. I thought she might add, quietly, 'I *think*.'

We continued the journey home in silence. At Tring Station, she phoned Aunty Beryl from a payphone to ask her to come and pick us up, as we were earlier than planned and Dad was playing golf all day. Aunty Beryl arrived in her Golf Polo. Cousin Tracey was sat in the back.

As I climbed in next to her, I saw Aunty Beryl mouthing to Mummy, 'Have you told her?'

And Mummy nodding.

I glared at Tracey. Who smiled back malevolently. She knew. She did. She *knew*.

And then Mummy, putting her seat belt on in the passenger seat, turned round and smiled at Tracey.

'Hello, Tracey! My little ginger minge! How are you?'

Aunty Beryl didn't speak to Mummy for two weeks.

ONE

2013

From the *Hemel Gazette*:

**ELSPETH JEAN SMITH (JEAN) Passed away peacefully
and with dignity on 26 April 2013, aged 73 years. Dearly
loved mum of Holly, and treasured wife of the late Ted. She
will be sorely missed by all who knew her. A service will
be held at St Dunstan's Church, Tring, on Monday 6 May
at 11.30 a.m., followed by cremation at Chilterns Crema-
torium. Refreshments afterwards at the family home.
Donations if desired to the Alzheimer's Society.**

I stared out of the window, at the path, a mirror in rain,
and pictured him standing there, as he was last night. He'd
come in his car, straight after his concert. He was still wearing
his tux and dicky bow, though it was untied, and the neck of
his shirt was undone. In his hand were twenty midnight-red
roses.

'Marry me, Holly.'

As the youth of today said, WTF?!

'Jude, the timing.'

17

His face crumpled, an unmade bed.

'What, my rhythm?' And he said it again, slightly more staccato: 'Marry . . . me . . . Ho . . . lly?'

I rolled my eyes. Typical classical violinist.

'No, Jude. It's my mum's funeral tomorrow. I wasn't expecting you till the morning.'

Which explained why I was stood on the drive in my nightie. Well, I say nightie – it was an oversized Care Bears T-shirt I'd found at Camden Market. Jude didn't like me wearing it in bed because he said it made him feel like a sex offender.

'But I thought this might cheer you up.'

He was a pathetic unmade bed now, yellow beneath the street light that used to keep Mum awake as her curtains were so thin.

'Jude, this isn't working.'

Now he was a pathetic unmade yellow waterbed that was going to spring a leak. I was sure he was about to start crying.

'I can wait,' he said, a white dove of a sentence, offering peace, pleading, *Please don't humiliate me, Holly. Not when I've driven all this way to see you.*

But I was resolute.

'I don't want to wait, Jude. It's over.'

His eyes had widened then, and that's when I saw he wasn't going to cry, but get very, very angry. Indignant that I'd dared turn him down. Hacked off that he'd driven all this way to be . . . rejected?

I was snapped out of the memory by Aunty Beryl.

'What's out there that's so interesting?' she enquired, peering through the net curtains.

'Nothing. Just thinking.'

She straightened out the nets and with a strain said, 'I'm very disappointed Jude couldn't come today.'

'He could. I just didn't want him to. We split up.'

She looked genuinely shocked. I didn't see why. Jude and I had only been together for four years. Compared to her and Uncle Norman, that was nothing. Jean and Ted had been together since Moses had a skateboard. Compared to that, me and Jude were the blink of an eye. I smiled to show I didn't care and headed off to the kitchen to get myself a drink.

The women from church were saying Mum had died of a broken heart. Shirley who arranged the flowers reckoned she'd heard someone on the radio claiming this was an actual thing now. Something about the heart becoming so enlarged when grieving a spouse that it inflated until it exploded. Betty who polished the brass, as well as working on reception at the surgery and therefore knowing a thing or two about All Things Medical, went one better and said what Mum had actually been suffering from was 'takotsubo cardiomyopathy'.

No one liked the sound of that. It smacked of the indisputably foreign. Amid murmurs of disapproval, Dilys from the choir claimed to have ordered it at the Chinese once; it had given her diarrhoea.

Oh, don't get me wrong – she didn't actually say the word. This being the women from church congregating by the breakfast bar, she just grimaced, pointed to her stomach and shuddered. And to be fair, give her her due, we were at my mother's wake. People were eating. There were vol-au-vents present.

Never one to be outdone, Betty counterattacked that takotsubo cardiomyopathy wasn't a takeaway meal but a medical condition whereby a traumatic incident triggers the brain to distribute chemicals around the body that weaken the heart.

She bandied the words about like nobody's business, thrilled to know something no one else did. And all with a mouthful of scampi.

I had always found Betty and her coterie deeply irritating, so tried to squeeze my way out of the kitchen and offer a tray of rather tired-looking cheese sandwiches to the other flock of people in the living room. I could still hear her chirruping away, though, as much as I tried to block her out.

'. . . Yes, she had takotsubo cardiomyopathy. I mean, the doctors didn't actually say that, Pauline, but how many times have we said it? I know more about the human body than the rest of those so-called professionals put together.'

And then more murmurs, this time of approval. That was very much how they operated, those women, liking to think that they had superior knowledge to everyone else on the planet. That's what came of going to church, I supposed. In the modern world, with decreasing congregation numbers and their beliefs more and more out of sync with current thinking, they didn't reflect and adapt; they clung to their beliefs. It gave them an unerring sense of their own rightness, and it drained by osmosis into all their other thinking too. They were always right. The rest of the world was wrong, and fools into the bargain.

I felt a tug at my arm. Geraldine from over the road.

'Are you OK, Holly?'

'I'm fine, thanks, Geraldine,' I lied, trying to mask my irritation with the breakfast-bar gossip. 'Cheese sandwich?'

'Ooh, lovely.' She took one. 'No Jude?'

'No, we split up.' I smiled. 'All good, though.'

Mum hadn't died of a broken heart. The death certificate proclaimed septicaemia, which was brought on by a chest infection she was too weak to fight. So any inferences that she'd gone because she couldn't live without Dad, who'd died a year previously, were medically inaccurate, no matter what the women wanted to believe.

'Is it true those flowers are from Sylvie di Marco?' Geraldine purred, tilting her head towards an ostentatious display of pink lilies I'd plonked in front of the fireplace.

I nodded. Geraldine's eyes instantaneously filled with tears.

'Isn't she kind? A global superstar and she even took the time to send flowers.'

'She's not really a global superstar, Geraldine,' I pointed out, irked that my boss, Miss di Marco, hadn't actually sent them but told me to spend a hundred pounds of her money on flowers for the house. It's actually pretty difficult to spend that much money on one bouquet. 'I mean, she's hardly Beyoncé.'

Geraldine didn't care. She shook her head. 'I saw her in *The Sound of Music* in Coventry years ago. No one can pull off a dirndl like Sylvie.'

As if on cue, I felt my phone pulsing in my pocket. Why? Why did I keep it on me today of all days? Wasn't it clear my dragon of a boss would be demanding some kind of attention . . . even when I was meant to be burying my mother? I ignored it, and Geraldine, though that wasn't hard, as she'd turned her back on me and was rhapsodizing about the bouquet.

I caught the words 'Sylvie di Marco, thank you very much' and 'never seen anything quite like it'.

I looked back to the kitchen, divided from the living room by a corrugated-plastic window, an original feature from when the house was built in the 1960s, and saw the shadows of the women from church, bent over their plates of vol-au-vents, heads ducked. With the light coming through behind them from the kitchen window, their silhouettes took on the shape of some scary shadow-puppet play. They should have been accompanied by sinister music. Something on the xylophone – I had always found that an unnerving sound – or that piece of music they used to play every time Alfred Hitchcock came on television with one of his chillers, or . . . No! I've got it! Something on the organ. Something dark and foreboding on the church organ.

Mum had continued to be the local organist over the years, till her dementia had got the better of her. And that had only really been in the last year. It was like when Dad had been here, he'd kept it at bay, made sure she was coping, no doubt doing everything for her when the rest of the world wasn't looking, but once he'd gone, she fell to pieces. It first became obvious at church when she played the opening hymn at one of the services. The vicar usually chose a shortish hymn that would cover his and the choir's procession from the back of the church to the choir stalls, one or two verses more and that was your lot. I believe the hymn in question was 'Guide Me, O Thou Great Redeemer'. When they got to the end and everyone put down their hymnbooks to consult their orders of service, Mum continued to play. And play. And play. And play. She just wouldn't stop, not realizing they'd finished. In the end the vicar had to walk over, shout at her and jab the on/off switch on the organ. Apparently Mum cried. After that the women at the church finally agreed with what I'd been saying for months: that Mum shouldn't really be doing so much.

On the mantelpiece, above the *look-at-me!* flowers, was a framed photograph. Mum's pride and joy. It showed her and the choir in their red robes standing on the steps of St Albans Cathedral when they had taken part in an episode of *Songs of Praise*. It was taken about ten years previously. I had no idea whether they still even made *Songs of Praise*. Mum looked so happy, so proud. Like this was the pinnacle of her life. It was the sort of smile usually adopted by gold-medal-winning Olympians. It was an infectious smile. I found myself mirroring it. Then I heard someone in the kitchen say, 'She seems to be taking it quite well, doesn't she? Can't be easy losing both parents in the space of a year.'

Were they looking at me, smiling at a photo of my mum? Is that what was deemed to be 'taking it well'?

'I know,' someone replied, 'but then she wasn't their own flesh and blood.'

That was like a shard of glass to my wrist.

I recognized the voice as Betty's, the know-all. I was tempted to return to the kitchen, pick up the unappealing Black Forest gateau she had brought as an offering for dessert – 'Your mum loved my BFGs!' she'd announced when she'd arrived – and shove her face in it. Actually, I should've dunked her in it for referring to it as a 'BFG', never mind getting so personal. It would have been such a rewarding thing to do. It would have marked the end of one era and the beginning of another. Mum was dead. Long live me! I wondered if by doing it, I would have received a round of applause. Mum worshipped the ground Betty walked on, but I had long harboured the suspicion that everyone else was slightly scared of her. I would have been standing up to the bully in the playground, and she would never have wielded her power again. But then I remembered this day was not about me, it was about Mum, and the last thing she would have wanted was a dessert-based contretemps, so I refrained.

Aunty Beryl was advancing towards me, dodging her way between doddery neighbours and people whose faces I recognized but whose names escaped me. Her hair was sandier now; the red had faded and a lot of grey had taken its place, like she'd been left out in the midday sun too many times on a hot Greek island. And since her daughter had opened her own tanning salon in St Albans, her skin did too.

'Holly, Holly, meant to say – did you get Tracey's card?'

'Er . . . yes, I think so. Yes, I did.' How could I forget it? It had been all about her.

Dear Hollie

She never spelled my name right. Mind you, I always spelled hers 'Tracie' to wind her up, so maybe she was just reciprocating.

I was so sorry to hear about Aunty Bracelet's passing.

I really did detest the way she called Mum 'Bracelet'.

Bless her, she was a love, wasn't she? But at least none of us has to keep traipsing over to see her now. I know it was a schlep for you coming from London, which is probably why you didn't do it as much as me and Mum.

I'm not sure you've ever forgiven me for clearing the loft out for her that time, though I'm sure you'll agree now that it's one less job for you to do, so maybe one day you'll thank me for it.

At which point I'd only skim-read the rest of the card. Something about not being able to come to the funeral because of wanting to be the next Hilary Devey. And something about childcare. Though more likely, the reason she couldn't come was because she was writing to random relatives, likening them to stuff she'd seen in the window at Ratner's. Aunty Beryl was wittering on about the demands of running your own tanning salon when Geraldine flew in as my fairy godmother and interrupted with her excitement about the flowers under the mantelpiece. As Beryl turned to view them, I slunk away and headed upstairs. As I climbed said stairs, practically gluing my back to the wall as there was so little space since the stairlift had been installed, I felt my phone pulse again. On the landing, I took it out. Two texts from Sylvie.

The first:

I can't find my reading glasses.

And the second:

Found.

I returned the phone to my pocket and hurled myself at the spare-bedroom door to open it.

The single bed I now lay on had once been mine. Since I'd left home, it had become a veritable *Generation Game*'s conveyor belt full of bric-a-brac. You see, when Mum had been admitted to hospital and I'd found myself coming to the house more often to clean or rifle through drawers looking for life insurance policies, et cetera, I discovered the following hidden under the duvet on the bed in the spare room:

- A Penhaligon's bath and body kit, fragrance: Elizabethan Rose
- A manicure kit in a burgundy leather pochette
- Square compact mirror, possibly from a Christmas cracker
- A DVD of the wedding of Prince William and Kate Middleton, still in plastic wrapper
- A mirrored Marks & Spencer photo frame, no photo
- A travel mini oil-painting kit, still in plastic wrapper
- Badedas bath oil, possibly opened as there was a sticky mess running down the neck of the bottle, which had stuck to the bed sheet
- A large box of Ferrero Rocher chocolates, none eaten, but seal broken
- A copy of Rosemary Conley's *Amazing Inch Loss Plan*, price scissored off the back cover
- A CD entitled *20 Top Ten Hits of the 80s*, a sticker on it 'Free With the *Daily Express*'
- Five cheap silvery bracelets (I hoped they were from Tracey)
- Thirty-five plastic bags. Neatly folded. Placed in another plastic bag.

The fitted wardrobe with the sticky door was crammed full of similar stuff, so too one of the drawers in the big chest that seemed strategically positioned so that whenever you walked into the room, you broke a shin on it. That is, if you could get into the room in the first place: Mum had chosen behind the door as the perfect place to store a human-sized teddy bear with a red polka-dot bow tie. I would have described all this stuff as tat, or crap, if it hadn't been for the fact that I had purchased some of the items for her (the Penhaligon's smellies and the photo frame), and it had quickly become clear to me what all this – oh, OK, I'll say it – crap was. They were all presents given to her that she was saving to stick on a stall at one of her beloved bring-and-buy sales at the church. I found it soul-destroying to think that rather than being cherished, the things I had given her over the years had been treated as money-spinners for the new church roof. But then I caught myself thinking, Well, how much effort had I really put into selecting that photo frame? I'd not even put a picture in it. So why shouldn't she do what the hell she wanted with it anyway? Not that she would now. So who had won?

And why, even now she was dead, was I viewing this as some sort of competition?

My phone pulsed. Again. I looked.

When are you back?

I should have ignored it, but there was something Pavlovianly canine about my response to anything from the Boss, so I quickly jabbed back:

Day after tomorrow.

I knew this would illicit no reply, but, horror of horrors, I felt it pulse again.

When does my new banquette arrive?

I sighed. Tapped:

Thursday.

Just as I was discarding the phone, yet again another pulse.
'*What?*' I hollered, and checked the screen.
But it was from Gracie, my flatmate.

**Hope it's not too vile up there. Sending love and call if you
need to chat. G x**

And just in case Sylvia texted again, I switched off my
phone. If I wasn't allowed some peace and quiet today, then I
didn't know when I was.

My mum and I had always had a very combative relationship. If I said something was black, she'd claim it was white.
And – as Betty had so kindly pointed out – she wasn't even
my real mum. I know that sounds awful, but since the trip
to McDonald's, Mum had been the first person to honk the
Adoption Klaxon if I'd done something that she claimed was
abhorrent (got drunk on Diamond White, sported a love
bite, criticized Gloria Hunniford). Then she would reel out
the stock phrases: 'Biggest mistake of my life, adopting you';
'What was I thinking of, choosing you?'; 'You're your mother's
daughter, and she was trouble.' Even though, actually, she
never knew my birth mother. Conversely, however, if I was
behaving myself and conforming to her expectations of how
a daughter should behave (playing the piano at a school
concert, wearing my hair in pigtails at the age of eighteen,
looking confused when people swore on the telly), then it was
as if she had given birth to me herself. The slightest hint of a
compliment paid about me to her by a neighbour or a friend
would elicit a snapped response of 'Yes, she gets that from me,
Betty/Geraldine/Dilys.'

She had the power to wind me up more than anyone else
on the planet, because of her ability to blow hot and cold so

much. And because of her competitive desire to put me down all the time. At any given opportunity. When Tracey had sent the initial letter about her being like a big, sparkly bracelet, Mum had come marching into my bedroom, brandishing the letter aloft.

'See? See?!' she'd squealed. She squealed well. 'Tracey says nice things about me. Tracey loves me!' Then she'd shot me one of her Exocet glances. 'Which is more than can be said for you, you ungrateful little . . . mole!'

Then she'd thrown the letter on the bed and stomped back out to the landing again. And once more I'd been left with the sinking feeling that nothing I could do for her would ever be enough. Maybe that's why I'd downed tools and come to keep an eye on her before the end, just to prove, finally, that I was a good daughter.

The invincibility I'd felt on our day out in London, the potential freedom I savoured on finding out I was adopted had quickly been extinguished, like a hot coal in the snow. Life had soon returned to normal. Actually, it became worse. I'd always felt like I didn't belong to this life, and now I had valid reason. I increasingly fantasized about the mother who'd given me away. Unsurprisingly she was the nicest woman on the planet, in my head, just a bit misunderstood. I tried a handful of times to question my parents about her, and each time was greeted with a wall, not quite of silence, but of 'We're not sure's and 'No idea, sorry's. I didn't believe a word of it. The day I'd turned twelve, I'd secretly squirrelled through all the boxes in the loft until I'd struck gold and found my birth certificate hidden away between some old copies of the *Church Times*. I slid it into the pages of a *Blue Peter* annual and said nothing. I didn't act on the information, but I committed it to memory, feeling like a spy, then returned it to the

Church Times one day when Jean was out at a meeting for a new design for cassocks and Ted was busy in the garden. Each night when I went to bed and said my prayers, I would recite the name and address from the certificate in my head, making sure I would never forget. It wasn't till I left home to go to university that I ever dared write it down. I biro-ed it in tiny handwriting in the corner of my Filofax. I would never forget who had given birth to me. And just as well I had trained myself to remember it, as I had returned home one day when Mum was quite poorly to find Tracey returning from a trip to the tip, and an empty loft.

'It was only a load of old boxes and bundles of newspaper, Holly. *God*!'

If only she'd known.

How could Betty be so cruel? Especially if she called herself a Christian? Was my suffering diminished because I was adopted? Blimey. I remembered her being hysterical with grief when the Queen Mum died. *And this was my mother!* Clearly she felt more closely linked to the royal family than I was allowed to be to my own. And my own they were. Or the only ones I knew. Not that there were any of them left anymore. I'd come into this world alone; now I was on my own again.

I hadn't shut the bedroom door. Remarkably, the sinister-looking teddy hadn't done his usual trick of toppling forward and wiping out a small village of knick-knacks on a nearby shelf. The chit-chat of the do downstairs floated up as general noise. I couldn't distinguish words, just sounds. Like a symphony of disappointment. Not disappointment that Mum had died, per se. More like . . . well . . . everyone that Mum knew just seemed continually disappointed. Nothing was ever good enough. Life, friends, family, television. The church might have offered some respite, but inevitably they'd always find something to be let down by. I lay there on the bed, feeling as if I was floating on their disappointment, and, I hate to say it, I felt disappointed too.

But what did I have to be disappointed about? Was I disappointed that today hadn't been a more glamorous, elaborate affair? It was the funeral of a woman in her seventies who lived on a suburban housing estate in Tring. It was never going to be the Royal Variety Performance. Was I disappointed due to a sense of anticlimax? Since she'd died last week I'd put every effort, Sylvie aside, into planning and executing this day. And now it was over and . . . what? But no, it wasn't that. It was more the sense that I still didn't feel bereft, distraught, desolate, as a grieving daughter was meant to. I thought I might have. I hoped I would do. But I was familiar with an overriding feeling that was possibly something I'd learned as a baby. *You're on your own, Holly, and somehow you have to get through this.* If I'd been posher, it might have been a case of *Stiff upper lip!* It wasn't, though; it was more a case of sink or swim. And if you get too upset, you might sink.

Why had Betty's words stung so much? I wondered. Possibly because there was a huge grain of truth in them. Jean and Ted had not been my birth parents. We'd spent a lifetime trying to convince each other we were a proper family, but the effort had been mostly futile. Unlike the majority of adopted children, I didn't feel I was of them. Don't get me wrong – I loved them both very much, and cared for them a great deal. I was certainly grieving in my own quiet way now they had both gone. But I had viewed both Jean/Mum and Ted/Dad as two elderly people I dropped in on from time to time to check they'd not fallen and broken a hip. I had cried a lot since Mum had died, but I was unsure whether I was crying because of missing her or for the missed opportunities, that sense that we'd never achieved the normality I assumed other families felt.

I'd certainly not cried when I went to see her at the chapel of rest. She'd looked funny in her coffin. Not funny like Joan Rivers, though admittedly she does look very funny, but funny like it wasn't her.

'It doesn't look like her,' I'd said to the funeral director, Amelia.

Her eyes had narrowed (Amelia's, not Mum's) and she'd insisted, 'No, it's definitely her. Everyone else in the chapel of rest at the moment's a man.'

I could tell it was her, of course. It's just that her nose looked bigger. I'd never noticed her having a particularly big nose before. And now here she was, looking like Concorde had crashed on a beach.

'Her body looks like it's on back to front,' I'd added, perturbed.

'It's definitely not.' Amelia had started to sound irritated.

I'd never noticed how big her tummy was before. She looked pregnant.

'She looks peaceful, doesn't she?' sighed Amelia, trying to make our conversation veer towards the positive.

'Yes. I took her to the Isle of Wight last month. She really enjoyed it.'

And we'd both stared at Mum, unsure what else to say.

I'd not been with her when she died. This had upset me slightly at the time, but then of course I was an only child, her closest relative, so I had done my fair share of sitting at her bedside at the hospital while she drifted in and out of consciousness. I'd returned to her house that night to sleep. A nurse phoned me at twenty past midnight to tell me what had happened. She was very sweet, although she sounded about fifteen. She had gone to check on Mum, had sensed something was afoot and decided to stay with her. She held her hand as she took her last breath. I didn't feel jealous that this stranger had shared something so intimate as my mother's final seconds. I was just pleased that she'd not been alone as she'd left.

I had said my goodbyes a few days before, when Mum was still lucid and responding. I had thanked her for being a wonderful mum, I had told her I loved her very much, and I'd thanked her for adopting me. I was holding her hand as I'd said it and I felt the faintest of squeezes in reply. I was glad I'd said it, even though it was only half meant. I hoped it would make it easier for her to let go. I hoped it was something lovely for her to hear, possibly as the final thing she ever heard. And in a way I *was* glad she'd adopted me. And even though our relationship had been, for the most part, fractious, I did love her – to quote Prince Charles – whatever 'love' means. The bottom line was, I didn't know anything else.

Of course, I had loved Jude, in my own sweet way. He was funny and kind and handsome – even if he had recently had a Mohican. Well, he called it a Mohican; I called it a midlife crisis – and talented. I loved watching him play the violin in his orchestra. They played in vast halls on the South Bank and maybe, I thought, that's where I preferred him. At arm's length. Away from me. On the stage. For me to observe but not connect with.

He would be upset. His music would be therapeutic, but he would be upset.

Was I upset? Strangely, about Jude, I couldn't tell.

To cheer myself up, I felt in the pocket of my trousers (there'd been a few raised eyebrows when I'd turned up at the church in a trouser suit today. Outrageous behaviour, clearly something I'd picked up in London!) and pulled from it a crumpled piece of lined paper. I smoothed it down, the action soothing me, like a crack addict preparing her apparatus. I knew this paper would be my balm, and after consulting it, I'd be able to head downstairs, smile painted on my face, invigorated. I looked at the words scrawled on it in my own biro-ed tiny hand.

Francesca Boyle, 32B Gambier Terrace, Liverpool 1

It was thrilling to think that one day soon those words were, hopefully, going to change my life.

TWO

My boss's penthouse flat overlooked Tower Bridge. In that flat there was a coffee table. On that coffee table lay a pristine copy of her autobiography, *Let Me Sing Cake*. She knew full well that if you opened the book and consulted the titles page inside you would see a subtitle:

Sylvie di Marco – Icon. Diva. Enigma.

But unbeknown to her, the woman who had my job before me had crossed out the last word and added another in biro so it read:

Sylvie di Marco – Icon. Diva. ~~Enigma.~~ TWAT.

The fact that it had lain undiscovered in the five years that I had worked for her tickled me muchly.

After leaving school, I studied music at Durham University. I had become rather good at both the cello and the piano; in fact I subsidized my meagre student loan by playing the piano in a wine bar three nights a week. On graduating, I started playing the cello in the orchestra for a string of West End shows. But after a few years of doing that, I grew bored.

Much as I loved my musical theatre (my adoration for Miss Salonga had never really died), I changed career and started to work in the offices of one of the theatre producers who had previously employed me as a cellist. I soon learned I enjoyed office work much more than sitting at the back of an orchestra pit. It also meant I had more time for a social life, as I wasn't spending most evenings playing the bass line accompaniment to 'Defying Gravity' or suchlike. After a few years of that the producer – I'll call him Titch, for that was his name – put on a production of a jukebox musical that was clearly trying to cash in on the success of *Mamma Mia!* It used the back catalogue of the Smiths and was called *Heaven Knows I'm Miserable Now*, which actually is what the audience was, mostly. Even the most hardened of Smiths aficionados were confused by the story of a boy called William and his journey through space to find the meaning of life and save his planet. All done to a soundtrack of guitar-heavy indie music.

The female lead in this ill-fated production – it ran for two months and got excruciating reviews – was Sylvie di Marco. She came off the worst in the notices, as the critics were confused as to why someone as hitherto successful as her would choose to be in something so shoddily put together. She played William's sister, Sheila, in the show. Originally Sheila had been William's mother, but she claimed she was far too young to be convincing and so asked for the part to be rewritten as his sister. The producers obliged and a star was torn. The one achievement the musical held was it made it into the *Guinness World Records* for being the show that featured the highest number of bows in a performance, as during the song 'Sheila, Take a Bow', Sylvie had to bow more than a hundred times. After the reviews came out, Sylvie claimed the bowing had put her back out, her understudy went on, and she never returned. It was during this period of recuperation that I was sometimes sent to her apartment on behalf of Titch with a basket of fruit, ostensibly to spy on her, but feigning support and concern. And it was during one of those visits that her PA had announced she'd had enough and was leaving and Sylvie, who appeared to have taken a shine to me, offered me the job on the spot. Fool that I was, and my interest piqued by the alleged increase in wages, and the photograph in her bathroom of her with Lea Salonga, I took it.

It was on the Smiths show that I first met Jude as well; he was playing in the orchestra. The experience stung him and he vowed never to 'play West End' again. He ran back to the safe confines of chamber music and symphonies, working for one of the better-known London orchestras. He actually wooed me by playing some Rimsky-Korsakov underneath my flat window one night. It was a touching moment. Till the woman in the flat above me threw a bucket of water down on him, screaming, 'Shut the fuck up – I'm trying to sleep.' The force of the water ripped the fiddle from his hands, causing it to smash on the pavement. It cost Jude hundreds of pounds to put right. I had to say yes to dating him then: something positive had to come out of the incident.

Two days after Mum's funeral I slipped my key in Sylvie's door at eight thirty on the dot and let myself into her apartment. I heard the soft pitter-patter of paws on marble and then saw her minuscule chihuahua, Michael, trotting towards me in a lime-green woollen cardigan, whimpering. I knew why he was whimpering – he needed a wee – so I unhooked his lead from the antlers of a deer's head on the wall and took him out straight away. As soon as we got out of the art deco building, he scampered to a nearby bush and cocked his leg. He seemed to stay there for ten minutes, emitting his own River Thames beneath him. Poor thing had been desperate. His business done, I scooped him up in my arms and carried him back inside. In the lift I tickled his bald tummy and he made pathetic baby licks to my hand as I did so. Don't get me wrong, I was a dog lover; I just never really 'got' chihuahuas. And the name Michael never did sit easy with me. Sylvie had named him after her good pal Michael Ball, claiming they both 'didn't look much but had mahoosive cajones. Ha!'

She had a habit of doing this: shouting, 'Ha!' at the end of a sentence to show you she was joking. A bit like writing 'LOL,' on a text. Only spoken, well, shouted.

As we came back into the apartment, I heard a toilet flush and went about flicking the kettle on and chucking a green tea bag into a mug that was emblazoned with the logo for *Cake!* on its side. I'll never forget the lecture I got on my first day when I was introduced to 'the Mug'.

'Holly, this receptacle is dearly, dearly precious to me. It was a gift from Cameron Mackintosh on the opening night of *Cake!* at the RSC all those many, many years ago. You do not need me to tell you that *Cake!* is still running *to this day* and has played in all four corners of the globe. And yet this is one of the original pieces of merchandise and is therefore incredibly special, unique. Wash it carefully, treasure it, cosset it and please . . . *never* put it in the dishwasher.'

'Yes, Miss di Marco.'

'If that logo ever fades, it'll be like the ravens leaving the Tower.'

'Yes, Miss di Marco.'

'I might actually die.'

OK. She liked her mug.

Sometimes I wanted to hurl the mug, or her, out of one of the picture windows. Her apartment was always bathed in light (except at night-time, natch) because of the floor-to-ceiling windows. And the views of Tower Bridge to the north and South London to the south were delicious. But surely the windows would look better with a Sylvie-shaped hole in them? This was awful. I had to stop my murderous thoughts about Miss di Marco.

Sylvie was a household name. ('Like Canesten,' I often joked to my flatmate, Gracie.) She had had a varied career in her sixty-five years (though Wikipedia still claimed she was only fifty-seven, and it was part of my job to keep it that way). She'd been an overnight success in 1977 playing Marie Antoinette in the musical *Let Them Eat Cake!* She had taken the show to Broadway and topped the British charts with the show-stopping torch song from it, 'Misunderstood Queen', the hi-energy version of which continued to be a floor-filler at many gay clubs even now. From then on she won leading roles on both sides of the Atlantic until the inevitable happened and she hit some God-awful age for a woman like fifty, or maybe forty – it might even have been thirty – and the roles dried up. Then there was the Smiths debacle. Now she toured the country and the world with her one-woman show *S for Sylvie, S for Star*. She continued to live in the style to which she was accustomed, in the penthouse apartment, people jumping to every click of her fingers (me, mostly), a string of younger lovers always at her bedroom door. ('Usually running for the hills,' I would joke to Gracie.) She had made a lot of money, slept with some very famous men and was the most insecure person I had ever met. Often insecurity can manifest itself in appealing shyness or self-deprecation. If only. Sylvie channelled hers into a kind of bombastic dictatorship. She didn't blow so much hot and cold, like my mum had, just a continual hot.

The only thing that seemed to make her happy was her son, Radisson. I know, *Radisson*. 'That's not a name – it's a hotel,' is what Gracie had said when I told her. Radisson was thirty-four (just three years older than me), aloof, grumpy, spoilt and devastatingly handsome. Not my kind of handsome: he was all floppy fringes and cheekbones like BMX handlebars; I preferred something more unconventional. But that didn't stop Sylvie assuming I fancied him every time he came to visit, which was fortunately infrequently since he'd moved to the States a few years back.

'I saw you looking!' she'd chirrup when he left the room. 'Well, I can't say I blame you, dear. If he wasn't my son . . . Ha!' and then she'd emit a throaty chuckle. At which point I usually changed the subject.

I knew Sylvie was going to be in a particularly foul mood this morning, as her manager, Monty, had emailed me overnight to forewarn me. Sylvie had been availability-checked for a new musical about the life of Dusty Springfield and had been overjoyed. 'Dusty, darling! Little ol' me! I love Dusty. Love, love, love her . . . She was so . . . iconic! So much in common, darling!' But then, to her horror, she had discovered that the producers were considering her for the part of Kay, Dusty's mother. Despite her insistence that she would only play it if Kay was changed to Dusty's slightly older sister, the producers wouldn't budge. Sylvie had then gone to the opening night of a new musical in the West End, which she was also furious about not being in, and had proceeded to get extremely drunk at the after-show party. Monty's email explained she had not been seen since midnight last night, when, while cavorting with one of the young stars of the show on the dance floor, she had fallen into an artificial fire.

As she trotted into the kitchen on her kitten-heeled slippers, sporting a headscarf (no wig for once), massive shades and a kimono, she growled, 'Is my banquette coming today?'

'Thursday.'

'Oh.'

I heard her rapping her fingernails on the marble counter-top. God, that hideous sofa she'd ordered. It was the most garish thing I'd ever seen.

She stopped rapping. 'How was the . . . thing?'

'Funeral? Oh, it went as well as can be expected, thanks.'

She clicked her fingers, summoning up the words. 'The flowers. They liked?'

I wasn't sure who 'they' were, but I nodded all the same. 'They very much liked, Sylvie, yes.'

'Oh good. Gooooood.' And then she emitted a wry, guilty smile. 'Sylvie has the teensiest of hangovers this morning.'

Despite being from Nottingham, Sylvie spoke with a trans-atlantic drawl. I couldn't help it. For bedevilment I ventured, 'So, what's the latest about Dusty?'

The smile froze on her face. She twitched a bit, then started pawing at my hair. She would do this a lot, invade your per-sonal space. Usually when she wanted something or was lying. This time it was the latter.

'I slept on it, darling, and I've decided. I don't wanna play lezz.'

I gulped. Did she actually just say that? She grabbed my arm. Tight. OK, so she was still making out she had been offered the lead part. Er . . .

'Don't get me wrong, I'm not homophobical, darling. Not me, not I, not Sylvie, no! Why turn my back on my fan base?

And let's be honest, I have drunk, myself, from the fur cup once or twice.' She looked around the kitchen, as if remembering, eyes darting across the floor. 'I had Melody Andrews on these very Fired Earth tiles.'

I had no idea who Melody Andrews was.

Sylvie turned her head quickly to look at me. 'It was when Radisson was very young. He was at kindergarten. I had to finish her off with one of his skittles. But no. Not this year. I don't wanna play . . . confuuuuuused sexuality, you know?'

I didn't know. But nodded all the same. 'Very wise. And at least it means you don't have to cancel Canada.'

'Exactly!' and she clicked some imaginary castanets and stomped her feet à la flamenco dancing. 'I cannot let my beloved Canadian fans down, darling. Canada's such a wonderful country, you know? It's so . . .' she searched for the right word, then found it, 'Canadian.'

Biting my lip, I managed a quick 'I couldn't agree more', then poured her some green tea. I was dreading going to Canada with her. I know most people would be thrilled about a trip abroad with work, all expenses paid, but the truth of it was, I would not get a minute to myself and would have no opportunity to see anything of the country I was visiting. Once out of the comfort zone of her Central London apartment, Sylvie was even more incapable of doing anything for herself. I would be with her twenty-four seven. The only time I'd get to myself would be when she was sleeping. And as she was an insomniac, that would be hardly ever.

Now my back was turned to her, I heard her say, 'Have you put on weight? Have you? Have you put a bit of weight on?'

Don't let it get to you, Holly.

I didn't respond, but she continued, 'Yes, you have. You're not . . .' She swallowed her breath. 'No, you can't be.'

She sounded so dismissive.

'Can't be what?'

'Pregnant, dear.'

'Why couldn't I be pregnant?'

'Well, you don't have a boyfriend.'

'Sylvie, I've had a boyfriend for four years. Although –' my voice faltered '– we recently split up. We hardly saw each other, but—'

'Why not?'

'I'm too busy.'

'Well, now your mummy's died, maybe you'll have time to find a new boyfriend. What was the old one? A fireman?'

'A violinist.'

She emitted a throaty cackle, sounding like the woman who used to say, 'Rrrrrené,' in *'Allo 'Allo!* and said, 'Excellent fingering technique, no?'

I said nothing. Of course what I'd meant was I was far too busy running around after her to go looking for love or nurturing love or, well, loving anything or anyone except the task in hand. Nannying her.

I knew this top was a mistake the minute I put it on. It's just I really fancied wearing it. The upside was, it was a really pretty, floaty white top with a sort of Indian paisley design and was tight at the top but all billowy at the bottom. It was too short to wear as a dress (unless you were incredibly racy) but looked great, I thought, with skinny jeans and bejewelled flip-flops. The downside was that from some angles it looked like a maternity smock.

'Or are you a little bit Dusty?' Sylvie cooed. And then

giggled. At least someone found her funny. I had no idea what she was talking about.

'Sorry?'

'You know. Maybe that's why you split up with your boyfriend. Maybe you're a little bit . . . Dusty?'

'No, Sylvie. I'm not even a teensy bit Dusty. Toast?'

'Bacon sandwich, darling. May as well join you in Team Porkypants. It's not like I'm going to be the ingénue anymore.' She sighed.

I couldn't help it. 'Well, you've still got to fit into last year's costumes for Canada,' I pointed out.

Even with my back to her I felt the dirt of the look she was giving me.

'Did your mother commit suicide?' she hissed. I turned and looked at her, stung. She shrugged. 'It's just you have a terribly vicious tongue sometimes. Very cutting. Almost knife-esque. Hope you didn't . . . upset her, darling.' I thought she had finished. Then she breezily continued, 'Make it two bacon rolls. I have company.'

And with that she spun on her heel and headed back to bed. Company. Poor chap.

Looking in the fridge, I saw that there was no bacon. I called through to her, 'There's no bacon, Sylvie!'

No response came. I heard a soft chuckling. Then what sounded like the muffled noises of a man waking up in a state of panic and realizing he'd made a really horrendous mistake, or maybe I just wanted it to sound like that.

'Sylvie! There's no bacon!' I tried again.

'Well, go to the fucking shop! Jesus! Or is that too much for your little brain to handle? In this life, Holly, you need things? You have to *go out and buy them*. No wonder your boyfriend left you!'

Her bedroom door slammed.

It made Michael whimper.

I cursed her aggressively under my breath and headed out.

Sylvie's favourite deli was wedged between a bookmaker's and a haberdasher's on a back alley off Tooley Street, a stone's throw from her flat. The avuncular owner, Frank, was past retirement age, past caring but not past it. He was Italian by birth and still had a strong undercurrent of the accent mixed in with his cockney. Every time I entered his shop, he called the same thing – 'Here she comes! When you gonna marry me, baby?' – and he'd hold his arms out like he wanted to hug me.

I'd always have to reply, 'You're a married man, Frank – I couldn't!' and then look to the till, where his wife, Esther, sat with a fat grin on her face, biro-ing bras on the Page Three girls in the *Sun*. I'm not sure which radio station they had vibrating through their tinny transistor, but it always seemed to be playing Duran Duran.

'What does that bitch want today, hey?'

I loved that he didn't just call a spade a spade, he called it a dirty great shovel.

'She's out of bacon.'

'Bacon, bacon. I cut you some nice bacon.' And he went about sawing thin slices of bacon off a big, leggy-looking hunk of meat. 'So, you gonna jack it all in and run away with me, baby?'

'Frank! Duh! Not in front of Esther!'

Again Esther chuckled, even though she heard this conversation almost daily.

'Oh my God, I did not ask you! How was your mummy's funeral?'

'Oh, it was . . . OK, thanks. Lovely service.'

'You will miss her big time, eh, baby?'

'Er . . . yes.'

'So sad.' He looked like he might cry.

'Yes.'

'Lot to sort out after funeral.'

'Yes.'

'Lot of shit to attend to. Know what I mean, baby?'

'I do. A shitload of shit.'

This tickled him.

'And your daddy, he's dead too, yeah, baby?'

'He is.'

'Little orphan Annie, innit?'

'Innit,' I replied, though my cockney was unconvincing.

'So . . . what's going on with the house they lived in, or was it council?'

'No, it was theirs. I've put it on the market. I got an estate agent round yesterday.'

'Bad times, innit?'

'Well, I don't want to live there.'

'And you get all the money from that, right?'

I nodded. Right. It felt wrong, somehow, me benefiting from the death of my parents. Before I could explore this further in my head, my phone rang. I checked the caller ID. It was Sylvie. I answered with a quick hello.

'I'm going to cook tonight, so I need two organic chicken breasts.'

'OK.' And I said to Frank, 'You don't do chicken breasts, do you?'

'No!' she was yelling down the phone. 'I want you to get them from Budgens.'

'Budgens?' I couldn't think where Budgens was.

'Yes, Budgens. In Belsize Park.'

'Sorry?'

'Are you deaf as well as stupid?'

'Belsize Park? It's miles away. I'm sure I can find somewhere round here.'

'Listen to me, Holly. I want you to take public transport – none of your taxi shit – and go to Belsize Park and get me two . . . organic . . . chicken breasts.'

'Why?'

I knew better than to question her, but I just didn't understand the reasoning behind sending me somewhere so far away for something so simple. Her voice was icy when she eventually spoke.

'I like them from there.'

'There must be a nearer Budgens, surely.'

'Belsize Park,' she yelped, and hung up. I followed suit.

'Go somewhere else, baby, and say you went up Belsize Park. She takes the piss, girl.' Frank was very put out on my behalf. Even Esther seemed to be scrubbing a little harder with her biro.

'No, she'll ask to see the receipt.'

'Tell her she can stick the facking receipt where the sun don't shine. You know what I mean, baby?'

He was funny when he was angry. I paid for the bacon and bid him and Esther farewell.

As I trudged beneath the twin castles of Tower Bridge, I wondered whether Sylvie had done this on purpose to keep me out of the apartment while she had some sexy time with her overnight guest. I became less bothered about it then, though I couldn't help but wish she'd just told me the truth and asked if I could keep out of the way for an hour or so. But then by doing that she would have been treating me as her equal, and no one was that, as far as she was concerned. A quick consultation on an app on my phone told me that if I walked to Monument Station, I could take the Northern Line direct to Belsize Park. The journey was going to take a good half-hour and, not for the first time, as I swerved the stressed businessmen and -women hurrying to and fro along too-narrow pavements, I decided that this was no job for a grown woman. I looked to my right, seeing the gleaming glass rockets of Canary Wharf. I had no idea really what went on in there, but I imagined a lot of people were rushing around doing deals with Asia and big, global, important stuff. Around me, the City of London buzzed with urgency. Life-or-death decisions were being taken. Behind me was the 1960s tower block-a-like of Guy's Hospital – how many operations were taking place there now? How many people were being cared for by doctors, nurses? Real life. Real stuff. And what was I doing?

Travelling six miles on a matter of the utmost urgency. To source two organic chicken breasts for someone's supper.

I hated travelling on the Underground. I wasn't claustro-phobic in any other area of my life, but stick me on a Tube train and I was liable to come out in a sweat of anxiety that only a general anaesthetic could dry out. It was the heat, the way everyone had to squash into carriages, the way there was never anywhere to sit, as the seats were always taken. It was the way they came to a sudden halt in a tunnel just when you needed a massive wee, and the driver could never explain why he'd had to stop, except that he'd seen a red light. *Jump it, for God's sake!* And the stations were no better. I always managed to walk behind an Antipodean with a maisonette-sized suitcase who had no idea where she was going, or a loved-up couple arm in arm who were taking in the scenery (crappy tiles and scrappy posters of Helen Mirren advertising jeans or a play), or a school party of under-twelves wearing hi-vis jackets and having either a bossy teacher who enjoyed shouting things like 'OK, stand close to the wall! Remember what I said about safety, yes?' or the trying-to-be-trendy type who attempted to laugh at their students' jokes, or feel their pain, and were all heart and no dress sense. And that was before you even tried to navigate your way around the different-coloured lines and the illuminated signs for South-bound, Northbound, Eggbound, et cetera.

So imagine my delight when I found myself in a beautifully underpopulated carriage. I had my choice of three seats. I chose the one nearest the door and settled down to at least try and enjoy the twenty-or-so-minute ride to sunny Belsize Park. I nestled my bag in my lap and took out my iPad and zigzagged my finger over it, trying to look important, as if I was on my way to one of those life-and-death meetings, instead of heading to source eco-friendly poultry. It was then Frank's words started ringing in my ears: *And you get all the money from that, right?*

It hadn't come as a shock to me that Mum and Dad had paid off their mortgage: I had had power of attorney over their 'estate', such as it was, since Dad died. But what had surprised me more, following Mum's demise, was just how many pots of money they had squirrelled away in various accounts. They had a funeral plan, life insurance, all sorts of ISAs. Basically everything was covered. It was money they had been saving for a rainy day and possibly to help towards the cost of their care if they ever needed to go into a home. Not that either of them wanted to. The funeral had cost a total of four and a half grand. Don't ask me how – it was hardly a lavish affair. We hadn't exactly hired Elton John to sing 'Candle In the Wind' and parade the coffin down Whitehall with a marching band. She didn't exactly have a pauper's burial, mind you, but even so. Over four grand for what we got seemed pretty excessive. Still, it wasn't my money, and it was what she wanted. To the letter. (Something she had planned before the dementia kicked in.) The house wasn't in a brilliant state, but nor was it falling apart at the seams. Just yet. But you could have knocked me over with a feather when the estate agent who came over yesterday told me he would put it on the market for £175,000.

Because if it ever sold for £175,000, that would be sitting in my bank account.

And with such a ginormous amount of money in my bank account, and the ISAs, I would no longer need to work for Sylvie.

I could break her *Cake!* mug.

I could chuck her wig out of the window.

I wouldn't have to go to Canada!

I felt excitement whirling up inside me again. This happened every time I thought about leaving. I'd fantasized about it for years, but now – with the prospect of being rich, rich, rich beyond my wildest dreams! – it was suddenly a possibility.

'Excuse me?'

I looked up to locate the voice. Lost in my reverie of kerching-style greed, I'd not noticed that the carriage had filled up. A woman was standing before me, tapping her left breast. How odd. She was younger than me, bit tubby, and wearing dungarees and the sort of haircut a nun might have on leaving a convent.

'I need your seat!' she gasped, as if she was about to collapse. I immediately jumped up. And as I did, I saw that she was wearing a badge, on her left breast, that said, 'Baby On Board.' She flung herself in my seat, took out a packet of Wotsits and starting munching away. Didn't even say thank you.

Baby on board. What was she, a Renault Espace?

Just then I saw her staring at my top. Her mouth froze mid-chew and she looked up at me guiltily.

'Oh my God, I'm so sorry,' she said, orange spongy bits spitting out of her mouth. 'I didn't realize. You should get a badge.'

And she stood up and offered me back my seat.

I was too embarrassed to say I wasn't pregnant, that it was just this top. I just couldn't say it. So I eased myself back into the seat and murmured my gratitude like I was in severe pain. A gallant gentleman stood up for Wotsit Face (surely they wouldn't be that good for the baby?) and she took his seat. We were both winners. Except I was a fat one.

'Hello, Sylvie? It's me.'

'Yes, I am able to read caller ID.'

'Well, I'm at Budgens. Belsize Park?'

'Still? Have you seen the time?'

'No, I've only just got here. I told you, it's a bit of a schlep.'

'For God's sake. Holly!'

'Only there aren't any organic chicken breasts left.'

'What?'

'I've asked and they've sold out. There are some normal ones.'

'No, it's probably horsemeat. Or they're pumped full of antibiotics. I know – I used to keep chickens.'

'So what would you like me to do?'

'Forget it. I'll do pasta.' And she hung up.

I kept the phone to my ear, frozen. For some reason, this

time her rudeness hurt more than usual. I could feel hot tears geysering up under my eyes, but I was determined not to let them fall. The man behind the counter was eyeing me suspiciously. Suddenly I realized how bizarre my one-sided conversation must have sounded to him and in that moment saw his look turn to pity. No doubt he thought I was a downtrodden wife in a controlling relationship, unable to buy anything without the say-so of my tyrant of a husband. Even if I had called him Sylvie. To regain his respect and evaporate all sense of pity, I smiled and shook my head.

'I don't know, *men*! It's his birthday and I promised him a treat. Oh well, why don't I take one of your lovely lasagnes?'

He visibly relaxed.

Oh well. Lasagne for supper tonight. For me. Just then I felt the phone pulse and checked my texts.

When's my banquette coming?

I tapped the screen like I was punching her.

Thursday, you forgetful horse.

And then thought better of it, deleted it and sent:

Thursday.

I always got home before Gracie. She had the sort of hotshot job in the City I was envying earlier. Something legal, something important. I didn't fully understand what she did, but I knew it involved something called underwriting. Truth be told, I hardly ever saw her. We'd not known each other before sharing the flat. She'd been there first and her flatmate had done a runner without paying a load of rent, so I'd answered an ad in *Time Out* and she'd snapped me up because I said I didn't smoke.

Which I don't. Often.

But never in the flat.

When I worked late, she seemed to be home early, and when I had an unexpected evening off, she would invariably roll in at 2 a.m. and collapse in a heap in the hall just outside her bedroom. Our flat was in Kentish Town. Again, I didn't get to see much of the area, as Sylvie was so demanding of my time, but it seemed nice from what I glimpsed as I ran home from the Tube each night, and like most places in London, we knew none of our neighbours. The flat was on the ground floor of an old Edwardian terrace. It had a small garden, which was communal and reached by the other flats in the building by an external spiral staircase. And sometimes the person below us in the basement practised scales on a piano. Loudly.

When I saw someone sat on the steps to the house as I turned into the path, I got a shock. At first I thought it was Gracie, home early and forgotten her key. But then a twitch of Mohican showed me it was Jude. He was sitting on the top step in a donkey jacket, baggy jeans and battered old pumps. I'd customized the elbow pads on that jacket with material from an old sofa. He stood up. He was wearing glasses. He hardly ever wore his glasses, preferring the vanity of contact lenses. I'd always said I liked him in his glasses.

'Jude, what are you doing?'

'I think you're being really unfair, Holly. Four years. Down the pan. Because I proposed to you?'

'Jude, I'm knackered. I've had a pig of a day.'

'All you had to do was say no.'

'And I did. Just . . . in a bit more of a final way than—'

'I didn't realize you were a heartless bitch.'

'I don't have to listen to this.'

I pushed past him and stuck my key in the door. I heard him behind me.

'Daisy says this is grief.'

Daisy was his mum. He didn't call his mum and dad Mum and Dad; he called them Daisy and Clint. They were greying hippies. They were sweet, actually.

'Daisy says I've got to give you time.'

I turned and looked at him. 'That Mohican looks ridiculous.'

'Daisy said it's not a hairdo; it's a cry for help.'

I smiled. 'Give Daisy my love.'

And in I went. As I fumbled through the post that had been left on a cabinet in the communal hall, I heard the letterbox go up.

'Now I know why you never wanted me to move in.'

I didn't answer.

'Coz you were planning on ditching me anyway.'

I was looking for a letter from my social worker. Nothing.

'Daisy says I've got to bide my time.'

I ignored him and headed to the door to my flat. I got a further shock when I heard voices in the lounge. Peering in, I saw Gracie huddled over on the couch, like she was texting or something, her mane of jet-black curls obliterating exactly what she was doing. The voices I'd heard were coming from the telly. Someone was shouting in *EastEnders*.

'Hey!' I called.

She looked up. It was then I saw that she didn't have her phone in her hand, so she wasn't texting. And when I saw the streams of mascara down her face, I realized what she was actually doing was crying.

'My God, Gracie, what is it? What's the matter?'

Suddenly she started sobbing very loudly. I rushed and sat beside her on the settee and put my arm around her. Had her mum died? Her dad? Had she lost her job?

'I'm pregnant!' she bellowed. I gasped. 'I know, it's horrendous!'

'Oh, darling.' And I hugged her and let her stain the shoulder of my faux maternity smock with her mascara. 'You know, it's funny, but a woman on the Tube today thought I was pregnant.'

And then another thought occurred to me.

'Whose is it?'

'Joshua's.'

OK, I had no idea who Joshua was.

'Who's Joshua?'

'My boyfriend!' she said in a very reprimanding kind of way.

'Sorry, it's just we . . . never see each other these days and . . . How long have you been seeing him?'

'Three weeks.'

'Shit. I'm so sorry.'

'I know.'

'Hey, I've got loads of friends who've had terminations and . . . you'll be OK. You don't even have to tell Joshua.'

And with that I got up and pulled out my iPad. It had a bit of cold lasagne on the screen from where the packet had leaked, but I was proud of how businesslike I was being, like I knew what to do. I actually only knew two people who'd had abortions, but still, neither of them was particularly traumatized about it. I opened the internet browser on my iPad and tapped in 'Abortion clinic London' . . . which is when I heard her say, 'I'm keeping it.'

I looked at her.

'Joshua's asked me to marry him.'

The horror on my face must have been evident. 'And what did you say?'

'I said I'd move in with him. Next month.'

THREE

You know when someone says, 'Who would you like to play you in the movie of your life?' and everyone gets excited and starts reeling off lists of people who are far better-looking than them? I don't, because I want to say, 'Why would they bother?' I knew full well that life stories on the big screen are usually about people who've actually done something with said lives: fostered eighty-nine children, saved a country from invasion by terrorists, that kind of thing. But my life was the most boring life in the history of . . . lives. I lived in a tiny, uncomfortable flat; I worked long hours for relatively little pay; I now didn't even have a boyfriend. I just existed, or that's how it felt. So why would anyone want to make a movie of that, unless it was a propaganda piece to encourage young people to get off their backsides and actually do something other than exist? And my movie for the time being was storylined so that I would stay in this grotty little flat, be bossed about by Sylvie till . . . Till when? Till what? Till I had the balls to walk out? Till I had my parents' money and I went on a world cruise?

So at times like this, when the script suddenly got rewritten without my consent or involvement, what was I meant to do? Was this latest development meant to give me the kick

I needed to be proactive? To do something for myself? This much was clear: I had to do something. Unless I sold Mum's house quickly and chose to stay on in this flat on my own, using my imminent wealth to cover two people's rent. But did I really want to?

This could not be happening, surely. In 2013 women did not meet a guy, get pregnant instantly and then walk them down the aisle plumping for the marriage in the ceremony book marked, 'Shotgun.' Did they?

Gracie clearly did. I couldn't quite believe it. As I lay on my bed a few hours later, the just-eaten lasagne sitting heavy in my stomach, I thought back to when we'd watched the film *Knocked Up* together with Jude on DVD. In it, the main woman found herself pregnant after a one-night stand, and oh, how we'd laughed when she decided to keep the baby and start dating the father, even though they were poles apart. We'd shouted, 'As if!' at the screen and, 'Yeah, right!', patronizing the character for not even considering any other options. We'd done a lot of 'Only in America!'s that even in a film as funny and edgy as this, with lots of swear words in it and drug-taking, it felt like the Right to Life lobby had won out. But then we'd reasoned that without her – in our books – naive decision to have the baby, there would have been no story. So eventually we'd overlooked that minor detail and had enjoyed the rest of the movie, all the while considering her a silly moo for not having been to the termination clinic. And yet here we were, maybe a year, eighteen months later, and Gracie was doing the exact same thing. Not that I knew that Joshua was her polar opposite; I just knew that she hardly knew him.

Or maybe she did. Maybe she had learned so much in the past three weeks that she was confident of their future together. Maybe it was me who didn't know Gracie at all. This would certainly indicate that. We had been ships that passed in the night. We'd rarely had nights out together. We just behaved like an old married couple on our rare TV-dinner evenings together, or the odd Sunday brunch together, and maybe we'd never dug deep enough for me to really get to know her.

She was a bit older than me – thirty-three, I thought – so it's not like she was over the hill and her body clock was ticking particularly loudly, so why the rush? Loads of women had babies in their forties now, despite what I'd thought growing up about my parents being ancient. It was much more the done thing these days. So why had she got it into her head that she needed not only to have the baby but to marry the father? And what sort of a man was he that he proposed to the first woman he got pregnant? That is, if she was the first woman he'd got pregnant. Maybe he had super sperm and he'd got a string of kiddies up and down the country, all the way from Plymouth to . . . somewhere in Scotland beginning with P. Perth, maybe. If Perth was indeed in Scotland. Geography was never my strong point.

I was well aware that this sort of behaviour would have been deemed chivalrous in the war years, maybe later, but now? In the twenty-first century? How times change. Maybe I was being too hard on him, but this old-fashioned behaviour seemed rather desperate in this day and age. But then I supposed at least he wasn't running at the first sign of trouble, like so many men might do. But still. Wasn't he suspicious? Wouldn't a lot of men assume, rightly or wrongly, that a woman who claimed to be pregnant so early into the relationship was trying to trap him?

Or maybe Gracie had become bored with the way the

movie of her life was panning out. Fearful of the critics walking out because they thought it was just plain dull, she was seizing this opportunity to give herself a better second act. Who knew?

Life sometimes didn't make sense.

As always happened when I thought or heard of anything to do with babies and pregnancy, I thought back to my birth mother. This woman I didn't know. This stranger who I could have quite easily walked past on the street and not recognized as the person who gave birth to me. Nor would she have recognized the baby she gave away. I wondered if her circumstances were like Gracie's. I very much doubted they were. I had given the circumstances much thought over the years and come up with two scenarios into which I was born.

OK. So I knew her name was Francesca. And she was from Liverpool. But beyond that I knew little else. But my two scenarios were as follows:

Scenario One: the Hollywood version

Hotshot up-and-coming lawyer Francesca Boyle doesn't believe in glass ceilings. In her quest for the top she will let nothing and no one stand in her way at the leading London law firm Harbottle & Deloitte & Judgey. That is till new head honcho Dirk Soliz is brought in to troubleshoot the photocopiers during a long, hot summer. (OK, it was obvious I didn't know much about law firms, but suffice to say Dirk Soliz was *hot*.) Oh yes, and in this version Francesca gets rid of her pent-up anger at the injustice she sees in the world each evening by playing the cello. She'll play anything on it: Elgar's Cello Concerto, the bass line from 'Pachelbel's Canon', 'La Cucaracha'.

She and Dirk have a combative, screwball relationship of one-upmanship, which concludes with Dirk taking her over a photocopier one night and making love to her till dawn. It's the best sex they've ever had. But the next day he drops down dead with an allergic reaction to the ink in the printer. Devastated, Francesca discovers she is with child. She soldiers on trying to take over the company with her ballsy but likeable ways, constantly covering up her pregnancy with a succession of increasingly large handbags.

One day she feels the first twinges of labour. She gets on her motorbike and drives to her family in Liverpool. She gives birth in the vestibule and insists her mother give the baby up for adoption, before returning to London for a three-o'clock board meeting. Francesca wins control of the company. She becomes a mover and shaker in the world of high finance and big business. But it has all been at a cost. One night she commits suicide. But then miraculously recovers, realizes she has got her priorities all wrong and becomes a nun and does good in the community. One day she is sent to be a missionary in Liverpool. There she meets her daughter and builds up a close bond with her before telling her the truth. Daughter Holly, now an orphan, is over the moon.

The end.

OK, so it had more holes than a doily, but I enjoyed it. I could see it as a movie too, with Anne Hathaway playing Francesca, George Clooney as poor Dirk and the little girl from *Les Mis* playing the young me.

However, the truth was probably far more like this:

Scenario Two: the gritty version

Francesca Boyle, a fourteen-year-old neglected crack addict, has a boyfriend who beats her up. One day he rapes her, then vanishes. She is left to bring the baby up alone and social services say she's not up to the job. She's a bit sad for a while when the baby has gone, but she soon adapts. Recently she has gone into rehab and has . . .

I didn't carry on. I wasn't a fan of that version; it made me feel sad. I contented myself with watching the first movie in my head. This time I saw it in Spanish with subtitles and a vivid palette of colours, as if Almodóvar had directed it. The motorbike ride from the City to Liverpool, up the M1 then the M6, was surprisingly exciting.

I had asked Gracie if she would change her mind. I wasn't requesting that she did, just checking whether she thought she would. The contract was up on our flat and we were meant to be signing the new one in a month. She claimed it couldn't have come at a better time for her. I wasn't as certain. I reassured myself that I wasn't going to be homeless. I counted my blessings that, due to my recent bereavement, I would, one day soon hopefully, be quids in at the bank. But what was I going to do then? I really should start climbing the property ladder and buy a place of my own, but if I did get the extortionate £175,000 for Mum's house, what might that buy me in London? A small kitchen on the outskirts of Peckham perhaps? If I was lucky?

My phone beeped. I knew who it would be before I looked at the screen. My wonderful lady and mistress. The wording of her text was suitably concise:

Wig. Plane. Yes?

I sighed. And quickly punched back:

On it.

No response came. No 'Thank you', or 'Cheers, sweetheart', or 'You're an angel.' Silence. I was officially her bitch. But for how much longer? Another text. I tutted and looked, but it was from Jude.

Take as much time as you need. I'll be waiting.

My fingers hovered over the phone.

Then I decided I would write to him. Tonight in bed. But what would I say? It's not me, it's you? It's not you, it's me? I prefer seeing you from a distance on the stage?

I could decide that later.

I flipped open my laptop and the screen blinked into life. I waited while the internet connection recognized the Wi-Fi. My job for this evening was to book Sylvie's wig a flight to Canada in time for the tour. She was having a new one made in New York and she needed me to get it couriered to the airport and flown to Vancouver ready for our arrival. I needed to book it a seat in the cabin and not in the hold, and I had to book it first class, presumably so the better breed of people there wouldn't be tempted to poke about with the box and wonder what was in it, then try and steal it. It was a ridiculous job, but someone had to do it. Instead of going straight to the British Airways website, however, I found myself looking at property websites. I was wrong: £175,000 wouldn't buy me a small kitchen in Peckham; it would buy me a small briefcase in Nunhead. Where was Nunhead? Just as I was Google Mapping Nunhead, I heard an email ping into my inbox.

God. Sometimes she did this. Sometimes she forwent her love of texting me to send me a missive via email. This would tend to happen when she was in a foul mood and wanted to rant about something. She found it easier to attack the keyboard of her desktop than the screen of her smartphone. I checked the time. It was just after eight. Maybe she was drunk and had forgotten she didn't have the chicken breasts and was incandescent that she'd had to make do with pasta and pesto. Nervously I minimized the web page I was on and brought up my emails.

Oh good. It wasn't from her. It was an email from Google. It showed a link to something I'd set up an alert for ages back. I'd almost forgotten that I'd done it.

Coincidentally, it was from an estate agent's website.

I clicked on it. And read.

Property for Rent: 32B Gambier Terrace, Liverpool L1 TBW

And in an instant, and with a rush of excitement, I knew exactly how my movie would play out.

I phoned the estate agent's the next morning from Sylvie's apartment. She was out with Michael doing a photo shoot for a new calendar called 'Stars and Their Dogs', in aid of Battersea Dogs Home.

A woman with a broad Liverpool accent answered with a confident 'Hello, pair o' net curtains. How can I help?'

'Sorry?'

'Pair o' net curtains. How can I help you?'

It was then I remembered that the estate agent's was called Perronet Curtis.

'Hello, sorry, yes. I was wondering if the property on Gambier Terrace was still available for rent – 32B. It came on your website last night and—'

''Ang on, love.'

I heard the click of fingernails on keyboard. It seemed to go on for ages, like she was breaking the Bletchley code.

'Number 32B Gambier Terrace. Yest.'

She did, she actually put a 'T' on the end of 'yes'.

'I'd like to rent it.'

'Ri-i-ight. I can arrange a viewing for that . . . this afternoon if you're interested.'

'No. I can't come today. I'd just like to . . . rent it.'

'Er . . . 'ang on, love,' and then she put me on hold. 'A House Is Not a Home' started to play down the phone. Shirley Bassey. It made me smile. I realized my phone was shaking in my hand. I was either nervous or excited, or both. I was on hold for quite a while. When that song finished, the Pet Shop Boys' 'Rent' started to play. It was quickly cut off.

'Hello. Can I take your name, pleeeease?' She elongated her 'please' to cover as many notes as doing a glissando on a piano.

'Yes. My name is Holly Smith.'

'OK, and can I take a contact telephone number from you, pleeeeease?'

I gave her my mobile number.

Could this really be happening? It seemed such a coincidence, too good to be true. It couldn't be, could it?

'Right, Mrs Smith, I'm gonna have to speak to the owner about this coz usually they want to meet their tenants before they go ahead and let it, you see.'

'I'll pay six months up front,' I said.

There was silence on the other end.

'I just really want to rent that flat.'

'But you haven't even seen it. We haven't taken any pictures of it yet.'

'I know. And I'm in London, so I can't come and look.'

She lowered her voice. 'But it might be a shithole. And you sound dead posh.'

'I'm not posh. I'm just Southern. And it's got sentimental value.'

'What has, that flat?'

'Yes.'

'Oh right.'

'Could you . . . could you tell me the name of the person who owns it?' I ventured. Because it could of course be Francesca Boyle, her actual self.

'I can't, Mrs Smith. On account of thingy. Data protection. Yest.'

I realized now that she was saying 'yest' because she was trying to poshen up her voice because she thought I was posh. It was quite endearing, if a tad bizarre.

'Is it a man or a woman?' I said. In a tone that said, 'Cut the crap!'

'It's a woman,' she replied, like she'd given a massive secret away and felt so guilty.

'Is it a Francesca Boyle?'

'Oh, don't do this to me, Mrs Smith – what are you like?' and then she lowered her voice. 'It's a Mrs Kirkwood.'

My heart sank.

'Right. Fine.'

Although that could have been Francesca's married name. It seemed churlish to ask this woman if she knew the owner's maiden name; it didn't feel like the sort of information you'd automatically divulge to a landlord.

'Mrs Smith . . .'

'Please, call me Holly.'

'Holly, love, you do realize six months' rent is an awful lot of money?'

66

'I don't care.'

'It's over five grand.'

'I appreciate that.'

I could almost hear her thinking, God, you lucky bitch, you must be loaded.

'And you could come in at some point and sign the contracts and . . . give us a cheque?'

'No. But I could do a bank transfer whenever you needed it. And I'm sure if you emailed me the contract, I could post it back to you. Or have it couriered.'

'Right. Well, I'll tell the owner.'

'Mrs Kirkwood?' I said, just checking.

'Oh, Holly love, what are you like?'

Desperate, I felt like responding, but I just chuckled instead.

'You do know it's partly furnished?'

'Yes, I read that online.'

'And you do realize that a lot of the stuff in these furnished flats is shocking?'

I loved the way she said 'shocking'. It sounded like 'shokkkin'.

'I don't care. I want that flat. What d'you think my chances are?'

'Well, you're not DSS if you can afford six months' rent, so I'd say they were pretty good.'

Good. Good. Oh my God, I was really nervous now. Maybe someone up in heaven was looking after me. Who, though? Could Mum/Jean really be my guardian angel? And if she was, wouldn't she be impeding this process of attempting to find Francesca?

'How soon can you speak to Mrs Kirkwood?'

'Well, I'm not sure if she works, so I don't know how easy

it'll be to get hold of her. You know, we do have some nicer properties on Gambier Terrace.'

'No, it has to be that one.'

'OK. Well, leave it with me, Holly love, and I'll see what I can sort out for you. Yest?'

'Yest,' I echoed.

Gosh, we were getting on well. Like giggly teenagers. It almost felt like we'd do a succession of 'You hang up' 'No, you hang up's, but she rather briskly cut me off and I stared at my phone wondering what on earth I had done.

Damn. And I'd still not booked the wig's flight to Vancouver. I hurried to Sylvie's computer and fired up the internet. I was just logging into the BA website, doing exactly what I should have been doing the previous night, had I not instead spent the evening Google Earthing the life out of Gambier Terrace, when the buzzer went, alerting me there was someone at the door. I skidded to the entryphone (wooden floors, over-enthusiastic Thai cleaner, recipe for disaster) and found it was some delivery men with Sylvie's new sofa. Or, as she liked to call it, banquette. I buzzed them up and three minutes later two burly lads in jeans and parkas were carrying the pink monstrosity into the main lounge.

Sylvie already had two white leather sofas facing each other across a coffee table as the focal point of this room, and she'd not said where she wanted it to go – and in all honesty I'd forgotten it was coming today as I'd been so preoccupied with my impending call to Perronet Curtis. So I just got the burly lads to place it at the end of the room, in front of an art deco sideboard Sylvie had had flown in from Miami that housed her Olivier awards. As they hacked off the brown cardboard the settee was wrapped in, I was reminded what a horrendous piece of furniture it was.

It was basically a massive pair of hot-pink velvet lips. It was allegedly based on a historic design by Salvador Dalí inspired by the shape of Marilyn Monroe's mouth. I saw the burly lads looking rather quizzically at it.

'It's based on a Dalí design. Apparently,' I proffered.

'Each to their own, darlin',' the more burly of the two said.

'Personally, I think it's hideous.' I smiled. And signed on their handheld electronic device. And they laughed.

I saw them nosing at Sylvie's gold discs on the wall in the hall on the way out. And heard the less burly of the two saying, 'Never heard of her,' as they headed for the lift.

An hour later, after speaking to several contacts in VIP services at BA, I had successfully booked first-class travel, plus couriering of a wig from Manhattan to Vancouver. I was feeling pretty pleased with myself when I heard the front door go.

'The sofa's here!' I called out perkily, hoping it would put her in a reasonable mood. Michael scurried in and ran round in excited circles at my feet. I bent to tickle his nose and something came off on my fingers. A brown stain.

'Is Michael wearing make-up?' I called again.

And then I heard it.

One of the most ear-piercing screams I had ever heard in my life. I jumped up and skidded through to the lounge. Sylvie was standing in front of the sofa with steam practically coming out of her ears.

'What . . . is *this*?' she snarled.

'Your banquette.' Why did I sound so frightened?

'I . . . *hate it*!' she screamed, and she started ripping off her faux-fur poncho.

'Oh. You liked it in the shop,' I said gently, trying to calm her mood. The poncho had stuck round her neck, so I ventured closer to help her off with it. She batted me away.

'I loathed it in the shop, but *you made me buy it*!'

'I-I didn't!' I stammered.

She turned to look at me. I thought she might hit me she looked so angry. I also thought she might choke, as the poncho was taking on noose-like proportions round her neck.

'What did you say?' Her voice was small now, which made it all the more threatening.

'Sylvie, I was never keen on it, but you thought it was camp.'

'Camp? *Camp!* Who do you think I am, dear? Danny La fucking Rue?'

'I'm sure you can send it back.' There I went again, ever the peacemaker.

'I never even wanted a new banquette in the first place,' she spat, and then went and kicked the lips. 'You've made this place look like a tart's boudoir!'

I couldn't help myself. I tried to remain strong, but the timbre of my voice belied my fear. 'With respect, Sylvie, we went shopping for a sofa because you were tired with the white ones. You wouldn't buy something just because I liked it. My opinion's not that important to you.'

She kicked it again.

'And anyway, my opinion was, and still is, that it's hideous.'

She spun round and in a flash I saw her arm swing back and before I could flinch she slapped me across the face. She almost span round herself afterwards. When she stopped, the poncho swirled about her like a dying maypole. I was so shocked I didn't do anything for a second. My face didn't hurt. I guess that was through shock.

'Get out of my sight! And ring the shop and tell them I'm sending it back!'

And in a flash, not that I meant to, I found myself hurling my arm towards her and . . .

Oh sweet Jesus . . .

I slapped her round the side of the face too. It knocked her sideways and she fell in a heap onto the couch. The force of my slap made her bounce up and down a few times. She choked a bit as the poncho caught her neck. She ripped it down, looked genuinely shocked, and sat there saying nothing. My face was now stinging from her attack as the reality set in. I'm sure hers was too. Her wig had gone a bit skew-whiff too. Oh dear.

'At least it's . . . well sprung,' I said, indicating her bouncing.

When eventually she spoke, it was almost a whisper.

'You're fired.'

I laughed. 'Oh no I'm not. Because I quit.'

And then she chuckled.

'In fact, Sylvie, you can stick your job up your egotistical anus.'

She gasped.

And I added, for dramatic effect, 'So far and with such vigour that I hope it pops out the other side.'

I tried to march out of the room, but it was more like a series of skids, and went into her office to get my bag. Michael was sat by the desk chair, whimpering. I bent and tickled his nose. I then grabbed my bag, pulled out the keys to her apartment, thumped them onto her desk and headed for the front door. I opened it. Then I called back, 'And for the record, I thought "Misunderstood Queen" was a pile of shite!'

I slammed the door behind me and went to the lift. I felt amazing, invincible; nothing and no one could stop me. This was what winning felt like. I was on top of the world!

Five minutes later I was sat on a bench overlooking the

Thames, bawling my eyes out. Panic rose in me. What had I done? Was I doing the right thing? But then I remembered the slap and tried to get some perspective. I took out my phone and jabbed in a number. I called the estate agent's in Tring.

'Oh, Holly, I'm glad you've called,' a guy called Guy said. 'I've shown a few people round, but I can never get the heating to work.'

'You have to thump the side of the box.'

'I see.'

'Anyone interested?'

'Well, someone wanted to offer one twenty, but I told him you wouldn't accept that. That's why I didn't call you.'

'Accept it,' I said quickly.

'Holly?'

'Take it. I want a quick sale. Take one twenty.'

'But it's worth fifty grand more than that.'

'I don't care. I want it off my hands. Are they in a chain?'

'I didn't even ask as I thought it was so low.'

'One twenty's fine. Thanks, Guy.'

'Well, I'll try to get them up. I've got targets to meet.'

'As quickly as possible, please.' And I hung up.

Oh God, Holly, I thought, what have you done?

FOUR

From: rkirkwoodmrs@longlivethegpo.co.uk
To: hollyjsmith001@hotmail.co.uk
Subject: Sunday

Dear Holly,

   Thank you for your email. Sorry I didn't reply sooner, but
I have been into Birkenhead to get my hair and nails done. I
am a trained hairdresser, so if you need to find a decent place
for yours, I can recommend several in Liverpool (where you
won't get ripped off).

   I am sorry to say I have never heard of Sylvie di Marco, but
I mentioned her to some friends and they had and were very
impressed. They reckon I'm renting the flat out to a celebrity
LOL. But don't worry – I am not a stalker. And I won't go
selling my story to the papers LOL.

   Everything is set for Sunday. I will be at the flat to meet
you at three with your keys, et cetera. Looking forward to
meeting you and welcoming you to the city. I am fine with you
bringing a dog – as you say, it is only temporary. Do not fret
about the washing machine: my husband has mended it only
yesterday. It's all looking nice and cosy in there, and I hope
you will be very happy. As you're coming such a distance, I will

make sure there is milk in the fridge and a loaf in the larder. I might even run to some teabags LOL.

I have to dash now, as my husband is taking me up the golf club for a karaoke night. I don't sing, but it can be fun.

In answer to your question, no, I don't own any other properties to rent. It's a small enterprise really. Personally I live on the Wirral. It's really pretty where we are – am very lucky.

Kind regards,

Rose Kirkwood

From: hollyjsmith001@hotmail.co.uk
To: judethefiddle@judetheobscure.com
Subject: Liverpool

Dear Jude,

I'm so sorry I've not been in touch. I haven't really known what to say, and didn't want to hurt your feelings with half-baked explanations, but a lot has happened in the last few days and I wanted to try and explain.

Jude, you're a wonderful man. Clever, talented, funny and handsome. You've often complained that I've not been there when you needed me because I was always at Sylvie's beck and call, and you deserve better than that. Well, I am going on a bit of an adventure now. Yet again being selfish, I am heading to Liverpool for a while to try and track down my mum. You know how months ago I contacted social services but they've been unable to find my adoption records because of boundary changes (whatever that means)? Well, my last letter from them said it might take another three months. I have got sick of waiting so am going to go up there and try and find out for myself where she is and what happened. I need to be on my own to do that.

I think if we were meant to be, then I would be asking you to come with me. As I'm not, I think that speaks volumes.

Thank you for saying you would wait for me, but I think you'd be wasting your time. Maybe I'm just not suited to a relationship, because if I was, you'd be my perfect match. But until I've put the pieces of my jigsaw in place, I don't feel I can move on. I feel I'm treading water.

I'm so sorry, Jude. Please give my love to Daisy and Clint, and all your lovely brothers and sisters. Sometimes they felt more of a family to me than my own. I bet D and C are having a blast on their round-the-world trip. And as they said in their card, they'd have been at the funeral in spirit.

All love, and goodbye,

H xx

'Ladies and gentlemen, this train will shortly be arriving at its final destination, Liverpool Lime Street. Hope you've got a snappy dress sense, the gift of the gab, and, ladies . . . if you're going out in the daytime, do make sure you wear humungous rollers in your hair. It's a look!'

I knew what Liverpool looked like. I had spent so many hours gazing at pictures online of the city centre and its distinctive skyline that I could have quite easily pencilled the twin domes of the Liver Building with its cormorants on top, the 1960s tower like a big sucked lollipop and the twin cathedrals in the style of one of those brilliant autistic artists. Although I was arriving by train, I'd somehow expected to sail majestically into the city on some form of overhead railway, taking in all the sights, the colours, the glistening River

Mersey speckled with ferries. But actually the last fifteen minutes of the journey we went underground, seemingly riding through a blackened sandstone tunnel. I only knew it was sandstone because I'd read as much online and knew the city centre was built on a ridge of the stone. So much so that the Anglican Cathedral – which my new flat overlooked – was made from that very stone. I gathered together my Everest of bags and clipped the dog lead onto Michael.

Yes, I had Michael.

Sylvie had blackmailed me into minding him for her while she went to Canada. She had turned up on my doorstep in her dark glasses with Michael in a handbag, claiming I had ruined her life, and as I wasn't accompanying her overseas, there was no one to look after her precious pooch. She claimed that if I didn't take him, he'd have to go into kennels and would probably end up slaughtered and sold to Romanians for dog food.

'It's dog eat dog out there,' I'd quipped. Though she hadn't laughed.

She then went on to threaten me that if I didn't take him for the month, she would report me to the police for hitting her.

'You hit me,' I pointed out.

'It's your word against mine.'

'I'm moving to Liverpool,' I said.

'So? They have dogs in Liverpool, don't they?'

She handed me the handbag. And then a bin bag.

'What's this?' I hesitated to look inside.

'Payment,' she said, then returned to her driver.

I looked in the bag. She'd given me her faux-fur poncho. As her car pulled away, I heard her call through the window, 'It's Alexander McQueen!'

Which is how I came to be moving to Liverpool with Michael in tow.

I'd been incredibly disappointed to discover that Mrs Kirkwood's first name was not Francesca when I'd been given her bank details to transfer the rent. But then I reasoned that Francesca had been living in the flat over thirty years ago, so the likelihood of her still having links with it today were pretty slim, bordering on anorexic. Just because my mum and dad had lived in the same house for decades didn't mean that everyone else had. Especially someone like Francesca, who wasn't one of life's copers. She'd not coped with me, so how would she have coped with paying rent, for instance? She may well have been evicted. Or repossessed. Or rehoused. I had no idea. She might even have died. I didn't dwell on this possibility too long, of course – I had to keep the faith that she was still alive, and that somehow I was going to find her.

But I couldn't work out the history of the flat until I was there and I could pick Rose Kirkwood's brains. I'd asked casually in an email if she owned lots of properties and she'd given me her response. So as she wasn't some big property tycoon, maybe she might know the history of the flat. Only time would tell. As I hadn't wanted to bombard her with questions via an email exchange, I would wait to see what she was like and ask her face to face. In my head, Rose Kirkwood was going to be the soothsayer who would unlock all the secrets from my past. She was going to be like one of those genealogy experts you saw on *Who Do You Think You Are?* I could just picture her in a dusty reading room in one of the records offices in Liverpool, lace gloves on, carefully turning the pages of an oversized book, showing me the history of

Gambier Terrace and the movements of Francesca Boyle via the censuses over the years.

'And this . . . Holly,' she would say solemnly, 'is where Francesca is today.'

I would sit in hushed reverence and then say, 'Son of a bitch!' – just like Kim Cattrall did in hers. Though admittedly in hers she was discovering that her grandfather had been a bigamist. I'm not sure calling Francesca a son of a bitch, whatever she had done, was completely appropriate. I still said it very well. And my American accent was second to none, even if Cattrall was Canadian.

'Son of a bitch.' Yes, I was very good. And, I now realized, I had said it out loud. Others in the carriage were looking at me. I looked down at the dog, as if I'd been aiming the words at him, but he was curled up at my feet, fast asleep. And now not only did people in the carriage think I was American, they thought I was an American chihuahua abuser. I'd be lucky to get off this train without the RSPCA arresting me.

I'd tried my best to travel as light as possible, but I still had a massive rucksack, my laptop bag and two holdalls – hard enough to carry at the best of times without having to keep one hand free to hold Michael's lead. It was challenging to say the least to mount all four bags about my person. The rucksack in particular was ridiculously heavy, and rocked my centre of balance. I was sure that at any point I would go toppling backwards like a hit skittle in a bowling alley. I yanked the lead and Michael jumped into action. From dreaming to trotting in the blink of an eye, bless him.

'Come on, Michael!' I chirruped as I tried to squeeze down the aisle. My attempt to get off the train first wasn't welcomed by my fellow passengers in Coach H as I knocked each of them out with my mass of bags.

'Sorry . . . sorry . . .'

'Watch what you're doing, girl!'

'Ow! Jeez!'

'So sorry, gosh!'

Then I heard, 'I thought she was a Yank?'

Eventually I made it to the section between the carriages where the toilet was and watched through the door as the platform zoomed smoothly into view.

'D'you need an 'and with your bags, love?' a friendly voice behind me said. I turned round, but judged it wrong and promptly knocked the kind man to the ground with my Mr Blobby-sized rucksack.

'Oh gosh, I'm so sorry!'

'Fuckin' 'ell, girl, what you got in there?' he said, scrambling to his feet. 'A dead body?'

I leaned to take his hand to pull him back up, but as I leaned forward, the weight of my rucksack hit me like a ton of bricks and I fell on top of him, and this time we both fell to the ground. My face hit his as I lay on top of him.

'Oh gosh, I'm really sorry about this.' Even in the most em-barrassing of situations I remained impeccably polite.

'You're all right, love – you had me at "sorry".' He winked. Our faces were so close his eyelashes grazed my cheeks.

'This is so embarrassing. I think you're going to have to roll me off.'

'First time for everything . . .'

The poor guy was only about twenty, a skinhead with swallows tattooed either side of his neck. He smelt of coal tar soap. Fortunately he laughed and pushed me to one side, but as I rolled off him, I got stuck again, as my rucksack wedged me between him and the toilet door. Other passengers were trying to leave the train now, but we were blocking their way.

'Can you hurry up, please? We need to get off!' called one antsy woman.

Fortunately Mr Swallows jumped to my rescue.

'All right, love, keep your hair on – we're trying our hardest. She's got loadsa bags.'

'I know. Bag city or what?' someone else commented.

'Oh, this is ridiculous,' sighed someone else.

'If you don't hurry up, we'll be heading back to Euston at this rate!' Someone else sounded irate.

I dared not look at them. 'I'm so sorry!' I bleated as Mr Swallows made a gargantuan effort to squeeze past me and up. And managed. A few in the queue gave a tepid round of applause and Mr Swallows took my hand and yanked me to my feet. All the time Michael just sat by the door, watching, bewildered or bored, one of the two. Mr Swallows grabbed two of my holdalls, pushed the button by the door and it hissed open. A bit unsteady on my feet, I stepped gingerly off the train and felt my feet on terra Liverpoola for the first time.

'Welcome to Liverpool,' he said.

'Thank you so much,' I said, and almost reached into my pocket to tip him.

'Nah, you're all right. Always wanted a posh bird on top of us.'

'Oh, I'm not really posh. I'm just Southern.'

'Nah, princess, you're well posh. You're like that Pippa Middleton. Shall I walk you to the cab rank or you getting the bus?'

'Cab would be great.'

'Cushty.'

And on we walked.

'You're very kind,' I said, though if I'm honest, I was slightly fearful this was all a ruse and he was about to sprint off with my luggage. I felt Michael stop, the lead getting taut, and I looked to see him taking a pee on the platform.

'Oh God,' I said, hoping no one would see.

Mr Swallows was in hysterics. 'Ah well, when you've gotta go, you've gotta go. What's his name?'

'Michael. Long Story.' And then I quipped, 'But I call him Michael for short.'

To which he burst out laughing again. Gosh, he was easily amused. And I was easily flattered.

When we eventually headed to the ticket barrier, he asked me what I was doing in this fair city and I found myself garbling, unnecessarily, about how I was trying to trace my birth mother and how I was moving into the flat where I was born and what an exciting adventure I was embarking on. Why was I even telling this virtual stranger this? His eyes widened and he did a bit of 'gee whiz' whistling out of the side of his mouth.

'Fair play to you, girl. Fate honours the brave an' all that.'

There wasn't actually a ticket barrier at the end of the concourse, just a partition in a glass wall, behind which lots of relatives, lovers, friends stood waiting for the new arrivals. I instantly appraised every woman over forty to see if they looked like me. I was so busy searching the faces of every passer-by that I almost didn't clock the view of the skyline as we bypassed the main pedestrian entrance. The sky was bright white; I had to squint to see the lollipop tower, which actually didn't look like a lollipop at all.

'What's at the top of that tower?' I asked, pointing.

'City FM. Local radio station,' Mr Swallows said. 'Think it used to be a restaurant too. Span round while you were eating. Dunno if it still is, like. This way,' Mr Swallows said, and nodded left.

I followed. The noise of the place was deafening, echoing around this cavernous space. We passed a bronze statue of an alarming-looking man with a feather duster – Ken Dodd, Mr Swallows explained – a coffee stand, a newsagent's, before arriving at a sweep of pavement that was still indoors where people were queuing for cabs.

'Can I give you a lift anywhere?' I thought it was the least I could do.

'Nah, you're all right, girl. I'm going the wrong way.'

Well, I really hoped that I wasn't going the wrong way. For all I knew, Francesca might have left Liverpool and gone to live somewhere else. For all I knew, she could have been living in the flat beneath me in Kentish Town, practising her scales till all hours.

'What's your ma's name?' he asked.

Gosh, thinking about it, Mr Swallows could be . . . my brother or something.

'Francesca. Francesca Boyle.'

He nodded, impressed. 'Posh, laa.'

'What does "laa" mean? Sorry . . .'

'Lad. Not that I think you look like a bloke.'

'I see.'

And I said it to myself in my head. Laa.

'Sorry. Never heard of her,' he was saying. Suddenly, as Mr Swallows placed my holdalls on the ground and he gave Michael a friendly tap on the head, I didn't want him to go. In the five minutes we'd spent together he'd shown me great kindness, and I knew that as soon as he'd gone, I'd be back on this scary adventure alone.

'I really appreciate your kindness. Thank you so much,' I said.

He rubbed my arm. 'Well, good luck, darlin'. I hope you find what you come looking for an' all that.'

'Me too.' I wasn't sure what else to say, but he could see that I was wary about something.

'You all right?'

'Yes. Fine,' I replied, sounding anything but.

'Tell you what, love. I'll give you me mobile number, yeah? You give us a shout if you fancy a guided tour.'

I was thrilled, but my face clearly didn't convey that.

'I'm not a rapist.'

'God, no. I know you're not.' Well, I didn't, but still. 'That'd be great.'

And so we did that familiar dance of 'You give me your number and I'll text you. Then you'll have my number' and 'What's your name so I can put it in my phone?' and 'What shall I put you in my phone under?' and so on.

Iggy. His name was Iggy.

'Wow, that's an unusual name.'

'Short for Ignatius. Good Catholic lad!'

I gave a rather dirty, ironic chuckle. And then realized he had described himself as a lad. Oh heavens, was I flirting with a *twenty-year-old*? And oh no, did he think I was some kind of cougar, or worse still that I was a MILF? Mind you, he had addressed me as 'girl' most of the time.

Of course, this could all still have been a ruse. He could still swipe away my bags and run for it.

Instead he saluted me. 'See you, babe!' he winked.

'See you, laa!' I winked back, causing great mirth. And then I watched him walk out onto the street, into the light. As he walked, he tucked his left hand into the waist of his baggy jogging bottoms. He had a swagger to his walk, a confidence, like he owned the streets. He sort of lolloped as he walked; there was something of the silverback about him. And just before he turned from view, he looked back, saluted me again and then disappeared into the day.

The chugging black cab swept me up a hill away from the station and I took in its road name: Mount Pleasant, though there was very little pleasant about it with its takeaway shops and overall greyness. The greyness gave way to some more appropriately pleasant Edwardian terraces further up, and then I caught my breath as I glimpsed Paddy's Wigwam for the first time. This was the name given to the Metropolitan Cathedral by the locals, and it was a startling, if surreal example of 1960s architecture – a brutal, fat wigwam of glass with a crown of thorns at the top. But I didn't glimpse it for long, as the driver swung right and took me into Hope Street. My heart was beating faster now as I was so familiar with these streets from my internet searches. We passed the Everyman Theatre on the left, which was being completely renovated – it was all hoardings and overhead cranes – and I strained my neck to see up ahead, because I knew that Hope Street linked both cathedrals. I knew that soon I would be home.

I looked at the houses and shops and pavements around me and tried to picture Francesca walking them, pregnant with me; maybe she even took me out as a baby in my pram around here. If only I knew what she looked like, it would make the image so much better. I imagined myself at sixteen, assuming that's what she'd been, pushing a second-hand pram around, baby Holly asleep below her.

Except my name wasn't Holly then. My name was . . .

Then I saw it. And it did actually take my breath away. I asked the driver to stop and he pulled over by the pavement. I wound down my window and strained to look up at one of the most powerful buildings I'd ever seen. A solid mausoleum of sandstone rock, the Anglican Cathedral sat at the top of a hill looking out over the pudding basin of the city centre. Its tall tower had eye-like windows halfway down that gave it the air of an imperious old lady keeping watch over her people, further down a circle of glass that looked like an open mouth. Was she shocked by what she saw? I certainly was. Although I'd seen many pictures of it over the months, and I'd read so much about its construction, nothing had quite prepared me for the reality. It looked so foreboding, yet beautiful, a sad beauty, but a majestic one nonetheless, and one for a city to be proud of.

I knew we must be close, as I knew Gambier Terrace over-looked the cathedral. I thanked the driver and we moved on. Seconds later we were pulling into the grove of houses that constituted the terrace. The Georgian sweep of yellow-bricked, bay-windowed, tall-chimneyed residences was also even better in the flesh, or brick, and I marvelled that the area was so well-to-do, or felt that way. How did a young girl from these houses get things so wrong that she had to have her baby taken away? The driver pulled up outside number 32 and I felt an instant connection. Whether that was because of some long-forgotten memory from when I was a baby or whether it was because I'd spent so long now looking at pictures of the houses, I didn't know. I imagined it was the latter. I rarely remembered anything before my fifth birthday.

'Did you know,' I informed the driver as he kindly helped me out of the cab with my bags and Michael, and walked them to the door, 'that this road was named after James Gambier, a royal admiral?'

The driver shook his head. 'I move here three year ago. I am Polish.'

'You like Liverpool?'

He shrugged. 'Gdańsk is very beautiful. Five eighty, please.'

Well, I had decided that Liverpool was very beautiful. I bet Gdańsk didn't have a cathedral like the one completely filling my field of vision.

'Keep the change,' I said as I handed him six pounds. I was sure he rolled his eyes. I turned to the green door. Looked at the bells beside it.

I was distracted temporarily by the noise of some screaming. An operatic wail, it ended almost before it had begun. Moments later a second came, longer this time. Where was it from? It seemed to come from up on high. I looked up to see if any windows were open, but couldn't locate any. And then, just as suddenly as I had heard it start, it stopped again.

Well, this was it – I was about to meet Rose Kirkwood. My journey of self-discovery could finally begin. The taxi chugged away, pulling out of the tree-lined slip road and back onto Hope Street. I felt the first drops of rain, and some clouds passed slowly above. I stared at the bell, and as the temperature dropped, so did my confidence. Excitement drained out of me like a cold flush, leaving me hollow. It was there, look at it, second bell down, 32B. But I couldn't press it. All of a sudden this felt like folly. What had I done? I had packed in my job, my life, travelled three hundred miles on a whim with a chihuahua that wasn't mine. This was madness. This was grief.

I looked back at the cathedral. The face on the tower seemed to gaze down at me quizzically now, as if saying, *Well, Holly, what are you going to do now? What next?*

Gosh. I was going mad, imagining that buildings could speak.

I toyed with getting a taxi back to the station and returning to London, but I had nowhere to go, nowhere to stay, and I'd impetuously paid the rent on this place for the next six months with my mum's life savings.

I had no choice. I could do this. I turned back to the door and stared at it.

It opened. Quickly. A mixed-race woman in her mid-twenties almost fell out, pulling up a trench coat and falling over a bulky handbag. She had a bright pink weave and far too much make-up. She then almost tripped over my luggage and had to jump clear of the dog.

'Oh God, sorry! I didn't expect anyone to be there!'

'No, I'm sorry – I'm in the way.'

Her eyes darted to the bags, to the dog, to me.

'Are you moving in?'

I nodded. She had a really squeaky voice. She *was* Minnie Mouse.

'Flat B.'

'Oh great. I'm Jax.'

'Holly. Hi.'

'Sorry. I'm gonna be late for work. Ah, I love your dog!'

And she ran off down the road towards the main street. It was then I noticed she was wearing mismatched shoes. Jax. With the squeaky voice. I tried to commit it to memory.

I turned to look at the door again and it slammed shut in my face.

OK, so I'd met a neighbour. I could do this. And for all I knew Rose Kirkwood was looking down from the flat window wondering why the hell I wasn't ringing the doorbell.

So I pressed it. And waited.

A man's voice crackled through the intercom. 'Hello?'

'Oh.' Had I pressed the wrong bell? 'I was looking for Rose? Kirkwood?'

I had – I'd pressed the wrong bell, surely.

But then I heard him say, 'She couldn't make it. D'you wanna come up?'

I heard a buzz, then the catch on the door go. I pushed against the door and tried to wedge it open with my body-weight to drag my bags into the hall.

FIVE

I really hoped that when I stepped over the threshold into 32B Gambier Terrace, I would be overcome by the dizzying drama of déjà vu, that I would glance at the floor and instantly recognize it, catch a corner of wallpaper and feel a euphoric rush of familiarity. I climbed the wide Georgian staircase, no doubt originally designed to accommodate ladies of the house and their maids, scurrying up and down it in their big, swishy dresses, but alas felt no surge of recognition. Now that the house had been divided into flats, the staircase felt a little over grand, a bit too big for its boots, and appeared to creak in a sinister way, whereas years before these creaks would probably have been endearing and a forerunner to calls of 'Ruby? Tell Filigree the butler the stairs are still creaking!'

Could I see their ghosts? No. But was I about to see some ghosts of my own? With every step the bar of my hopes was raised more and more. I was going to see that floorboard, that chance of wallpaper and immediately memories buried deep within me would come bubbling up and flood my brain. In an instant I would see her, my mother, leaning over my cot, smiling. I would remember her for the first time and all would be well in the world.

As I reached the first floor, I saw the stairs continued up, but a small landing led me a few footsteps to a wide wooden door, painted something that was either faded hospital green gone dirty or something posher and National Trusty that probably had a quirky name like 'Melancholy'. As I struggled up with my bags, Michael straining on the lead – he wanted to keep running to the top of the house – I heard a man inside the flat calling, 'Oh God, I should've given you a hand. Sorry!'

No. I didn't want him to open the door just yet. But I could hear latches being switched, a spring of key in lock. I wanted to stand in front of the door and consider it. Just for a moment. Find out if I could remember ever having seen it before.

In my mind's eye I could see her. I could see Francesca hurrying up these stairs. She was in an astrakhan coat and a headscarf. It was raining outside and she clutched the baby – me – to her, wrapped in a blanket. She was going in a pocket for the key. In my mind's eye the door was grey then, but I knew I was making this up, because I was seeing this all from this vantage point, outside the door; in reality I would have been the hours-old baby wrapped safely in her arms. But of course, how safe could I have really been if I'd eventually been removed from her?

The door opened and I realized just how dark the hallway was. I could barely make out this man's face, silhouetted as it was against the bright daylight from the flat behind him.

'How ya. You must be Holly,' he said, outstretching a hand.

Still unable to see him clearly, I shook it.

'Hi.'

'Come in. Come in. Hello, little fella.' I assumed that was directed at Michael.

I followed the man in.

And then a thought struck me. A thought so ridiculous but at the same time so compelling in that very moment I had to see him. I had to see him turn round so I could see if my face was mirrored in his.

This could be my father.

Was this to be how I would spend every waking hour in Liverpool? Wondering if every stranger that crossed my path was related to me?

But this man, the man with the voice, was standing in my birthplace. So it could be.

Then as we moved into the living room, light flooded us and I saw him for the first time and was sure he wasn't related to me.

The man the voice belonged to was a late fortysomething with the air of a dodgy car salesman about him. The only reason I say this is he was wearing a sheepskin coat. I didn't even know they still existed outside of reruns of *Minder* or vintage clips of *EastEnders*. Nothing else about him screamed second-hand motor, but there was something about putting a man, any man, in a cut of sheepskin and I always imagined him trying to grease my palm in an attempt to offload a Morris Minor. He was affable enough, quietly spoken, a lilting Irish accent, polite and incredibly apologetic that his wife was unable to meet and greet me as he showed me around my new apartment. This was Alan Kirkwood, Rose's husband.

'Everyone calls me Irish Alan. Except back home, where they call me English Alan, coz they think my accent's gone on the boil.'

And even though I'd never met Rose, I imagined she saw Alan as a definite catch. He held doors open for me, insisted on helping me with all my bags, found a bowl to fill with water and put down for Michael, and all that with the perma-tanned, over-muscled skin of an ageing porn star. It was odd. He had the personality of a courteous village priest, the body of a former Mr Universe and dressed as if he was going to a fancy-dress party as Del Boy Trotter. Confused? I wasn't. He was really rather lovely, actually.

But he was definitely not my dad. Different nose. Different eyes. Different face shape. Different lips. Just . . . different. I didn't feel a crushing disappointment that I could tell this, more an interest, like I had a pad in my hand with every man of a certain age in Liverpool listed. He was the first to be ticked off. With the comment 'Too porny' next to him. I hoped he didn't misconstrue my eyes flitting over him as me checking him out. I couldn't afford to start off on the wrong foot with the landlord. I needed to be accepted here. I needed to be allowed to stay.

Sadly for me, the apartment was clearly not how it would have been in 1982, when I was born. I could tell it had been renovated in the last few years. The bare floorboards were too glossy, the handle-less white kitchen units too chic, the wooden blinds at the window too 'now'. Any other tenant would be overjoyed at the fashion-forward beauty of the place; I have to admit, though, I was crushed.

'It is all right, isn't it?' he was saying. My face must have relayed my feelings.

His voice trailed off, possibly worried I was going to sue him under the Trade Descriptions Act.

'No, it's lovely, Mr Kirkwood. Who wouldn't want to live somewhere so tasteful?'

And he visibly relaxed. Like he was actually melting into his sheepskin coat.

'And Rose is really sorry she couldn't be here today to show you in and all that. Only it's this friend of hers. She's quite old and she's had a fall. So Rose has had to go up the hospital, you know.'

I nodded. I did know. I knew only too well what that was like, having rushed more times than I cared to remember from Kentish Town to Tring each time Mum had had one of her scrapes, and I told him as much.

He was very sympathetic about Mum dying, surprisingly so for a man, but then I wondered whether this was a Liverpool thing, that men wore their hearts on their sleeves a bit more. Iggy had certainly been more upfront than most men I knew; maybe Alan was the same. Oh, but then he was Irish.

I explained that in the wake of Mum's death I had fancied a change of scene and a change of life, hence Liverpool. He didn't ask why I had chosen Liverpool; it clearly made complete sense that I would go to his illustrious city to 'start again'. Well, at least that meant he didn't ask too many questions. I wanted to tell him the real reason for coming. I wanted to blurt out, 'I'm here to find my birth mother.' But it seemed so weird, such an odd, impulsive thing to have done – to chuck in your life and move to a new city on the basis of a name on a solitary certificate – that I couldn't actually bring myself to blurt.

Alan showed me the electric and gas meters and how the central heating and hot water worked. He showed me the airing cupboard and where the instructions were kept for all the white goods, and then he handed me a card on which it said:

PERM SUSPECT
49 Glenda Jackson Parade
Belle Vale, Merseyside
L25 0GH
0151 484 6128
Email: appointments@permsuspect.co.uk

I looked at him quizzically.

'It's Rose's place. She says pop in anytime for a hairdo. Mates' rates.' I must have looked wary because he added, 'She's good.'

I nodded politely. 'That's very kind, tell her.'

'Or, you know, pop in for a coffee and a gab. She'd love to see you. Just, like I said, she's had this emergency today.'

'That would be lovely, thank you.'

'Ooh. He's friendly.'

I didn't know what he meant. Then I looked down and saw that Michael was humping his leg, well, his ankle.

'Michael!'

And Michael ran away.

After Alan had gone, I had a major panic when I realized I now couldn't find Michael anywhere in the flat. I ran from room to room, calling his name, unable to see him, fearful he had slipped out of the main door as Alan had left. But then I saw the door to the airing cupboard ajar and so I opened it wider and peered in. Michael had made a nest in there, next to the boiler, and in a small pile of old tea towels. He was fast asleep. It seemed a shame to wake him, but I knew I didn't want to be stuck inside on my first day. I had a new city to explore!

I have always found it easier to formulate plans or organize my brain when on the move. Many's the time I'd sit at Sylvie's computer screen staring blankly at the screensaver trying to work up the enthusiasm to actually do something, trapped in a careless catatonia that not even a hot slurp on a Costa latte could pierce, but as soon as I set foot outside her block, Michael on his lead, ideas would come to me in the blink of an eye. Maybe I just needed to get the blood circulating, the wind in my lungs to function. And today was no exception.

Where Gambier Terrace stood, behind the Anglican Cathedral, it appeared to perch on the rim of a big bowl that looked down into the city centre of Liverpool. As I stepped out with Michael, and headed down the slope towards the town, I fancied I looked a little like Reese Witherspoon in *Legally Blonde* with her chihuahua. I'm sure I didn't, but I also didn't care. The weather was so fresh, the sun so bright, and my shades were on as we practically sailed downwards towards the city. I knew exactly what I had to do.

Before I went on my mad quest to find Francesca Boyle, I had to get my bearings. What was the point in searching this city for someone if I didn't know this city in the first place? The other idea I struck on was ingenious, even if I said so myself. It might have been the startling sun going to my head, but . . . I decided I was going to become a yes-woman. For so long I had spent my life, or so it felt, saying 'yes' to one person – Sylvie – and now it was time to say 'yes' to me. So, in the next few days if an opportunity arose to have a new experience, I decided I would say 'yes' to it. I was so not used to that, but thought it was the only way I was going to get to know my new city and some people in it.

My first attempt at being a yes-woman wasn't particularly brilliant. I stopped to get a coffee from a burger van and they asked if I wanted sugar in it. I never had sugar in coffee, but as I'd made a promise to myself, I said, 'Yes, please.'

They asked how many, so I stammered a 'T-two, please.'

It was hideous.

As I carried on down the hill into the bustling centre, I wondered if I had turned down any opportunities since my arrival a few hours ago. Or whether any had fallen into my lap.

Two had.

At the bottom of the hill we were walking down was a bizarre shell of a church building with trees growing in it. I recognized it as something I'd read about on the internet. It was a bombed-out church from the Second World War that had been left derelict as wildlife grew inside. It was obviously a symbol or something. Outside sat a bench. I pulled Michael over and sat down, took out my phone and jabbed in a number.

I heard it ring twice and then a raucously jovial voice boomed to me, 'Pippa! Blimey, that was quick, girl!'

I laughed, 'Strike while the iron's hot, Iggy.'

To which he laughed; of course he laughed. To this guy, I was on a par with Joan Rivers.

'I don't want you to think I'm stalking you or anything, Iggy . . .'

'Bollocks – don't be daft.'

'But if that offer of showing me around the city's still open, I'd love to take you up on it.'

'Nice one, laa. When?'

'Well . . . tomorrow? I could buy you some lunch?'

'Great.'

Only when he said it, it sounded like 'grace' . . . with a very elongated 'sssss' sound.

'Why don't you have a think about where we could meet and what time and drop me a text later? I'm staying by the cathedral. Gambier Terrace.'

'Ah, nice one, Pips. That'd be sound.'

Again, when he said it, it sounded like 'sounzzzzzzzzzzzzz'.

'Unless you're working or something.'

Which made him almost double up with mirth by the sound of it.

'Nah, I think I can squeeze you in, Pips.'

I wasn't overly keen on being called Pips. It reminded me not of Pippa Middleton, as he intended, but of Pip from *The Archers*, an immature character who only ever seemed to moan, a character who seriously annoyed me.

But I was a yes-woman now, open to new experiences, and if Iggy wanted to give me a pet name, no matter how annoying that was, maybe now was the time to embrace it. Pips/Pip/Pippa I was!

Next I took out the business card I had put in my purse. I dialled Perm Suspect and asked to speak with Rose. However, as I expected, she was still up at the hospital, so I booked myself in with her for a wash and blow-dry in two days' time. I decided I wouldn't worry about crossing the Mersey to Birkenhead for now. I was sure Iggy could offer sage advice about that.

When I hung up, I felt excited. As the salty air from the Mersey hit my nostrils, I felt like a proper woman about town.

Look at me, I thought, I am a woman living in Liverpool with plans for the next two days. And I've only been here an hour. It felt good to have a full dance card. I wanted to shout out to passers-by, 'Sorry, what was that? What am I doing for the next two days? Well, it's funny you should ask, actually, because . . . Let me get this straight . . . Oh yes! I'm seeing my pal Iggy tomorrow for a bit of a scout around the city, and then the day after I go and see my landlady, Rose. Bless her, she's going to do my hair for me at her salon. Ciao, darlings! Have a great day!'

I had read online about a vast shopping area called Liverpool 1, so I followed some pedestrian signs for it and eventually found myself in open and covered multilevel walkways lined with all the usual shops you'd find in any given city centre.

Why this was seen as a particularly glamorous jewel in the city's crown I would never know. But though the backdrops seemed familiar, the people populating them seemed more startling.

The first time I realized I wasn't in London, let alone Tring anymore, was when I clocked a young woman, possibly early twenties, caked in make-up eating chips at the bottom of a pyramid of stairs that led to a food-court area. Nothing odd about that, you might think, except that this woman was wearing fuchsia-pink leggings, a fuchsia-pink poncho, had fuchsia-pink nails and lips, and then her jungle of blonde hair perched atop her head was carefully arranged in a construction of humongous fuchsia-pink curlers. I was startled by her and, I'm embarrassed to say, I stopped and stared, mouth open, as if she were an exhibit in Madame Tussauds. It took her a couple of seconds to register my gawping. And when she did, she froze, chip mid-air between paper and mouth . . . At this point I noticed her unfeasibly large eyelashes – they were like paintbrushes – and she said, 'Are you a model scout?'

I shook my head. She looked disappointed, then resumed eating. I hurried on. I tucked Michael into my shoulder bag when I entered the shops. If people noticed, maybe they'd think I was an It Girl. Or a WAG. He didn't seem to mind. He seemed to be ten per cent chihuahua, ninety per cent sloth.

The shops were busy, considering it was a weekday and not half-term. Also, considering there was a recession on, there were plenty of people browsing. But maybe they weren't buying. And the more I looked, I realized there was quite a lot of time-killing going on here. Three teenage boys had clearly settled in for the afternoon in one games shop, standing playing Xbox around a pillar. In John Lewis, a bored woman was playing with all the locks on a row of Samsonite suitcases. After doing some time-killing of my own – I must have sprayed myself with at least ten different tester perfumes, so much so I was making myself sneeze – I decided to head home.

Home. It felt funny thinking of it like that.

The traipse back up the hill wasn't as pleasurable as the brisk catapult down it, and by the time I arrived back at the terrace, I was definitely looking forward to putting the kettle on and making myself a decent cup of coffee. No sugar.

When I put my key in the main door of the house, I was relieved to find that it worked. Although Alan had previously assured me my keys worked, it was one thing I'd not checked before he'd left.

'Come on, Michael, in we go,' I said, sounding so Home Counties it was untrue. Amid all the Liverpool accents I'd heard on my stroll, I felt like I sounded posher than Nigella Lawson. Michael trotted in and his obedience was moving. Poor little thing. Sylvie had been gone for weeks now and hadn't once checked that he was all right. Oh well, stuff her. It had all been quite fortuitous really; at least with a dog I would never be truly alone in my new residence. I was just climbing the creaky stairs when the door on the ground floor opened and a shock of pink hair blurred out. Jax.

'Hi, Holly, babes!' she chirruped. 'Did you move in all right, love?'

Oh. How kind.

'Oh. How kind,' I said, echoing my thoughts, not the most original of retorts, but it made her smile. 'Yes, thank you. Everything all right with you?'

'Oh God, yeah, babes. Everything's fab. I was thinking, if you were at a loose end, whether you wanted to come round for a drink? Let me welcome you to the house and all that.'

Again. Oh. How kind. And I had to say yes, did I not? I was now, after all, a yes-woman.

'Well, that would be lovely. When were you thinking?'

She pulled a phone from her pocket and checked the time on it.

'Er . . . now?'

'Oh. Well, let me just go and drop Michael off upstairs and freshen up, and I'll be down in . . . fifteen mins?'

She nodded, unperturbed, it would appear, by my – to my mind, anyway – rather annoying use of the abbreviation 'mins'.

'Bring the dog, though. I love animals, me.'

So bring the dog I did.

If I thought Jax's appearance and voice pitch was a little Minnie Mouse, then her ground-floor flat maintained this quirky feel. When I came down, she had changed into a bright red dress with white polka dots on, which matched the tablecloth on her dining table. Her flat seemed somehow smaller than mine, even though I reasoned it must have been the same size as it was directly below me and covered the same floor space. But then I had only been shown her living room. It appeared smaller because it had so much . . . well . . . tat in it. Heavy red velvet drapes masked the tall sash windows, blocking out so much light. There were three sofas in clashing colours that formed a U-shape facing a fireplace full of dried flowers. There was a dusty rocking horse in the corner, a mannequin dressed in a Hawaiian skirt and a garland of flowers, and several marionettes hung from the ceiling so that you had to duck when you moved around the room. On one wall, there was an old payphone.

'Oh my gosh, does it work?' I exclaimed.

'God, no. But I love the look of it, d'you know what I mean?'

I did. And then I saw the slots on it for two and ten pences and realized it really was a museum piece.

She poured, from a Cath Kidston teapot, what she claimed, and what proved to be, pre-mixed gin and tonic into over-sized pink teacups, and handed me one.

'Cheers, baby face!' she sang.

'Cheers!' I giggled. I had never, *ever* been called 'baby face' before. I looked into a narrow hallway that must have led to her bedroom and bathroom. A massive suitcase appeared to block it, its cover-up, a big mouth spewing dresses from it onto the floor. Seemed she was packing for something.

'Oh. Are you off on your hols?' I asked.

Her eyes narrowed and she gently but firmly pulled the door to.

'No,' she said. She was looking at me disapprovingly. I wasn't sure why. Then she smiled and said, 'Is there something you wanna ask me?'

This wrong-footed me. I had just asked her something. And she'd replied in the negative. There was, of course, something else I wanted to ask. So I did, though I no doubt sounded startled by her directness.

'I was wondering how long you had lived here, actually.'

'Oh right. Er . . . three years?'

'Oh,' I echoed her. 'OK.'

'Why, babes?'

'Well, I was interested in tracing someone who lived up-stairs many years ago.'

'I've only known the Greens. They were the people be-fore you. Solicitors. But then she fell pregnant and wanted a garden.'

I nodded.

She continued, 'Fuck knows why. Maybe she wanted to give birth on the grass. Holly?'

'Aha?'

'Are you . . . here on a quest?'

Which wrong-footed me, again.

'Er . . . well, yes. A bit.'

'Don't be scared, Holly,' she said, advancing towards me in quite a scary way, 'only I've got a gift.'

'You have?'

She nodded and sat on one of the sofas. She patted the space next to her and I joined her.

'I'm psychic.'

Oh gosh.

'And . . .' she continued, 'someone's trying to speak with you.' Just then she abruptly looked to her left, the other side to me, and barked, 'Yeah, all right. Can I handle this my way, love?' Then she looked back to me apologetically. 'Some people in spirit. They aren't half gobby.'

I found myself swallowing. Possibly because I was starting to feel uncomfortable.

'Now tell me, Holls. Can I call you Holls?' But before I had a chance to answer she continued, 'Has someone close to you recently passed? Is it your dad?'

'Er . . . my mum.'

'Oh.'

'Mm.'

Jax tried another tack. 'Has she got a deep voice?'

'No.'

Jax took this in. Then tried again. 'Did she die of throat problems?'

'No, her heart.'

Jax nodded, as if this all made sense. 'Think she's got a

bit of a throat problem at the mo. And you've been trying to contact her, haven't you?'

What madness was this?

'Well, no, I haven't. I'm not sure . . .'

'Oh God, am I freaking you out, Holls?'

'No!' I shrieked, sounding completely freaked out.

'Oh God, I am – I can tell.' Then she added, 'Coz I'm psychic. I sometimes forget this isn't to everyone's taste. I'm sorry.'

And then she got up and crossed the room. 'Shall we talk about something else?' She took a packet of cigarettes from the mantelpiece and lit one quickly. 'You don't mind, do you?'

I shook my head.

She nodded. 'I knew that.'

'Jax,' I felt the need to explain, 'you didn't freak me out. My mum did die recently, but . . . well, it's not her I'm looking for. It's my birth mum. I was adopted.'

Jax's eyes widened as the penny dropped. She took another drag on her cigarette and then hastily jabbed it out prematurely in a conch shell on the dining table. She hurried and sat beside me again.

'I know,' she said.

'You know what?'

'I know you don't believe.'

'Well, no, I don't really.'

'But you've just got to open your heart, your mind, to the universe. To what's around you, babes.'

And because I was a yes-woman, I found myself nodding.

'Tell me everything you know,' she said.

She listened intently as I told her all that I knew. Which admittedly wasn't much. She held my hand while I spoke, and as I finished, she started to breathe heavily and nod slowly.

'I think we need to go up.'

'Right. Is that a . . . spiritual thing?'

'No, Holly. Upstairs. Bring the dog. And the teapot.'

Once we were in my flat, she made a big song and dance of moving from room to room and whispering to some invisible force, sometimes shaking her head sadly, sometimes chuckling mischievously. Sometimes she would go and touch a wall with both hands, again, breathe in and emit a low kind of hum.

Michael went and lay in the airing cupboard. I didn't blame him.

I followed her round like a spare part. She even sat on the toilet.

'Oh sorry, did you need to . . . ?'

'No, I'm communing!'

I stayed there. In the bathroom. As she sat on the toilet, eyes closed, deep in thought. After twenty seconds of doing this, which actually felt a lot longer, she opened her eyes and smiled awkwardly.

'Can I get you a top-up of gin?'

'No, I'm fine.'

'I need one.'

And she hurried through to my lounge, where she'd left the teapot. She topped herself up with a shaky hand and a smile. A particularly false smile. You didn't have to be psychic to work out something was amiss.

'Is something wrong?' I asked.

'No!' she said quickly.

'So . . . nothing came through?'

'How long have you rented the flat for?'

'Is there something you're not telling me?'

'No!'

'Jax!'

And then she swung round, panic on her face. 'I'm sorry, Holls. It's your birth mum. She's dead.'

I looked at my teacup, rattling in its saucer. I lifted it to my lips, knocked it back in one, then asked for another.

SIX

'What d'you think of John Lennon?' Iggy said to me as I showed him round my flat the next day.

I kept pointing to things: the space-age kettle that lit up when you switched it on, the view of the cathedral completely filling the windows, the dog. Each time he would nod, but nothing would deter him from his train of thought.

'Are you, like, a fan or what?'

At least he wasn't pretending to commune with spirits like Jax had.

'Erm. Yeah, he was . . . yeah, he was great,' I said, sounding non-committal, which completely went against what I'd actually said.

Could Jax have been right? I kept thinking. Even though she gave the air of being completely inept and away with the fairies, and even though she had got everything else absolutely wrong, could it be that she had been right about one thing and one thing alone? Francesca was in fact dead?

Only time would tell, I guessed.

Iggy stood in the middle of the living room and placed his hands firmly down the front of his jogging bottoms. Although it looked like he was about to start fiddling with himself, he was so engrossed in his train of thought I found it doubtful.

'See, most people say Elvis was the King. But he wasn't. In my eyes it was Lennon.'

'The Lennonmeister,' I proclaimed. And I had no idea why I did. I couldn't even speak German, and I wasn't a hundred per cent certain what it meant.

Iggy was nodding, though, so it must have made sense.

I had to be honest, I'd never given John Lennon too much thought over the years. Yes, he was a superbly talented musician, taken too early, and in tragic circumstances, but he wasn't exactly of my generation, and a part of me had slightly dismissed him as a hippy man with a beard, long hair and bottle-bottom specs. But then Iggy had to be at least ten years my junior, and to him, this man was a god. I had to embrace this; I was a yes-woman now. Heavens, I'd even let this practical stranger into my new home. I was alone with him; I could so easily have been in danger. I could hear Mum's voice in my head. And, what's more, she was appalled.

Holly, you let a strange man into your apartment? When you were on your own? But . . . anything could have happened!

And yet somehow I felt safe with Iggy. Possibly because he was that much younger and he had the air of a frisky young pup who could become excited by the slightest distraction, and also, despite the window-dressing of tattoos and – now I noticed – piercings to the eyebrow, physically he still felt a bit like the runt of someone's litter. And yes, anything could happen, and that was precisely the feeling I wanted to savour. Now an adventure could begin.

And also I suppose a part of me felt, well, I've lain on top of him in a railway carriage. What's the worst that can happen?

And so, continuing the Lennon theme, Iggy proceeded to take me on a magical mystery tour. Though having said that, had he just taken me to the local sweetshop, that would have been a magical mystery tour, as I was in a city I only knew virtually. The streets around Gambier Terrace felt comfortingly familiar as we stepped out with Michael into another bright day. I wanted to think it was because I had seen these pavements, these houses from my pram, but it was because I had crossed them so many times via the magic of the internet and Google Earth that I felt instantly at home. I'm not sure that Michael was doing much for Iggy's street cred: every time he looked down at him wiggling along beside us, he emitted an embarrassed high-pitched laugh and shook his head, probably disappointed that I didn't have a Staffie or a pit bull, though that was probably unfair of me.

'Iggy, do you believe in the afterlife?' I asked as we ambled along.

'What, like ghosts and all that?'

'I suppose so. You know, when you speak to dead people via psychics?'

'No fuckin' way!' He didn't even apologize for swearing. I found this refreshing. 'Why? Do you?'

'No. I don't think so. I don't know really.'

'So why d'you ask, like?'

'The girl who lives downstairs from me claims to be a psychic.'

'Oh aye? How much did she fleece you for?'

'Oh, nothing. She didn't charge me. But she did say my birth mother was dead.'

'Nutter. They wanna send her up Rainhill.'

'Rainhill?'

'The arl looney bin. Here we are.'

Oh good. Iggy was dismissing her as a bit lulu. That I could live with.

A few streets behind Gambier Terrace was Percy Street, and now we were at number 9, Iggy informed me that Lennon had lived there when he'd been at the local art college. We stood reverently for about five minutes on the pavement outside the yellow Georgian terrace.

'Looks a bit like a castle, doesn't it?' said Iggy, demonstrating the observation of someone who had looked at something for too long far too many times.

I nodded. 'Yes. I suppose it does. A bit.'

It didn't really, though it was quite an imposing edifice with its pillars. But there was only so long I could look at a building and imagine someone having lived there and what they got up to without actually stepping inside. For a minute I imagined John strumming a guitar and calling to a flatmate, 'Hey! Think I've just worked out the bridge for "Imagine"!' . . . but I knew this was clutching at straws. Iggy, however, was transfixed, hands down the front of his pants again, a mesmeric glint in his eye.

'Have you ever been inside?' I ventured.

He shook his head. 'Don't wanna mess with the magic,' he replied, and tapped the side of his head. 'Coz if I seen it now, it wouldn't be like what it was like when he was there. Sometimes what's in your head's, like . . . better than what it actually is.'

Well, I could identify with that, as I thought about the new decor in 32B Gambier Terrace. A huge part of me preferred it in my imagination. Why hadn't it been kept as a museum piece, like Jax's payphone?

'It's like there's his childhood home,' he continued, 'the National Trust own it now and they've done it all up to look just like it would've done when he was a kid. You can go round it, on a day trip. But how do they know? How do they know what it was like? It's only what they think it was like. It's only, like . . . pretend.'

There was real sadness in the way he was speaking.

'So I just prefer to make it up in me head. It's better then. I like to stand outside here, or outside the other place, and just see it all in front of me. And that's better than anything anyone else makes up. D'you know what I mean?'

I didn't fully, but it did somehow make sense.

From Percy Street we walked down the hill again and then snaked our way through some backstreets to a minuscule pub called Ye Cracke, where Iggy allowed me to treat him to a pint of bitter while I had a half of Guinness. Then he proceeded to tell me how John Lennon used to drink in here and how, once, he swam on the floor in some spilt beer.

The image was surreal. A grown man pretending to do the breaststroke on the floor of a spit-and-sawdust pub in a puddle of ale. It must have been like performance art. Iggy went on to tell me that his grandmother had been one of the screaming schoolgirls who used to slink off from lessons and go to the Cavern Club to see the Beatles play. How all she ever talked about was her love of the band. Iggy had never known his granddad, or his parents for that matter (I didn't ask why – it felt impolite when he offered up the facts so barely) and so for a long time he used to fantasize that John Lennon was actually his granddad, which is why he'd always taken an interest in his childhood as well as his songs. Growing up, his gran had had a framed photo of Lennon over the mantelpiece as if he was the head of the family. They observed a three-minute silence on the anniversary of his murder each year. Some might have thought this erred on the bonkers, but I couldn't help but think . . .

That sounds a bit like me.

Here I was, going in search of who and where I came from, going in search of an island I could call home. Being brought up by people who weren't really mine. Idolizing an image, a fantasy maybe, of who my mother could have been. And then visiting the place of my birth. Being disappointed that so much had changed in thirty-odd years. Maybe I too should have just stuck with standing outside and imagining. Maybe that meant there would be less heartache in the long run.

Maybe Iggy had been sent to me by the same guardian angels who secured the flat for me, as a cautionary tale. There was another way to go. Stand outside and pretend. Imagine. The fantasy was always better than the reality.

But somehow I knew standing outside and imagining was never going to be enough for me. Fantasy would not suffice. I craved cold, hard reality.

'Iggy?'

'Yeah, Pips?'

'How do I get to Belle Vale?'

Twenty-four hours later I was standing outside Perm Suspect and trying to imagine what it would be like inside. The windows were frosted and had the shop name written across them in transparent glass, like someone had scratched on the logo. I imagined behind it a cornucopia of kitsch, possibly because I'd been up close and personal with Alan's sheepskin jacket. I saw all the dryers and curlers being a lurid pink, like the vision at the mall. And then I saw Rose gliding in with a 1980s Joan Collins bouffant for some reason. Well, that reason would be the sheepskin coat again. Anyone who loved a man who wore a jacket like that surely had to have some level of kitsch about them. I bet she wore Anaïs Anaïs and knew all the dance moves to *Saturday Night Fever*.

I was wrong. On all counts. The decor of the salon was understated, subdued. The dark polished wooden floors were almost identical to the ones in my flat, and there was a distinct overuse of granite surfaces. 'Relaxing' pan-pipe music floated quietly in from some speakers in the ceiling, which jarred slightly with the attempt at classy, but other than that I was impressed. I waited a few moments on a low, grey Fifties settee while flicking through a *Homes and Gardens* magazine from a coffee table before me as the various stylists and receptionists flitted around in matching black Japanese dresses. And then, from behind a beaded curtain, she appeared.

Rose Kirkwood was a lot more beautiful than I had imagined her in my head. She was immaculately presented, which was reassuring as she was about to style my hair. She was quite tall, though very slim, and she had a poker-straight long, black bob that suited the Japanese look perfectly. She also had so much make-up on she could have passed for a geisha. She extended a hand and told me it was a pleasure to meet me. She had an odd accent, like that of someone who had been to elocution lessons to lose theirs but hadn't quite succeeded. She showed me to my seat and wondered if I wanted to look through any of her styling catalogues with her, which is when I told her I only wanted a wash and blow-dry. She didn't seem to mind. And it was then that I realized there was a calm, icy detachment about Rose Kirkwood that made me wonder if I had overstepped the mark here. Had the invitation to get my hair done just been made out of politeness, with no expectation of me taking it up? That's certainly how I started to feel: for a hairdresser, she was very low on small talk. If I said something, she would respond politely, but she never instigated a conversation, and seemed more comfortable with silence than without.

She brushed my hair for what felt like an age, as if familiarizing herself with what she was about to mould, while we waited for a sink to become free for my wash. As a result I found myself chatting on, more and more, as if to make up for her reluctance to engage. And then, and I don't know if it was out of a desire to kick some life into her or to shock her or just to get some reaction from her, I blurted out the real reason I had come to Liverpool. I told her about being adopted, and the birth certificate, and the address, and the real reason for being at 32B Gambier Terrace. And it worked – she looked suitably stunned. She stared at me in the mirror, our eyes meeting.

Eventually she said, 'I'm very sorry to hear that, Holly.'

And I smiled back. At last, some emotion from the Japanese doll.

'What was her name again? Your mother?' she said.

And I told her, again.

She thought for a while, then shook her head. 'Sorry. Wish I could help, but . . .'

'How long have you had the flat?'

'About ten years.'

'Who had it before you?'

She stumbled a bit around her words. 'Well, some kind of . . . letting agency.'

'So not Francesca Boyle?'

'No. Sorry, love,' and with that she looked around the salon and we both saw that a sink was finally free. 'Jasmine? Can you wash Holly's hair for me? Thanks.'

I went to the sinks and sat with my back to one as Jasmine lowered me down, my neck reaching into the U-shape of the basin. As my head lowered, I saw Rose disappear through the beaded curtain.

When she reappeared to dry my hair and style it so that it looked almost identical to how it had when I had walked in, Rose yet again felt no need to engage in any chit-chat. She was professional, she wasn't a bad stylist, but her detachment was very unnerving. When eventually she had finished and I had eulogized about her prowess with a hairdryer, she took me to the counter to pay.

As I did, I said, 'If you can think of anything, like the name of the previous landlord, it'd be really helpful. I'm going to be looking it all up on censuses and things, but . . . you know.'

'Of course.' She smiled. 'I'll look through my paperwork tonight. I must have something for you.'

I nodded, grateful. She was beginning to become human. It was then that I noticed her eyeshadow had changed. I was sure that when I had come into the shop, it was midnight blue. And now it was definitely green. Why had she changed it? And when?

'I'm really sorry to hear what you've been through, Holly. I am, you know. And I will try and help you.'

Yet again something wasn't right. It was like she was reading the lines from a cue card, like she didn't quite own them.

'Thank you,' I said, as she handed me back my credit card. 'And thanks again for the do.'

She smiled. 'You're really pretty.'

And that time she sounded genuine.

Something about my encounter with Rose had unnerved me. When I got back to the flat, I felt crushed. I started to wonder if there was more to her than met the eye. I started to feel she was in fact hiding something from me. I opened a bottle of wine and poured myself a glass, which was when I realized that Michael hadn't come and greeted me on my return. I went in search of him. He was in his now usual hiding place of the airing cupboard. He was fast asleep, so I left him there and paced the flat, sipping at my wine. I felt lost. Now I had absolutely no plans for the rest of my life. My busy two-day stretch of guided tours and hairdos had come to an end. What did I have to look forward to? Nothing.

Alan had left the Wi-Fi details on a card near the router. I decided to log on to the internet on my laptop and see where I might go in Liverpool to look at censuses or certificates. I wanted someone with white lacy gloves to open huge tomes and direct me to magical information about my past. Just like they did on the television. But try as I might, I just couldn't get the computer to log on.

Oh well. I would call Alan or Rose tomorrow and ask them if they might be able to help.

I put the television on and channel-surfed for a bit. I felt a buzz of excitement when I saw an advert for the new series of *Hell Hole*. It was one of my favourite shows, my guilty pleasure. Each year fifteen people were incarcerated in a prison-style TV studio while hidden cameras filmed them twenty-four hours a day. Their petty squabbles, rows, friendships, affairs gripped me, and each day they were set hideous tasks to do by the telephone-voting public. As it was on television late at night, when I got in from work, and with my complete lack of social life, I didn't dare admit it but the young folk of *Hell Hole* became my virtual friends for the six-week run. I made a mental note to make sure I was home for the launch show.

I switched off the telly and mooched from room to room. I knelt on my bed and looked out of the window. An odd domed building hit the skyline from my right. I would have to try and find out what that was. Ahead, more houses in brown and yellow brick. This area had clearly been very well-to-do in the past.

I had thought I would find some peace, some happiness coming here. Now I was just experiencing that all too familiar feeling of being hollow. Maybe I needed to eat. I went to the fridge and realized I had only bought thus far a couple of bottles of wine and half a dozen eggs. I located a pan and poached one of the eggs, badly.

Poached eggs and wine. Sylvie's favourite square meal.

'Good for the figure, darling,' I could hear her say.

I wondered what she was doing now. I wondered if she was wowing an audience of ageing gay men in Vancouver with 'Misunderstood Queen'. Bizarrely, in that moment, I missed her.

Oh, this really would not do. I returned to the airing cupboard to wake Michael.

'Come on, you,' I told him. 'The least you could do is give me a hug.' And then I added, for extra effect, 'I'm an *orphan*.'

I chuckled. Possibly the effects of a glass of wine on an almost empty stomach. I tickled Michael's chin and he woke instantly. He stretched a bit and then happily stood and pushed past me out of the cupboard. I flattened down the tea towels that made his makeshift bed. As I did, I felt the floorboard underneath wobble. I pulled up the towels and saw that one of the boards had risen up a bit. I pushed it back into its place, but it slipped instead to one side, revealing a hole underneath the floor. A picture of a woman's face was looking back at me. Intrigued, I put my hand into the hole and felt around. In the hole beneath the boards was a tin. I put my other hand in and slowly pulled it out. It was a very dusty biscuit tin. On the front, once I'd blown off some more dust, was a picture of a smiling woman in Welsh costume playing a harp. I shook the tin. Something fluttered inside. I brought the tin into the living room and placed it on the couch next to me. Michael, lazy as ever, was now asleep on an armchair. I wiped the lid of the tin with my sleeve and then slowly prised it off. A light spray of dust blew up into the air. It made me cough. I peered inside. There I could see a pile of papers. They had yellowed with age, but the top one was covered with some neat handwriting. In turquoise ink I read:

She's always out there earning and it does my head in.

Coz when she's out there earning he always comes round. I don't even like ritin his name. He don't even ring doorbell coz he's got a key so I hear the door go and I'm like panickin.

I'm like. What you want ____?

And he's like. You know what I want Daz.

He's the only one who calls us Daz and even that gets on my tits.

I'm like. You can't have it ____.

And he's like. Fine. I'll wait for your Robbie to get in.

I'm like. Piss off ____ you big nonce.

And he's like. Piss of yourself Daz. Have you seen your Robbie lately? He's really grown up.

So I'm like. All right. And we go and get in his car.

I felt excited. Fascinated and excited. Who had written this? When? It looked like the box had been there for ages. Years. I looked under the top sheet and saw there were reams and reams of paper, each covered with the same neat scrawl.

It felt impolite reading it. Maybe I shouldn't, I thought. The old me might not have. Maybe I should call Rose and tell her.

This was her flat after all. But then I had decided to become a yes-woman. A yes-woman would have a good old nose and read on.

But I couldn't, could I?

I decided to take Michael for a walk. On my walk I would decide what to do.

Obviously, on my walk curiosity got the better of me and I decided that I would spend the evening reading the papers. I was quite excited when I returned to the flat, but just at that moment my mobile started ringing. It was a local number I didn't recognize.

'Hello?'

'Hi, Holly. It's Rose.'

'Oh, hi, Rose.'

What did she want?

'I was wondering if you could meet me tomorrow. By the Antony Gormley statues on Waterloo Beach.'

Where?

'Er . . . OK. Let me just write that down.' I grabbed a pen from my bag and wrote on the top of a newspaper. 'Sorry – what was it again?'

'What was what?'

'Where you want to meet.'

'The statues. Antony Gormley. Waterloo Beach.'

'OK.'

I scrawled it across the top of the paper. 'Why?' I asked. Maybe she thought we were going to be friends. Well, if this was the case, she had gone an odd way of going about it at the salon.

'Well, the thing is . . .'

'Yes?'

'I know Francesca Boyle.'

I froze.

She continued, 'I can take you to her.'

And for a moment the world seemed to stop turning.

Then I heard the operatic voice again. The same brief squeal. It seemed to be coming from heaven.

DARREN

She's always out there earning and it does my head in.

Coz when she's out there earning he always comes round.
I don't even like ritin his name. He don't even ring doorbell coz
he's got a key so I hear the door go and I'm like panickin.

I'm like. What you want ____?

And he's like. You know what I want Daz.

He's the only one who calls us Daz and even that gets on
my tits.

I'm like. You can't have it ____.

And he's like. Fine. I'll wait for your Robbie to get in.

I'm like. Piss off ____ you big nonce.

And he's like. Piss of yourself Daz. Have you seen your
Robbie lately? He's really grown up.

So I'm like. All right. And we go and get in his car.

Coz he's a copper he knows where to go where you don't
get caught. Favourite at the moments down by the Cazzy.
I don't even wanna think bout what he does coz it hurts but I
try an zone out an look at the Mersey and think of our Robbie
coz he's probably in by now and he's doing his homework or
something and if I wasn't doing this Robbie would be and it's
not fair on him. Today he was doing the front bit when I seen
some bizzy car come into the car park.

123

I'm not arsed if he gets caught. But I am arsed if I do so I'm like. ____ there's a bizzy car coming. So he sits up and goes Don't call it a bizzy car you tit.

The bizzy car comes over coz he's in a unmarked one. It pulls over and arlarse winds down his window and he's like. Don't worry. Plain clothes.

And he flashes them his badge or whatever it is. I don't look.

And the other ones like. Who's that?

And this ones like. Grass mate.

And I wanna go. Nah I'm no grass. I'm sat here with me kex halfway round me knees but the other ones not arsed and drives off.

And arlarse is like. Now where were we?

He tells me I'm better than his Mrs. And he tells me I'm better than most birds. Coz I don't say nothin.

But he always says this when he wants something. He says his Mrs goes on and on and on and sometimes he wants to slap her one to shut her up. I don't say nothing.

He tells me he wants to go round the back only I say I've not had a bath today even though I've had. Sometimes it works sometimes it doesn't. Today it does. He makes me do him round the front and when he's done he tells me to pull my kex up then tells me to get out.

I'm like. We're miles away.

Only he's shrugging.

I get out. He drives off. Makes a cloud of smoke coz its not rained for days.

I get an ice pop on the way home.

Boring today.

Sitting in kitchen. Ma at sink, singing. Slow song with bitsa French in – sounds like nothing on earth. Ma drops plate on floor n swears. Starts moaning coz she broke her finger nail.

So what? I think.

Then she sings the song I like. Ma wiggled her hips in the boopoopeedoop parts. I join in.

Ma stops and turns round.

Shut it Darren. You can't sing for toffee. Your tone deaf.

I shut up, go all quiet and twist the spoon in the sugar bowl.

Ma? I ask when she stops singing.

What?

Ma turns round with that piss off look on her face.

Who's my Dad?

Ma turns back and pulls plug out of the sink. I'm leaning forward like I'm gonna retch or something, think she's going to tell me.

We made a deal Darren. She says.

I remember her deal. She's gonna tell me when I'm eighteen.

You eighteen yet lad? She asks.

You know I'm not.

She makes some stupid noise like Huh and started wiping the drainer. She smiles dead wicked then giggles, looks at me then back at the drainer.

Darren?

She sat down aside me. She brings the big blue sauce pan. The heavy one. It near crashes on the table when she put it down. She sits there polishing it with the cloth. She loves that fucking pan.

She loves that fucking pan more an me.

What Ma?

You want me to tell you who your father is?

I nod my head n try an look all angelic.

Ma smiles. Your father was sin. She laughs.

Sin?

Dunno what she's on about there. But its making her laugh.

Yeah. He may as well've been, coz your as ugly as sin. Ma laughs. Some joke.

I get up and get out. I wanna say to her. I'm not ugly. If I was ugly why does _____ wanna do me? But I know there'll be murders so I don't. All day long I hear the laughing in my ears. Makes me wanna cry.

I go down into the gardens by the Cathedral. Sit on the tooms. Is dead quite here and no one ever comes. It's like another planet. Flowers. Weeds. Grass. Paths. And shitloads of dead people.

Yeah well a least dead people don't take the piss.

I read a name on a toom.

HORATIA DELAMERE   1812–1845

I can't get over how weird that name is. For a second I see my own name there. But then I think as if they'd ever have a Darren in here.

I head back. Go to Umed's shop and get an ice pop.

I love ice pops me.

When I get home Robbie's sitting in front of the telly. Grange Hill.

Your gob's all orange. He goes.

Had an ice pop. I goes.

Your off your head. He goes.

Your a nob. I goes.

And we both giggle.

Then I see Ma crying.

What you crying for? I ask.

Sad. She sniffs.

Sad?

Grange Hill. She goes.

Robbie looks up like he only just seen her then looks back at the screen.

Ma gets up and goes to her room.

Wake up Darren.

First thing I heard this morning. Ma leaning over me. What jew want?

You got a tenner to lend me Darren.

A tenner?

Yes. A tenner. What are you? Deaf?

I sit up in bed. Why?

I haven't got any money Darren, give me a tenner.

Stop yelling Ma, you'll wake the whole house up.

I get her a tenner.

Oh who gives a fuck about this house. She screams. With the nig nogs downstairs and Fatty Arbuckle up top.

I'm like. Don't let them hear you call them that they're nice.

And she's laughing. Coz she knows its wound us up.

She's got a posh coat on. Not one she goes earning in.

Bad night? I ask.

No night. She says, holding the tenner up to the window.

Yer all right Ma it's not counterfit. Why weren't you earning?

Mind your own. And then she leaves.

Strange. Ma doesn't usually have night offs usually.

Where's Ma? I ask Rob later.

Gone the doctors.

Ma sick?

Rob shrugs his shoulders.

We hear a car pull up outside. I go the window an look. It's him.

Am going out. I go. I won't be long.

*

Lucy come round today. Everyone was out so she come round. Drew the curtains so can't see the cathedral and she just sat and played the tennis game on the telly then went. Her hair was a mess and she didn't really do much. Think she was in a bit of a mood. She gets like that.

Bored bored bored. Always the same. Lad downstairs bored too. We go the pub. Rigby's.

Some fit birds here. He says.

Yeah.

Askin for it.

Yeah.

I don't even know what his name is. Only ever let on to him before, hardly ever spoken. Know his Ma though. She's nice. Hair like brillo pads in the kitchen. Ma's mate Margy says she could sort that out with Frizz ease or some conditioner but I reckon his Ma's not arsed about stuff like that. She's like really into God. Always gives me a big smile. Always up early on a Sunday to go the church on Percy Street.

Ma says she's screwing the Priest.

I say no.

I wonder what him downstairs would make of Lucy. Wonder if he'd think she was asking for it.

Some girls walk over.

Hiya Richie. One of them goes.

So his name downstairs is Richie.

These girls glamruss.

Who's your mate Richie?

Richie interduce us.

This is Darren. He lives upstairs to me.

Hiya Darren.

Alright I says blushing probly red like a pillar box.

Darren this is Smantha and Lu.

I laugh.

What you laughin at?

Lu. I says. Your name's the same as our bog.

Smantha and Richie laugh. The Lu girl gets all fuming.

You cheeky get.

Thought she was gonnarit me. But no.

Smantha starts going on about how her Dad has lost his job at Tate and Lyle and how he is going to do something called the March for Jobs. Loads of people are going to walk all the way from Liverpool to London to protest at the government. Smantha says me and Richie should go on it coz her and Lu are. Richie makes out he's intrested but I don't. How can I tell them I hardly never go out? This is a one off. I live in town. Furthest I go is town. How can someone like me walk all the way to London? Smantha says it's important. Lu doesn't look so sure. She's wearing high heels and leg warmers.

Best not do it in them shoes. I go. And the girls laugh.

I drink too much as usual. Smantha and Lu catch last bus home to Wavertree. Me and Richie walk home. Walk like a pair of weebles. Wobbling everywhere and falling off the pavement into the street.

Goodnight Darren. Richie says by the stairs.

Richie's ok.

Room spins round and when I wake up me throats all dry.

Ma's trip to the doctors must have made her better coz she's earning again. It's raining bad. I try not to think of her. Rob should be in bed, but he's in here watching my telly. I look out at all the goldy blocks of light in the houses opposite and wonder if she's in any of them. Rob says nothing. He's gone dead quite to me recently.

There's this fella. Rob goes suddenly. I look back at him. Hanging round by the school. I think he's watching me.

What's he look like?

Old. Dunno. Forty?

Has he talked to you?

Nah.

Just keep away from him. Stick with your mates. You'll be all right.

I look back out of the window. I'll kill ____.

I was like. You been spying on our Robert?

And he was like. No. Fuck off. What d'you think I am some perv?

Which actchally made me laugh. And he give me this look. And the look was like he didn't understand what I was laughing at. And it was then I realize he thought this was all fine and not pervy and completely normal.

Some bloke's been hanging bout. Staring at him.

Where?

School.

Teacher?

Outside.

Want me to look into it?

No.

He might be a nonce.

I think now might not be the time to point out I'm 15. But I don't fancy a black eye so don't.

When I get home Lucy comes over. She's quite chatty today. Rabbiting on about this and that. Most of it bollocks. She puts one of Ma's records on and has a little dance.

Why jew always draw the curtains? You ashamed of me? That's what she says.

You know why Lucy.

And she just keeps carrying on dancing. She's a boss dancer. Well. She's a better dancer than me. Not that that's saying much.

I look at the clock and its half two. I have an idea and I ask her to leave. She goes. I draw the curtains back. And then get the bus to Rob's school.

Rob goes to this posh school in Allerton. Red bricks. Clock tower. Boss place and it's got trees in the grounds with pink flowers on it. Like something out of a movie about private school only this isn't private. But he did have to pass an interview to get in. There's a phone box over road from the school so I goes and stands in that to see if I can see the fella watching our Rob. When school starts to let out I look about but can't see nothing. When I see our Rob I come out the box and stick me hands in my mouth and do my whistle. He looks over. He's dead surprised to see me but comes across the street.

What you doing here Darren?

Wanted to see if that fella was here.

Rob looks about. Then looks back to me and shakes his head.

Oh well. Mays well get the bus with you.

And we walk down to Penny Lane and wait outside the bogs.

Shit. I hear Rob say.

What?

He's there.

I look where he is looking and outside the charity shop over the road I see this fella looking in the window.

You sure?

I'm not thick Darren.

And before I really know what I'm doing I'm marching over

131

the road and giving it large to the bloke by the charity shop. Rob's coming too but he don't say nothing. I start screaming at the fella.

What you doing hanging round the boys school laa? And why you so fucking interested in my fucking brother you nonce?

And I carry on like that. All angry and scally and not like me really and this man actually looks scared. For once in my life I have thrown my weight around and actchally made someone scared. Someone who isn't me. Is scared of me. When usually it's me scared of . . . so many things.

And while I'm banging on he sort of stammers something and I don't hear. But Rob is looking pale as a sheet.

You what? I go.

And he says it again. And this time I hear.

I think Robert might be my son.

Rob's got a Dad. He don't have to wait til he's eighteen to find out. Not that I know that's the deal Ma made with the golden child. Rob does everything right. I never do. Rob stays at school. Rob works hard. Rob behaves hisself. Rob's good looking. Some people have all the luck. And now he's got a dad.

He doesn't go on about it coz he knows it makes me sad.

I tell him he can talk about it if he wants to but he says he doesn't.

He's seen him twice now. But I'm not allowed to tell Ma. His name is Cameron and he lives in the Wirral which is posh. I wanna ask loads of questions but coz Rob don't wanna talk it's hard. All I know is it wasn't Ma who told him coz he's not seen her for years but he knows someone who knows her and that's how he heard. He is married now and his wife don't know and he needs to keep it that way and Rob's cool with that.

I don't get Rob some times. If that was me I'd be made up, over the moon. But he just seems non plus. Not arsed. But that's him, takes everything in his stride.

Some days I wonder. Would Rob rather go and live with Cameron and his wife in the Wirral. They probably got a nice posh house, maybe a cottage, with gardens and trees and flowers everywhere. Stead of living here with me and Ma. With me indoors all the time and Ma out earning.

What would it be like for me living with Ma on my own? I don't like the idea. Maybe I'd leave. But then I don't really like going out so I don't know where ad go.

And sides. It's not like Rob is gonna go live with his Dad when his wife don't even know he exists.

But one day Rob is gonna be old enough to go and then where will I go? He's clever. He'll go off to University or big careers and look at me then. Sat in here like a massive gobshite with tenners from Ma like Billy No mates.

What's gonna go on with me then?

The march for jobs was on the news. I tried to see Smantha but I couldn't. But that's probably coz by the time the march got to London there was like a hundred thousand people on it or something. Like looking for a needle in a haystack.

Is really hot today. Have to open all the windows in the flat. Wanna get a gun and shoot down the cathedral so it don't block the breeze from the river. Lucy was gonna come round but too hot for her. She don't like the heat.

Seen Richie before at the bottom of the stairs.

We'll have to go for another drink some time. I say. Richie laugh.

Yeah. Not at the mo Darren, I'm skint.

Know the feeling. I say but I'm lying. Ma always gives me

money when I want it. Always got a tenner in me pocket. Never tennerless.

Ma singing in her room tonight. Brass in pocket. She don't sound too bad. I stand outside her door and listen in. Suddenly she stops.

I can here you out there you know.

I creep away.

Later she comes out and she looks a million dollars.

You look nice Ma. Goes Robbie.

Tar laa. Goes Ma.

Dead nice. I go.

She just looks at me.

Goin out earning?

She shakes her head. If you must know I've got a date.

What's his name Ma?

Geoffrey.

And me and Rob burst out laughing.

What? Theres nothing wrong with the name Geoffrey.

Is it someone you met through the earning? I go.

No it's not now do this necklass up for us.

I help her fasten it round her neck. I'm a bit fingers n thumbs at first and she's like. What you tryina do Darren? Murder me?

And I go. If only.

And I can tell she's in a good mood and excited coz she actchally laughs.

She smells of perfume and ciggies. She checks herself in the mirror over the fireplace and I think you know what, Lucy would love that dress.

The lady in red. I goes. Coz she is in a red dress. Her hair is up in red combs and she is wearing red high heels.

Scarlet woman. Ma agrees and then she heads out.

Robbie sits in his room doing his homework and I watch telly bored when doorbell goes.

It's Margy.

Where's your Ma? She's not earning.

I know she's on a date.

A date?

I know.

Not like your Ma.

I know.

She's a giddy kipper. Where's your Rob?

In his room.

And she just goes and sees him without knocking. A few seconds later I hear her laughing really loudly. She never laughs like that with me. I carry on watching the telly and she's in with him for the whole of The Hitchhikers Guide to the Galaxy.

When she comes out she's like. See you Darren. And off she goes into the night. Everyone wants to talk to Rob and no one wants to talk to me. Story of my life.

When Ma gets back she's in a boss mood. Giggly and friendly til I tell her Margy's been round.

What she want?

Wanna see you.

How long she here for?

Half hour? Dunno. She was in with Rob most of the time.

Then she goes into Rob's room and puts the light on and wakes him up. Five minutes later she comes out and heads into her room.

You gonna see him again? I shout.

Who?

Geoffrey.

Mind yer own.

And she slams her door shut.

*

Rain today. Feels nice coz it's been so hot lately. I'm off out to the betting shop and there's this girl on the doorstep.

Hiya Darren.

She know me? I look at the face under the umbrella.

Smantha! You calling for Richie?

Yeah.

I let her in. She says she's been ringing his bell for five minutes but no reply. I take her to the door where his family live and she knocked.

Richie not in.

Nobody in.

Smantha pulls a face. He said he'd be in. I got a taxi n everything.

She seemed upset.

Your wet. I said.

Smantha laughs. Your very quick on the uptake. It's people like you go on Mastermind.

I say she can go up to ours to dry out til the rain goes off and she's made up.

Smantha surprised at the size of the house.

Ay its big Darren.

Mm.

Where's the family? She ask.

Erm.

Smanthas looking out of big window at the street below.

Me Ma's at work.

What she do? Smantha sitting down now.

She sings.

Sings? Is she famous?

I shook me head.

She's a cabaray singer.

She used to be so I'm only half lying.

Ooh Darren. I've always wanted to be a singer but am tone deaf.

So am I!

Smantha looks like a pop star. Fit. Pretty face and funny smile. She sees me staring at her legs. Nice legs. She gets embarrast.

I asked her if she wanted a drink. Tea.

Ma drinks tea. I made her a tea. Two sugars.

Nice tea. Smantha smiles. Tar.

Not many people say that to me. Tar. I was chuffed. Made up. If anyone has said thank you its ages ago. Ma never. Rob hardly never.

Does your Dad work?

Dunno.

Yewa?

Me dad's dead. I say.

Now Smantha blushes. She spills the tea.

Am sorry Darren. I never know. Oh God a feel ashamed now. Sorry.

Smantha's a nice girl. I'm surprised she'd be friendly with Richie coz he's dead hard and always getting in fights. Police always knocking on his door.

How jew know Richie? I ask.

Lu used to go with him.

Oh.

Underneath he's a softy.

Smantha is smiling. She says she's surprised I hang round with him. I say I hardly don't.

I tell her I seen the march for jobs on the telly and she says she didn't go in the end but her dad did. She had it all out with him and she's got exams coming up so she wanted to concentrate on them coz she wants to go to university so she needs to go get her o levels so she can go the 6 form college and do her a levels. I ask her what job she wants and she says she doesn't want a job she wants a career. I just smile at her coz I'm all impressed.

Smantha is staring at me and smiling.

I wonder what's wrong. I wonder if I got something on my face.

But next thing I know she pulls me to her and starts kissing me. Tongues n all. She puts her arm on my shoulder and rubs it and I don't like it. I don't like people touching me. So I pull back.

Oh sorry Darren.

S'alright.

It felt weird that. Nice weird. But weird all the same. Nicer than kissing anyone else. _____ never wants to kiss. Says its for girls. But I like it. Well I like it with her.

We sit by the fire on the floor and talk about this n that. She's a student doing her A levels. I knew she'd turn out clever the minute I met her. She can read French. I can just about read English, let alone different languages.

I tell her I'm thick. She says av been let down by the education system which makes me laugh.

I was in the unit.

I don't care.

She's had a good education. Brainy, like our Rob.

Smantha had to leave in the end. She give me her number. So I can phone her.

Trar Smantha. Trar.

Before she leaves she goes. My mum and dad met round here.

Oh aye?

Yeah Rialto Ballroom round the corner. It was dead classy in them days.

It's a furniture shop now. I go.

I know. She goes. You can picture it being glamruss though cant you?

I know.

The domes n that.

I know yeah.

And she goes.

From the window I watch her goin down the street. Seen her bum waggle as she walk. Can't stop looking at it. Her blondey hair cut like Lady Di. Feel like I'm smiling non stop.

I go for a walk. Go and look at the Rialto. Imagine it in the sixties. Smanthas mum n dad on the steps. Going in giggling. In my dream she's drinking milk – don't ask me why. Short socks. Big skirt.

The twin domes on the top. The pillows holdin it up. The white tiles. So smart. Like a palace. Curving round the corner. Everyone knows the Rialto, like they know Dicky Lewis, like they know the Adelphi.

One day am gonna go in the Adelphi. Go and drink tea with Smantha. There's a big hall in there where people sit n drink tea and wear fair coats and talk all posh like. When I win the Littlewoods pools I'm there.

The Adelphi's in my favourite joke.

Bloke gets on a bus. Goes to the driver: Jew stop at the Adelphi?

Drivers goes. On these wages? Jokin aren't yer?

That's like my favourite joke ever.

I look back at the Rialto.

Course it's not a dance hall now. Those days are long gone. Now it's a place called Swainbanks. Tables chairs in window. Sofas carpets. All good things must come to an end. Sign outside says this

Second hand furniture emporium.

But in my head the dome on top spins round and fire works hit the sky. And Smanthas mum n dad are in there dancing.

Why am I thinking about Smanthas mum n dad?

Why am I thinking about Smantha so much?

Feelings I don't understand. But not bad feelings. Pointless pushing them away.

Emporium. I don't no that word. It's like magic.

Emporium. I think I'm saying it right.

It's magic like HORATIA DELAMERE.

I like words.

I get an ice pop and go home.

Lucy comes round and is all jealous about Smantha. Wants to know all about her and doesn't look that impressed when I tell her. She takes the piss out of me. She tells me I'll never take my clothes off in front of her and so it's going nowhere and I should stop it now before it gets out of hand.

I tell her she's been over dramatic and we have a row.

She tells me am stupid. I was in the unit. I got no exams. I will never amount to nothing.

I tell her to shut up.

She goes. Well go on then. What you gonna do? What you gonna do with your life except sit in here playing silly games and watching telly and watching the cathedral and hardly never going out.

And I say it back to her. Well what you gonna amount to? Coming round here all the time. Not out there are you. In here aren't you.

Your ashamed of me. She says.

I just want to have a nice time with Smantha.

She's a slag. She says. Then she goes.

When she has gone I stand in front of the long mirror in Ma's room and look at myself. She is right. I don't want Smantha seeing this. I don't want anyone seeing this. My skin is so white. It's the body of a dead person. The body of someone else. And where I've cut myself on the leg it's like norts an crosses. Who would want to look at this?

I decide I am gonna knock it on the head with Smantha like Lucy says. Before it all gets out of hand.

Went the shop for milk. Fatty Arbuckle's in there. She don't like us coz of Ma's job. Every time she sees me she's like looking away like there's a bad smell in the air. And is funny coz she smells like cheese. I don't like cheese. Today she's no different. Pulls her cardigan too her and wrinkles her nose up like that bird off the telly in the 60s. American. Her mouth's moving like Ermintrude the cow like she's saying stuff but no words actchally come out.

Scuse me. I say so she'll move for me to get past. She leans about 2 millimetres forward so I have to shape shift to get past her to the frdgey bit. Anyone would think I had asked her to lie down in the path of a train to Lime Street.

While I'm choosing milk I hear her making a big song and dance about getting her money out of her purse. Like we've never seen a five pound note before.

I hear next year there bringing out twenty pence pieces Umed. She goes to the shopkeeper. Whatever will they think of next? This country's going to the dogs.

And she looks over at me. I bold it out and take the milk to the counter. Not gonna let her make me feel shit.

I didn't realize it was half term. She goes, flicking her eyes at me.

I say nothing. Not rising to it.

Is it half term? She goes, now looking right at me.

I just shrug.

Someone should tell the authorateas. And she gets her change and walks out, which coz she is so enormous takes about half an hour. She can hardly lift her feet off the floor. You just hear her flip flops slowly flipping and flopping like two snakes sucking slowly. When she go through the door she sort of have to dance through it. Left a bit right a bit shifty shifty.

I don't like Fatty Arbuckle. She is not a nice person. She don't think families like us should live in what she still sees as posh houses from long ago.

I do a detor walking home coz if I go normal way I will bump into Arbuckle coz she walk so slow. I go round the block. It's no problem like as it's a nice sunny day. Pavements look yellow as custard. There's an orange cat outside the church on Percy Street who's lying slap bang in the middle of the pavement enjoying the heat and licking itself. Oblivious to the rest of the world. I walk round him and he doesn't flinch.

When I get to ours Fatty Arbuckle is long gone. Seen Richie in the hall instead. He was like

Smantha says you haven't called.

I know.

Smantha's a nice girl Darren.

I know.

Ringer now.

Looked like there was no getting out of this. Richie and his Ma have got a phone in theirs that you put money in so I called her from there coz Richie was giving me daggers.

I dialled the number. I still had it in my pocket. Richie said that was a sign. It wasn't. I just didn't want Ma finding it and taking the piss. Had a small chat with Smantha and arranged to meet her two o'clock tomorrow under Dicky Lewis.

Nice one Darren laa. Richie goes while I'm leaving his.

What you doing using junglebunnies phone? Ma says when I gets back upstairs.

Ma don't like Richie's family. Richie's Ma always calling round to see my Ma and trying to convert her. Make her change her ways. Ma tells her where to go.

Richie's Ma's nice though. She is always smiling and she has nice white teeth. White as the paper I write this on. And her laugh is loud as a lorry. She tells us about Jesus who's one of her friends. She wants me to be his friend as well but like I say to her. I've never even met him. Which always makes Ma laugh.

Don't call them that. I say.

She tuts.

So I told her about Smantha. I wish I hadn't.

She some sort of fruit loop is she? She said. Sideways on.

No.

She like a bike is she?

No Ma. Smantha's nice.

Well why's she going with you then?

Just then I hear Rob's voice.

Ma don't be an arlarse.

Ma turned round to look at Rob in the hallways. Rob goes all pale.

You spoke? She says all hard.

Don't be tight on our Darren Ma. He's not ugly and Smantha's nice.

How jew know? Ma goes.

I've met her actchally. Rob smirks.

Oh have you ACTCHALLY? Gasps Ma. Well I say she's the local bike.

She's from Wavertree. I go.

Just coz you're a whore doesn't mean everyone else is a whore! Yells Rob dead violent like and angry.

Ma slaps him straightaway. Like she's hittin the words right out of his mouth. Rob stops dead.

Silence.

Ma's looking at her hand. She never usually hits like that. I think she's surprised herself. Rob starts shaking.

Watcha do that for ay? I asked in a whisper.

Ma looks back at me like she's scared an all. Then she ran out fast as her legs'd carry her. Door slam. Ma's outside.

Rob started crying. I put me arm round him and hug him. He stuck up for me he did. He's sound.

I hate her. He screams and pushes me away. Then he screams it again and again.

No Rob. She's your Ma.

I hate her. She's a whore.

Nah Rob she loves you.

She hit me.

Snot the first time.

It is.

Is it? I didn't believe it. You mean Ma never hit you before?

No Darren.

Ma's always hitting me. Ever since I was little. I don't cry though, not like Rob, though usually I feel like it. I'm good at not crying. Ma doesn't hit me much now though. Now am older. Rob's small though. Thirteen.

Rob says he's gonna run away and see his Dad. I say no.

144

Leave it. Ma'll be ok. Rob's not too sure. Ma loves Rob though, she'll say sorry soon.

Ma hasn't said sorry to Rob.

Rob says he couldn't give a damn but he's sad really.

Seems like she's hitting everyone at the moment. This morning I went to get milk and when I was coming back I seen her on the corner of Huskisson Street. A car slowed down and I seen her getting ready when who comes round the corner but Margy. Ma ignored the car and went flying at Margy and pulled her down to the ground by her roots. I jumped and hid in the entry coz I didn't want her to see me and I didn't really wanna see her. She was shouting all sorts at her and calling her all sorts of names and saying how could you how could you? I waited a bit.

By the time I come out Ma was in the car driving off and Margy was getting her breath back leaning against a wall.

Yalright Margy? I goes as I went past.

She nodded. Yeah I'm fine lad.

What was all that about?

Think your Ma's got the wrong end of the stick as per.

Her face was all red and her hair was a mess. I wanted to say sorry but I thought of the things Ma said to her and I thought well if there true she can get to fuck.

See you Margy.

You're a good lad Darren.

When I got back to ours there was a bizzy car outside and the front door was open. When I went inside I seen ____ in the hall talking to Richie's Ma.

Mrs Eustace I need to speak to your son.

He ain here.

Mrs Eustace I have a search warrant.

145

I ran upstairs but I knew he seen me. I couldn't settle knowing he was in the building. I thought about going out but I didn't wanna bump into him in the hall again. But then he knew I was in so I expected the key in the door at any minute. I just sat on my bed thinking of nothing. I hadn't even had a bath. That was good. I was probably stinking. All good. I sat there and realized I really needed a piss. But I couldn't get off the bed. Suddenly I needed it bad. I was frozen. I knew I should go to the bathroom. Knew I should fight my way cross the landing with the stalactites of slips n tights hanging from the ceiling that Ma always had drying. Go in there and relieve myself.

Stalactites. I remember Miss teaching us that in the unit. I never forgot it. Coz when she said it was like tights hanging down I could just picture our landing.

I looked down. Thinking about Miss I'd taken me eye off the ball and I had let a little pee come out. A dark patch sat on my jeans. Dirty bastard Darren I thought. Pissy pants Darren.

And then I realized what might happen if I just pissed myself so I did.

Let him knock now. Let him knock now and see what he says when he sees I'm a mess. Come on you dirty bastard knock for me I dare you.

I must've sat there for half hour or so. Nothing. Not like him. Maybe I was losing my touch. Good.

The piss had gone cold on me now. I slowly got up and went into the living room. Quietly I lifted up the window and slowly stuck me head out. Nothing. The bizzy car had gone. I went to the door and opened it. Downstairs I could hear Richie's Ma crying.

Lucy came round. Didn't say much today. But she washed my jeans and my undies for me and hung them up to dry on the landing.

I tell her I've decided not to see Smantha again.

She says it's probably for the best.

Turning the corner to Hope Street I see orange. Orange dress. Orange dotty skin. Orange hair. Long. Like her off the telly who sings the songs. Her who Ma wants to slap. And Ma'd want to slap this woman too. What's she doing here?

Hello Darren. She say.

Hello Miss. What you doing here?

I came to see you.

Why Miss?

You know why Darren. You haven't been to school in months.

Am nearly 16 Miss.

Can you take me into your flat Darren?

No Miss. It's really messy.

Is your Mother in?

No she's out at work.

What time will she be back?

I don't know Miss.

I've written a lot of letters Darren. Social services have been in touch.

They don't care Miss. Coz I'm nearly 16 Miss.

I care Darren.

And I can see it. She does. She likes me. She's been good to me. Better than Ma really.

I think your wasting a valuble opportunity Darren.

Miss I'm thick Miss.

You are not thick Darren.

But it's no point arguing with her. I know am thick.

You always liked to write your stories.

Can't spell though Miss.

You have a good imagination Darren. And you had the best spelling in the unit.

Not gonna put bread on the table is it though Miss?

What are you going to do with your life Darren?

There's no jobs Miss.

How are you going to make yourself happy Darren?

Bloodyell she was like a dog with a bone this one. And I wish she'd stop saying my name it's getting on my tits.

I know your different from other lads Darren.

How d'you mean?

Your more sensitive. Struggle to cope sometimes.

I'm fine.

Good. Good. I didn't mean anything by it.

Miss I've gotta go.

And I just ran. She calls after me but I ignore her. What does she mean? She didn't mean anything by it. Why say it then? But when I get in I sit in my room and think. Well I bet Richie hasn't got norts an crosses on his legs.

Smantha came today. Out of the blue. Ma in. I was really embarrass.

You never met me. She goes. Under Dicky Lewis. She goes.

Sorry. I goes. I forgot.

She knows I am lying.

Smantha said hello to Ma and Ma just murmured something stupid. Smantha bought a can of coke with her so she sips on it. Bit noisy like. Am thinking I best get her out the flat so I head for the door when Smantha goes. I hear you're a cabaray singer.

A what? Laughs Ma looking at me.

Darren said you're a cabaray singer.

I'm no singer love.

Smantha looks at me confused then goes. Oh what is it you do then?

Ma walks about all tutting and strutting.

To be honest love. I don't think it matters what I do. Whatever it is I do I'll bet I do it a damn site better an you. And what I do do is me own business. So Smantha. Stop poking your massive fucking beak into thingsat don't concern you.

Smantha looking hurt.

Sorry. She says all funny. I'm frowning looking this way that way. Staring at the wallpaper. Blowing out me cheeks like bubbles as if I heard nothing.

You've got a big nose. Ma says. Smantha looks gobsmacked. She puts her can down on the table. More like she didn't know what to do rather than thinking it was a good thing to do.

Am sorry about that too, but it's the only nose I've got so I can't do much about it.

You wanna watch it doesn't get broken love with a gob on you like that.

Am going. Smantha goes to the door. By Darren.

You've left your coke love. Ma goes.

Smantha looks back.

Oh you can finish it for me. Love.

And she walks back, picks up the can, then chucks it in Ma's face.

Cheeky little bitch!

But Smantha's already gone.

I keep laughing all day about Ma covered in coke stains. Funny.

And I've got a date with Woody. She kept going.

Has Geoffrey changed his name? I go.

149

Geoffrey's a knob. Woody's his mate. Proper.

Then she goes into her room to get changed. For Woody.

Ma's a bitch. I've decided.

Sometimes I wish she weren't my Ma. Most times I wish she weren't my Ma. I wish Richie's Ma was. She's funny. Giggling on about the gospel she have to proclaim. Makes me giggle.

Don't never feel lonely Darren my friend. You have a friend in Jesus.

Just as well. Goes Ma. Coz you haven't got any others.

Today though she crying. Sat on bottom stair crying.

What's up Mrs Eustace?

Police day say Richie had drugs in the house. He didn't have no drugs in the house. I'da known if he had drugs in my house. He's in trouble.

But if they found them. I say.

Den who put them there. Mm?

Richie?

No. Police.

But. Why?

Are you colour blind or something Darren?

No.

I don't know what she means.

There's something wrong with Ma.

She lies in bed all day and won't earn. Tells me to piss off if I go near. She's not eating. She'll be sick if she carries on like this.

Men knock at the door. Where is she?

I go. She's sick.

They say shit.

I go. You shouldn't be coming round here.

Having her here all the time makes it hard to have Lucy round.

Margy called this morning.

Where's your Ma? She says. Why hasn't she been out all week?

Margy's wearing a fair coat. Business must be picking up. I say it to her and laugh only she gives me daggers.

Margy wanted to see Ma. I go to her room and call. Ma it's Margy. Come to see you.

Silence.

About a minute late I call. Ma.

Ma spoke. Let her in.

Margy comes in like she owns the place. Walking like Ma n checking her face in the mirror. Brushes her fair coat then goes in to Ma.

Eventchally Margy comes out.

She sick? I go.

Margy laughs. She's not sick Darren. She's pregnant. And by the looks of it she's got pre natal depression.

And Margy heads out.

Not sure what I think about her having a baby. She says it's his. Woody's. I said what if it's someone from the earning. She said she knows. I don't wanna know. If she has another baby I'll end up looking after it. She'll go out earning and I'll look after it like I look after Robbie. But Ma reckons all that is going to change because Woody wants her to have the baby and give up work and she is going to be something called a kept woman. As far as Ma is concerned this means she will go shopping all the time and meet friends for coffee and then have long baths and go to dinner dances.

What's a dinner dance? I go.

It's like a dinner. Only you dance as well. She goes.

In fact, she reckons she's already given up earning.

This is gonna be a nightmare. She is never gonna be out now. She lounges round all day smoking and watching telly and listening to her records and putting face packs on and bossing me about saying she can't do anything coz of the baby. Now don't get me wrong, she is being half decent to me. But she also keeps going on about moving in with Woody in his big house near Runcorn Shopping City. Though she says dead quick it's a nice bit by Runcorn Shopping City. Though I have never been to Runcorn Shopping City so fuck knows what Runcorn Shopping City's like. Ma reckons it's a magical place of space age shops. But she also admitted she'd not been since I was a toddler. I don't remember her taking me. Must've been when I stayed with Nan.

I wish Nan was still alive. She thought Ma was common.

I was sitting in today doing nothing staying in my room when I heard the key go in the door. Ma was already in and I knew it wouldn't be Rob coz he was at school. I freeze.

I can tell it's ____. I hear him raising his voice. I hear him calling Woody for everything. I hear him calling Ma for everything.

I keep quiet case he realizes I'm here.

Then I hear him hit something. Sounds like he has hit something against one of the big cushions on the couch. Then I hear the front door slam.

I stay in my room.

When I eventchally come out Ma's in the bath with the radio on.

Richie knocked today and said him and Lu were going Formby Beach with Smantha and did I wanna tag along. Beats sitting in with Ma moaning on so I jumped at the chance. Don't usually like going to far from home but it was such a nice day I thought it'd be nice to go the beach and see the sea.

On the train Smantha was dead quiet. I wondered what was wrong with her. She went the loo at one point and Lu said she was in a mood coz I hadn't called her.

I goes. Last time I seen her she threw a can of coke over me Ma.

I know. Goes Lu. That's why you should've called her.

Felt a bit of an arlarse then.

Smantha had sandwiches she'd made in a plastic bag and we went down the sand dunes and sat on the sand. There was a wedge of rock behind us that was red. Smantha starts going on about how it was called the Nicotene trail coz it's where the old nicotine factry used to pump its waste. Richie said she was full of shit but Lu said they'd done it at school.

Do you know why the Cazzy's called the Cazzy? Goes Smantha.

No. I goes.

Short for the cast iron shore.

Is it? Goes Richie.

The sand on the sea front went red coz of all the iron in it from the rust from the ships n boats they scrapped on the front at the Dingle there.

Smantha. The fountain of all knowledge. I goes. And she laugh.

Darren. The more you know. The more you can do with your life.

Don't suppose there's no arguing with that.

Like. One day I wanna live a broad. She goes. A do. I'd really like to live in Osstralia.

Why? I goes.

The whether. The space.

The kangaroos? I go and we all giggle.

Lu ast Richie about getting arrested the other week. He swear blind he didn't do nothing and he says its coz he is black. He says the bizzies just pick on black kids, young men mostly and just nick em for nothing. He says everyone's had enough but I don't know weather to believe him. There's no smoke without fire. But then I think the only bizzie I know is _____ and he isn't exactly Mr Nice Guy.

It becomes clear that someone has told Smantha what Ma's job is.

She's like. Darren your mum needs to be careful you know. Coz like prostitutes are in really vunrable positions with men.

And she starts going on about the bloke in Sheffield or somewhere who has been nicked for nearly 20 women. Killing them. And how she has read in the papers that some of them were earning.

I'm a bit embarrassed so change the subject.

Lu says she wants to paddle in the water. So her and Smantha head off towards the water.

Jew fancy Smantha? Asks Richie.

I nod. Though I don't know if I do.

Only Darren lad I wanna do Lu while we're here so give us some space man yeah?

I nod.

You can get nice and private in these dunes, know what am saying Darren lad?

I nod.

Tell you truth. He goes. I always thought you was a queg.

I shake me head.

When they come back from the sea they've got bear feet and have their shoes in their hands.

I go to Smantha. Jew wanna go for a walk? She like shrugs. Lu practically dives into the dune with Richie as we walk away.

We end up lying in a dune looking at the sky.

Baby blue, Smantha says it is. In Osstralia the skies are terqoize.

I think about that for a bit. Maybe skies are all different colours in all different places. Then she rolls on top of me and starts necking me. I neck her for a bit. Then she stops and giggles quietly.

What you laughing at Smantha?

You just make me laugh coz your so funny.

Am not funny. Am not Russ Abbott.

I didn't mean funny like that.

Jeez. Another one who thinks am weird.

So I showed her I wasn't.

I didn't enjoy it. But she did.

Halfway through she goes. Get off at Edge Hill.

Edge Hill's the last train station before Lime Street.

Rob come and sit on me bed today and watched telly in my room coz Ma has taken over the front room.

After a while he goes. My Dad. His wife found out about me. She hit the roof.

I have visions of his Dad's wife getting the ladders out and going on the roof and hitting it. I laugh. Rob tuts. He thinks I'm skitting.

Am not laughin at you.

He looks at the telly again.

It's ok though. My Dad's gonna see me in secret.

Oh.

Says nothings gonna stop him now.

Oh. Right. You like your dad then.

Yeah.

Good.

But Rob can tell I'm jellus. He leans over to me.

Ah Darren don't be like that. I know it's dead arlarse on you but I cant help it can I.

He looks back at the telly.

I wish. He says.

Then he shut up.

What jew wish?

Rob smiles at me like he smiles at Ma.

I wish he was your Dad an all.

Ah. Rob can be dead nice when he wants to be.

When I went back to the living room its empty. Ma's sat at the kitchen table drinking something brown. Bottle of whiskey on the side.

A can't keep goin on forever. She goes. Thirty five. Crows feet. Weather beaten skin. Out in all sorts. Varicoats veins. Hard skin. More pricks than Ker Plunk. I don't wanna be like the old whores round here. Seventy years of age on the corner of Huskisson in the pouring rain. Hair scraped in a pineapple to take the skin up and ten years off em. Holes in their leggings. Stinking a bit pissy. Who wants an old whore Darren?

Have you been drinking Ma?

Ten years left in me. Fifteen. Twenty.

How much you had?

Some just wanna talk. Sit in the car. Tell you about their lives. Wife in an iron lung. Wife doesn't understand. Can't get a fucking wife. One likes me to sing. Remembers me from the clubs. Remembers me pregnant with you. Top of the bill. The Coconut Grove.

Ma you shouldn't be drinking coz of the baby.

How the mighty have fallen. May as well fall down the hill.

Into Cathedral gardens. Lie on a toom stone and let them get on with it. But the look in his eyes. Him in the car. Despising. All that promise. All that beauty. Where's it gone? Even if it was only fleeting. Even if it was only smoke n mirrors.

Not really heard her speak like this before. Maybe I shouldn't worry coz she's been nice to me. Anyway I say nothing but I go and put the whiskey back in the cubbard.

What you doing with that?

Ma it's bad for the baby.

Her eyes are like glass eyes.

What baby? She goes.

His baby. Woody's baby.

She gets up. She comes to me and opens the cubbard. Gets the bottle out and pours a large one.

There is no baby.

And she goes back to the table and sits down and takes a big swig.

What happened Ma?

But she doesn't tell me. Instead she just goes. Not gonna want me now is he?

And then suddenly she crying.

I love him Darren. He was gonna change everything.

And she don't stop crying. And even though I hate her. And even though she's usually so vile to me. And even though she's so horrible to me and hates me so much I can't help myself. I go and stand by her and put my arms round her and hug her.

Oh Ma. I goes.

And she sobs into my arm. And my arm feels warm where she berries her head in it. Ah I think. She is alive. She isn't a reptile. And I think she's never gone stop crying.

I hate it. She goes.

What jew hate? I goes.

Everything. She goes. And sighs. An am gonna have to get back out there aren't I?

She wipes her eyes now. Not crying so much.

Were you not pregnant then? Did Margy get it wrong?

Oh I was pregnant. But I lost it.

And she takes another swig of the drink. And it seems to warmer. And I know. Al probly lose her to the drink for the rest of the day. But for now she's being all right. I suddenly get an urge to tell her something.

Ma?

What?

You know ____?

She nods.

Well.

But I can't say it.

She's like. What Darren?

And I'm like. He just sometimes comes round here. Snothing.

She doesn't look so sure. So I say it again.

Snothing.

He's a nasty piece of work. She goes. Like I don't know. He's too powerful with us girls. The amount he earns off us.

Jew have to sleep with him? I goes.

She shakes her head. Thank fuck.

Is he your pimp? I goes.

She shakes her head. But if we don't pay him. We get hassle from the bizzies. Bastard.

Yeah. I go. Bastard.

If only she knew how much.

Ma's back earning.

She'd only been out a few hours when she come back.

Its all kicking off out there. She goes. Bizzie nicked a black

158

lad on Selborne Street and it's all kicking off. I don't like it. Don't go out.

We got no milk.

I don't care. Your not going out. Where's Robert?

Bed.

All I can think of is it must be serious coz she said black lad and not some slag off word.

Later on we hear Richie and his Ma screamin at each other. Doors banging. Mum stamps the floor and yells at them to pack it in.

Didn't call them black people then.

All day we here the door going downstairs. People coming in and out of Richie's flat.

Was going on down there? I go.

I dunno Darren. On account of the fact I can't see through floorboards.

All day long we hear slam slam slam.

I don't want either of yous going out. Ma goes. So we stay in. Suddenly there's a knock at the door.

Who is it? Goes Ma.

Me. Goes Richie's Ma. So she opens it. Richie's Ma stands there and burs out crying.

Am really worried bout Richie. She goes.

Mum's like. Your his mother. Mothers jobs to worry.

Like all she does about us is worry. Rob looks at her like she has said the weirdest thing in the whole wide world. Like she has said the world is made entirely of cheese.

And then Richie's Ma throws herself at Ma and cries. Ma gides her in and sits her on the couch.

Get her a whiskey Darren.

So I do. And she has it. And she talks.

Richie says there not taking any more shit. They stood up to the police and they saying enough is enough. The police they call for more of them. Reinforcements they come but the lads stoned them. Stoned them like something out of bible. Is gonna get worse today and tonight – they making petrol bombs.

Ma dint like the sound of that. She looks to me an Rob.

Yous two are staying in again.

During Summertime Special Ma said she had to go out earning. She'd been gone five minutes when the bangin started. Me and Rob look at each other.

I wanna go out. He goes.

I wanna go out. I go. But we'll have to leave it a bit case Mum sees.

So we wait.

She might come back. I go.

She might. He agrees.

And if we're out? I go.

Rob laughs. Was she gonna do? Stop being so nice to us?

And that make us both laugh. Loads. So we think fuck it less just go.

Come out of the terrace an look down Hope Street see if Ma's still there but she's not. Bingo.

Voice from above goes. Typical. I look up. Fatty Arbuckle is hanging out of her window. Surprise the bloody building don't capsize. We heads off.

Nothing round by our way, but further up by Park Road and Windsor Street suddenly there's loads and loads of people. Fellas. The noise of the shouting does your ears in. Shouting Thatche'rs Basterds at the bizzies. Big line of bizzies with plastic shields. As far back as Parly Street. An then suddenly the bizzies start beating their trunchons on their shields. An the noise from that is terrifying.

I don like this. I goes.

Me nider. Rob goes.

So we legged it back down the entry and headed to ours.

Sunday and Rob makes up a cock n bull story bout going the Wirral to see a mate of his from school. Ma doesn't want him to go coz she reckons it's all gonna kick off again tonight. She doesn't wannim coming home late and getting caught up in it which I thinks fair enough but he doesn't coz I know he is lying and really he is going to see his dad coz his dads wife has gone to Portsmouth to see her sister who has got the cancer.

But Rob goes. No no no I can stay overnight and get a lift to school in morning.

And Ma seems made up like she's getting him evacuated during the war and this mate from school is saving his life. Not stopping to think why the fuck would a lad from the Wirral be going school in Wavertree or Allerton or wherever it is. So Rob packs a bag and goes.

In the evening Ma goes. I've put some spuds out in kitchen. Peel em for us will you. Fancy doing a roast tomorrow.

On a Monday?

There's no law against doing a roast on a Monday Darren.

No I know.

Well then. Stop going on like an arl woman. Yer are. Yer like an arl woman.

I say nothing.

As darkness fall Ma goes to work and the banging starts.

Lucy come over but I couldn't concentrate coz of the noise outside. So she went. She weren't very happy bout it have to say.

I put telly on but it's worse tonight and I switch it off and go to my room. Kneel on bed and pull the blind up on the window.

I don't halve get a shock when I see the sky. Pink. Dark red. And thick black smoke swirling overhead. To the right when I squeeze my head round I see the buildings like sillooettes. Above them flames of fire. Orange. Purple. Green even. Like a fucking rainbow. Must be the tire factry by Parly Street. There's a petrol station there too.

I have to go and look. Mi not be safe to stay in. What if this building goes up an all?

The streets are busy. At the end of Hope Street I get the biggest shock. The Rialto is on fire and suddenly it explodes like there's a bomb in it.

Kids run past with shopping trolley full of bottles of booze and some shoes.

Black lad runs past with face red with blood. Runs so fast the force of the wind round him near nocks me over.

Round the corner the shops are on fire. Lit up. Yellow flames pushing out. Further down I see a row of burning cars. On their sides. Blocking the street. A wall of cars.

From nowhere a line of bizzies came and stormed into a gang of lads, knocking them to the ground with their trunchons and shields.

On the other side of me the bizzies tried same thing but that side there was more people and they ran at them an knocked them to the ground.

A milk float come flying down the road with no one driving it. Went straight at the bizzies which got a cheer. I ran cross the wasteland, dint no where I was going now. Further into it or trying to get home. Warnt really thinking. Then I seen it.

I seen Richie.

Lying on the wasteland tryina put his hands over his face as this bizzy was hammering him with his trunchon.

Richie's screaming.

An then I notice who the bizzy is. It's ____.

An I just seen red and ran straight in.

Get off him you cunt get off him thats my mate get off him ____ you fucking basterd!

And he looks round and pushes me away. Not like he's hitting me but just to get him off him as I started tryina hit him. An while he was working out who I was an realizing it was me Richie seen his chance and got up and legged it. And suddenly a load of other bizzies appeared and ran towards us only ____ screams at them to leave me alone.

He's me son. He goes. And the bizzies looked weird and ran away.

I freeze.

What did he say? I look at him.

He looks at me. Hisses. What you fucking waiting for Daz. Get fucking home now. NOW.

I leg it.

I can't breathe. I can't breathe. I can't stop but I can't breathe.

This must be what the war was like.

Is like I've stepped into the end of the world. Is like I've actchally stepped into hell.

Can't sleep when I get in. I goes downstairs and knock but there's no reply. Just wanted to check Richie was ok. But I know he must've been because he ran off when I seen ____.

I go and sit on the couch. Noise still going outside but as the hours pass it dies down.

But am not thinking about out there now. Am thinking about in here. In my head. Am thinking about what ____ said.

He's my son.

Am shaking like a shitting dog.

He can't be my dad can he? ____. No. No way. He can't be my dad or else why did I go with him all those times in his car? If I was his son how could he do that? He wouldn't. Nah he was just saying it to get other bizzies to fuck off.

And when I think that I stop shaking.

But then I think. He knows Ma. Him and Ma go way back. She always said is coz he like protected her but he told me they done it. Loadsa times. What if he done it and that's how she had me?

But then I remember she wasn't earning when she had me. That came later. When she had me she was the cabaray singer. Her name was Penny Lane. She sang in the clubs in Liverpool. She was gonna be famous but then she fell pregnant with me and it all went tits up. That's why she hate me. She blame me. Every day I remind her what might have been.

____ is a bizzy.

She only knows bizzies from earning. From earning round here. From standing on street corners waiting to get plucked n stuffed. ____ offered protection and she took it up. Loads of whores get cut. Smantha was right. No one care for whores. But Ma done all right for herself. And she says that down to ____. Well, she says that in her better moods. Rest of the time he's an arlarse and worse.

Am shaking again.

I know what'll calm me.

I go to bathroom and shut the door and lock it.

I know what to do.

Am shaking now but for different reason. Am shaking now coz am excited.

I kneel down in front of the basin and open the door of the little cubbard. Behind the spare bog rolls n cloths I find a small clump of faded pink bog roll. I pull it out. I stay kneeling and open it in the parm of my hand. Like am opening a precious Christmas present. But right now this is better than every present put together.

I expect it to shine. To dazzle me. To glint in the light. But it don't. It's dull from under use. Almost black. I stand up and run it under the hot tap. Like that's gonna make a differents. Takes a while for the water to run hot and as it does I see the light outside is getting lighter. The sun is coming up.

I dry it carefully with a flannel. Slowly. Then rest the flannel on the side of the sink and rest the blade on that.

I takes a towel from the radiator and place it on floor.

I step back and pull my T-shirt off. Then kick my trainers off. Socks. Then down my jeans. I stand there in my undies for a bit then eventchally pull them off too. Now I don't look. Now I just close my eyes. Take a deep breath. Open them again. Breathe out. No. Still not feeling calmer. My shaky hand reach out and take it from the flannel. I kneel down. Bow my head like in church or something. Deep breath. Eyes shut. I dig it into me and immediate its piercing me and hurting but is beautiful too. I feel the warm blood trickle down my leg and onto the towel.

It's nice.

I feel calm.

Out with the blood and the panic goes to.

Blood comes easier than tears tonight.

Calm. The noise has stopped. A seagull sings. ____ is not my Dad.

I remember I said I'd peel the spuds.

I bring Ma's record player through to the kitchen and put one of Ma's records on. Only soft like coz it's six in the morning and everyone else will be in their beds. I stand at the drainer and start peeling the spuds. I wander how Rob has been getting on with his Dad now that his Dad's wife has gone to Portsmouth to see her sister with the cancer. I bet they got on like a house on fire.

I don't know where that saying came from house on fire but now I've seen houses on fire tonight I think it's a bit sick and I don't understand it. Who on earth come up with that? Houses on fire don't get on they destroy. Nah. Something not right there if you ask me.

I was just thinking Ma must be having a good night when I heard a key in the door. Then footsteps in the front room.

Hiya Ma am in here. Am doing the spuds for tomorrow. Couldn't sleep.

I slice the side of another spud and put the peel in the sink and the spud in the pan on the drainer.

Ma don't say nothing. And when she come into the kitchen I get a smell. And I imediatley know. It's not Ma.

I think you owe me an apology Daz.

I put down the peeler. Am shaking again. I don't turn to look at him. I can't.

Look at me Daz.

I can't. I don't say it I just can't.

Daz.

I don't wanna look at you. I say after a bit.

Why not lad? Don't you fancy us?

I shake my head.

You do fancy us.

I do nothing.

You do.

I say nothing.

Why did you say you was my Dad?

You could do a lot worse than me lad.

166

Why?

Aren't you gonna offer me a drink?

Like am on automatic pilots I go the cubbard and then pore him a whiskey. Can't even look at him. Go back to the drainer and turn my back on him again.

Yer didn't think I was serious did you? He goes.

No. Course not.

Yer think I'd fuck me own son?

No.

You dirty bastard.

And then he jumps towards me and pushes me into the drainer an starts rubbing hisself against me arse an I feel sick and I feel scared but the worst of it is I start responding and I hate myself for it. He reaches round and grabs it.

Fuck off ____.

Well what's this then?

Nothing.

Fuck off it's mine that. I own it.

Why? Why does my body always let me down? Why does it do shit I don't want it to do? Be a way I don't want it to be?

He rips my PJ bottoms down with his left hand as he slaps it with his right.

And without thinking I lift the pan with the spuds in and I spin round and punch the pan through the air like I'm serving in tennis and I hit it straight over the side of his head. I hear a really loud crunch. He immediately goes backwards and falls on the floor and there's another crunch.

There's water and spuds everywhere.

Ma's favourite pan is still in my hand.

He is lying there with his eyes open staring at the ceiling.

I have to put the pan down. It's so heavy. It makes a big bang as I drop it onto the drainer.

I look back again. The shakes have come back.

____?

But he is just lying there with his eyes open. Staring up.

I slowly kneel down. I need to see if he is breathing. But am scared coz I think this is a windup and at any minute he will jump up and leather me. But he don't move and I edge closer. I lean in next to his face. I can't hear nothing. I stand back up and I just don't know what to do.

The record is still playing. It has hit a scratch. I should go and tap the record player but I can't actchally move.

Which is when I hear another key in the door and then Ma coming in.

She comes into the kitchen and her eyes go wide. Jaw near hits the floor. She calmly puts her bag on the side. Looks at ____. Then looks at me.

Fuckinell Darren. What've you done?

Woody came over. Never met him before. Brought two mates with him. All speaking quietly work out what to do. Ma had called him from the box round corner. No one seemed that bothered he was dead. Ma told me to go in my room. When I come out later Woody and his mates had gone and ____ had gone. The rug in the living room had gone too. Ma had finished peeling the spuds. I didn't know what to say.

You owe me one. She goes. Not even looking at me.

He touched us. I goes.

You owe me one. She said again. Making sure I got the message.

Just then the doorbell goes. We both freeze. I look to Ma. She looks to me.

Well go and get it.

I shit meself going down them stairs. Convinced it would be

bizzies askin where ____ was. My heart beating in my chest. Like it would explode like the Rialto. I come down the stairs. The door to Richie's flat is a bit open. I half expect to see a load of bizzies in there going What you done to ____. But I don't. I can hear their telly though. I hear Margret Thatcher. Just hear her voice.

She goes: Those poor shopkeepers.

I get to the front door. Take a deep breath. Open.

Smantha's standing there.

And relax.

Hiya Darren.

Hiya Smantha.

Then I didn't say nothing coz of the relief. But she doesn't look that happy. In fact she looks dead uncomfortable.

She goes. I got something to tell you.

HOLLY

SEVEN

It was an odd sensation, walking onto a deserted beach yet seeing several naked men, ten metres or so away from each other, legs slightly apart, staring at the incoming tide. Had I not heard all about the statues from Iggy and just wandered unknowingly onto the beach, I would have been unnerved. The statues were bronze, mildew green, proud, faceless, and poor Michael was petrified of them. Who were these human beings who didn't move, flinch or breathe? He danced around the first one we passed, growling and baring his teeth – something I'd never seen him do before. I yanked him away with the lead and broke into a trot to put some distance between him and the iron man.

The wind hit my face with brisk, hard slaps and I was grateful for them. They were the caffeine facial my body craved, as I'd slept so poorly the night before. Thoughts and questions had quickly become obsessions. I could not get the boy from the diary out of my head. I couldn't stop thinking about him and his life and his family and what had happened to him. I couldn't stop thinking full stop. About him and today and Francesca and Rose and the beach, and today. It was all about today. Today I was finally going to meet my mother.

At around two I had had to put the diary down. There was

more to read, but if I'd carried on, I'd never have slept – that was my rationale – and I didn't want to be exhausted today of all days. I wanted to know what happened next to him. I had fallen asleep with ease, but the sleep was fitful and I'd woken frequently, unable to get him out of my head. Each time I'd been tempted to put the light on and read some more, but I decided sleep, elusive though it was, was more important.

Each time I woke, I'd become increasingly niggled. My niggle started as a glowing magic bean that then grew and grew till it became a massive neon beanstalk, lighting up my head, the flat, flashing and flashing so much I'm surprised the whole of Liverpool hadn't been lit up. And it was telling me, the boy in the diary, Darren. He must have lived in the flat I was born in. And if he was caught up in the Toxteth riots, that meant he was living there in 1981. (Thank you, internet search engine.) And if he was living there then, he was living there not long before I was born. Which meant he was my brother. Francesca was his mother. His 'ma'. She had been desperate to have a baby, it seemed, as a way out, possibly, of her 'career'.

No wonder I had been unable to sleep properly. I had just discovered that my mother was a prostitute. And, on top of that, a not very nice prostitute. I felt for Darren. I liked him. I had so many things I wanted to ask him. I wanted to put my arm round him and tell him that everything was going to be OK. How ridiculous was that? Here I was, thirty-odd years later, wanting to reach out to him. He would be in his forties now, no longer the little boy, that's for sure. But could he really be my brother?

And could I really tell him that everything was going to be OK? For all I knew, nothing had been OK. For all I knew, he could well be dead by now.

I wanted to tell him that killing the unnamed person, well, it wasn't his fault. Well, it was, but he was provoked.

Had I really found my brother's diary under the floorboards? Had it really lain there for thirty years unnoticed, unread, untouched? And why did Darren leave it there when he left? Why on earth would you choose to leave a diary lying around that contained such . . . such incendiary information in it, that he had killed someone?

Well, I would ask Francesca. I would ask her today and we would sort it out and I would check that Darren was still alive and was happy and sane and . . .

A wave of nausea hit me. My mother was not a nice person – that much was clear. And judging by how she'd treated Darren, I'd had a lucky escape being shipped out to Ted and Jean. No wonder Francesca had rejected me; she didn't appear to have a maternal bone in her body. So much for the romantic notion of the poor naive girl who couldn't cope. Francesca probably didn't want to cope.

I had to face facts. My mum was a bitch.

But then, maybe it wasn't her. Oh, the constant toing and froing in my head was exhausting. But addictive. She was living in the flat a year before I was born. She had been pregnant and lost the baby, so maybe she fell pregnant again shortly after.

Or maybe this family moved out and Francesca moved in. My mind started playing tricks with me. I couldn't remember whether anyone in the diary had ever referred to Darren's ma as anything other than 'ma'. Had he at any point called her Francesca? I knew that I had known the night before, but now I just couldn't remember.

Years ago I had placed my name on the Adoption Contact Register. If my mum had ever tried to trace me, she would be on it too. She wasn't. And her name had never appeared on it.

Oh yes. Bitch.

I wanted to know how Rob was. I wanted to think that he had gone to the Wirral and was living with his father. I wanted to know that both those boys had escaped. Maybe I was being harsh; maybe I was overanalysing because I was so shocked that my mother was not some Doris Day, apple-pie-wielding Sindy doll.

Unless Sindy was a street-walking prostitute.

She had to be my mum. She had to have lived in that flat when I was in her tummy. Darren had been to the flat below him and used a payphone. I had seen that payphone when I had gone to Jax's for teacups of gin. She was living in Richie's flat and I was in Ma, Darren and Rob's. It was the most peculiar feeling, having had a tantalizing glimpse into someone else's life. Someone who was my own flesh and blood, I thought.

Or maybe they had moved out soon after he kept the diary and Francesca Boyle moved in.

And if she was my mother, who might that make my father? I'd not given him much thought at all before. Now I wondered if he was some anonymous punter – great, my dad was the sort of man who drove around red-light districts picking up women off street corners – or was he one of her gangster-type boyfriends, one of the ones who had helped conceal the dead body? Which made me some kind of Holly Soprano. It didn't bear thinking about.

I had so many questions to ask Francesca, but the question in my head just now was, 'What does an ageing former prostitute look like?' Or maybe she wasn't former. Maybe she was still working.

No wonder Rose had been coy about admitting she knew

her. Francesca might have had a string of babies by her punters. And who wants to admit to being pals with a hooker? No wonder she had clammed up in the salon when I'd told her: she was probably gobsmacked that an old hooker would have had a child. Furthermore she was probably worrying about upsetting me. How easy must it be to say, 'Oh, you know your mum? The one you're looking for? She sells her body on street corners. Must be a joy to find that out. It's been an absolute privilege being able to let you know.'

I felt a bit sorry for Rose Kirkwood.

I had to steel myself. If Francesca was the mum in the diary, then chances were she was going to be hostile towards me. Hostile with an overcurrent of vile. I just had to get in there, ask my questions and get out.

The madness of what I had done struck me like the wind. I had uprooted myself to go on an adventure, and by the looks of it, it was over before it had even begun. I had discovered my identity. It wasn't particularly fragrant; now it would be time to move on. So what if I had nowhere else to go? I would go somewhere. On another adventure. And like the old prostitute, I would survive.

Even without giving it too much thought, I felt I had come to a decision. The search was over, my mother was found, but I didn't want an ongoing relationship with her. If that was snobbish of me, I didn't care. Would it have been different if she'd worked in a bank, a shop?

I tried not to think about this. She didn't do either of these things; she was a prostitute. And she had been rather ghastly to my brother, Darren.

It felt so odd thinking that. Me, the only child, suddenly, potentially, having siblings.

It was pointless trying to avoid these blessed statues. They were everywhere. I yanked Michael's lead again and headed away from the water, back towards dry land.

As I turned, I saw her. Where the beach ended, there was a rather gaudy-looking brick esplanade, raised above the beach, green dunes behind it. Rose was walking along the esplanade in a very long leather jacket, with the collar turned up. All she needed was a massive fur hat and she would have been every inch the Russian spy. I instinctively waved and she nodded. I headed over, running with Michael to give him some more exercise, trying to tire him out so that he could sleep through my meeting with Francesca.

But the nearer I got to Rose, the easier it was to make out the look of apprehension on her face. She kept flitting her eyes down to the dog.

'Sorry. Is something wrong?' I asked, before even saying hello.

'I didn't think you'd bring the dog,' Rose said.

'Oh. Sorry. Is that a problem?'

I started climbing some steps up to the esplanade now.

'Well . . .'

Clearly it was.

'Does Francesca not like dogs?'

Rose shook her head. 'No, it's not that. It's . . . where she is . . . they're not allowed.'

I gasped. 'Oh, is she in hospital? Is she OK?'

'She's fine. She was. But she isn't now.'

Rose was confusing me. And she could tell.

'She was in hospital, but now she's out.'

'What's the matter with her?'

'She had a fall.'

'Oh right. And why can't she have dogs, er . . .'

'Come with me.'

'Where are we going?'

'You'll see.'

There was nothing green about the Greenacre Nursing Home when we arrived five minutes later, a tall, narrow Edwardian mansion slightly set back from the main sweep of a road called Mersey View. The brickwork was greying, but I could see that it had once been a proud yellow. 'Faded grandeur' was the phrase that sprang to mind. Not unlike the feeling of Gambier Terrace, now I thought of it. The shrubs and bushes surrounding it appeared to be grey also; gnarled fingers of branches poked out of crumbly dry soil. I didn't get a particularly good feeling from the Greenacre Nursing Home.

'So, this is where Francesca is,' Rose said solemnly.

'What's the matter with her? Is it old age? How old is she?'

'A woman never reveals her age,' Rose countered, which I found a ridiculous thing to say.

I felt a sudden rush of anger. I wanted to spit back, 'No. And she clearly never revealed she'd put a daughter up for adoption. She possibly hasn't even told you she's a prostitute. Unless you're one too. You weird bloody geisha!'

I didn't, though. With my Home Counties restraint, I bit my tongue and said nothing.

But I knew what I looked like when I was feeling angry and I knew that a telltale rash would be seeping up my neck. I could tell that Rose saw it too.

'What I mean is, I don't really know.'

I nodded, placated.

'But the reason she's in here is . . .'

I looked at her.

'She has a form of dementia.'

179

Dementia. A form of.

'What d'you mean, a form of dementia?'

'Well . . . she's got early onset dementia.'

Dementia. My old friend. Or maybe adversary was better. The condition that had cloaked my mother and now hid my birth mother. Like Harry Potter's invisibility cloak, it completely wiped out any signs of a personality . . .

'What stage is she at?' I asked.

'She's had it a few years now. Some days she's reasonably lucid, other days not at all.'

'Have you told her I'm coming?'

'Yes.'

'What did she say?'

'It didn't register. Holly, I think you have to prepare yourself for her not remembering you at all. She's away with the fairies.'

I nodded. 'Shall we get this over and done with?'

Rose looked to Michael, wondering what I was planning on doing with him, so I tucked him under the front of my coat, gripped my stomach so that he was sitting on the ledge of my arm and in we went.

Francesca's room in Greenacre was a modest affair with a three-quarter bed tucked against a wall, a couple of armchairs, a small sink in the corner and a massive television, which stayed on throughout our visit. The decor suggested a set designer had visited and offered up things that you might assume you'd find in an old person's room. The throw on the bedspread was crocheted; the flowers on the bedside table were paper; on a shelf on the wall sat a pair of porcelain praying hands. It all seemed a bit too old for the woman who sat before me with a twinkle in her eye.

This was it. This was the moment I had waited for since that fateful day in McDonald's all those years ago. I was finally meeting the woman who'd given birth to me. I'd expected a fanfare, trumpets, a roll of thunder, the axis of the earth to shift. Instead, we were sat in a poky room with the curtains drawn and *Loose Women* showing in the background.

I had hoped and expected that when we finally met, I would have a déjà vu feeling, that I would look at her face and be shocked that I wasn't looking into a mirror. Or that seeing Francesca would be a bit like one of those apps people have that can make a photo of them look fatter or older or uglier. Or all three. I would see a morphed version of my own face looking back at me nervously. The sort of nerves that come when a birth mother is worrying, I rejected her years ago. Will she reject me now?

I knew. I'd seen every episode of *Long Lost Family*.

But then, those birth mothers, of course, didn't have dementia.

Francesca looked to be in her mid-sixties, possibly older, well preserved, hair recently dyed – I wondered if Rose took care of that – the wrinkly terracotta skin of someone who'd seen too much sun. She was dressed simply but elegantly in a cream blouse and green skirt, but her foot was up in front of her, encased in plaster.

Oh, and she was sitting in a wheelchair.

She didn't look familiar at all.

'This is Holly, Frankie,' Rose said, as I sat myself in an armchair opposite her.

Francesca smiled politely with a nod of the head. 'You all right, love?' she asked brightly, as if she had known me all her life and I'd only recently visited.

'Good, thanks. You?'

And she nodded, then looked to the TV. As if I was so familiar she didn't have to stand on ceremony.

'Well, you've broken your leg, Frankie,' Rose pointed out, with a slight *Duh!* in her voice.

Francesca swung her head round, surprised. 'Have I?'

'Course you have! Look at your plaster!'

Francesca looked to her leg and seemed genuinely surprised.

'How did you do that?' I enquired politely.

Francesca looked confused and turned to Rose.

'You had a fall, didn't you, Frankie.' And it wasn't a question; it was a reminder.

Francesca looked to me and nodded earnestly. 'I had a fall. It was terrible.'

'Gosh, I'm sorry.'

Then Francesca leaned forward, towards me. Urgently, she whispered, 'Can you take me home? I don't like it here. They're trying to kill me.'

I didn't know how to respond to that. I looked to Rose.

'Nobody's trying to kill you, Frankie. This is a good home. You like it here.'

'I don't,' she said to me. 'They poison the food. Everyone's dying.'

And as I just looked blankly at her, she turned and watched the screen for a while. I felt Michael wriggling beneath my coat, so undid some buttons and he hopped into my lap. Francesca shrieked, then laughed.

'Oh, isn't he comical?'

The abruptness of her change in mood brought me up sharp, reminding me as it did of Jean.

'Sorry. This is Michael. I'm minding him for a friend.'

Francesca looked to Rose. 'Oh, isn't he comical, Marg?'

It took me a second or two to register. Did she really? No, she did. She just called Rose 'Marg'. Margy from the diary.

'What did she call you?' I asked, short of breath suddenly.

'What did you call me, Frankie?'

Francesca looked to her. 'Y'what?'

'What's my name?'

Francesca looked blank.

Rose looked to me. 'I think she called me Marg. Sometimes she calls me Margy.'

'Why?'

'I think it must've been the name of a mate from when she was younger. I don't know.' And then Rose looked to Francesca and raised her voice. 'Who knows what year your head's at, eh, Frank?'

I looked at Rose again. Could she be lying? Could she actually be the other prostitute from the diary? The one who Francesca battered in broad daylight on the street? And if so, why was she lying? Had she reinvented herself as 'Rose' to cover up her embarrassing past?

Or was she – which was more likely – just telling the truth? I knew from personal experience how Jean had called me myriad names during her illness. Each of them made sense in their own way; each had been the name of someone important to her at some point in her life. I'd found some comfort from this at the time.

'Who's Margy?' I asked Francesca.

'Sorry?'

'Who's Margy?' I repeated.

Francesca shook her head, like it wasn't important, and turned her face to the television again.

'Did you work with her?' I asked.

'I think she's tired,' Rose said, seemingly apropos of nothing. 'Maybe we should come back another time.'

'We've only just got here,' I said, voice raised, and Rose shifted in her seat. My tone told her I was not to be argued with. 'Francesca, Rose has brought me here today because, as she's explained before, though you might have forgotten, I am your daughter.'

She looked at me. Stunned.

'My name is Holly. And I am your daughter.'

Her face remained impassive as she said, 'I haven't got a daughter.'

'You had a daughter who you gave up for adoption. Or maybe she was removed from you. It was a very long time ago – 1982. And now I'm . . . all grown up and I'm here and I just came to say hello really.'

Francesca continued to stare at me blankly. 'I don't have a daughter.'

'You've forgotten. I've got my birth certificate. Mother: Francesca Boyle, 32B Gambier Terrace. That's you.'

Francesca returned to the television.

'Have you got *any* children?' I asked.

Francesca studiously ignored me.

'Frankie, answer her. She's come all the way from London.'

But Francesca was saying nothing. I looked around the room. No photographs in frames. Nothing personal, come to think of it. *Loose Women* came to an ad break and this seemed to please Francesca, as she smiled and turned round and . . . well, it was like she was seeing me and Michael for the first time.

'Oh, look at that. Isn't that comical, Margy?' she chuckled, pointing out the dog to Rose.

'I'm Rose,' Rose replied sadly. And this time I believed her.

'And who's this pretty thing?' she said, looking at me.

'My name's Holly,' I answered, possibly blushing.

'Are you from the Co-op?' she asked, and she looked so pleading I felt I couldn't upset her.

'Yes,' I replied, 'that's me.'

And she turned to watch the adverts.

'See?' said Rose bitterly. 'I told you she was away with the fairies.'

And I couldn't help but detect a hint of cruelty in her tone. Like she thought Francesca wasn't just ill but stupid. Or deserved it. And it made me not like her very much.

Afterwards we sat in Rose's car. I didn't particularly want to share such an intimate space with her, but as I didn't know the way from Greenacre to the railway station, I didn't have much choice.

'Well, you've seen her now. You must be gutted,' Rose said, as she fiddled with some make-up in her handbag and attacked her lips with some lip liner.

'It's not ideal,' I agreed.

'Oh well. Some things are best left in the past. Did you have a nice adoption?'

She said it with the casual ease of someone asking if I'd had a nice holiday. I just nodded. I had no desire to tell her anything about myself. She almost seemed to be enjoying this.

'Well, you know, if I were you, I'd just keep it in your head that they're your family and her in there –' she pointed at the nursing home '– well, I'd forget she even existed.'

'I thought she was your friend?' I couldn't help but be surprised at her harshness.

'She is. But you seeing her again won't do you any good.'

'I'll see her if I want to,' I said, sounding like a completely petulant child.

Rose sat in silence for a bit. She was still staring in the rear-view mirror, checking her face.

'How do you know her?' I asked.

Rose froze for a bit, looked away from the mirror and down into her bag again.

'I used to do her hair,' she said sadly. 'Holly, the thing you need to know about Frankie is, dementia's softened her. She used to be a right hard-faced —' and she stopped herself from swearing.

'You're saying she's not a nice person?'

'She is now, but then, she's not herself.'

I wanted to say, 'Yes, I know – I have read her son's diary,' but I didn't want to tell her how much I knew.

'Does she have any family?'

Rose shook her head. And she blushed. I knew she was lying.

'Only my mum and dad – Ted and Jean – they were always of the opinion that she had sons. Two sons.' Now I was lying: Ted and Jean had said no such thing.

'Well, if she has, then . . . she's not seen them for years.'

And this sounded plausible.

'As I said, Holly, she wasn't very nice. So it wouldn't surprise me if she had kids and they didn't speak to her.'

Again, this sounded plausible.

But for some reason I still didn't trust Rose Kirkwood.

'So, will you go back to London?' she asked, completely out of the blue. I was affronted. It was like she was trying to get rid of me.

'No.' My voice had a steely edge. 'She might be away with the fairies, but she's still my mother.'

186

Rose licked beneath her lips, erasing any lip liner from her teeth.

'And besides,' I added, 'I want to find my brothers.'

She didn't have to say anything. Her body language shouted it all. She crumpled into herself as if to proclaim, *I give up*. Like she was my careers adviser and I was the first girl in the school to want to be a welder. And I wouldn't let anything stand in my way. So any fight on her behalf, even though she thought it futile was . . . well . . . futile too. Just then my mobile rang. I checked the caller ID: 'Jax calling.'

I answered, trying to ignore the passive-aggressive ice queen sitting next to me.

'Hi, Jax!'

'Babe! Where are you? Can you get home?'

'Why? What's the matter?'

'There's a load of water pouring through my ceiling!'

'Oh no!'

'I know! I thought it must be coming from your flat!'

Stopping myself from saying, 'Well, you're psychic, don't you know?' I instead beamed, 'Well, fortunately I'm sitting here with my landlady!'

I turned to Rose and smiled.

EIGHT

As Rose and I arrived at Gambier Terrace, we saw Irish Alan pulling up outside number 32 at exactly the same time. Rose had made me call him en route and tell him to drop everything and come and meet us. Again, the sheepskin jacket was on, and I nearly held on to it as I followed him up the stairs, two at a time.

Jax was having a very noisy nervous breakdown in the hallway.

'My favourite Cath Kidston wallpaper *ruined*!'

'I'm really sorry!' I called back, even though I had no idea if this was my fault or not. I could hear Rose running behind me. Then Jax started pacing up the stairs too, not wanting to miss out on the drama, no doubt.

I had to get to the flat door first. I knew there was something I had to hide.

Eventually I barged past Alan as we reached the landing by my door and I almost screamed, 'It's OK! I'll open the door!'

In fact I nearly took him out as I lurched to the keyhole and slotted the key in the door.

'Are you OK, Irish?' I heard Rose whimper.

She called him Irish? How odd.

'In we come!' I trilled, and we all fell into the flat.

'Get the stopcock, Irish!' Rose gasped, and I dived into my bedroom and bellyflopped onto my bed, arms out, as if on a crucifix.

As I heard Rose and Irish Alan scrabbling around in the kitchen, I heard footsteps behind me.

'What are you doing?' It was Jax.

'Just . . .'

I was about to say something ridiculous like 'Just lying here.'

But what I was actually doing was covering Darren's diary so Rose couldn't see. I instinctively knew that she would want to confiscate it from me and I wouldn't ever know what happened next. I didn't want her to know about my family. They were mine, not hers. And here were all his papers, laid out on the bed, messy and out of order some of them, as I'd left them this morning, after I'd slept with them. I felt Rose was keeping secrets from me, that Darren and Rob were smackheads, in and out of rehab. Well, I would keep secrets too. I knew something else about them, about a time from long ago, and I would keep *that* from *her*.

I saw in Jax, suddenly, an ally. I sat up.

'Jax, can you do something for me?' The urgency in my voice clearly excited her. She practically clapped her hands.

'What is it? Sure.'

'I need you to take this biscuit tin and hide it.'

She looked wrong-footed, as well she might. I scrunched up the papers, trying as hard as possible to keep them in some semblance of order, and squashed them into the tin, then handed it to her.

'I don't want Rose to see it.'

She nodded. 'I'll put it in my flat.'

'Can you do it now?'

She nodded again and, without further ado, scarpered, tin in hand. As she did, I caught a glimpse of Irish Alan running past my door, then heard him running upstairs to the flat above. It felt like the whole house was banging, with Jax running downstairs and him running up. Rose came into my bedroom, looking agitated.

'What's the problem?'

'Oh, it's not here. It's the woman upstairs. You've water pouring through your kitchen too.'

'Oh God, no!'

'But don't worry – Irish'll sort everything. That's our job.'

'Thanks.'

And then she came and sat on the bed next to me, completely uninvited.

'I don't like the woman upstairs,' she offered.

'Right. Why?'

She shrugged. 'Just something about her.'

Maybe I would get on with her, I thought.

'I wouldn't talk to her if I were you. She's very standoffish and can be rude. Very rude.'

And it hit me. Possibly thanks to my lack of sleep, I'd never even thought of the woman upstairs. The one in the diary. The one Darren called Fatty Arbuckle. He had found her rude. She had been rude. She'd looked down her nose at him.

'Save you being offended,' she added, as if that would swing it for me.

I nodded, but I knew I was definitely going to seek her out.

'How long's she lived here?' I asked.

'I'm not sure. I only took over looking after this place once Frankie got ill. She was here then, but I'm pretty sure she'd just moved in.'

I didn't relish this close contact with Rose, her sat right next to me.

'So this place isn't yours?'

'No, it's Frankie's, but I've got power of attorney.'

'What, she gave power of attorney to . . . her hairdresser?'

'As I said –' Rose was getting defensive now '– she'd really isolated herself.'

I took this in, though it was an odd one to swallow. Frankie must have thought she was some stylist.

'Holly?'

I looked at her.

'If you like, I can ask around for you, see if I can find anything out about the sons.'

'Would you? That's very kind.'

'I know a couple of people who've known her a while, but . . . well, the impression I always got was that she'd cut herself off from everyone she knew. Become a bit of a recluse. I don't know why she took to me, really. I'm nothing special.'

She still managed to do it. I could be feeling apathetic about her, almost negative, suspicious, and then she'd say something that made me warm to her. She was an odd mix.

'Before the illness she was very . . . loud. Aggressive. She drank a lot and . . . swore a lot and . . .'

'Did she work?'

Gosh, my faux naivety was good.

'Not while I've known her. I think she must have. She was never short of money. But again, she was a very guarded woman.' And then she added, 'I'm so sorry.'

'It's not your fault. Looks like I landed on my feet, being adopted.'

Rose nodded. 'I know she's my friend and everything, but I'd say you had a lucky escape.'

And with that she stood, smoothed the creases in her skirt and almost floated out of the room.

I heard footsteps hurrying up the stairs. Then Jax hurtled in the hallway. I rushed to meet her and she went to whisper to me just as Rose popped her head round the living-room door. Aware she was being listened to, Jax raised her voice and said, 'I've got to go out. I'm doing a reading in Bootle. D'you need that thing back?'

'Later'll be fine,' I replied with a tight smile.

Rose interrupted, 'The water appears to have stopped running. I think Alan must've located the source.'

'And what do I do about my wallpaper?' Jax actually folded her arms and tapped her foot.

'If you phone your landlord and tell him, and we'll see if her upstairs can claim it on her insurance.'

'Okey-dokey.'

Rose disappeared back into the living room.

'Jax!' I whispered urgently.

'What?'

'The woman upstairs. What does she look like?'

'I dunno. Why?'

'What, you've not seen her?'

'Well, yeah, I've seen her, but . . .'

'Look, is she really fat?'

'No. Why?'

'Oh. Nothing.'

Jax looked confused and turned to go. She then quickly looked back. 'Any news? Sorry.'

'About what?'

'Your mum.'

'Long story.'

Jax nodded, then turned again and ran down the stairs.

Rose popped her head round the door, again.

'I don't think your kitchen appliances are going to work, you know. I think it's done something to the electrics.'

'Oh right.'

'It's OK. Irish can sort it tomorrow. He knows a man who can.'

'OK. I'll get a takeaway tonight.'

'Well, I thought we might go one further.'

'How d'you mean?'

'Why don't you come to us for dinner? Get to know each other a bit better.'

'Erm . . .'

'I do a lovely chicken curry.'

And because I was now a yes-woman, I found myself nodding.

'Yes, Rose, that'd be great.'

Rose drove behind Alan through central Liverpool, but then we lost him at some lights. She drove in silence, the radio on, playing a local station featuring an overenthusiastic DJ who sounded like a cross between John Lennon and Timmy Mallett. It made me think of Iggy. To get to the Wirral, where Rose lived, we had to drive through the Mersey Tunnel.

'It's a tunnel that goes under the River Mersey,' explained Rose, needlessly. I had already worked that out for myself.

As we drove underground, Rose switched off the car radio and we were engulfed by the sound of engines bouncing off gas-chamber tiles. It was like hearing the scream of pollution. The temperature dropped, I pulled Michael closer to me like a tiny hot-water bottle, the yellow lights above lit our faces sporadically, and with the lack of daylight and air, I started to feel trapped. Anxiety rose in me slightly and I fidgeted in my seat. The tunnel became a metaphor for what I was currently doing with my life. The strange city, the strange people, the strange mother. And now I was going for dinner with a couple I hardly knew and didn't really want to, frankly. I wanted to wind the window down, get some air, but worried that all I would get in this subterranean drainpipe was carbon monoxide. I looked to Rose, her face flicking from yellow to grey in the lights. She looked imperious, regal almost. There was something about her profile that was a little too perfect and I wondered if she had had a nose job. As if reading my thoughts, she turned and looked to me. It was an unnerving sight, the driver of your vehicle staring at you and not at the road ahead, especially in such a confined space as the tunnel, and she held my gaze for a little too long. She didn't speak. She looked like she wanted to. Like she was building up to saying something. And then she didn't. And then it was gone. And I worried about what it might have been.

Relax, Holly, for I am driving you to your death. Alan and I are serial killers. And you are my next leather coat.

Or: *I am actually your mum's very old friend Margy. I cannot bring myself to tell you, though, because Alan knows not I was a working woman. Keep away from your mother. She is evil.*

Although, as she was a hairdresser, it could just as easily have been: *You know, lowlights would really bring out the shape of your face.*

Eventually we saw light at the end of the tunnel – literally – and as we drove up into the daylight, Rose started talking. She had been so winsome and reserved driving from Gambier Terrace to the tunnel, then stoic in the tunnel, but it was like she'd given birth to a new personality now she was on the Wirral. The tunnel had been her egg and now she'd broken free, she could fly. She became garrulous, relaxed; her driving even picked up the pace. She was becoming excited, it seemed, or nervous. Heavens, she'd only promised to cook me a chicken curry – what was there to be nervous about? Or was she regretting inviting me? Like I had felt trapped in the tunnel, maybe she too was now fearing this was a bad idea. I was quite prepared for her to do an emergency stop, ricochet Michael off my knee and say, *I'm sorry. I don't think this was a good idea. I felt sorry for you today, finding out your mother was a bit bonkers. But now I . . . well, I'm just not bothered.*

But the emergency stop never came, and her mood continued to brighten.

The street that Rose and Alan lived on on the Wirral was on a sweeping hill called Derwentwater Drive. It was remarkably similar in feel to the street in Tring where I had grown up, except these properties were 1970s built. They still exuded the same suburban ennui as Tring, as if their tight little frames were constricted by their narrow minds. All in my head, of course, but my lasting impression of home nonetheless. But whereas I saw Ted and Jean's place as humdrum and ordinary, it soon became clear that Rose believed she lived in Buckingham Palace itself. It was evident she saw Derwentwater Drive as a destination address. As we drove up the hill, she gave a running commentary of who lived in each house, 'Judy. Daughter's a doctor . . . The Patels. Very competitive. Hot tub . . . The O'Haras. She's had a breast removed, and he's been caught getting up to mischief in toilets.'

There were no fences between the gardens in Derwentwater Drive and the houses seemed to pile up the hill on top of each other, like a trail of beige dominoes about to fall. Rose treated me to a 'hilarious' story about how Alan and she had minded a neighbour's dog once when they went on holiday. (The Valentines. Number 43. Immaculate blinds.) Only the dog was a bit burly and he dragged Alan down the hill across every single garden. Rose could hardly get the words out she was laughing so much and she kept accidentally putting her foot on the brake, so we juddered up the hill as we went, and Michael bounced on my knee.

'Oh, it was comical, Holly,' she said, which reminded me of Francesca.

'And here we are!' she announced as she swung into the narrow drive in front of a very ordinary semi-detached of yellow brick, grey tiled roof and white wood panelling around all the windows. Concrete steps climbed to the front door and on each one Rose had planted a tub of brightly coloured flowers. Irish's car, she informed me, was already in their up and over. (Garage, I presumed.) Rose made a big song and dance about putting the handbrake on as the drive itself was on a steep slope. And then she sort of fell sideways out of the car and staggered towards the house, almost holding on to the brickwork to steady herself. It was the first time I'd not seen her be ladylike.

'I know it doesn't look much from outside,' gasped Rose as she uprighted herself to launch up the steps, 'but wait till you get inside. It's very deceptive.'

I nodded, pretending to be excited to enter this amazing Tardis-like house. She shot Michael a look.

'He doesn't eat butterflies, does he?' she asked, wary.

I shook my head. 'No. Not that I'm aware of. Why?'

'You'll see,' she said.

I followed her up the steps. It was then that I realized Rose was wearing cherry-red, shimmery, footless tights. Why had I not noticed them before? She had had her neck-to-floor leather jacket on all day and maybe only now was I getting a flash of her legs. They struck me as garish for someone so dainty and refined. Or trying to be refined. I had even started noticing that Rose's accent went around the houses a bit. When she was distracted or agitated, she had a very broad Scouse accent, but most of the time she appeared to rein it in a little, as if she'd been to elocution lessons and was trying to remember for the life of her what they'd taught her. A bit like when I'd originally spoken with the estate agent and she'd added a 't' to the end of her 'yes'es. It was then I realized that maybe this refined act was possibly for me, being a Southerner, a breed apart. But why would I be someone she wanted to impress?

As she fumbled around in her handbag for some keys, the wind blew her coat up again and I saw the tights. Heavens. And just then the front door opened and Alan was standing there with what looked like two chintzy highballs of gin and tonic.

'Welcome . . . to the madhouse!' He grinned and handed me one.

I dreaded that inside, somewhere, there might be a poster of a chimpanzee in a suit on the phone saying, 'You don't have to be mad to work here, but it helps.' Actually, though, the reality was even more surreal. Every single nook and cranny of this otherwise ordinary three-bedroom semi's hallway was covered in anything and everything to do with 'The Owl and the Pussycat'. Figurines, framed drawings, stuffed toys, cushions – if you could get it with an owl or a pussycat or both on it, Rose had it here in her hall. I now noticed the front door had a stained-glass image of the owl and the cat; the bannister had black owl and cat shapes painted up its spindles; cuddly cats and owls hung from the ceiling. Even the beaded curtain between the hall and the kitchen boasted hanging metal silhouettes of owls. I think I'd have preferred the chimp poster.

'Told you it was a madhouse,' laughed Alan.

'I see you like . . . "The Owl and the Pussycat",' I said.

'And the award for stating the obvious goes to . . .' Alan laughed again. Oh good, it was going to be an evening of Alan laughing. At everything. 'Anyway, it's not me, it's her. She's obsessed.'

'Oh well, at least it's just one room,' smiled an embarrassed Rose. 'Anyway, makes me easy to buy presents for. Show Holly the garden, Irish, while I check on the slow cooker.'

Of course she had a slow cooker. Of course it had been on all day. Rose Kirkwood was Mrs Suburbia. In footless tights.

Alan pushed through the beaded curtain and I followed with Michael into a gleaming white kitchen infused with the smell of curry. There were framed posters on the walls showing various paintings of white Greek houses, sunsets over Greek villages. Each one had the word 'GREECE' written at the bottom, just in case you had been born under a stone. Alan then opened the back door and led us across some crazy paving towards the garden. To reach said garden, Alan had to open a mesh door in a mesh fence, a bit like we were entering a tennis court. I then discovered that the first third of the thirty feet or so garden was encased in a mesh. It was like we were standing in a cage. It was full of the most beautifully coloured flowers, and juddering between them a host of delicate butterflies.

'Rose also likes the butterflies,' chuckled Alan.

'Amazing,' I said. I was pretty stunned. It just wasn't what I expected to see in a suburban back garden.

'Neighbours call her the Butterfly Lady.'

There was another door leading to the rest of the garden, and I opened it to let Michael out in there. Alan and I followed him and stood on the other side of the mesh, watching the butterflies dancing.

'Come here and look at this,' Alan said, sounding enthused.

I followed him to the far end of the mesh cage and he pointed out what looked like some nuts hanging from sticks.

'They start off as caterpillars. Then they wrap themselves up in that stuff and turn into pupae – that's what they are. Then one day they break free and become the butterflies.'

I nodded. I knew all this from primary school, but seeing it first-hand did bring back to me what an amazing feat of nature it was. I looked back at the house. Bizarrely the back of the house looked nothing like the front. Continuing the Greek theme from the kitchen posters, the rear of the property looked like it had been ripped away from Pathos, tossed by a tornado and landed here on the Wirral. The pebbledash was all painted white, and the back door a vivid royal blue. Before I could pass comment on it, Alan was speaking.

'Hear you've had a shit of a day.' He said it casually but sympathetically. There was something so soothing about his Irish accent that he was instantly more likeable and empathetic than his wife.

'Well, I came here looking for answers. Got a few. Don't think I'll get any more.'

'Ah, never give up. Rose was saying she's bound to have family, so she's going to do some digging for you. See if she can't find where they are.'

I nodded. Oh well, at least Rose appeared to be taking this seriously. If she'd told Alan that's what she was going to do, maybe there was a silver lining to my cloud. Why was I being so unfair on her? Thus far she had taken me to meet my mother, offered to make me chicken curry. What more could

I ask for of a landlady? And poor Alan and Rose, managing a flat that wasn't even theirs.

'Seems like you do an awful lot for my birth mother,' I said, genuinely trying to praise Alan.

'Ah, it's no big deal. And neither of us has any family. Rose has a kind heart – she'd do anything for anyone.'

I felt bad. I'd been getting Rose all wrong, just because she was so different to me.

'Plus . . .' he left a dramatic pause, 'Frankie's leaving everything to Rose in her will.'

And he threw his head back and laughed. And it all made sense. But still unnerved me.

'She must've thought a lot of her perming skills,' I said.

And he laughed even more. Suddenly Rose appeared in the butterfly house.

'What are you two laughing about?' she said severely.

Alan was brought up short, a schoolboy caught gassing in class behind the teacher's back.

'Ah, nothing, Rose. Just this and that.'

Was he scared of her? Rose smiled, relaxing. She pulled the bangs of her long bob out of her eyes and said, 'I'm just getting the rice out of the microwave. Why don't you come through?'

The curry was an insipid yellow colour and boasted sultanas, chopped almonds and some coriander dandruff. It was so Seventies it was untrue, but served not with a *Look at me – I'm retro* pride, more *This is how chicken curry is made, end of.* It was tasty and homely, but I couldn't eat it. Alan was talking away about his weekend fascination for car booting. Cue lots of horrified raised eyebrows from Rose: in her book you clearly bought new and it lasted. Although most of her taste seemed to have been bought new in the 1980s, it still looked brand new. But I wasn't really listening. I found it hard to concentrate with the crashing noise in my head of everything finally slipping into place. I understood now why Rose had been so reluctant, at first, to take me to Francesca. I realized now why she zigzagged between being kind to me and being cold. I had to say something. I had to explain I wasn't the enemy. Maybe then she'd . . . like me a little bit more.

'Rose?' I interrupted Alan mid-flow.

She seemed grateful for it. 'Aha?'

'I have something to tell you.'

She seemed to pale.

'I want to put your mind at rest about something.'

She cleared her throat. What was I going to say?

'I just want you to know that when my adoptive parents died, I inherited their house. A considerable amount of money.'

Still she said nothing, but continued to look afraid.

'And so I'm reasonably comfortably off. I was an only child.'

'This is none of our business,' Alan interjected.

'I just don't want you thinking I've come to try and get money out of Francesca.'

Rose looked confused.

'I know you stand to inherit Gambier Terrace when Francesca dies . . .'

Rose shot Alan a look. 'What've you said to her?' and she sounded *so* Scouse you could have broken plates on her accent.

'Nothing! Just . . . just mentioned it in passing.'

Rose rolled her eyes.

'I won't be asking for anything from Frankie.' I tried to sound reassuring. 'I won't be . . . contesting any wills or . . . saying she owes me or . . . you know.'

'I find it vulgar to discuss finances,' Rose said, almost swallowing the words.

I wanted to say, 'I find it vulgar to cake your hallway in nursery-rhyme memorabilia when you're in your forties,' but I kept it zipped.

'I'm sorry. I just didn't want you to view me as any competition. A contender to your crown.'

'Alan shouldn't have said anything,' she reiterated. And then she shot him another look that told me there was going to be an almighty row later, once I had left.

'I had a stroke a while back. In hospital for months, I was. Think it sent me soft in the head,' he said, by way of explanation for why he might sometimes get things wrong. 'It was touch and go for a while.'

Rose continued to eat in silence, as if unmoved by his story.

'But the bad news is, I survived,' he added with a twinkle. A twinkle I returned.

Rose became even more guarded than usual following my recent blurt. Everything I asked her she batted back to me like a Wimbledon pro, as if my questions were unimportant, banal.

Where did you grow up? Liverpool.

Which part? All over. We moved a lot.

Are your family still alive? My mother lives in Greece. That's her in the photo there. Everyone else is dead.

I looked. On an alcove shelf was a framed photo of a rather glamorous woman in close-up, her face sunkissed.

Oh, but Alan said you both had no family. Ignore him – he had a stroke. He talks rubbish sometimes. Just listen to me.

How did you get into hairdressing? It's really not that interesting.

Did you ever want children? We have lots of godchildren.

Where did you get your hideous tights from? The most vile shop in the world.

I may have made the last one up.

Alan was a bit more forthcoming. He'd been a bit of a bad lad, ducking and diving, more diving than ducking, but following his stroke, he had taken things a bit easier and erred on the right side of the road. I wasn't sure what this meant, but I assumed it was his way of saying he'd been a bit criminal and now stayed on the straight and narrow.

Rose was far more at ease grilling me, and they were both interested to hear more about my job with Sylvie di Marco. Alan had vaguely heard of her but couldn't profess to name anything she'd been in. Rose had hazy memories of her having had a record out once, though she couldn't name it. I told them about my contretemps with her and how I'd walked out on her/been fired and they seemed amazed that a boss could treat an employee like that and get away with it. They asked politely if I had anyone special in my life and I told them about Jude and how I'd felt there was a distance between us and I'd not known how to breach it, and maybe it was the sweet wine that I was drinking with the curry but I found myself saying things I'd not hitherto acknowledged. How I'd never really under-stood how close he was to his family, to his brood of brothers and sisters. And how only now was I beginning to understand how important it was to me that I might be part of a similar brood, that I might have siblings. And how I felt guilty that I'd abandoned him, when now I was starting to understand why that might be a comfort. And I told them how I didn't really have many friends. How I'd let most of my relationships slide over the years, blaming the pressures of work, of having Jude, anything, when really I knew the reason. I didn't see the point in investing in people, because eventually they would reject me, just as Francesca had. When you come into the world and are unwanted, who else could possibly want you? I felt tears in my eyes and saw that Rose also was moved. She dabbed at her eyes carefully (so much make-up) with her napkin. I saw Alan give her leg a squeeze under the table.

'And have they?' asked Alan.

'Have they what?'

'Has everyone else abandoned you?'

I thought. And had to be honest. 'No. I guess I've abandoned them.'

The words hung in the air.

'All my life I've felt there's a question mark running through me.' Rose nodded, as if she completely understood what I meant. 'And because I know so little about my birth and the first few months of my life, I don't feel fully formed. I feel like . . . like I just appeared one day.'

Rose nodded and said, 'The girl who just showed up.' Like it was a concept that was one she was more than familiar with. And then it was my turn to nod.

After a dessert of Arctic roll and tinned apricots, I excused myself to go to the bathroom. Alan went about getting his coat on as he was going to drive me home in Rose's car. I could hear them having a hissed row downstairs when I came out of the bathroom. I stopped, embarrassed to go back down as they were spitting venom at each other, and I looked around the landing. The door to their bedroom was open; another bedroom door was shut; a third was shut and had a padlock on it. I looked through the first, open door. I could see there was a framed photograph on the bedside cabinet. I could see a boy in it, smiling. It drew me in. I tiptoed so that they wouldn't hear me downstairs, and then I sat on the bed and looked at the photograph.

It showed a handsome blond boy in a smart blue uniform. He must have been about thirteen, fourteen, maybe younger. He was smiling at the camera while wrinkling his eyes up at the flash of the camera. There was something about his smile that reminded me of Rose, even though her smiles had been few and far between. And then it hit me. The ice of her, her distance, how she could appear aloof. How she'd grown combative when asked about children.

Something told me this was her son. Had she and Alan had a child who had died?

I must've become a bit too transfixed by the photo to not hear footsteps coming up the stairs. Because the next thing I heard was Rose's voice saying, 'Holly? What are you doing?'

I looked up. She was standing in the doorway, looking paler and angrier than ever.

NINE

'Did you have a son, Rose? Did he die?'

She looked flustered. 'You shouldn't go snooping. You've got no right to come in here and go sniffing around. I'm not Francesca.'

'I'm sorry, Rose. I could hear you rowing with Alan, so I waited a bit and . . . then I saw this and . . . well, he's so handsome I couldn't help but . . . Who is he?'

She hurried towards me, snapped the photograph off me and jammed it in the top drawer of the bedside cabinet, slamming it shut.

'I don't want to talk about it. OK?'

'I'm sorry.'

I'd clearly overstepped the mark.

'I know you've had a tough day. I know you want answers. But please. Stop asking me so many bloody questions. I'm doing all I can to try and help you. I'll find out about your brothers, I will. But you know . . . life isn't a storybook, Holly. Ask yourself this. Why were you taken off Frankie?'

'I don't know. Social services haven't been able to find my adoption records yet, but they will.'

'Well, if she wasn't up to looking after you, maybe she

wasn't up to looking after them. Maybe you were all taken off her at the same time.'

'I know life's not a storybook.'

'There are no happy endings. Like my butterflies.'

I looked to her, confused.

'They start off as caterpillars, then mutate into these beautiful winged creatures.'

'A happy ending!' I insisted.

'And how many weeks do they stay alive? Happiness doesn't last forever. It's squashed out of you before you know it.'

I was right. That picture was her son. Why else have such a negative view of life?

'You come up here. You lift up rocks. Then wonder why there's creepy fuckin' crawlies underneath them? If life was such a mess back then, don't be surprised that it's gonna be a mess right now.' She was like a preacher, jabbing her finger in my direction, emphasizing everything she said. I'd never seen her so energized. I'd certainly never heard her swear.

'I'm really sorry,' I said. Now it was her turn to look confused. 'I can't imagine what you've been through. I'm sorry.'

Tears pricked her eyes. She bit her top lip. Her arms tensed at her sides, and she went out onto the landing. Then I heard her lock herself in the bathroom. A few seconds later I heard Alan calling from downstairs. I shouted a goodbye to Rose, heard nothing back, then hurried down the stairs to get Michael and my lift home.

Alan said very little in the car on the way. Neither did I. I felt exhausted by the last twenty-four hours. The diary, the lack of sleep, the anticipation of meeting Francesca, meeting her, the bitter disappointment, Rose's bizarreness, it all felt too much for me to handle. I wanted to get back to Gambier Terrace and go to bed. It was well past eleven. I wouldn't even knock for Jax and ask for the diary back. Right now I didn't care. No doubt I would eventually read it and it would devastate me. I'd read Darren's description of Francesca giving birth to me and then . . . and then . . . neglecting me, or abusing me. Who knew what she got up to with the infant me? It certainly wouldn't have been exemplary maternal behaviour, or else why was I removed from her? Or maybe Darren described her not loving me and leaving me on a doorstep or . . .

Enough. I'd had enough. For now I wanted to go to bed in Gambier Terrace and wake up in Tring. Ted and Jean would still be alive and I'd love them much more than I ever did before and be more grateful to them for saving me from Francesca than they'd ever know. I'd conform. I'd be nice. I'd wear my hair in pigtails, anything, to say I was sorry for not appreciating their kindness like I did now.

I had come to Liverpool, turned over a few stones, and yes, Rose was right, felt squeamish at the creepy crawlies festering beneath. It was time to put those stones back and just . . . sleep.

When I got back to the flat, Alan wanted to come in and inspect the damage in the kitchen again. Everything looked fine, apart from the stains to the ceiling, floor and one wall-papered wall. He pulled at the wallpaper and tapped some wall units to check they were stable.

'I'd plug the kettle in in the bedroom if you fancy a cup of tea, love. Not sure the wiring in here's safe,' he said, then re-assured me someone would be round soon to put it all right.

Before he left, he said, 'You know, Rose might have her faults, but she's got a heart of gold really. I knew her for years before we got together. I had to grow up a bit before I was worthy of her really. Before that I'd always been drawn to high maintenance.'

I nodded, unsure why he was telling me this.

'These days I don't even want high maintenance in the flat I rent out.'

I smiled.

'She's had a hard life. Go easy on her.'

Again I nodded. Though I wasn't sure that I'd been particularly tough on her. Still, this was a man marking his territory, protecting his brood. There was something of the lovable caveman about it and it was actually rather appealing.

When he'd gone, I climbed into bed and snuggled up to Michael. He went out like a light and I lay staring into the darkness. The futility and humiliation of what I'd encountered in the last few days slayed me. I'd had such high hopes, and now, nothing at all. Again Rose had spoken sense. For a child to be removed from its mother meant that there was mess or chaos around that child's birth. To return to the scene of the crime, it was unsurprising to find mess and chaos again. Why on earth had I expected to be Little Miss Different and miraculously find a Utopia of regretful mothers? Again like Rose said, I should be grateful Francesca had Alzheimer's. At least it had softened her edges. I'd met her – she'd been away with the fairies, but at least she'd not been the bitch I was now more than aware she could be.

I heard a knock at the front door. I ignored it. I heard Jax calling through the letterbox, 'Holly? Holly, did I hear you come in? Holly, d'you want your tin back?'

I ignored her. She called my name a few times more. Then, 'I'll get it back to you just as soon as I can!'

I heard her let the letterbox drop shut. Then footsteps

retreating downstairs. I lay in the darkness, staring at a ceiling I couldn't quite see. I heard a group of women passing, drunk, singing Daft Punk, and then what sounded like one of them being sick. Then laughter from her friends. Eventually they moved on. And then I heard it, what I'd heard the day I'd arrived and I'd pulled up outside in the cab. A brief scream. It seemed to come from more than one person. And it seemed to come from upstairs. Then a roaring noise. Then another scream. What was that woman doing up there?

I located some earplugs in my washbag. Eventually I slept.

Fortunately I woke the next morning with my batteries re-charged and the first thing I did, before even getting dressed, was run downstairs and knock on Jax's door. I waited. No reply. I knocked again. Either she was sleeping or she had already gone out. I checked my watch. It was half past eight. Was she really the sort of woman to be up and about so early? Maybe if I tried ringing her mobile. I returned to the flat and called her. I heard it ringing downstairs. It rang out and then went to answerphone. She must have still been asleep.

I got out my laptop, powered it up and entered the name 'Darren Boyle' in a search engine. The first said there was a Darren Boyle on Facebook. I'd set up an account years before in a vain attempt to keep in touch with people from school and my time in the orchestras amid the madness of working for Sylvie, but rarely ventured on. I logged in and re-entered the name. Of course, it was not an unusual name and soon I was inundated with hundreds of Darren Boyles. What should I do? Send each of them a message saying, 'Sorry, you don't know me, but . . .'? It seemed an impossible task. I entered another name, 'Robert Boyle'. The leading name was that of a philosopher from the seventeenth century, but then there were, again, gazillions of names to skim through. I shut the page down and opened the search engine again. I entered, 'Richie Toxteth riots.' There was lots of information on the riots and on Nicole Richie without her make-up on. I re-entered, 'Red-Light District Liverpool.' I found a 'delightful' blog by a man who discussed the difficulty of finding prostitutes on the street and how annoying it was to have to go online to procure oral sex these days – he didn't mind going online to write about it, of course. And then my eyes were drawn to a paragraph about the red-light district in Liverpool in the 1970s and 1980s. One sentence made my eyes practically pop out on stalks: 'I lived there for a while in the 1980s. I have fond memories of meeting prostitutes in Hope Street next to the Anglican Cathedral.'

Hope Street, the street that linked the two cathedrals. Hope Street, the street that Gambier Terrace curled off. Francesca had only had to step outside her house to tout her wares. I had to admire her brass neck, it had to be said. Aside from working at home, that was one quick commute to the office.

I entered the words 'Policeman missing after Toxteth riots.' This time, lots more info about the riots. Nothing about a missing policeman. This surprised me. Surely someone must have realized he had gone missing. Surely he had friends, a family. He certainly had workmates – did none of them report him missing? Surely it would have been noticed that he hadn't turned up for work the next week.

I thought about what Darren's teacher had said to him that day outside the house. How he liked to write stories. He had kept a diary, after all. So now I entered the words 'Darren Boyle writer.' Lots of articles came up about the film director Danny Boyle and his thoughts on writing. Again all roads led to zero.

I remembered that on the TV genealogy shows they were always looking up the census to see who lived where at a certain time. I entered, '1982 census.' Nothing. But I did find many links about the 1981 census, so I re-entered, 'Gambier Terrace 1981 census.' This time I learned that all censuses were kept secret till a hundred years later. Boo, hiss! However, I did discover that Stuart Sutcliffe had lived in Gambier Terrace. I clicked on the link thinking this was the Yorkshire Ripper, but it wasn't – it was someone who had been in the Beatles before they got famous. Another link was titled 'Your Memories of the Riots.' I clicked on it and read:

> I was living in a basement flat in Gambier Terrace in Liverpool in 1981, just behind the Cathedral. I was living with my wife and twin sons. A policeman was killed nearby on Friday 3 July in some incident involving a car.
>
> The tension in the city on the Saturday was palpable and when we came back from a club at 3 a.m. we found Toxteth in the grip of the riots. Sunday deteriorated. From a neighbour's flat we could see Upper Parliament Street alight, the Racquet Club up in flames, and the Rialto too. The police were everywhere. It was so frightening, it affected everyone. And when we woke up the next morning the devastation was incredible.

Even though I had already read Darren's disturbing account of events that hot weekend in 1981, I suddenly found this secondary evidence unsettling. It hadn't just affected the Boyles; it appeared to have devastated a community. Of course, I already knew that from reading different bits and bobs online, though thus far I'd not had chance to spend any proper time really digesting what had happened that weekend and how it had shaped the area in which I was now staying.

I spent the morning reading account after account of the riots online. The articles were full of grainy black-and-white pictures of policemen with shields, burnt-out buildings, burnt-out milk floats. On some of the pieces, there would be a photo of the same view now, sometimes unrecognizable from the original image, as buildings had been razed to the ground. I saved some of the pictures and emailed them to myself so that I could view them on my phone, then decided to spend the morning walking around the area looking at them with Michael.

I suppose what shocked me most was just how close everything was to my new home. The first place I visited was what had been the Rialto ballroom. Darren had made it sound magical when he'd stood outside it imagining Samantha's parents meeting there. I had the picture of it burning on my phone. I held it up and compared the then and now, and was hit by a wave of sadness. They'd kept the original shape, a curved corner, a cylindrical tower, but there was something so inauthentic about the replacement building. As if the designer of Toytown had said, 'This can be your new Rialto.' There was little magical about the municipal-blue window frames and the tiny blocked prison-like windows either side of it.

I wondered where Samantha was now. What did she have to tell Darren? She was clearly bright. Maybe she was telling him she was leaving Liverpool to go to university. I liked that idea. Girl power! I wondered if her parents still passed this corner and marvelled at how their palace of dreams had changed.

From there I went to Upper Parliament Street, or 'Parlie', as the man in the article had described it. The beautiful, elegant Georgian terrace still stood. If only Samantha's parents had met there, their palace of dreams would still be intact. This was an area that had once had a lot of money passing through it, perhaps when Liverpool was at the centre of the slave trade. I didn't know. But I thought of Fatty Arbuckle and her disappointment that the area had gone to the dogs. Maybe she had too. If she really was the size Francesca claimed she was in the diary, maybe she was six feet under by now, dead from a heart attack. I wondered if she was so huge they'd had to winch her rotting corpse out through one of the upstairs windows.

After these two views I gave up comparing the then and now and just walked around the streets. Thus far I had known parts of the area through Google Maps and trying to imagine Francesca walking about with me in her pram; then I had explored a nearby street and pub with Iggy, reminiscing about John Lennon. Now, however, I felt an emotional tie to the area. My family had lived here and seen the area change forever during the riots, the year before my birth. Though it still felt rather alien to me, dare I say it was beginning to feel like home? Was I becoming an adopted Scouser? An adopted-out Scouser certainly.

I felt less like a local when I walked past several young men in tracksuits, their hands stuffed down the front of their pants, like Iggy, with various Staffies and pit bulls on or off leads. I think had I not met Iggy, I might have felt intimidated by them, but I didn't. I gave them all a smile and a cheery 'Hi!' and they giggled and gave me 'All right's back, each time with a guffaw at the state of Michael compared to their butch beasts.

As I returned to the terrace, I passed the Rialto once

again and fantasized some more. Samantha had gone to university, gained a first at Oxford, in politics, and then returned home and married Darren. I made a mental note to look up Samantha Boyle online when I got in. But then I thought, No, Lucy would never have allowed that.

Lucy. I had forgotten all about her. Who was she? And how did she fit into the pattern I had established in my head? When I thought of 32B in 1981, I pictured the building as a doll's house with the front off. Richie and his mum on the ground floor, Fatty Arbuckle lying on her sofa on the top floor, eating a selection box (all year round), Darren and his ma and Robert in the middle. And yet Lucy seemed to appear out of nowhere when she knew that Darren was on his own. Did she live there too? Was there a flat I was yet to discover? I hurried home and saw, no, I was right – there were only three flats at number 32. Maybe she lived in one of the adjoining houses. Or maybe – and this thought excited me – she lived with Fatty Arbuckle or Richie. Was she Fatty's daughter? Or was she in fact Richie's sister? Richie's family had a surname. I'm sure Darren had mentioned it in the diary, but I couldn't for the life of me remember it. I had to find it. I had to wake Jax. I hurried into the hall, dragging Michael with me so that he hit a skid on the tiled flooring. I banged on Jax's door, no longer standing on ceremony, and called her name. I banged again. Then called her mobile. Again, I heard it ringing inside the flat. Oh God, was she OK? If she had gone out, why hadn't she taken her phone? And if she was in, why wasn't she answering the door? I banged again, this time with a ferocity that could have woken the dead.

'Careful, dear, you'll take the door off its hinges,' I heard a voice boom from the top of the stairs. I looked up to locate the owner of the voice. Coming down the stairs now was what

I can only describe as a symphony in puce. Her voice was commanding, even if her walk down the stairs was less so. She looked about seventy and was dressed as if going for a jog – sportswear, headband, bottle of water in her hand, tidy rucksack strapped so tight to her back I was amazed she could still breathe.

'Sorry,' I gasped, and the woman sort of harrumphed and continued on past me. I grabbed my chance. 'Excuse me, sorry, but I'm Holly. I just moved in, Flat B. I was wondering . . .'

I was wondering what all that screaming was last night.

I was wondering if you ever knew Fatty Arbuckle.

The woman looked back. Just then my mobile rang. Convinced it was going to be Jax phoning me back, I hit 'accept'.

'Hello?'

'Darling, how's Michael?'

I knew the voice instantly. Of course.

'Sylvie?'

I was so shocked I turned towards the wall, feeling like I was imploding. I might fall at any second and headbutt the mustard wallpaper.

'Who else?!'

I turned back to face my neighbour, but just caught sight of the front door swinging shut. I sank onto the bottom step of the staircase.

'Oh, he's fine. He's . . . he's sat here with me.'

'Put him on.'

'Sorry?'

'Put him on. I want to speak to him.'

'Erm, OK.'

I held the phone to Michael's ear, where he now sat between my legs. Sylvie's voice was so loud I could hear it rattling out of my mobile.

'Darling, it's Mummy. Is Holly looking after you OK? I bet she's spoiling you rotten. Oh, Mummy is missing you. It's so cold over here I could do with a massive hug.'

And then she rattled off into peals of laughter. I couldn't quite believe I was sitting at the bottom of a staircase holding a phone to a dog's ear so his 'owner' could have a word.

'Are you eating OK, my lovely? Is she giving you enough food? I know what a fussy eater you are, dear heart. Oh, I can hear you whimpering.'

He wasn't.

'It's like you're talking to me. Oh, I can't bear it. I had a feeling. A knot in the pit of my stomach. And I just knew I had to call you because I knew you were missing Mummy.'

And then I could hear her crying. I waited for the tears to subside, knowing they would take quite a while. Now that Sylvie didn't get much acting work, she often moaned about not having a cathartic space to get any pent-up feelings out of her system. Some days she had even said, 'I am going to my room to scream and cry. No disturbing.' And though it was completely bonkers, me sat there holding a phone to a dog and listening to someone cry, it also felt reassuringly familiar, and for the first time in a good few days I felt myself relax. Because even though Sylvie had treated me like dirt, even though I hated her guts, I knew where I stood with her, knew who I was (her slave, of course). Up here in Liverpool with my dreams of discovering who I was and where I'd come from, I'd felt confused at best, sinking at worst. Sylvie was a reminder of more straightforward times and I never thought I'd relish any contact with her.

Eventually the tears ran dry and I heard her sigh heavily, calmer now. I returned the phone to my ear. Michael hadn't budged during the whole call. Maybe he was deaf.

'I hope I haven't agitated him too much.'

'He's . . . looking a little worried,' I lied.

'Oh *God*. That is beyond. I can't bear to think of him upset.'

'He's . . . calming down now. I think he'll pull through.'

'Do you? *Do you*?'

'I think he's . . . Oh my God, yes, he is – he's smiling.'

Somebody section me now!

'Awwwww, my little lamb chop Mikey plops.'

Actually, somebody pass me a sick bucket now!

'How's Canada?' I continued.

'Hellishly cold. I've nipples like chapel hat pegs. How's London?'

'Liverpool,' I corrected.

'Oh, what've you gone there for, darling?'

Why was I doing this? Why was I even entertaining her? I should just hang up and be done with it.

But maybe she was ringing to arrange her getting Michael back off me.

'Oh, just some personal stuff. I did tell you.'

'You know, Holly, I have the world's most ineffective PA out here.'

'Oh, really?' I couldn't help but smile.

'Marybeth. What sort of a name is that?'

'I think it was one of the cops in *Cagney and Lacey*.'

'Of course! The wonderful and eponymous Tyney!'

'Sorry?'

'Tyne Daly! We did *Jane!* together.'

Was she spilling more sexual exploits of a lesbiotic nature?

'Jane who?'

'No! *Jane!* The musical version of *Whatever Happened to Baby Jane!* Tyne is wonderful and so, so, *so* eponymous.'

I wasn't sure she knew what eponymous meant. Still . . .

'I loved her so much, you know, Holly. She was such an eponymous actress. I have no idea why she stopped speaking to me once the reviews came out. Little bit jealous if you ask me. And how was I to know she was dating Igor?'

I chose not to go there.

'Anyway, I've got to—'

'Oh, don't go, Holly.'

She was being overbearingly chummy. She sounded a bit like Miranda Hart in *Call the Midwife*. And it would be impossible to put the phone down on *her*.

'You'll never guess what she did between Montreal and Quebec.'

'Spontaneously human-combusted?' I was feeling mutinous.

'Sorry?'

'Nothing. What did she do between Montreal and Quebec?'

'Lost my fucking costumes, darling.'

I stifled a giggle, trying to find some comradeship with poor Marybeth, and stopped myself from saying, 'I'm sure it was the airline that lost them Sylvie, not your PA.'

'I had to wear off the peg. Off the peg, Holly, in *Quebec*! Have you ever been to Quebec?'

'Not since your last tour.' But she wasn't listening.

'It's a ball gown *desert*.' And I could hear her anger bubbling over across the miles.

'What time is it there?' I asked, suddenly realizing it must be really late.

'Four a.m. I have jet lag and Marybeth's gone to A and E. Or whatever they call it over here.'

'Oh, what's the matter with her?'

'She walked into the wall of my suite. No doubt she'll say she was pushed, the little bitch.'

I said nothing. My heart went out to Marybeth.

'Is she Canadian?'

'Allegedly. Keeps going on about family in Leeds. Like I'm interested. Anyway, here's the thing.'

I hated the phrase 'Here's the thing.' One of the good things about Liverpool is not a single person I had met had used it. Which was a thing. And I hated that phrase 'Is that a thing now?' Grrr.

'I've been thinking.'

Oh God. Here we go, I thought. The doors to hell just swung open.

'I think I may have acted a little hastily over that horrendous sofa you made me buy.'

'I did no such thing.'

'Mea culpa, as they say in Spain. Mea culpa.'

'You chose it, Sylvie.'

She powered through, not letting me sidetrack her with a little thing like the truth.

'If I double your wages and fly you here first class, would you consider taking your job back?'

Shit. *Shit.*

'But, Sylvie—'

'Don't say yes now. Sleep on it. Think about it. Let me know. Sylvie needs you.'

'You said I was useless.'

'I was mentally unbalanced.'

'Just for a change.'

'Sorry? This line . . .'

'Nothing.'

'I think I've been suffering from depression. It clouds the judgement.'

That was another thing I hated. People jumping on the

depression bandwagon. Some people had one bad day or were a bit fed up and bandied the word 'depressed' about like nobody's business. Yet true depression could be crippling.

'What sort?' I asked, the devil in me.

'I'm not sure. Post . . .'

'Natal?'

'Possibly.'

'Sylvie, your son's thirty-four.'

'Maybe it was delayed. It's post something, anyway.'

Yes, post nobody wanting to hire you.

'If I was at all unfair with you, then you need to hear it wasn't my fault. It was because I was undiagnosed.'

'Have you been diagnosed?'

'Yes. It's clinical.'

'By a clinician?'

'No, not a clinician, per se . . .'

'Have you self-diagnosed, Sylvie?'

Her voice was small now. 'Yes.'

'I'll think about it.' And I hung up.

I stared at Jax's front door. There were four different Yale and Chubb locks on it in a line from the bottom to the top. Talk about Fort Knox.

And then I was hit by a flashback to last night. Standing on Rose's landing. I saw the bedroom door ahead of me, one of the ones I didn't go through. And I wondered, Why would someone put a padlock on a bedroom door?

TEN

'Maybe they're kinky,' said Iggy three days later, as he lifted his second pint of Guinness to his lips, before smacking the moustache of froth it left away with his sleeve.

'Kinky?' I said, ripping the corner of a spare beer mat and wondering at how translucent his skin looked when the light from Ye Crack's windows hit his face.

'You know. They're into S and M. Loads of people are getting into it now, coz of that book.'

I loved the way he said 'book', like it was spelled 'buke'. I was marvelling at this instead of answering him, so he explained.

'*Fifty Shades of Shite*.' And he winked. And I giggled.

It felt very bohemian, drinking in the middle of the day, no work to head back for, few responsibilities. And it felt novel, drinking with a *friend*, having a *social life*, and above that my friend was a *cheeky scally Scouser*. How my life had changed! Two men who looked to be in their eighties were the only other people in our back room of the pub. Gaunt, caps on their heads, shiny old suits, they wouldn't have looked out of place in a Lowry painting.

'What, you mean like a dungeon?'

Iggy nodded. I wrinkled my nose.

'From what I can imagine, that was their small front box

room. Not much space in there to be whipped or . . . chained to a crucifix. Not enough room to swing a dead cat-o'-nine-tails.'

Iggy laughed. 'Oh, so you know how it works, then!'

'Not from personal experience, Iggy, no.'

'Ah, man. Thought you was gonna be the bird of most men's dreams then. Posh and a little bit dirty!'

And we both laughed at that.

'Oh, I don't know, Iggy. Maybe I'm overthinking things too much. Do you ever watch *Hell Hole*?'

'*Shit Hole!*' he corrected playfully.

'Well, last series they had this girl in, Ronnie, and she'd been a policewoman before entering the Hole, and she was so paranoid and suspicious of everything?'

'Yeah, but she was a massive knob, though,' he pointed out.

'Oh, so you do watch it!'

'Launch show on Friday, laa.'

'Well, maybe I'm like her – creating suspicions where there really needn't be. There could be any number of reasons why someone would have a padlock on a bedroom door.'

'Maybe it's where they keep the dead bodies.'

'And maybe I should just . . . give up the ghost. Maybe it's good I've not been able to read that diary again. Maybe I should just . . . be content with the fact that I've met my birth mum and . . . look to the future.'

'Yeah, but if you've got two brothers out there . . .' His voice trailed off.

'Who's to say they weren't adopted too? Or removed from her? Last thing they might want is a reminder of her.'

'If I had two brothers, I'd wanna meet them,' he said wistfully.

'I want doesn't always get,' I said. He nodded, taking this in. 'My mum used to say that.'

He winked. 'Which one?'

I took a crisp from our open packet and fed one to Michael. He took it and placed it on the floor between his paws and licked daintily at it.

'So no sign of her downstairs, then?'

'No. I toyed with calling the police. Her landlord's been knocking for days, trying to gain entry. He wants to inspect the damage from the flood, but she's added an extra lock on the door and he hasn't got a key.'

'She might be dead in there!'

'I know. He didn't seem unduly bothered. I keep sniffing through the letterbox. No putrefaction yet.'

Iggy pulled a face. 'I wonder where she's gone.'

'Well, I saw a suitcase in her hall. I asked her if she was going on holiday, but she said no.'

'Lying bitch.'

'She's vanished off the face of the earth,' I said dramatically. And in that moment, the two of us sat across a rickety table in a backstreet boozer, I felt we were some crack-nut TV-detective duo. Holly and Iggy. Though we weren't having much luck with our latest case. We even had a gimmick, a chihuahua with links to the stage!

'You gonna go to Canada?' Iggy took another sip of his pint.

'I don't know.' And I meant it. 'On the one hand, it's lovely not having to be at her beck and call, but on the other, I'm not finding too much out here. And if I strike while the iron's hot, I could go back to her and make her sweat. Issue demands, more money, better hours. I just don't know if I have the energy.'

'Have you heard any more from the hairdresser?'

'No. And I'm glad, really. She brings something out in me.'

'Eczema?'

I chuckled. 'No, I turn into Ronnie from *Hell Hole*. Remember how she thought Conrad was a mole? She didn't believe a word he said. Felt he was being inconsistent. That's how I feel around her.'

'And at the end of the day Conrad was sound.'

'He was lovely. Just a bit shy and nervous. I was so glad he won.'

'So the hairdresser's probably sound.'

'Exactly.'

'And yer ma?'

'Why d'you call her that?' I gasped.

'Eh?'

'That's what Darren called her.'

'It's just another way of saying "mam".'

'Oh.' Disappointment drained through me. I got angry with myself. 'See? I'm overanalysing every bloody thing. I thought maybe . . .'

'Maybe what?'

'You knew Darren and weren't telling me.'

'Bloody 'ell, Pips. You need to get a grip.'

He was right. I did. Instead I tightened my grip around the beer mat in my hand and crumpled it to a mess.

'I'm sorry.'

He pulled a face that told me that wasn't necessary. 'So are you gonna see your ma again?'

'I don't know. What's the point, Iggy? She doesn't make any sense.'

'Maybe she will without Rose West breathing down her shoulder.'

'Her surname's not . . . Oh . . . I get it.'

Iggy winked. 'I reckon you should see your ma again and then fuck off to Canada.'

'Oh what, trying to get rid of me?'

'I'd love to go to Canada.'

'Not with Sylvie di Marco you wouldn't.'

A man had entered our room. He scoured the lists on the jukebox. He wore a monocle and a cravat. He wore other things too, but these were the things that made Iggy stare at him.

'It's rude to stare,' I whispered.

'Professor Plum in the library with the taser or what?'

And I smiled. 'This whole thing is folly, Iggy. Coming to Liverpool, thinking I'd find answers in the flat where I assume I was born.'

'I thought it was on your birth certificate thingy?'

I shrugged. 'But everything changes in thirty-two years. Nothing stays the same. That's not my birthplace anymore. That place doesn't exist. I don't exist.'

'Bit deep for me, that, Pips.'

I sighed and drained my pint. 'What I need, Iggy, is a sign.'

He nodded. The monocled man returned to the bar and pulled up a stool. As he did, his song choice started to play on the jukebox. The two Lowry men groaned loudly. Mr Monocle looked over as if to say, '*What?*' I felt sick.

'Can we go, Iggy?'

He nodded. 'Why?'

'Come on, Michael!'

I yanked the dog out of his dream and got up to head to the door. I could hear Iggy slamming down his pint and screeching back his chair. As I hurried from the pub, I heard Sylvie singing the opening bars of 'Misunderstood Queen'. And more groaning.

I didn't want that to be my sign. I couldn't let it be. Every fibre in my being was screaming, *No, not Canada*. Every bit of my DNA – if you're able to break DNA into bits; I'm sure you can – was pulling away from all things Canadian. Had I seen a maple leaf, I might have been *sick*. I made a deal with the universe: *OK, Universe, I asked for a sign and you sent me one. Can I exchange it for another, please?*

What did I think the universe was? Marks & Spencer? I returned to the flat with an agreement to see Iggy on Friday night – we were going to watch the *Hell Hole* launch show together – and went and sat on my bed. Was Iggy right? Should I go and see Francesca one more time, or should I stick Michael in kennels and book myself on a first-class flight to Canada? But the thought of Michael in some desolate cage, shivering, ruled that out.

Nobody had been to check the electrics in the kitchen since the flood. I was sure that was illegal and my landlords should by now have rectified the problem, but I just didn't want to phone Rose to hassle her.

But maybe I should. I now had the kettle and microwave in my bedroom and kept a carton of milk in the bathroom sink filled with cold water. For the rent I was paying on this place, this was hardly on. Maybe I should email. Then I wouldn't have to speak to her.

I felt tired. Maybe it was the two pints I'd had at lunchtime, but I felt my eyes closing and my head lolling forward, so I plumped up the pillows and lay back to surrender to the fatigue. Just as I closed my eyes, I heard an almighty crash coming from the kitchen. It made me jump.

'Michael?' I gasped, unable to see him. Was he all right?

I jumped off the bed and hotfooted it to the kitchen. I passed Michael in the hall, so knew he was fine. But in the kitchen I immediately saw what had made the noise. One of the wall units had fallen off and onto the floor, knocking a work surface on its way, which was now chipped. There was a massive scratch on the tiling on the floor too. But my eyes were drawn to the patch of wall where the cupboard had been. Whereas the rest of the kitchen had tiled walls and trendy wallpaper, the cupboard had exposed what was behind it. Damp, of course, from the flood, but I could now see some other wallpaper. Dated wallpaper. Eighties wallpaper. Like pinstripes but diagonal. One line red, one black, one white, varying widths. And I immediately recognized it. It was incredibly familiar to me and I didn't know why. But the more I stared at it, embarrassingly open-mouthed, I realized what it must have been. I must have recognized it from my childhood. I had lived here. This had been my home.

I did exist.

Two men were stood outside the Greenacre Nursing Home in navy overalls with what looked like space-age packs on their backs, power-washing the brickwork, slowly erasing the greyness and exposing some welcome yellow sparkle. I called a cheery hello to them, which they ignored, and pushed my way through the heavy front door. A care assistant called Yvanka – I know this for she wore a name badge saying, 'Yvanka Care Assistant' – was guiding a white-haired old soul in a dressing gown through the entrance hall, moving at approximately minus twenty miles per hour.

'I'm here to see Francesca Boyle,' I said brightly. 'Family friend.'

Yvanka didn't seem that fussed and nodded. So I tried to remember the way to Frankie's room. I eventually located it, after walking into a stock cupboard and a laundry room, but after I'd knocked on the door a few times and got no reply,

Yvanka and the old dear passed by and Yvanka said, 'She is in garden.'

I really wanted to say, '*The* garden, Yvanka, *the* garden!' but just nodded a polite middle-class thank-you and tried to find it.

About six hours later – well, that's how it felt – I found Francesca sitting in a wheelchair in what was a surprisingly pretty garden. There was a large terrace with a mishmash of garden furniture on it, then a lawn that sloped down and seemed to drop into the Mersey. Not the safest of gardens for people with dementia, with that drop, but the view was nevertheless stunning.

I dragged up a greying plastic chair and sat beside her. The screech of the legs on the paving made Francesca look at me. A dart of recognition jolted across her face and she smiled as if seeing an old friend.

'Oh, hiya.' Her voice was soft and warm. It was so hard to equate it with the Frankie I'd read about in the diary.

'Hi, Frankie. How are you?'

'Have you come to take me home?' She said it as if that was her sole purpose for being outdoors, as if her bags were packed and at her feet, as if I was a cab driver.

'No.'

She looked crestfallen.

'Had any visitors?' I continued. I had no idea what I wanted to say to her, but just gave in to the moment. I would soon find out where this would lead.

'No.'

'Not even Rose?'

'No.'

'How's Darren?' I said this quickly, as if slipping his name in would force her to remember him.

'Oh, he's good, yeah.'

'Seen him?'

'No. I don't see anyone.'

'Robert? Rob?'

'No.'

'Your little girl?'

She hesitated.

'You had a little girl, didn't you, Frankie?'

'Pretty little thing, she was.' She was smiling. She was smiling, remembering me. Suddenly I had a huge sense of belonging. It seeped through my body, upwards, a whirlpool of warm water.

'They took her off you, didn't they?'

She looked away from me, stared at the Mersey.

'Frankie? Look at me.'

Frankie turned. 'Take me home.' The water started to subside.

'Where is home?' I asked. I was beginning to sound like an undercover reporter, which I suppose in a way I was. To the outside world, I appeared like any other concerned relative, visiting, when actually I was digging for the scoop of the century. Well, my century.

'Oh, you know. Big house. Flat.'

'By the cathedral?'

She stared at the river. I cleared my throat. I now knew what I had to say.

'I'm going to say something now, Frankie, and I want you to hear it. I'm your daughter. I was adopted. And whether you gave me up or they took me off you, it was a good thing. And I've had a nice life.'

I wanted it to sink in. Through the blankets of confusion I wanted there to be a place somewhere where she would take information in and let it rest there. When Mum had been ill, I had interpreted her confusion as if she was hearing lots and lots of white noise, interfering with what she was receiving, cutting out the here and now, forcing her to a deeper place, where only memories from long ago were kept. I wanted to interrupt the transmission, cut through the white noise and allow some lucidity. It would never happen, but then maybe I was doing this for me more than her.

'I just want that to sink in,' I reiterated, sounding terribly like I was clutching at straws, which I was.

'Sinking,' she said with a knowing smile. I suppose she knew a thing or two about that. Her face clouded over. I wanted to know what year her head was at. I took a gamble.

'These riots are terrible, aren't they?'

She looked quickly, alarmed. I had scared her.

'Do you go to work when it's all so . . . dangerous?'

She looked panicked. Her mouth opened, as if she wanted to speak, but no words came.

'What about the kids? Where are they?'

'The kids are fine.'

'Are they? Who are they?'

'Will you just leave me alone?'

'Who are your kids, Frankie?'

She started trying to get out of her chair.

'No, Frankie, your leg's bad.'

But still she tried. I jumped out of my seat to try to get her to sit back. She screamed out in fear.

'Frankie, I just don't want you to hurt yourself.'

I heard footsteps behind me. I swung round.

'Is everything all right?' A rotund woman in a crumpled power suit, red of face, was looking stern.

'She was trying to stand up. I . . .'

'Come on, Frankie. Sit back down, love. You've broken your leg.'

The rotund woman went and stood in front of her. She more or less blocked out the sun. Behind her frizzy split ends, there was a virtual eclipse. Frankie wouldn't dare try and get past her, so rested back in her seat, the struggle dissipating out of her.

'Oh, hiya, Margy.'

'I'm not Margy, love. I'm Veronica.' Then she looked to me accusatorily. 'And you are?'

'It's a long story.'

'Perfect,' she said. Her voice was so loud it practically echoed off the Mersey. 'I've got all day.'

Veronica took me to her office and gave me coffee and Rich Tea biscuits, a ghastly combination, and I explained honestly and in detail why I was there. I kept calling her 'Matron', then getting embarrassed as she explained she was the manager and that matron was a bosomy Fifties thing, but I kept doing it, possibly because she reminded me of Hattie Jacques in the *Carry On* films. It was the booming voice more than anything, which completely sat at odds with the caring, kindly things she was saying. She was saying everything I already knew, but for some reason, possibly because she wasn't Rose and I didn't think she had a secret agenda, I listened, took it in and believed. She asked if there was anything she could do to help. I didn't think there was. Though I did ask if Frankie had many visitors. Veronica didn't even have to think about it. She wasn't aware of Frankie having any children. Rose had power of attorney. Rose was her only visitor apart from a few volunteers from the local church. Veronica didn't really see the point of this, as they had no history with Frankie and therefore never knew what to say to her. She told me Frankie was very sweet-natured but prone to outbursts of anger, which she said was common with people with any form of dementia. She asked if I wanted to see Frankie again before I left, but I declined. I was only going to confuse her more and it didn't seem fair.

'Poor woman,' I said, rising from my seat. 'Only ever seeing the same faces. No contact with the outside world.'

'Quite. Who'd be old?'

As Veronica showed me out, she suddenly stopped and said, 'Mind you, she did get a letter once. Not so long ago. From America.'

'America?'

Veronica nodded. 'It was lying on my secretary's desk when Rose arrived.'

'Who was it from?'

'Well, I was interested to find out. Frankie never gets personal correspondence, so we were all quite excited in the office.'

'Who was it?'

Veronica laughed. 'Such an anticlimax. It was from Rose's daughter, would you believe? All that excitement over nothing.'

'Rose hasn't got a daughter.'

Veronica looked pained. 'Oh. Maybe she said niece.' And then she brightened, her work here done. 'A relative of some description, anyway. Though I'm sure she said daughter. Oh well! Maybe I'm losing my memory too!'

'Did you read it? The letter?'

'We're not a prison. Rose took it to read to Frankie. Lovely meeting you, Holly. If there's ever anything we can do to help, please get in touch.'

'Thank you. I think you've been more than helpful already.'

Veronica shook my hand. Her fists were like baseball gloves. And then she led me to the main hall.

ELEVEN

'She's gotta be back soon,' said Iggy, raising a shot glass to his mouth. 'She's been gone a whole week, laa.'

'Unless she's gone on holiday for a fortnight.'

'S'pose.'

Iggy had come round to watch the launch night of *Hell Hole* with me. He'd arrived with a bottle of vodka and two shot glasses. Five minutes into the show we'd started a drinking game, knocking back a shot of the hard stuff every time someone said, 'Oh my God.' Iggy had invented the game when the first contestant entered the Hole and kept saying, 'Oh my God.' She'd said it quite a bit, but thankfully, the following two contestants hadn't, so I was able to take a much-needed vodka break.

Jax was still away. Her phone was now going to answerphone. I was starting to think I'd never see her or the diary again, but something told me Iggy was right – she'd be back soon enough, no doubt full of apologies.

'D'you fancy something to eat?'

I had finally been to a supermarket and filled the fridge with some long-overdue provisions.

'Yeah, if you want, Pips.'

I hauled my backside from the couch and slid through to

the kitchen in my socks. A builder-type person had been in a couple of times in the week, rehung my wall cupboard and verified that the electrics were OK. I had taken a photo of the 1980s wallpaper on my phone, before the cupboard returned, and now used it as my screensaver. I bunged an oblong rustic pizza in the oven and started preparing a salad.

When I heard someone shouting, 'OhmyGodohmyGod,' in the living room, I realized contestant number one was back with a bang and allowed myself a childish chuckle. The slam of glass on coffee table told me Iggy had taken another shot.

I could then hear a roaring crowd and the over-toothed presenter shouting into a microphone, 'Are you ready to meet contestant number four? Are you? *Are you*?'

And then more roars.

I drifted off to the one thing I hadn't been able to stop thinking about for the last few days. Rose. And her daughter. She had told me at the dinner at her house that she didn't have kids. Irish Alan had said something in the garden about neither of them having any family. Why had she then pointed to a photograph of her mother in the living room? And why had she said to Hattie Jacques that the letter from America was from her daughter? Had she been lying to me? Did she have a secret child, or was she lying to Hattie? Who had sent Francesca a letter, and why did she feel the need to lie about the sender? I started humming 'Letter From America' to myself, singing only the words: 'Lochaber no more . . .' Which were my favourite lyrics *ever* in a song. Then I stopped. The voice in the living room sounded familiar.

'People say I'm mad, but basically I'm really kooky, quirky. You name it, I've bought the T-shirt, worn the high heels!'

No. It couldn't be.

'The other thing you need to know about me is I have a

gift? I'm, like, totally psychic? I have a spirit guide with me. She's here now, and basically I talk to the dead *a lot.*'

I put down the balsamic vinegar and slid to the living room.

'Look at this knobhead,' said Iggy. 'And she's from Liverpool. Silly bitch, giving us all a bad name.'

'Ssshhhh!' I hushed him with a finger to my lips.

'Eh?'

On the screen, larger than life, was the one and only Jax.

'I'm really loud, I'm really zany, and I'm really, really deep. Like the ocean? Or the deep end of a swimming pool?'

My neighbour Jax was on the television.

'I don't think I'd have sex in the Hole, coz . . . I'm really moralish?'

Moralish? Really? Did Jax just invent a new word?

Jax was on the telly as a contestant in *Hell Hole*.

Jax who I was hoping would be home soon to return my biscuit tin to me.

'But I'd never rule out finding true love. I'm dead romanticky?'

Jax was locked away in a TV studio for a show that ran for six weeks.

'What is it, Pips?' asked Iggy.

'It's her.'

'What?'

'That's Jax.'

'You are *joking*.' He sat forward in his seat and stared in disbelief at the screen.

'. . . Oh my God! I'm getting a message through!' And then she closed her eyes and put her finger to her ear. When she opened them again, she said, 'I hear there's loads of spirits in there. Something tells me I'm gonna love it in the Hole.'

The programme then cut to the over-toothed presenter standing atop an artificial crater.

'People of Great Britain, I give you contestant number four, the one and only . . . *Jax*!'

Jax was then lowered towards the crater on a harness and chain, waving desperately to the crowds of people standing round the crater. She was wearing one of her zany Fifties polka-dot dresses and a tiara. She had a faux-fur (at least I hoped it was faux) shrug on her shoulders and Nineties platform trainers. The crowds were, understandably, booing her.

'Jax, it's time to go –' and the crowd joined in now '– in the Hole!'

And then, suddenly, the chain was released and Jax fell down into a hole at the bottom of the crater. I looked to Iggy. He looked to me. And he said what I was thinking.

'How the fuck are you gonna get your diary back now?'

On screen, Jax was tumbling down the slide that led into the Hole. I plonked myself beside Iggy, unable to take my eyes off the screen.

'This is a disaster. She could be in for six weeks.'

'Nah, the irritating ones get voted out first these days.'

'But what if everybody likes her? What if she *wins*?'

'Pips, she's mental. She's looney tunes. They'll eat her alive.'

'But she might. Remember Jaydenne? Series six? She actually had a nervous breakdown on screen and ended up winning.'

'I know. Section Night was mental.'

'Literally.'

'But it's different now. People like wielding their power with the dickheads. The quiet ones stay the distance. The loud ones . . .' and he made a hacking action at his throat.

He might have been right. I really hoped he was.

'Well, there's only one thing for it.' I picked up my phone. 'I'm going to have to phone to evict her. What's the number?'

I watched the rest of the show with a scowl on my face. Usually I would have been excited to know someone in *Hell Hole*, but the fact that she had taken something of mine and not given it back was barring my enjoyment. Why, oh why, oh why hadn't I just answered the door when she knocked that night? I couldn't dislike her too much: she had at least tried to return it to me. And the suitcase of clothes made sense now – she was packing in preparation for her television debut. It was beyond a joke.

A beep from my phone told me I'd received an email.

'Someone's popular!' grinned Iggy as I picked it up. I half expected it to be from Jax, which is when I realized I was a little bit tipsy. Well, who wouldn't be when contestant number one, Geena from Surrey, was OMG-ing like nobody's business? I thought it would say, 'Sorry about the *Hell Hole* hellish nightmare. Get the diary back to you ASAP. Jax xxx'

But when I looked, it was from Rose:

From: rkirkwoodmrs@longlivethegpo.co.uk
To: hollyjsmith001@hotmail.co.uk
Subject: Hello

Hello Holly,

Haven't heard from you in a bit, so thought I would drop you a quick line to check everything was OK with the flat. I believe the kitchen is back together now LOL. Hope everything's OK, anyway. Sorry about the other night. Hope it didn't spoil what for me was a lovely evening. You're a great girl and your parents must have been very proud of you.

Bye for now,

Rose x

My fingers hovered above the screen. Dare I? Dare I?

'What you thinking, Pips?' Iggy enquired. He didn't miss a trick.

'Sometimes in life, Iggy, you have a "fuck it" moment.'

'You what?'

'When you do think, Fuck it, and then do something impulsive.'

'You sound hilarious when you swear.'

'This . . . is a "fuck it" moment.'

And I typed:

From: hollyjsmith001@hotmail.co.uk
To: rkirkwoodmrs@longlivethegpo.co.uk
Subject: Re: Hello

Hi Rose,
    All good here, thanks, and yes, all is good in the
kitchen now LOL.

LOL? I never wrote, 'LOL'!

    Something bizarre happened the other day. I visited F in
her care home and got chatting to the matron. Or manager.
Or whatever it is she's called. She said F had had a letter
once from America and you said it was from your daughter.
I was a bit confused. Thoughts?
    H x
P.S. I was just asking her if anyone ever got in touch.
Wondered if either of the sons had contacted her, etc.

I pressed 'send' and heard it whoosh out into the ether. I had wanted to add, 'And why do you have a padlock on one of your bedroom doors?' but I didn't want to appear too nosy. I waited for her to reply. And waited. And eventually put the phone down. Maybe she was one of those middle-aged people who visited the computer once a week and therefore didn't know when emails had arrived. But then I heard another ping. Yes, she'd answered.

From: rkirkwoodmrs@longlivethegpo.co.uk
To: hollyjsmith001@hotmail.co.uk
Subject: Re: Re: Hello

Blimey, you're a proper Miss Marple LOL. I don't have a daughter, of course. I was just fibbing to shut that woman up – she is SO nosy. And at the time things were going missing from F's room and I thought it was her, but it wasn't. So yes, I was being a bit cautious. Sorry for the confusion. I haven't forgot that I said I'd ask around for you about the boys. I am doing a cut and colour on someone tomorrow and am hoping she will be able to throw some light on the matter. She used to know F years ago, I believe. Will keep you posted.

Take care,

R x

Again my fingers hovered over the screen. Buoyed by the booze, I felt the need to reply and make everything OK between us. It was lovely, this warm feeling I had about Rose that hitherto I'd never experienced. And just as I was toying with what to say in return – 'Hey! Let's go to an "Owl and the Pussycat" convention *soon*' for instance – another email pinged in.

From: judethefiddle@judetheobscure.com
To: hollyjsmith001@hotmail.co.uk
Subject: I Know I Said . . .

Hey Holls,

   I know I said I would wait for you, but I got the message
from you loud and clear – don't bother! Anyway, just in case
you hear it from anyone else, I am now seeing Henrietta from
the wind section. Remember? You met her at the cheese
and wine evening we went to. Anyway, she says hi, as do I.
Things are going really well for us and I'm sure you'll wish
us well.

   Keep happy,
      Judith x

Judith. That was my pet name for him sometimes. I reread
the email. Even though he knew why I had come up North, he
didn't make reference to it once. I wasn't sure how I felt about
what he was telling me. Relief, in part. And yes, there was a
little pang of anger. And, oh, blame the shots, but I replied
quickly:

From: hollyjsmith001@hotmail.co.uk
To: judethefiddle@judetheobscure.com
Subject: Henrietta

Fatty Arbuckle?
   X

Hahahahaha. Thank you, Darren, for the perfect put-
down. Jude replied instantly:

From: judethefiddle@judetheobscure.com
To: hollyjsmith001@hotmail.co.uk
Subject: Grow Up

That's offensive.

To which I replied:

From: hollyjsmith001@hotmail.co.uk
To: judethefiddle@judetheobscure.com
Subject: Deal With It

She's offensive.

And almost immediately he retorted:

From: judethefiddle@judetheobscure.com
To: hollyjsmith001@hotmail.co.uk
Subject: And Anyway

She's stick thin now, actually, because she had a gastric
band fitted. Not that it matters. I'm not that shallow, as
I thought you knew. Clearly we should never have been
together.

I didn't reply this time. Because two of the words in his
mail jumped out at me from the screen. Gastric band. It was
as if they were written in neon. I instinctively looked up to the
ceiling as I wondered . . .

What if the woman upstairs had been here forever? What if
it was Fatty Arbuckle? And she has had a gastric band fitted?
And therefore lost loads of weight . . . ?

Iggy was speaking. I looked over to him.

'What was that, Igs?'

'I think I know how to get your diary back.'

'How?'

'Break in and take it.'

I thought, then shook my head. 'Nice idea, but I couldn't condone breaking the law for it.'

'I don't mind.'

'She's got four locks on her door.'

'I'll break a window.'

'No. It's a really bad idea. We can't. We can't. We're pissed. It's the worst idea in the world.'

An hour later I was standing outside Jax's door, waiting for Iggy to let me in. I was swaying a little – someone kept moving the wall I was leaning on – but I have to say this felt like the best idea in the whole history of ideas *ever*. It could not fail. Iggy was a genius and we were a crack team. We were *the best*. I even did a little air punch. And went, 'Yay!' in a tiny voice, in case any police were passing and did a spot-check to make sure no one was breaking into their neighbour's flat. I also hoped that he'd get a move on so we could head back upstairs for some more shots. *Shots rocked*. And they'd really helped me see things more lucidly.

Iggy had climbed out of my kitchen window and slowly lowered himself, via a combination of drainpipes and brickwork, to the garden below. He'd then indicated for me to head downstairs. I was hopeful that Jax, being the scatty type, would have accidentally left a window open while she was away. Yes, she was bound to have done that.

Just then I heard a smash. Breaking glass.

Oh well, so she hadn't. So what? It's not like she was going to come back tonight and find the window broken: the first eviction from the Hole wasn't till tomorrow night, and then she'd probably be cooped up in a hotel for a few days doing interviews for *Heat* magazine, and then she'd make her guest appearance on the spin-off show, *Hell Hole: You're Out!* So she wouldn't be back for *ages* and there'd be plenty of time to get a glazier round and pop in a nice new pane of glass.

I heard the locks of the door turning one by one. And then the door swung open and Iggy was revealed in all his glory. He had a startled look on his face as he said, 'Bloody hell, Pips. This flat is mental.' He stood aside and I ventured in.

The chaos of Jax's interior design meant finding the diary was going to be a bit of a challenge, as it wasn't immediately obvious where it might be. I had hoped she would just have left the biscuit tin out on a table or a bedside cabinet, but a quick scour of the premises revealed she had not left it on show. And so we began looking in drawers and under beds and down the back of sofas. We worked quietly and diligently. I joked that we should be wearing white paper suits because we were like a forensic team at the scene of a crime. At one point Iggy appeared in the lounge in a pair of Jax's polka-dot heels and a humongous bow in his hair and called, 'How do I look?'

It was just then that I heard footsteps behind me. I was near the open door to the hallway and turned, panicking suddenly, to see who it could possibly have been. But the carpet must have been loose, because as I moved forward, I tripped, falling to my knees with an embarrassingly girly squeal. I landed on the floor with a loud thud and felt the carpet burn my knees and hands. When I slowly looked ahead of me, I saw a pair of slippers appear in the doorway. As I looked up, I saw they had legs in them. And those legs belonged to the woman from the top flat. Helen Chance. I knew that was her name because I'd seen post for her in the hallway this week. She had a face like thunder.

'What on earth is going on here?'

I scrambled to my feet as I heard Iggy running back to the bedroom, no doubt for a quick change.

'Oh. Hi. It's not what it looks like, Mrs Chance.'

'Ms Chance. And you're Holly, yes?'

'I am. You see, we just staged a little break-in.'

'Yes. I heard the window smash.'

This woman was furious. I think maybe we'd woken her, as she was dressed in a dressing gown and had a curler in her fringe.

'But there's a really good reason why we did.'

She folded her arms and raised an eyebrow.

'You see, I gave Jax a box of mine for safe keeping. A biscuit tin, actually. And it's got some really important papers in it. Only, we put *Hell Hole* on tonight – I know, guilty pleasure – and she was in it, and I really need my tin, so I thought we better get it back.'

'So you decided to break in?'

'Yes.'

Suddenly I felt myself sobering up. This was perhaps not the brilliant idea I'd thought it was. In fact, it might have been a particularly stupid idea.

'I'm going to get a glazier round first thing tomorrow. She need never know we did this.'

'And have you found the papers?'

Her voice was imperious, her vowels cut from a bygone era. She might have looked like a beanpole, but she had an air of Margaret Rutherford about her.

'No,' I said, sheepish.

'No. And shall I tell you why you haven't found it, Holly?'

I heard Iggy coming back into the lounge. I could sense him loitering.

'Sorry?'

'Shall I tell you why you've not found it?'

'Er . . . yes, please.'

'Because she gave it to me.'

And then she gave this tight smile. It was so fleeting. It was a real 'fuck you' smile. Which is very different from a 'fuck it' moment. Maybe those were best avoided, I thought.

'I beg your pardon?'

'She came to me before she left and explained that she was minding the tin for you. She had tried your door many times and not found you, so she wondered whether I would keep it and return it to you when I saw you. I am now seeing you.'

'You've got my tin?'

'It isn't your tin, but yes, I have it. Might I ask where you got it from and what your connection to it is?'

'I . . . I found it in my flat. Under the floorboards. In the airing cupboard.'

'Finders keepers,' butted in Iggy, bless him.

'I came here looking for my mum,' I said quickly.

'It's like a quest,' Iggy chipped in again.

'I was born here. In 1982. Have you looked inside the tin?'

Helen Chance nodded.

'I think it might be my brother's diary.'

Helen Chance nodded again.

'Did you read it?'

Helen Chance nodded again, and this time her 'fuck you' smile lingered a little too long for my liking.

'And I tell you what . . .'

'What?'

'I didn't like the way he described me.'

It was at this point that my jaw kind of hit the floor.

TWELVE

I had the mother of all hangovers. And unlike my own mother, it was right there, in my face, screaming at me, giving me grief, telling me what a disappointment I was. My woozy recollections of *Hell Hole* and breaking into Jax's flat and the confrontation with Ms Chance made my stomach cramp and my whole body groan. I tried to think positive – if the ends justified the means, then at least it had been worthwhile: today I would get the tin/diary back. Ms Chance had flounced off to bed after I announced I felt I was going to be sick, telling me she would 'see me tomorrow'. Michael was lying next to me on the bed, on his back, stock still, and for a second I thought I might have rolled on him in the night and suffocated him. But then his little legs started to kick and I realized he was dreaming. If only I had dreamed the previous night. I swung my legs round so they hit the floor and then attempted to stand up. I stumbled through to the lounge, which looked like a bomb of booze and pizza had hit it, and saw Iggy sprawled on the couch, fully dressed, also looking like he was dead. This was when I realized that I too was fully clothed.

I walked carefully to the kitchen and flipped on the kettle. Tea, I needed tea. Oh God, and I needed to find a glazier. Had I slept all night while leaving Jax's flat with a gaping wound in one of her windows? Panicking, I ran downstairs, but her door was, once again, locked. Light with anxiety, I raced back up the stairs. As I went back into my place, I noticed an envelope on the floor by the front door. It had my name on it. I opened it. Inside, it said:

Dear Holly,
I have 'your' biscuit tin. I am working all day,
then away from this evening, so if you would care
to meet me in the Anglican Cathedral gift shop at
midday, when I go on my break, I can return it
to you then.
Helen Chance

I heard a cough in the living room and skidded through to see Iggy yawning and stretching, still prostrate on the settee.

'Iggy, did we leave the flat all night with the window broken? Oh, Iggy! What have we done?'

He screwed up his eyes, then chuckled. 'No, Pips. I stuck some cardboard over it. Relax. I'll get a glass fella round today.'

'But you won't be able to get into her flat without breaking in again!'

'I nicked a key, didn't I? How's the head?'

'Oh, I feel absolutely fine,' I lied.

Despite having lived in the shadow of the cathedral for a fortnight now, I'd still not ventured inside. Although she appeared to follow my every move, staring down impassively, this old nun in specs, I hadn't yet paid her a visit. Leaving Iggy a hundred pounds in cash to sort out a glazier, I headed off feeling slightly better thanks to a double Berocca, a bacon sandwich and three mugs of builder's tea. Although the weather was bright, it was crisp out. The breeze whipping up from the Mersey might have played havoc with my hair, but it certainly blew away the remnants of my hangover.

Despite the building itself creating quite the shadow over Gambier Terrace, and despite the fact that it looked like I could reach out of my window and actually touch it, it was still quite a schlep round the side of the cathedral to get inside. But once I was in, well, it had certainly been worth the wait, and I wondered why I'd not come before. Everything about it seemed otherworldly; the atmosphere felt different, like I was suddenly in outer space. Sounds altered, the light changed, the temperature dropped, yet I didn't feel cold. My footsteps on the marble chessboard floor echoed round the vast open space that was just so big it was hard to believe I wasn't outside. I looked up. A light display shot up into the tower, vast arches of sandstone disappearing into the clouds were hit by vivid blues, reds, and the lights through the windows made the red bricks everywhere glow like hot amber.

I found the gift shop easily, on the other side of the knave to the entrance. Helen Chance was handing someone their change when I tiptoed in. She saw me immediately and turned and whispered something to her co-worker, then glided out from behind the counter, picking up a holdall on her way. I felt like I was in a spy movie again. She would now approach and whisper in my ear, 'Red Fox says take the ostrich only flies at midnight,' before placing the straps of the holdall in my hand.

But she didn't. She said quite loudly, 'Shall we have a salad?'

The word 'salad' echoed round the space, whirling about as if through a megaphone.

I nodded and followed her up a spiral staircase to the cafe.

Perched up high above the knave, we got a bird's-eye view of the cathedral as Helen tucked into a small Niçoise salad and I had an orange juice.

She took the tin from the holdall and placed it on the table in front of me. I opened it, not sure why, and she commented, 'I haven't stolen it. I'll leave the law-breaking to you.'

'Have you read it? All of it?'

She shook her head.

Oh good, she wouldn't know that Darren had killed someone.

'Whereas it might be of understandable interest to you, savouring the incoherent ramblings of my former neighbour are not how I wish to pass the time.'

'Do you mind if I ask you a few questions?'

She shook her head, a leaf of rocket dangling from her mouth.

'You've obviously lost a lot of weight.'

'That's not a question. Unless you wish to ask how I did it, to which I'd answer, "Mind your own business."'

I nodded. Fair enough. 'What was Darren like? How long did they live there for?'

'The Boyles were there for years. He must've been a toddler when she moved in. Soon she was pregnant with the other one.'

'Do you remember her being pregnant with me?'

'No, but then, I didn't pay much attention to them. She was never in, and he was never out. I'd see the little one go to school, come back from school. I think she'd trained them to be surly with me. I paid them little heed.'

'What did he look like?'

'The little one?'

'Darren.'

'Puny. Runt-of-the-litter type. Dickensian almost. Very pale-skinned, like he'd never seen daylight. I was forever reporting her to the authorities. He never went to school, and she was always out.'

'Working.'

'It had not escaped my notice that she was a prostitute. Hope Street was the epicentre of the red-light district then. The pavements were soiled with her ilk littering them up, awaiting kerb-crawlers. I didn't like her, and just because she is your mother, I will not pretend I did to make you feel better.'

'Clearly.' But I added, 'I don't think I'd have liked her either.'

This seemed to please her. Maybe she would warm to me now.

'Holly, I don't know what your experience of adoption was like, but mark my words, if they took you off her, you were very fortunate.'

I nodded. It was odd, sitting here in this cavern of a building, her voice echoing round the walls when this all should have felt so intimate.

'Do you know where Darren went?'

She shook her head. 'They were all there one day; next day they weren't. The flat was empty for months, and then she came back alone. Never saw the children again. I assumed they'd both been taken into care.'

I let this sink in.

'So they disappeared?'

'I really didn't give it much thought. I really didn't care. Maybe that's unchristianly of me. So sue me – they weren't nice people.'

'Do you remember me as a baby?'

'I was only ever aware of two children. Two boys. I'm afraid that's all I know.'

'I have found her – Francesca Boyle. She's in a nursing home. She has dementia.'

'Probably a blessing if she can't remember her past misdemeanours.'

'What about the family downstairs? The black family? They were there around that time.'

'Oh yes. He went to prison for drugs. She maintained he'd gone back to her family in the Caribbean, but everyone knew that was a lie. The council moved her to a smaller flat, I think.'

'Yes. I think the police framed him.'

'Your positivity must be quite draining for you, Miss Smith.'

'Not really. Is there anything else you can remember about Darren?'

She thought. She dabbed the corner of her mouth with a napkin, then shook her head sadly.

'I didn't even know his name was Darren. I knew they were the Boyles, little else.'

'He had a girlfriend, Samantha. Does that ring any bells?'

Again a shake of the head. 'It was thirty-odd years ago.'

And I nodded back. 'I know. I don't know what I expected to find, coming here. I guess I wanted to walk into that flat and . . . I don't know . . . see it all right there in front of my eyes. As if nothing had moved on. If only the walls could talk, but they can't, and even if they could, there's been thirty years of life and memories going through there. Everything's changed.'

'I used to think Darren looked so brittle, so angry. But I was walking back from the bus stop – I was quite large in those days; it took a while – and he came walking past me with a plastic bag and he tripped. The contents of the bag spilt out into the street. It was all . . . make-up and blusher and . . . stuff for his mum probably, but he scrabbled around for it, shoving it back in the bag. And he looked up at me. And he looked so scared. Kept apologizing.' She let the image hang in the air. 'And I remember thinking, What does she put those kids through, if they can get so scared about dropping something?'

A wave of sadness engulfed me. Francesca must have sent him out to do her shopping. Why was he so scared of her? Was this before or after the murder of _____? Why was he so in her thrall like that?

'Anyway, you have your diary back. I trust the window will be mended today?'

I nodded. I couldn't speak.

'Good. I am away for a few days from this evening. Don't need to worry about burglars getting easy access.'

I didn't ask where she was going. By now I wasn't interested. I couldn't stop thinking about Darren on the street, scared.

'Since my weight loss I like to keep active. Turns out I'm a bit of a thrill-seeker. I'm now a member of the Roller Coaster Club of Great Britain. We're doing the Loopathon tomorrow. Two parks in one day – Alton Towers and Drayton Manor.'

I must have looked startled. She added, 'I'm seventy next birthday. There's life in the old dog yet.'

I remembered the intermittent screams I'd heard coming from her flat.

'I hear noises. From your place. Screams. Quick screams, then . . .'

She smiled. 'I film every ride I go on. Love watching my movies back.' And then boomed at the top of her voice, 'Scream if you want to go faster!'

I decided now was my cue to leave. I clutched the precious tin to my chest as I walked quietly from the building. It felt strange, holding so many long-forgotten memories to me, clasping my family history, the clues to my existence. Modern technology beeped around me, texts coming through on phones, emails, and here in my tin was a time when all that was alien, space age.

A beep told me that one of the emails coming through was on my phone and was for me. I pulled the phone from my pocket and opened it. It was from Sylvie. I didn't read it all, just skim-read the odd sentence: 'Might have been a bit overgenerous with the double-your-wages thing . . . Come anyway and have some fun . . . Could keep Marybeth on and you could manage her . . . Michael can go and stay with my dear friend Teddy in Putney.'

I was just putting the phone away when, sod's law, it started to ring. I should have put it on silent, I know, and some tour guides and ushers cast me evil glances, so I hurried outside. I checked the caller ID: 'Rose calling.'

I answered. 'Hello?'

'Hi, Holly. It's Rose.'

'Hi, Rose. How are you?'

'Good. Holly, I've got some news.'

Hope bubbled inside me.

'It's about Frankie's kids.'

'Yes?'

'There's no easy way to say this.'

'Aha?'

Fear gripped my throat. A vice-like grip. I could hardly breathe.

'Robert, the younger one, emigrated to America many years ago. Darren . . .' Her voice faltered.

'Yes?'

'Holly. Darren is no more.'

Darren is no more. Such an odd choice of words. And even

though I didn't know him, and even though I possibly never even met him – who knows? Your guess is as good as mine – that was still a crushing blow.

'Really?'

'I spoke with an old family friend and they didn't know anything about you. I'm so sorry, Holly.'

Darren is no more.

'OK. I've . . . I've got to go.'

I hung up and ran down the wide red steps of the cathedral. I stopped by a small building with railings over the curvy road. A sign told me this was the oratory. I tried to stare at the wording, to take my mind off things, but it was futile – I couldn't hold back any longer. Hot tears geysered down my cheeks. I leaned against the railings and surrendered to the pain.

When I got back to the flat, Iggy could see I'd been crying. When I explained what Rose had said, he stepped forward and hugged me. I fought the tears again and shrugged him off, realizing something.

'What is it, Pips?'

'All this time . . . I've been obsessing about the past.'

'That's understandable, though, like.'

'And Darren's dead. That's in the past. And I've completely been ignoring what's going on in the present. You've shown me such kindness since I got here, Iggy, and I don't really know the first thing about you.'

'There's not much to know, girl. Brew?' I nodded. He switched on the kettle. 'I live with me nan in Anfield. I do painting and decorating every now and again for me uncle's firm. Do a bit of plastering as well. I smoke a bit o' weed. Got a daughter called Casey.'

'A daughter!' I gasped. I had no idea. I thought of him as being . . . well, so *young*.

'I hardly ever see her, though. She lives near Crewe. Her ma was a one-night stand I had three years ago. Ma's a bit mental, but I keep in touch for Casey. Wanna see a picture?'

'You bet!'

He took his phone out and scrolled through several images of a pretty little toddler with a snub nose and ringlets.

'Oh, Iggy, she's gorgeous.'

'Yeah, but I'm nothing special. All a bit boring really. See, you've been scratching away for stuff about your family and maybe there's not much to find out in the first place.'

I considered this.

'Apart from my brother killing an off-duty policeman and his mother covering for him with her dodgy boyfriend. Yes, it's just another boring story of suburban Scousers.'

And that made him laugh. A lot. I looked out of the window. Suddenly it irritated me that the massive cathedral blocked out all the light. No longer the imposing building, it was now the place where Fatty Arbuckle worked, and the place where I found out my brother had died.

'Oh God,' I said, 'it's started.'

'What?'

'I've now grown some associations.'

'You wanna see a doctor about that, Pips. Are they painful?'

I smiled. 'I thought this was going to be my new home.' I shook my head. 'Not so sure now. My mum's away with the fairies; my brother's dead; the other's in the States. What's keeping me here?'

Iggy handed me a mug of tea. Steam rose from it like whispers.

'Me,' he said. 'I'd hope that I'm keeping you here, Pips.'

I looked at him, alarmed. Was he proclaiming undying love for me? He looked longingly into my eyes, then did an odd shake of his head, like he was taking in my beauty. Oh *God*. But . . . then . . . thank God, he broke into a massive grin and erupted into the biggest peal of laughter I'd ever heard.

'Your face, you knobhead!' and he literally bent double he was howling so much.

I slapped him on the back lightly. 'Bastard!' and my swearing made him laugh even more.

'Ladies and gentlemen, this train will shortly be arriving at its final destination, London Euston. Watch out for the pearly kings and queens, apples and pears everywhere you turn and urchins dancing through the city streets singing Lionel Bart songs. You have been warned – strike a light!'

I felt a mixture of emotions as I stepped into the cab at Euston – after first pushing my rucksack in and hiding Michael in the folds of my coat – a little bit 'tail between my legs', part pride that I'd actually got off my backside and done something for me for once, and part numb at how much and how little I'd discovered about my humble beginnings. As the cab spun out onto the Euston Road, I thought back over the last few days. Well, I was doing it – I was taking up Sylvie's offer and heading to Canada, once I'd dropped Michael off at her friend's in Putney. She was paying for this cab; she was paying for my Thames-side hotel tonight; she was paying for my first-class flight to Toronto. And I intended to enjoy every minute, because no doubt I wouldn't once I was there. She claimed she was thrilled by my decision and had even used the sentence 'I grudgingly admit sometimes you were a very reliable assistant.'

What an accolade! And after the shenanigans of the past

few weeks, I was actually looking forward to returning to the lion's den – at least it was familiar, and at least it was the devil I knew rather than the devil I was tracking down only to be rejected by it once more. It didn't have to be for ever, but part of me felt so bruised by what had happened in Liverpool that I was convinced all was going to be fine. What I was going to do post-Canada I had no idea.

Iggy had understood. Of course he had. He was such a delight, old Iggy. I really hoped that I would keep in touch with him. He had offered his friendship to me gladly and openly, and wanted nothing in return apart from to help me. He was a proper little knight in shining armour and I really hoped I wouldn't let him slip off the radar, as I had done with so many friends over the years.

Jax was still in *Hell Hole* and had rapidly gained the reputation of being the worst contestant ever. The tabloids were full of her latest crazy antics every day, especially as she was going round upsetting her so-called friends in there by claiming to be able to speak to their dead relatives, then passing on information that would anger or upset them – 'Your mother killed herself coz she hated you, babes. Don't hate me, I'm just passing it on!' et cetera.

Rose and Alan had been amazingly supportive about my change of plans and had – wonder of wonders – even refunded me all the money I'd paid up front in rent. I had no idea why they were being so kind, but I took it as a feather in my cap that I must have come across to them as a decent human being for them to treat me so generously. After all, they'd not asked for six months' rent up front; I had offered it to make sure I got the flat.

The biscuit tin and Darren's life sat in my rucksack. I'd not been able to face reading the rest of it yet, but I knew I would one day. Maybe he wrote about me going into care; maybe he didn't. Maybe it finished a few days after the last entry I read. But all the same I had developed feelings for my brother and it would be too upsetting now to explore his optimism all those years ago.

Rose had driven me to the station to get my train, and as she helped me to the platform with Michael and my ridiculously large kit, she had handed me a teal-green envelope and told me to 'read it later'. In the struggle to get myself onto the train and subsequently find a seat where someone wasn't moaning about the presence of a chihuahua, I had completely forgotten about it.

I located it in the side flap of my rucksack and pulled it out. Michael snored faintly on the seat next to me. She had printed my name on the front from her computer, very formal, and as I ripped open the envelope, I ripped a bit of the card too.

The front showed a peaceful scene, a country cottage in watercolours, roses round the door. So far so predictable. I opened it and read the message inside:

Dear Holly,
    It was so lovely to welcome you to Liverpool. I'm sorry your stay was brief and that you never got the answers you come looking for. Like I said before your a great girl and you've done really well for yourself. If you ever find yourself this way again do let us know and don't go wasting your money on a hotel, come and stay with us. I enjoyed our time together and am actchally going to miss you. You probly think I'm mad lol!!
    Take care Holly
      All best and love
        Rose xx

For a moment the world stopped turning. My heart pounded in my chest. My temples throbbed. I could barely breathe. I had not seen her handwriting before. Without the cloak of a computer's spell-check I saw in an instant that she had been lying to me. As a million crazy notions rattled in my brain before slotting with a jolt into place, I knew in that instant that Darren was not dead.

DARREN

All the way to Rigby's pub I've been panickin. Smantha's not been chattin and is like she's got the wait of the world on her shoulders.

Outside the pub there's a pigeon on the ground. He's only got the claws on one leg. The other ones a stump and he's slowly goin round in circles.

Someone should put him out of his misery. Goes Smantha. An I think that's a bit harsh.

But then I think of ____. And I think the pigeon's better off than ____. And I have a little panick on.

Ah don't say that. I goes. Like that's gonna make the last twenny four hours go away. Like that's gonna bring ____ back to life. Not that I really want him coming back to life but just so it means that I've not done what I did.

Its ten o clock in the morning and Smantha orders coffee. She looks at me funny coz I order whiskey. Don't even particularly like whiskey but I hear it's good for shock.

And she's got another of those.

Am pregnant. She goes.

And we just sit there for a bit. All I can hear is noise. The punch of a fruit machine win. Rorcuss laughing from a woman at the bar who's always in here. She's dead fat and she's got a red face but she's proud of her ankles. She's always like that. Always sayin – My ankles are dainty. Don't you think my ankles are dainty? But truth be told she always smells a bit pissy. Music on the juke box going all jumpy and I realize it's that knobhead off the telly I hate who bounces round in his denim jacket goin on about the green door. Shakey they call him. He's been number one for weeks. You can't move for him right now. And then I think I don't really hate him. He never done nothing bad to me like some people. All he did was make shite music.

Well say something then. Goes Smantha.

So I say something and she's not best pleased coz what I say is why are you telling me, are you sure its mine. And she's like. Of course its yours. And I'm like. Well I didn't know. And she's like. I'm not a slag Darren. And I'm like. No I know I'm just saying. And she's like. Well your not saying much are you.

But we've only done it once. I eventchally say.

And she says. Well you only need to do it once apparently. I'm like. It's a lot to take in.

And she's like. I know.

Even though what I meant was it's a lot to take in when you've had the twenny four hours I've had. And even though she's not had that she still thinks it's a big one to get your head around.

As the whiskey warms me I start to relax for the first time. Been a bit jittery with not sleeping. Now I stop. And I don't think about the baby growing inside her. I think instead about the fact that that bastard won't be touching me anymore. And I mustve smiled coz Smantha goes. You happy about it?

So I stop smiling and go. I dunno. Are you?

And she shrugs.

What you gonna do Smantha?

And she shrugs. I dunno. I don't like the idea of killing a child.

It's not a child though is it. I go. It's a cluster of cells.

Cluster. She goes. Get you.

This couldna come at a worse time. She says. And I wonder if she means it or if its just something she's heard people say on the telly. Like in play for today or something where people sit in pubs like this all the time going. I'm having a baby and I don't know what to do. But she carries on. I've got plans. I wanna do me A levels. I wanna go travelling. I wanna make something of my life. I don't wanna be stuck round here forever Darren. If I have a baby it'll keep me here.

What's wrong with round here? I goes.

People fighting. I'd hate to live where you live at the moment.

But it's only coz they've had enough of being treated like shit. I goes. I thought you were all four standing up and being counted. Like the March for Jobs. I goes.

I just don't know. She goes.

So. The million dollar question, I'm thinkin. What you gonna do about it?

And she circles the coffee cup in her hand. Starin at it.

A dunno. I need time to think.

Well you haven't got forever. And I don't even know why I said it.

A do know that Darren.

If you had it. What would you want me to do?

What would you want to do?

Well would you want me to like . . . marry you?

And she shrieks. Laughin.

It's not that funny.

It is.

And am a bit hurt if you must know.

Well would you want me to have a part in its life and that?

I just don't know Darren. But I'm not getting married. And then she sighs. And she's like. This is such a mess.

I could bring it up. I go. You could go to school. Then travelling. Then uni. Then work. And I could stay at home with the baby. I don't mind.

Darren. You never go out. You'd sit in with it yeah but the baby'd be a recloose. Just like you.

She's making me sound a bit weird. Ah well. Spose I am.

I need time to think about it.

Rob comes back from his Dad's. He's worried Ma's gonna ask to many questions about where he's been. He tells me he's got his lies all worked out but I tell him he needn't bother. He doesn't know what's gone on here today and last night so little does he know Ma's made up he wasn't here so she's not arsed where he's been. Sleepover Lil she keeps calling him.

Rob doesn't even ask where the carpet's gone.

Ma talks to him. But she don't talk to me. At first am a bit para about it.

But then I think. Story o my bleeding life.

That night Ma cooks a roast.

Spuds are nice Ma. Our Robbie goes.

Darren peeled them. She goes.

Every single one of them makes me want to choke. But I have to eat them so Rob don't know.

I wonder if I should be thinking about getting a job. If Smantha's gonna have a baby I'll have to provide for it.

But then I think. Babies have the traits of the parents. That baby would have half my chromozones. That baby would be half me. I wouldn't wish me on my worst enemy. So why would I wish it on a poor innocent baby? I think of me stood in front of the mirror last night. The norts an crosses on my legs. I know that's not good. I know I'm not normal. I see Lucy laughin at me and think. I can't have half of that in a kid.

But it's not really down to me. It's down to Smantha.

Ma sees am miles away.

What you thinkin about Darren? She goes.

Nothing. I goes.

Well you wanna snap out of that. She goes.

So I do. And I spose it's the first time I realize that Ma being hard is a good thing. Nothing wrong with being strong.

What jew do with him? I goes later when Robbie's in bed.

Ma looks up from doin her nails and goes. You don't need to know.

What? I goes.

She ignores me.

Five minutes later she's like. I'm going earning.

You haven't got protection any more. I goes.

An whose faults that ay? And she is gone.

It's three days since I hit ____. I should really be feeling bad by now and hating myself and feeling guilty but the weird thing is I don't. Alls I feel is thank god he won't be nocking at the door or ringin the bell and I don't have to panic when I hear footsteps on the stairs. I've not been in the cubbard under the sink in the bathroom. No more norts an crosses. Well no more n what I already have. Ma buys a fan for the flat now. Big old movie star thing that clicks when it spins but it keeps the flat cooler. Everything's nicer now. Only thing to worry bout now is Smantha.

I just no she's gonna come round an say she's keeping it.

What would you do if you needed to get some money Richie? I ask him while we sit on the step at the front of the house in the sun.

Everything's quietened down now since the trouble the other night. Their calling it the Toxteth riots now. Been on the news and everything. Keep especting to see _____ on the news and his Mrs wondering why he aint come home but no.

Richie shrugs. Nick something?

Wouldn't you go n get a job laa?

Aint no jobs man.

Keep thinkin he's gonna ask about that night. When _____ let him go. But he doesn't. Guess he's got bigger fish to fry.

So I ask around. I ask Umed in the shop. Any jobs goin? He laugh in my face. But he didn't do it in a horrible way.

Maybe I should do what my teacher said that time and go back to school. But if I go back to school or go to college first off I am not the best speller. And second off even if I got loads of qualitications they would take me ages and qualitications aren't what the baby needs. The baby needs cold hard cash.

You could sell yer arse down Limey. Goes Richie. But I don't laugh.

He don't even know what I want money for. I haven't told no one.

But what I do know is that any day now am gonna get a knock at the door and Smantha will be stood there looking all fat and going. Am keeping it Darren. And I'll be like ok. And I'll have to go out and support my new family.

I can't sell my arse down Limey. Well I could. Isn't nothing I've not done before with _____. But I don't want to. I did it with _____ and I don't want to do it ever again. Plus I don't want to bring a child into the world the way my Ma brought a child into the world. I don't want to bring a child up on the proseeds of earning. And I won't.

If I have to I'll go out and rob a bank.

I've got to hatch a plan though. I've got to hatch a plan to provide for the baby.

Lucy's not been around for ages now.

Think I know why.

____ was on the news. Only local. And in the paper. His Mrs been interviewed goin on about how he has disappeared. He told her he was leaving her then he went out to work and never came back. Had all sorts of money worries and the house about to be reposesed. Gambling detts. Branding him a coward coz he has left her and hasn't told anyone where he was off to.

Rob is watchin the telly with us when it comes on.

Coward. Ma goes. Fancy running off on her.

I know. I goes.

Rob says nothing. Of course.

I haven't got to hatch a plan no more.

Well I have. But I've got to hatch a different plan.

Smantha finally comes round and I brings her up to the flat coz Ma is out and Rob is at school so we can talk. I make her a cup of tea and I can see my hand is shaking so I must be nervous. I think she'll wait til I've at least stirred the sugar but she says it while my back's turned.

I'm getting rid of it.

Shit.

I'm having an abortion.

I looks at her. You sure?

She nods.

Jonathan Harvey

Why jew decide that then?

What I said last time.

What jew say last time?

You know what I said last time.

Remind me.

Not sure why I'm being this arsey.

It's a woman's right to choose. She goes. Like she's the first ever person to say this.

And what about my rights? It's my baby too. I say. Like an arlarse.

I don't even know why I'm saying it, truth be told. I haven't exactly been into the idea. But then I've been thinking. And hatching plans. So maybe I am into the idea. And I just hadn't aloud myself to say it or think it to myself.

Am sorry Darren. You don't come into it. You wouldn't have to carry it for nine months.

I nod. I know she's right. I finish the tea for her in silence. I realize am tryina stop myself from crying.

This is pathetic.

Having a baby is daft. It's stupid. Why am I so upset that she wants rid of it?

I hand her her tea and we sit in the living room on the big couch.

She can tell how I'm feeling.

Darren. I don't wanna get rid really but it's the worst decision I could make.

Keeping it?

She nods.

I wanna go to college. I wanna go travelin. I wanna do stuff, you know?

I know.

Us two having a baby, it's . . . it's stupid.

I know.

I haven't come to this decision lightly.

Am sure.

Darren I ate the idea of an abortion. I ate the idea of killing it stone dead. But we can't bring up a baby. We just can't. And if we try an make out we can then we're just kidding ourselves. I wanna go to college. I wanna go travelin. I wanna do stuff with my life and a baby'll hold me back.

I could look after it.

How?

I could.

Darren you never go out. You sit in this flat watchin telly and rowing wit yer ma and cooking for your Robbie and every blue moon you go the pub with Richie. You never go school. You never go nowhere. What you gonna do? Keep it cooped up in here twenny four seven? I don't think so. And I don't think you want that. You haven't got a job. You haven't got any money.

All right all right I get the picture. I goes. Jeez. You chose a right bute when you chose me ay?

And we both laugh.

Sorry. I didn't meant to be harsh.

I nod. She's right.

Asides. She goes. My mam and dad would go spare if they found out I was pregnant. You don't know the pressure am under.

I shake my head. I don't.

You don't know how lucky you are.

I nod. I don't.

But actchally I wanna say, you don't know how lucky you are Smantha. Id give anything for a mam and a dad who put pressure on me to do well or even do anything. My Gran was like that but she's not here any more.

Ok. So she's gonna get rid of it.

Oh well. Least I won't have to get a job.

Shame. Was quiet lookin forward to that.

Only thing is now. She goes. I don't know where to go.

Go your doctor. I goes.

He'll tell my mam. She goes.

Go to a hospital in town then.

Which one?

I dunno.

Won't they tell my GP?

I dunno.

I think. And then I realize something. But before I can say it she's like. I can't let my mam and dad find out Darren they'd kill me.

I know who we can ask. I go.

She goes. Who?

I goes. Ma.

She rolls her eyes.

But this time I know am right.

Ma knows everything to do with stuff like that coz girls in her business. Girls who go earning. There always having to have abortions and no one ask any questions. She's always joking that Margy has one a week though I don't think it's true. She will be able to tell us where to go and how much it'll be. And I don't think she'll take the piss now coz if there's one thing she likes its being the hexpert. And on this she'll think she is the hexpert. She'll love nothing more than showing off to Smantha that she knows more than her. And she'll love nothing more than making Smantha feel that she's messed something up and needs her help.

Oh yes. Ma is gonna love this one. Make no mistake.

*

It's Ma's birthday. Every year we have to do the same thing. Every year we has to go to a wine bar restraunt place on Lark Lane. We go in a taxi and have to let Ma lord it over us as she makes out she's all well to do even though Rob always says the fella what runs the place is probly someone she knows from the earning. Ma's always in a good mood on her birthday. And this year she says Smantha can come for the meal an all.

More the merrier. She goes. Like she loves a party.

Woody's coming to. She goes. Oh Darren your gonna love him. He's decent. You know he's decent, he's really looked out for you.

Even when Rob drops the biggest clanger ever. He has arranged to go and see his Dad on the same night. Not that he says that. He says he's going skating. Ma laughs it off like is not important. And I know why. She's so excited Woody's coming she's not that arsed about anyone else.

Smantha comes over after school and has brought Ma a book-A of flowers.

Oh aren't they pretty love. She oohs and ahs. All the time lookin at the clock wondering where Woody is. Darren stick em in some water lad.

So I do.

She runs down to Richie's Ma's to use the phone and find out where Woody is.

You ok? Goes Smantha. I nods.

We'll ask her when she gets back up.

But Ma don't come back up.

Darren? Smantha? Taxi's here! She shouts from down the stairs so I lock up.

In the cab she's like. Woody's running late. He's gonna meet us there.

But once we've been sat in the restraunt for an hour and Ma won't let us order is pretty clear he isn't turning up.

I think Ma is gonna get all moody and mad but she smiles a lot and tells us to choose what we want. Smantha looks at me and I shrug. Ma's reading the menu. Smantha gives me this look. It's now or never.

Ma? I go.

Aha? She goes. I might have the duck.

Ma. Smantha's pregnant.

Ma looks up.

Yjoking!

We both shake our heads. Ma lights up a cigarette. She looks to me.

Is it yours?

Yes. Goes Smantha.

All right love I was only askin. Are yous keepin it?

I shake my head.

Smantha shakes her head.

So I wondrin. I goes. If you knew somewhere Smantha could go.

Ma takes this in, twirling the ciggie in her hand like a majorette with a baton. Nervous.

Only she don't want her mam and dad and that to know.

Ma takes this in. Then stubs the ciggie out all of a sudden. She takes a swig of her wine.

Smantha burbles on about what she wants to do with her life and how she hates doing this sort of thing but she has no choice. Ma doesn't look at her once but looks like she is listening. She lets her warble on til she hasn't got any more words to say. She sits there thinking.

Then goes. Smantha. I don't know if Darren's told you. But we're Catholics.

Since when?

Shut up Darren, we've always been Catholics.

Granny was a Catholic but . . .

We are – like that was the end of it – and therefore Smantha I can't condone what you wanna do.

Right. Goes Smantha, looking at me coz this wasn't part of the plan.

But don't worry love. She reaches out her hand and takes Smantha's in it. Help is at hand.

How jew mean?

I'll bring it up.

You'll bring the baby up?

I'll bring it up as my own. Then you won't have the shame. Your parents won't know. And then you can see the baby whenever you want.

Smantha is taking this in now. Silence. The waiter comes to take our orders.

In a minute Manwell love. Goes Ma.

Me name's Peter. He goes.

And she gives him this look that says fuck off, loud and clear. So he does.

Smantha looks at me. I shrug again.

I need to go the loo. Goes Smantha.

Off she goes.

I look to Ma.

What's this all about Ma?

I'll bring the baby up.

But why?

I'm tryina be kind here.

But . . .

Stop saying but, Darren. But nothing. Just remember. You owe me one. You owe me more than one.

Shite. She means that.

So when Fanny for lodgers comes back from the bogs you better convince her. To give that baby to me.

And she looks across the restraunt and shouts for the waiter.

He comes. She orders the duck. Then orders the same for me and Smantha. Like what we actchally want doesn't come into it. Then just before he goes the kitchen to give in the order she ast him where the nearest payphone is.

I need to phone Woody. She goes. Looks like I've got some good news.

48 Round Hey Road
Childwall
Liverpool 16

15 August 1981

Dear Darren,

I've thought about nothing else since Frankie first mentioned it on Lark Lane that night and no doubt I'll think about nothing else in the coming months and years. You know at first I was a bit wary, because I've never really seen eye to eye with your mum before. But you were right — I just had to give her a chance.

Whenever I've met her since it's been like meeting a different person. Kind, caring, funny and warm. I'm sorry my first impressions weren't up to much, but as you say, she has been a bit down lately. And I have to salute her desire to leave her current work and marry this businessman, and when I think of all the opportunities that could bring the baby, well, for the first time since finding out, I now feel positive about this pregnancy and that there is some sort of light at the end of the tunnel.

278

So this is just to say, on consideration, yes, I would like to go ahead with your mum's kind offer. I am a bit nervous about my parents noticing the bump as it gets bigger, but Dad is now working in Birmingham and so is away a lot of the time, and Mum has taken extra hours cleaning and quite a bit of it is in the evening, so I am hopeful I will get away with it. Then, as your mum says, we can go to Southampton for the birth and no one will know.

I keep imagining myself at uni. Or in the souk at Morocco. And I get really excited. I'm sure it'll be really hard to hand over the baby. But as your mum says, it's for the best for everyone.

I see your mum put some money in my building society account yesterday. Will you tell her thank you – it'll be a real help.

See you later in the week.

Sammi x

48 Round Hey Road
Childwall
Liverpool 16

1 March 1982

Dear Darren,

Further to our phone conversation last Thursday, I will see you at the coach station on Friday at nine in the morning. Rita spoke to Mum last night and she has bought it, so all is good. Can you tell your mum the latest payment is a bit late? Hate to bring it up, but it will just give me peace of mind before going to Southampton. I will check the balance again on Wednesday to be sure.

See you Friday,

Sammi x

SOUTHAMPTON March 1982

Cockney Carol is Ma's best mate from way back. She's got a deep voice n sounds like a fella off Minder or The Sweeny. She gabs ten to the dozen and smells of like ciggies n air freshner. Her and Ma were bezzies back in the day when they both worked Hope Street together when Cockney Carol lived in Liverpool. Now she lives in the arse enda nowhere as she calls it. Otherwise known as Southampton. She come down years back when she met a bloke called Smoky Joe and she give up the earning and he treated her like a queen.

Oh yer he treated me like a queen. She goes. One o them what gets behedded or flung in a tower.

Ma says Smoky Joe got his name coz he set fire to people that crossed him. Carol says to take no notice.

It's every hore's dream, accordin to Carol. You meet a fella who wants to wisk you away from the earning and cover you in diamonds. An that, she goes, lookin me strait in the eye. Is why I've gotta help your old girl. It's so romantic. Init romantic Darren mate?

Her voice cracks me up. The way she says mate is like — maaaaaaaay.

I shrug.

No it is. She goes. It's dead romantic.

Now we're in Southampton I practically live in the pub. Carol's local is a place called The London. She treats it like her office. She goes in there first thing, necks a brandy, heads off to work. I went with her one day for something to do and coz I was bored in her flat and now I go every day. She heads off to do some earning and then when she is done she comes back and leaves the money with me. She says I've got a trustworthy face n no one will suspect me. Suspect me of what I don't know.

Few days after doing this her mate Rita started doing the same thing. And then after a while another one done it too. Now I look after the money for four different girls and they like me keeping an eye on their earnings for the day coz it stops them spending it on shite and if they get attacked or robbed, they haven't got much on them.

Ma is still going out earning but she stays in a bit to. Don't think she likes being out of her usual patch and doesn't no the fellas like she does at home so doesn't no if she can trust them or not. She don't give me her money to keep an eye on either. Probly doesn't feel it would be right and I no what she means.

Carol says the scene is changing. She says in her day working women did the job to put bread on the table but these days it's all about them getting money to pay for heroin. This is why she and her mates like me looking after there money. She says the younger ones will rob your money to pay for there latest fix so it's good they don't carry to much cash on them. She says her and Ma are part of a dying breed. Though Ma says Carol's livin in a fool's paradise because she reckons all Carol's mates are on heroin anyway. I have no idea. Ma's probly right though.

Carol is always sighing and going on about how many years she's got left. She reckons blokes don't want women like her and Ma now coz there too old. Ma says there's a few women in Liverpool who are still working in there sixties but even she admits they don't get much attention. I'd never really thought much about the future. But Smantha having the baby has made me think about it more. Everything changes. Ma can't go on working forever and when I think about it, I can't go on staying in Ma's flat forever. This place has opened my eyes to that. Just been in a different place has made my head feel in a different place. I didn't even want to come here. I wanted to stay in Liverpool and look after Rob but Ma was adamant. Rob has gone to stay with his Dad for a fortnight while we are here. Rob was honest with Ma. He told her he'd met Cameron and he thought she'd go like mad. But she was so hexcited about this baby she wasn't arsed. Weird or what. Think Ma wanted me here in case Smantha had second thoughts. But I know she won't.

Smantha hates being pregnant. Any fool can see that. She just sits in Carol's flat moaning. Everything I say to her gets on her tits. Last night she goes. I wish to God I'd never done this with you.

I just keep out of her way. She's turning into Ma.

Last night I found her crying in the bathroom. She thought she'd locked the door and I walked in on her and she was sat on the side of the bath with her head in her hands.

Whats the matter? I goes.

Leave me alone. She goes.

I'm sorry about all this. I goes.

I just miss my mum. She goes.

Jew wanna go home?

She laughs at that. And tells me to leave her alone again so I do.

She can't go home. I know that, she knows that. Her mum thinks she is in Southampton on work experience. Carol has a mate who runs a charity for working women and Carol nicked some paper from the charity and wrote saying Smantha was doing work experience here. Coz Smantha has fed her mother stories saying she wants to be a social worker and coz she managed to square it with her 6 form college nobody thought it was odd when she told them she could stay with relatives of mine. Ma even phoned Smantha's mum and did her la dee da voice and Smantha's mum bought it.

But Smantha says there are seven of them and she's the quietest and brainiest and causes them the least bit of trouble so Smantha's mum didn't ask too many questions. The clever ones are always overlooked.

Personly I can't believe she's got away with no one realizing she is having a baby. But Ma's like. No she's skinny. You can't tell unless you know. And all them baggy jumpers she wears. Perfect. Thank fuck it's not summer.

Smantha says she has been wearing baggy jumpers all year. And now she's in 6 form she has folders instead of exersize books and so she says she's been carrying them in front of her stomach all year and says no one thinks nothing of it coz its how girls do it in movies in America so no ones none the wiser.

But Smantha is bored. She says she's fed up of watching Crown Court and Pebble Mill every day. She's sick of the smell of take away. Ma says she should go for a walk but Smantha says everyone stairs at her.

Ma says I have to keep her spirits up but on my life, all she does is give me daggers and moan about the honk of Chinese from the place downstairs and all she ever does is tell me to shut up so I just get out of her way every day. Anyway it's not like she's going anywhere. She can't go home. Like she says. I've come too far to turn back now. And she doesn't sound particularly happy when she says it.

Carol says she prefers the London coz it's a gay pub which means the men don't give her hassle. I'da thought she'd want men to give her hassle. How else does she get paid? I like it in there coz the staff are friendly. They all call me Lucien after the fella in the Liver Birds coz of my accent. And they all don't believe me when I say am not gay. I've stopped saying it now coz they just take the piss and really I'm not arsed what they think. And some days I wonder if ____ made me a bit gay but I don't think I am. I never enjoyed it. (Talking of being arsed) Not that I enjoy thinking about ____. Still get nervous when I think about him but I can't help it at the moment as if it wasn't for him I wouldn't be here now. Ma knows now I write stuff down in the tin and she says am an idiot for doing that in case anyone finds it which is why I keep it hidden at all times. I always know where it is and I always make sure it's safe. Some days I think about burning the papers but I have no one else to talk to so I don't want to stop writing. Some times I write nothing and I miss it. Carol calls us Oscar Wild coz I'm always writing. I been reading loadsa books from the libray. Cant get enough of em. Lace was the best. I couldn't put it down like.

When I go back to Liverpool maybe I will chuck it all away. It's not like I ever read back what I've written. Well I did once. Read a page or two. And I just sound like a sad soft melt.

I am. Am gonna burn it when I get back. Ma's right.

But then if someone found it. And someone found out what I'd done and they sent us to prison then it's only what I deserve.

Maybes I want someone to find it.

Like I said. Too much time to think down here. Time enough to make decisions and good ones I hope but also too much time to dwell on everything I've done wrong in my life. Everyone thinks am a mouse. Don't say boo to a goose.

If only they knew.

Anyways. Enough of this shit.

We've been here two weeks now and we're still waiting.

Am sat in the pub wondering weather to go back to Carol's – it's near five o clock and I've been here all afternoon drinking orange and lemonades and minding the money when Gina comes in. She's one of Carol's mates. She's all excited and she passes us a piece of paper. It's been ripped from a pad and on it in biro it from Carol and says – Darren go the wash house over road from flats and get towels from dryer. The baby's coming.

Gina gives me a little smile and I say something like fuckinell. And off I hurry to the laundrette.

The laundrette is called Sunset Bay. There's a massive photo on the wall of palm trees and blue skies like you've come to paradise to do your bag wash. There's about a million machines and driers and I look through a load of round windows before I find Carols towels. I open the door and the hot air hits me. I pull out the towels but they're not quite dry. Mind you, I don't think Smantha is gonna mind. And anyway. What gets wetter as it dries?

As I pull them from the machine the woman who works there starts yelling at me. Oi leave them. There not yours.

I'm getting them for Carol. I goes.

And she looks a bit gob smacked. And stops. And then goes. Oi. You. Gizza job.

Like that fella on the telly. Yozza Hughes.

Oh well. Makes a change from the fella from the Liver birds. I roll me eyes. Grab the towels and leg it.

Outside the Chinese the woman who works there is sweeping the pavement. She ignores me as I run passed to the entrance to the flats. The lift is still broken so I go up the stairs. I drop one of the towels in a puddle on the landing but pick it up quickly so it's not to stained. I hammer on Carol's doors rather than get me keys out coz my hands are so full of towels. Before I even get to the front door I could hear her screaming. I thought they were supposed to be keeping everything quite. Talk about drawing attention to yourself. After a bit Carol answers the door and grabs the towels. She shuts the door in my face. After the door is shut she shouts. This is womens work.

I wanna be inside. I wanna be with the women. I wanna help if I can. We've waited so long and now it's happening and it's like a little bit of history is being made. That's my baby being born in there but I am not wanted. The papers are full of test tube twins been born and how history has been made but history for me is behind that skuzzy door above a Chinese on a busy shopping street.

I treat myself to a spring roll. But I'm too excited to eat it. I go for a walk and feed it to the seagulls down by the water. I like the water. It reminds me of home. Even though I never go down to it really back there I see it every day and it's always there in the corner of my eye. Shining like a smash window. There's always something reflecting off it or that's how it feels when you walk round by ours. Feel so strange stood out here with nothing to do. I don't know how this is going to work out. I look at the water and it looks choppy and angry though the seagulls don't seem to care as they peck at the spring roll I've chucked on the floor. Funny how quick excitement can turn into fear.

I don't know how this is going to work out. That's all I can think about. I don't know what is going to happen next. I keep thinking of the baby that is being born back in that flat and it makes me feel sick. I feel faint and hold onto the railings.

I am letting Ma bring up the baby and I know it is wrong. She wants the baby coz she is going to pretend it is Woody's and she thinks that will keep him. She's been wearing baggy jumpers and moaning of back ache and Woody's over the moon or so she says and I just can't bear it.

But maybe she will change. Maybe it's the earning that's made her hard. Maybe with the baby she will become soft and Woody will look after her and it and . . . but there is a massive alarm bell ringing in my head. I know it's not right. I want to run to a phone box and phone the police or the social and tell

them what's going on and they will come and the baby can be
adopted by people that will love it and not use it as a porn and

But I can't.

Like Ma says.

I owe her.

Big time.

I can't swim. If I jump in the water now the water will swallow
me and I won't have to worry any more. I grip the railing harder.
I don't even know if I could climb it I feel so weak. I'm not
sporty enough to just hop over it. I was crap at PE at school and
everyone used to laugh coz I am such a weakling. I'm so pathetic
I wouldn't even be able to get over the railing without falling back
or something. I wouldn't even be able to drown myself properly.
Typical. Can't swim but can't even drown myself.

If I made that call Smantha would be in the shit. And Ma
wouldn't hold back and she would kill me for what I'd done
to her and Woody coz she'd be shown to be a liar. And then
that'd be me banged up. And the thought of that puts the fear of
God into me.

But then I think. Maybe prison could only be as bad as living
with Ma.

I know when she takes the baby back home I will have to
move out. I don't see how I can live there and keep up the lie. But
then maybe the baby will need me there to make sure it is ok.

Too many thoughts. Too many thoughts going on in my head.
Am I too much of a weakling to end it all and force myself over
this railing? Does ending it all mean you've got to be a strong
person? What does the coward do?

I could do it. It would be so easy. There would be no one
about to laugh and take the piss if I fell back off the railings.
Even if it took ten minutes to clamber over am sure I could do it.
And then all I'd have to do is flop down.

Knowing me I'd probably be unlucky enough to float.

I'm just picturing myself bobbing about on the water. Some tug boat coming to my rescue and me going. Nah am all right. Leave me to drown – when I hears a voice.

You went off with our money you knob.

I look round and Gina's there.

I realize I've ran off from the pub with the girls money.

Think she's fuming but she's smiling so I realize she's not. She says I should go back the pub with her. I look back to the water. It looks too bloody cold anyway. And then push away from the railings and jog over to walk back with her.

I know babies can pop out in seconds or spend ages coming out. Gina says Carol will phone the London when its ok to go back so I stay in there with her and she spends her earnings. I have a couple of pints but I make them last. I don't wanna be tree sheets to the wind when I go back in case it all kicks off. Smantha might say she wants to keep it and Ma will throw an eppy. I don't think that will happen but you just never know.

My bladder is about the size of a pea when I'm boozing so I'm forever heading off to the bogs.

On my third time of coming out the bogs I see her.

She's stood at the bar at first getting something see through. She's tall. She's slim. And she's so so glamruss. She looks right out of place in here. Not saying it's rough but she looks like something out of a movie. The hair the clothes everything about her says class to me and I can't take my eyes off her. She takes her drink and goes and sits in a booth. She gets a book out and starts reading.

Gina sees me starin at her when I gets back to the bar.

Jew know her? I go.

She shakes her head.

Wonder what she's doing here. I go.

Gina laughs. She's a tranny mate. And I look back.

She's sat there. Reading. Totally oblivious to everything that's going on around her.

Barman sees me staring as Gina talks to some mates.

That's April. He goes.

Does she come in here often? I've never seen her before. I goes.

Barman shakes his head. Comes in twice a year. Night before a cruise. Stops at the Pollygon hotel and always comes in here for a couple.

The Pollygon. I've seen that. It's the other side of the station. It's got a revolving door and is really posh. No wonder she stays there. She couldn't stay anywhere else if am honest.

I've never been through a revolving door.

What's she like? I go.

Dead friendly. He goes.

Jew think she'd mind if I talked to her?

I had no idea why I said that.

Or maybe I did.

April? No. She might look all hoity toity but she's all right really.

And so I head over.

I clear my throat and she looks up.

Anyone sittin here? I go.

She shakes her head.

Mind if I join you? I go.

She shakes her head again. So I sit down. She puts her hand in her book, keeping the pages open but looks at me.

What's the matter? I go. Have I got a welly on me head?

She smiles. And goes. You have the most excuisite cheek bones.

And two things hit me.

One. No one had ever said anything nice to me before about

the way I look. Not that I blamed them. But having good cheek bones is hardly something to write home about I suppose.

And two. She has a Liverpool accent. Soft. Disappearing. But defo from there.

Are you from Liverpool? I goes.

She smiles. A very long time ago. What's your name?

Darren.

April.

Then she holds out her hand. I don't know what to do with it. But coz it all looks so elegant like she's a bally dancer or summat I take it and hold it to my mouth and kiss it.

Ah. She goes. Old school. I definitely approve.

I ask her where she's going on her cruise and she tells me somewhere called Santa Reeney. She says I'd love it there as it is divine. Only when she says divine she says it like Dee-viiiine.

She says it's like an old volcano and the houses and streets are built right up on the top of it. She tells me about the sunsets and the black sand and the white houses and the blue doors and how some of the houses are caves in the side of the rock. And she tells me how there's loads of stray dogs and she takes the food from the boat and she goes round feeding them of a night and how it brakes her heart that she has to leave them there and how she'd ship them all over if it wasn't for the cuaranteen. She says she's not really goin on a cruise, she's just going by boat because she has a fear of flying. She tells me about the rosay wine and the salads and how you haven't had a lamb chop til you'd had one in Santa Reeney. And then she stops. And as if realizing what she's said a few seconds ago she goes – looking me straight in the eyes – a bit weird. What are you scared of Darren?

And I honestly don't know what to say. But it's like she can read my mind. It's like she can see that an hour before I had

been stood at the dockside staring at the sea and thinking I'd be
better off in it.

I don't know. I say.

Are you scared of me? She goes.

No. I say, really quickly, she's the most amazing thing I've
ever met on this planet. No course not.

She nods. Like she's letting it go. And starts talking about
Santa Reeney again. And how she wants to live there. She
wants to live in a place called . . . I forget where she said it was
now but it sounded like she was saying Hiya I think. And she
tells me about this place which sounded like Hiya but it wasn't.
About the narrow streets and how you can reach out from
your window and almost touch the sun. And how if she doesn't
meet a rich man soon who'll take her there she is going to jack
everything in and move there anyway. And then after a while
she probly doesn't have much more to say about Santa Reeney.
And so she stops speaking.

So Darren. She goes. I don't think you came over here because
you want me to take you back to my hotel and make love to me.

That makes me blush.

I didn't think so. So why did you come over?

Again. I don't say much. I'm working up to it. She looks like
she has all the time in the world. She takes a packet of cigarets
from her hanbag. There weird cigarets as it happens because
they're actchally pink. Pink. She puts one in a holder – mother of
purl she informs me – and then lights it up. She takes a big drag
on it and raises an high brow like she's waiting.

And so I tell her.

I do.

I tell her what I've never told a single soul in the whole wide
world.

I tell her about Lucy.

Jonathan Harvey

THE POLYGON HOTEL
SOUTHAMPTON

My dear Darren,

It was so lovely to meet you in the pub this evening. I had only imagined popping in for a quiet drink and a read of my book. I didn't expect to make a new friend. I sincerely hope this gets to you. I am going to drop it into the London tomorrow and ask the barman to pass it on next time you are in, as I didn't get any contact details for you as you had to rush off.

What we discussed has stayed with me. I'm sure you understand why. I shan't mention it here as pieces of paper can fall into the wrong hands. But, Darren, I would love, when you return to Liverpool, to go to the library and read up about a woman called April Ashley. She is an incredible woman, also from Liverpool, who has inspired me a lot in my life. It's why I took her name. She was born a boy, joined the merchant navy, but later became April and became a world-class model and film star. If you read about her, I am sure you will find her the inspiration I have. And she will be someone to tell your friend Lucy about.

The thing you need to tell Lucy is that she is not alone. She may feel she is; in fact I know she will be. There is a lot of stigma attached to what she will go through and the powers that be are, on the whole, bastards. She may find more tolerance abroad. I did. We are the silent minority, but there are many people like her out there. It's just that often we cannot be seen. And though the path ahead for her might be difficult, she needs to know that one day there will be light at the end of this arduous tunnel. Eventually the caterpillar turns into a butterfly.

I hope that Lucy will always view me as a friend. I enclose my card. She or you can call me anytime. It is a lonely world and we all need friends. One thing she will need to be prepared for are the questions. Where are you from? What sort of childhood did you have? What sort of little girl were you? And yet I am a mystery to many. And so often I feel like the girl who appeared from nowhere, the girl who just showed up. Although, having met me, you will know my 'girl' days are long gone.

I will think of you as I sip some rosé wine on the terrace in Oia. I will raise a glass to you and wish you and Lucy every success and happiness in the future. And who knows, one day maybe you will join me there in the sunshine.

All best wishes and love,

Your friend,

April xx

P.S. I really hope you don't mind me writing. You are a charming, polite person, but I sense an air of fear and confusion about you. You remind me so much of myself at your age. Bet you don't like me saying that!

P.P.S. Also, Lucy needs to know that there is nothing new about us. People like us have existed throughout history. Maybe also look up the Roman emperor Elagabalus at the library. (I hope you have a good library!)

The baby is perfect. Ma is calling her Ruby after the nurse mate of Carol's who helped deliver her and coz she was born on a Tuesday.

Smantha has gone back to Liverpool.

We go back tomorrow.

I don't bother with the tin much at the mo coz I am completely besoted with this baby.

LIVERPOOL June 1982

Ma's getting married. She's got the dress and everything. She wants Margy to be bridesmaid and our Robert to be page boy. Am going to hold Ruby who will be flour girl. Not sure what that makes me but living here has really changed. It's like a different flat. Ma's dead easy goin. Laughin all the time. All interested in anything I have to say. It's like she's white washed the last fifteen years out of history. She isn't goin for nothing ponsy (her words) like Lady Di wore but something simple and elegant. Says she wants to look as good as she can.

Why not wear a Punch n Judy booth. Goes Marg.

And Ma laughs. Really laughs. Cheeky bitch.

That's how much Ma's changed. She's not been earning for a few weeks now. She says Woody's not that keen and it gives her more time to get the wedding ready. Her and Marg lie on the sofa all day flickin through magazines about brides and weddings and white dresses going. Oh isn't that nice Marg. And Marg going. Oh look at that Frankie. And then they go oooh like they've seen a dead cute puppy needing a home.

Actchally they both make me feel a bit sick.

Why do women act like this just coz a fella is bein nice to them? I don't get it. I don't even think Woody's that nice. I can't espress that opinion of course coz if I say anything negative about him what so ever then Ma gives me a sly look and goes. Remember what he did for you. So I keep it shut. It's times like that when I see the old Ma coming back.

But I can't help feeling the way I feel about Woody. He comes round here lookin like something out of the 60s with his rainmac with the coller up and his hands in his pockets like a flasher.

Proper little Derk Bogards. Goes Marg. And her and Ma laugh.

Behave yous. Goes Woody. And then he does this like movie star matiney idol pose. And that makes them laugh even more.

Don't get me wrong he's a handsome bastard. I can see why Ma likes bein on his arm. I think she thinks she's like that Nancy in Oliver. The one in the red dress who works in the pub n keeps singin. And Woody's the big fella with the ugly dog breakin into houses. Mind you. Look what happened to her before the end credits.

And I'm not messin. I did actchally hear her singin along to a record in her room. And I swear to god it was as long as he needs me.

Not that Woody is anything other than nice to me. Always tryina get me to talk. But i get embarast. Ma goes. You gotta be nicer to him. He's dead nice.

Rob's spending more n more time at his Dads. Ma's not even bothered about that. If he's not here she doesn't even ask half the time. If am honest she's not that fussed over Ruby neither. Sept when he's around. Then she walks round with her wedged on her hip like she's mother earth and doing everything with one hand and humming songs to her and going. What's the matter with you ay Ruby Tuesday? And then she's bouncing her on her knee and going. Horsey horsey don't you stop. Does my head in. Rest of the time it's just muggins here who's with her.

Smantha doesn't want to come round. She came round like twice like but each time she would cry before she had to go and now she says she is to busy with her course work and it is probly best for all concerned if she stays away which of course Ma is more than happy about and is all – good riddles to bad rubbish. And of course we cannot mention Smantha's name or Southampton or Carol or the Chinese or any of it in front of Woody. As far as he is concerned we went on holiday and Ma suddenly give birth. It was all a total surprise. But to be honest wit you he doesn't seem that arsed. He certainly don't seem that arsed with Ruby. He pats her head n squeezes her cheeks but thas about it. Ma's always goin on about how she can see him in Ruby and how she takes after him but it's in one ear and out the other with Woody. Its clear little Ruby was gonna be the glue that got him stuck to her. Once she's got his ring on her finger she thinks life will be made. But I worry for little Ruby. Will Ma need her any more?

At first Ma n Woody rowed about where they would live after the wedding. Ma was like. Am moving in with you. He was like. What, you and the kids? Jokin aren't you. (Thanks Woody. Actchally I was releeved when he said that coz there's no way I'm living with him and callin him Dad or any of that shit) and she was bangin on about how as a married couple they had to live together. But he didn't see why that changed things. And she said it changed everything. Now they have a greed that they will live together with Ruby n Rob n I have decided to get a place of my own and Ma will give this flat up. I can't really see that happening. I don't know why. It's just a feelin in me waters.

Rob is not impressed with Ruby. Months back Ma tried to convince him she was up the duff but he was having none of it. He smelt a massive rat. In the end I told him what was goin on. It's one thing lyin to everyone else, it's one thing lyin to Woody. But Rob is proper family. Snot fair. He was completely increjulus. Ever since he's had his nose in the hair about it and wants nothing to do with it. Wouldn't surprise me if he moves out permanently and went the Wirral. Now the baby's here he just keeps out the way. And when Woody's here. Which ammitedly isn't that much. Rob is a liability. Always bein dead sarcy going – Oh god yeah when Ma is saying Ruby looks like him. And – Yous two could swap heads Ruby.

Which makes Ma look at him like she wants to slap him and Woody think our Rob's not all there.

But of course Ma can't keep giving him daggers or else the games up so if Woody looks over Ma's daggers turn to a narrow eye nod like she's really concentrating on what our Rob is saying. Like he is the prime minister spouting bollocks that we are meant to believe.

Rob then looks at me while there not looking and goes gozzy with his eyes.

Sometimes though he can be dead nice. Ushally when Ma ain't here mind. Its then I see him. Leanin over the carryin cot. Sayin dead quite. Am not your brother baby. Am your uncle.

Then he blows a fart on her nose and she always does this noise which sounds like a gurgle but I know is a laugh.

Makes me feel weird when I see them doin that. Nice weird. But weird still.

Then other times he's like. Woody's far to young for Ma.

I hadn't even noticed. Maybe is coz he's built like a brick shit house.

He your toyboy Ma? I go.

And she laughs. Really laughs. Like she really likes the sound of it.

Not seen Richie for ages. I nock for him and ast his Ma if he wants to take the baby out with me. She says he's not here. She says he's gone away. I ast where he's gone and she stutters and says he has gone to stay with her family in Jamaica.

It's not good for him here. She goes.

Ma doesn't believe a word of it.

He's been banged up. Any fool can see that. She goes.

I don't know what to believe. But if he has why would Richie's Ma lie about it?

But then I suppose we've all got our secrets.

I went and sat on the stairs today. The stairs from Richie's to ours. With the front door shut its dark as midnight. In the stillness of the hall I thought of all the secrets that this house holds. I look up to our land in. I feel tired. Sometimes secrets can take it out of you. Sometimes they feel like ghosts. Hovering in the air around you. Ghosts of people. Ghosts of ideas. Ghosts of what might have been or what should have been. There's not one person in this house who don't have a secret.

I hear a door open at the top of the house. Then a tap. Suddenly the hall is full of light. The switches are timer switches. Thirty seconds later I will be in darkness again. Then I hear slow steps coming down. And a front door slam. It must be Fatty Arbuckle. I want to stay on this stair. It feels all right on this stair. But sooner or later she will be down here. Later probly coz the fat bitch takes so long to walk. But here she will be. Maybe if the light goes out and I squeeze against the wall she won't see me. She will walk past me like I am a ghost to. And to her we are ghosts probly. Lives goin on around her which she ain't interested in. Ghosts can be like that can't they.

I get up. I don't know why but I don't go up I go down. I tiptoe into the hall and tuck myself at the far end of the hall. Opposite the front door. She won't see me here. True to form the light snaps off. I hear her come down. There's another light switch at the bottom by the door but she doesn't belt it. She just opens the front door. More light. Fresh air. Salty air. Sound of a car going past. She stands in the open door. A round sillooette. She looks back. I can't see her face coz it's in the dark and the light is behind her.

And she just says. Your very strange, ghost child.

Why she call me that? Is it coz I'm a ghost? I look like a ghost? I'm not all there? I'm not really living?

Fat she may be. But daft she ain't.

Other day Rob calls us into Ma's bedroom while she's gone for a run out with Woody. Ruby's awake in her carryin cot.

Look at that. He goes. And he's pointin into the carryin cot.

I look in and don't know what he's showing me.

She's got a bruise. On her arm.

He points. She has.

Jew do that?

No. Piss off. Course not. She musta just banged it.

Rob gives me this look. And my stomach does a cart wheel. I know immediately what he's saying. Coz it looks so wrong. It is obvious it shouldn't be there. And how does a baby bang her arm coz that baby is either in the cot or with me and I don't remember her banging her arm unless she banged it with Ma.

She musta banged it with Ma.

Rob rolls his eyes and walks out the room.

My Dad says if she hurts that baby I've gotta take it to social services. He says it's not safe having a baby in here.

Your dad some sort of hexpert is he? Ay?

No but he's got a brain in his head, knobhead.

Well he doesn't mind you living here and you haven't done to badly for yourself.

He hates me living here actchally. And he says the sooner I get out the better. He says what Ma does is child abuse.

Oh behave.

He does. So there.

So where?

Oh shut up Darren.

Ma wouldn't hit Ruby.

299

Why not? She hit you. She hit me. Why wouldn't she?

Coz she's a baby you knobhead.

Like that'd stopper. She's hit her Darren laa. And I want no part of this.

And with that he spins round and goes to his room and shuts the door.

Fuckinell. I call after him. Drama queen or what?

Piss off. He shouts through the door.

I love that phrase drama queen now. The lads in the London learned me it.

And the other thing one of them used to say was me thinks the lady dust protest to much.

Which I could say about myself right now.

And I know why.

Am getting all arsey coz I know Robbie is right.

I go to his door and speak into it. Like am sharing a secret with the wood.

Rob. If anything like that ever happens. I'll take her the social meself.

Hear a noise. Don't know if it's a grunt or he's saying good or what. I go back to the baby. And pull the blanket over her arm so you don't see the bruise.

I seen April today. She is up in Liverpool visiting her family. Although they get on she doesn't stay with them as she says they get on each others tits to much if they spend to much time together. So guess where she is staying. The Adelphi. I couldn't believe it when she told me. She phoned us on Richie's Ma's phone and ast me round for afternoon tea. Which is when you drink tea in the afternoon.

I put our Ruby in the pram and wheel her down the hill. I get there a bit early but am to nervous to go in and wait so I hangs

around outside by the bus stop. Which is when I see April
arrive. I don't know it is her at first. I just see this dead posh
car pulling up outside the hotel, goin up the little hill to the front
steps. You can't see into the car coz the winders are black. A
man in a funny coat and a top hat rushes down the steps and
opens the car door. Which is when I see our April getting out. I
know it's her immediately. The hair's the same but she's wearing
sun glasses and she's got this massive swingy fur coat on. She
waits while he pulls some shopping bags out of the boot – and
am not talkin Kwik Save here – and then he carries them up the
stairs for her.

I look at what am wearing and feel a bit embarast. I have
put jeans on to be smart and my really smart Sergio Tacchini
top. Its starting to rain and my hair is no dout stickin to my face.
Oh well. In for a penny in for a pound.

Afternoon tea isn't just tea. You have cakes as well and they
bring it to you on like a shelf of plates. On each one there is
cakes or sarnies. And each sarnie has the crusts cut off it so you
can more or less eat the sarnie in one bite. The tea comes in a
funny shape silver tea pot and the room. Don't get me started
on the room. It's no wonder people joke about how expensive
it is to stay at this hotel coz the room we had our afternoon tea
in was absolutely out of this world. I've never seen anything like
it, not in real life.

When you look up its like looking up at the sky. The ceiling
seems miles away like you'd have to get in a helly copter to
go up to touch it. And it's not a normal ceiling with paint or
wallpaper on it. No woodchip here. No artex. Instead there's
like windows in the ceiling so you can actchally see the sky.
And everywhere you look there's shandyleers and pillars and
the room stretches as far as your eye can see.

Me and April sit on lether settees and Ruby sleep in her

pram next to us. Maybe April can tell am feeling a bit out of place coz she prattles on about this n that n her holiday n her travels n what she's been up to. I don't have to say much at all. Eventchally I tell her I've always wanted to come here but never had the reason to.

She smiles and says. Well look on me as your fairy godmother. Speaking of which. Has Lucy ever been out in public?

I shake my head.

Don't you think it's time?

I don't shake my head. Just then the baby starts to cry.

She's gorgeous. She's beautiful. And I can't believe she's a part of me. I can't believe I helped to make something so perfect. She's the best thing I have ever done. She is my biggest achievement. My only achievement. I look into her eyes and I see so much for her. Worlds. Planets. The cosmos. It could all be hers. I want it to be hers. And then I look around the flat. And I don't know where to start.

48 Round Hey Road
Childwall
Liverpool 16

13 June 1982

Dear Darren,

I am just writing to let you know that I am going to be leaving Liverpool sooner than expected and go on my travels, not because I want to but because my dad 's job in the Midlands has worked out and they want him permanently now. He is at the Bourneville factory near Birmingham and a house has finally been laid on for us. He thinks all his Christmases have come at once, but the rest of us aren't

looking forward to moving to Brumland. Anyway, he says it's
a job for life and there aren't that many of them around so
he has to take it. Apparently we will be living in a house that
looks like a cottage and is really old. I am not happy about
interrupting my sixth-form studies, but they won't let me stay
in Liverpool on my own. You know what they are like.

Please give Ruby a kiss from me. I'm sorry I've not been to
see her, but it's probably for the best. I thought I could cope
with her growing up just down the road, but actually I can't.
I find it dead hard. So this move is probably best for all of us
all round.

I won't come to say goodbye. I would be too upset and
that would then upset her and that's not right.

I'm sure our paths will cross again sometime in life. And
till then I wish you and Ruby all the best.

Take care of her,
     Sammi x

It is Lucy's first time going out. April says I don't need to bring
a thing, she has all bases covered. I get to her hotel sweet
and she has everything laid out on the bed. Everything. I can't
believe how kind and genruss she is being. She is right, she is
like a fairy god mother.

Ma's lookin after Ruby. I made sure I ast her in front of
Woody so she couldn't say no. She was like. Of course you can
have a night out. Course you can. And of course I'll have Ruby.
God Darren. Like you have to ast!

Then she looked at Woody and was like. We can have a
quite night in can't we Wood?

And he laughed and went. Jokin aren't yer?

Which is how I got the night off from the baby and how
I end up here in a posh massive sweet in the Adelphi.

An hour later and a few glasses of shampayne down and Lucy is set to go. April says she looks so pretty. That's what she says. So pretty. But she leaves a massive gap between the two words like she is looking at the moaner Lisa. Lucy steps in front of her full lenth mirror and has a little cry. She never knew it was possible to look so beautiful. April says it's time to go.

Lucy is nervous walkin through the hotel. She thinks everyone will be pointin and starin but they don't and she realizes it's much easier to be in front of other people when she's got April linkin her arm.

Lucy is shaking. April knows but doesn't say nothing. Just squeezes Lucy tighter to her. And with April at her side, Lucy slowly starts to think like she can take on the world. The lobby of the hotel is busy but no one bats an eye. It's the same walkin down into town. Some people look but I know there lookin coz April is so stunning. April has booked a table in a place on Bold Street called the Cafe Tabac. She says its cute and bahemian and Lucy's gonna love it. Lucy does love it. It's lit by candles which means she thinks people won't stare so much but the thing Lucy loves more than anything is the walk. Walking around this city she knows so well a whole new person. A whole new experience.

Liberating isn't it? ast April.

And that is the only word to describe it. Liberating.

It is like an earth quake has ripped the city open. Like the sky has turned orange. The air tastes different. Everything is new. It feels good. Liberation.

It feels less good for Lucy when she has to order her food at the Cafe Tabac because the voice is a give away but April has chose the right place to come coz the fella servin didn't even bat an eye.

He's nice isn't he? Says April as the waiter goes away.

304

Lucy nods.

April says something about the third person. How Darren has got to stop talking about Lucy in the third person.

Lucy shrugs. Maybe one day.

Baby steps. Goes April.

April tells Lucy all about her life. Childhood to now. It's like the longest and greatest story ever told. She's still telling it when there having there puddings. And even though Lucy understands why she is telling her all this – to make her feel better about herself – it's still really interesting. Lucy tells her she should write a book.

April lives all over coz she married a man from Jordan and he was minted but then he died. He left all his money to her but because of tax she can't stay in one place to long. Also his kids from a previous marriage didn't take to kindly to April and think they should have got more money than they did so they are taking her to court and she thinks she may well loose as she is the sort of person she is and no one looks favrably on people like April and Lucy. She says tonight is on her and slips the waiter a roll of notes and her and Lucy head off into the night. It's dark by the time they come out and April says Lucy is more confident than Darren. And it's true. Maybe it's the wine with the meal. Lucy's never really had wine before, but she's all confident and giggly as they walk down Bold Street and head down one of the side streets to a club that April wants to take her to.

The club is called Sadie's Bar Royal. It's on Wood Street. And a building less like a club or a royal bar you couldn't imagine. It's just a door. A big black door. April rings the bell next to the door and waits.

Bit of a come down from the Adelphi. Lucy says.

But before she can reply there's a noise. A window is

opening above them and a narled lookin fella pops his head out and goes. What the fuck do you want?

But then he sees it's April and he cackles his head off.

He then screams. Lerrem in.

And they hear a bolt going on the inside of the door and it's opened by some bouncery looking bloke. A smell of noise hit them as music seeps out from upstairs. He hushes them in and Lucy follows April up some stairs. At the top of the stairs – it is like goin into someone's house – there's a lad in a booth takin coats who looks pissed off that April and Lucy have come out without them. April takes a right and Lucy follows her into this room. It's obviously a club coz there's loud music playin. But the room itself has velvet wallpaper and tartan on the other and paintings hung on like this is someone's front room. Not very nice paintings neither. Lucy is no artist but even she can tell that a picture of a Spanishy lady and a boy crying are not high art.

I hate that picture. Says April. Don't they say whenever houses go on fire. It's always that picture that survives amongst the ruins?

Lucy looks at the ugly crying boy and chuckles. Even though it reminds her of Darren. April gets some drinks. Lucy tries to look around without making it look like she's looking around n being nosey when that's exactly what she is trying to do. It has to be said. There's hardly any women here. Loads of fellas. In another room neon lights sillooette men dancing. Lucy finds it all very exciting. Everyone is gabbing and laughin. A few fellas look over but look away. Just the usual checking to see who's there probly.

There's a man in the corner. Lucy doesn't see him at first. He's wearing a camel coat which looks daft in June. But he's handsome. There's no denying that. And he's looking at her.

He takes a swig of his pint. Dead slow. But doesn't once take his eyes off Lucy.

Lucy's heart goes in her mouth. Her stomach does a summer salt. She wants to run but she is literally frozen to the spot. April is chattin away but Lucy doesn't hear. He keeps on starin.

April senses something's up. She looks to the man.

You've got a fan there.

But Lucy can't tell her why he's really starin.

She knows him.

He's getting up out of his seat. And oh shit. He's coming over. With every step that he takes Lucy feels herself getting more and more faint. This is the worst thing that could ever have happened. Her first night out and she is found out.

He arrives. Gets his wallet out. And goes to April. I'll get these April.

Lucy looks to April. She's just about to pay for the drinks. But she lets Woody pay.

Oh. Thanks darling. She goes. Like the queen.

So who's your friend?

This is Lucy.

Not seen you before.

She's new.

Lucy says nothing.

Cat got your tongue Lucy?

Lucy nods.

Lucy's shy. Goes April.

And he nods. Like that's fine.

And Lucy has no idea if he's playing mind games with her. Does he recognize her? Does he not recognize her? Shorely he must recognize her she can't look that different. Lucy has started shaking.

He puts his hand out and squeezes her waste.

307

No need to be scared darling.

He never calls Ma darling. He gives her another squeeze. Then heads back to his seat.

He likes you. Goes April.

April can we go?

Why?

I just need to go.

Of course.

Lucy and April leave. At the door Lucy looks back. He's still lookin straight at her.

I can't say anything. I can't say anything to Ma or she'll kill us. If I say something then I'll have to tell her about Lucy which I can't do. And if I say I seen Woody in a gay bar then she will say am interfering, which is what she sort of said after I told her the truth about _____ , she said I'd messed with her work. Even with him dead on the floor and the pan on the side and the blood on the lino she made some comment about protection. Even though she could see I hated the fucker. Even when she knew he'd hurt me. So if I was to say I'd seen him out and about, Woody, she would turn it into something else. And as she says. She's got shit on me. April says she's known Woody a little while. He likes to flirt with the girls. He likes to by drinks and be the big I am. And he likes a pretty little thing. And if April is to believed. And Woody's eyes were on storks. Lucy is a pretty little thing. Prettier than me that's for sure. If I say anything to Ma she will just say I am tryina ruin the wedding.

I was really worried Woody would say something. But when he come round he did his usual trick of slapping me on the back saying all right fella and then ignoring me. Does Lucy look that different from me? Obviously she does.

I have got away with it. I better keep my gob shut.

Maybe he is just bein nice to people by drinking there and bein kind. Yes. That's what he does. And that is why I can't say anything to Ma.

But then I find myself starin at him. And thinkin. He wanted me. And it doesn't feel bad or scary like with ____. Coz the way he done it was wrong. I remember one time he hit me round the head with something like a kosh. I honestly don't know what it was. I blacked out. And when I woke up he was inside me. I threw up over him and he punched me in the face.

It wasn't like that with Woody.

Old school. That's what Ma says he is. Old school.

Well maybe he was bein old school with Lucy.

Sometimes I want Lucy to be here when he comes round. See how he reacts. And then I hate myself. He's marrying Ma. And when I think of him like that it makes me think of ____ and I worry that maybe with ____ it was my fault and I put out a signal I didn't know I did and then I feel really last. There's no one to talk to about it and when things like that fizz round in my head they feel like there gonna make me explode. I've never had no one to talk to. Then I had April. But she's gone on her travels again and now there's no one. No one would understand. And why should they?

It's all to much.

I go to the bathroom. I lock the door. I kneel in front of the cabinet. Blood comes easier than tears.

I'm in the corner shop. Rob's mindin our Ruby. I'm reading through the magazines when I hears a voice I recognize.

Twenny Marlbros.

I look round. It's Woody.

I puts the magazine down am readin and walk past him like am heading out.

Oh hiya Woody. I goes.

Oh oright Dar laa. And he slaps me on the back as is his wont.

We step out together.

Where you goin? I go.

He shrugs. Just shootin the breeze. Yer Ma in?

No.

Oh rice.

We walk along. It's sunny. He puts sunglasses on.

Mate a mine seen you the other night. I goes.

Fuck. Why did I say that?

Oh I? Who's that?

Oh this girl I know. Lucy.

There. I've said it. Feel like am kacking my pants it feels such a massive thing to be saying.

He looks none the wiser.

Where was this?

The other Satday. Place in town. I forget what it's called but you have to knock on the door to get in and this weird lookin fella shouts you up.

Woody went pale. He stops. He lights a ciggie. Offers me one. Even though he knows I don't.

Is it called Sadie's? I go – and fuck me they should be givin me the Oscar.

Nah snot called that. He goes.

Oh rice. I go.

What does she look like?

Dunno. Pretty. Brown hair in a long bob. Was with an older mate. Think she was wearing a red dress and matching heels.

How jew know her? He goes.

I just do. I go.

Have you told yer Ma?

No. Forgot. I go.

Woody's lookin well freaked out. He takes his sunglasses off and looks at me. Like he's tryina work out why am saying this.

She said you bought her a drink.

I never.

She didn't mind.

And I said that a bit too quickly. And it startles him. He freezes. Lookin at me. and then I add. For good meshure. She really didn't.

His face changes. It goes from shock to dawning to shock again. And he's still sayin nothing. He suddenly jolts into life and starts walkin away.

Where you goin? Am shouting after him.

He doesn't reply.

Woody?

He just keeps on walkin down the street.

Am an arlarse for doin that. But something tells me. He won't say nothing.

Ruby looks so pretty in her flour girl dress. But Ma had Ruby's ears pierced yesterday and she don't like it. And on top of that she is makin her wear this flour thing on her head on a piece of elastic and them two things combined I think are makin her grouchy. She hasn't stopped all day. She's only three months old. I may as well have a doll in my hands bein flour girl for what she can actchally do. She just has to lie there bein a baby while I hold a basket of flours in my other hand and scatter them on the ground in front of Ma.

I know. Feel a cunt for myself.

The church round the back of us has agreed to do the

weddin. Ma and Margy have been goin every Sunday in there best clothes and comin back raving about Father Parr and his wise cracks.

There's only an hour to go and Margy is doing Ma's hair. She looks ridiculous. She looks like Kiki Dee in the 70s. The flick is back with avenjance. The dress is nice. And the flours are nice. Ma called in a few favours from her punters. She's draggin on a ciggie as Margy messes with her hair. Rob sits board on the couch in his school uniform and I try and shut our Ruby up.

How do I look? Goes Ma.

You look beautiful Frankie. Goes Margy. Someone needs there eyes testin.

Tina Charles is playin on the record player. Ma keeps nocking back a voddie and then singin along. Her and Marg do a little dance round the living room when there done. Giggles. Never seen Ma so happy. But jittery. She's all on hedge.

It's a bright sunny day and the sun is streaming in through the open winders. Not even the cathedral can block out the sun today. The music's blarin. The baby's cryin. There all laughin and dancin when suddenly there's this noise and a black thing has bombed into the room. It's a pigeon. It's flown in through the winder. Its flyin everywhere tryina get out but Ma's screamin and Marg's laughin and Rob's jumpin up. Ma's screamin. Get it out get it out before it shits on me dress. An she runs into the kitchen and comes back with the broom and the pigeon's goin mental flappin around everywhere. It's bedlam in here an then almost as soon as it come in it's gone out again. And the music stops. And then we hear a man's voice.

Frankie?

We all look round. Some fella stood there. In a track suit.

Ay. You wanna get a move on. Ma goes. We're meant to be

at the church in fifteen minutes. Everyone this is the best man. Billy. Why haven't you got your glad rags on Billy?

Only Billy just shakes his head. Ma takes Ruby off me. Like she wants to look like the devoted mother.

Shut your gob Rube. She goes.

He's not comin. This fella goes.

Ma says nothing.

Y what? Goes Margy.

He's not comin the wedding. This fella goes.

How jew mean? Goes Margy.

No one can find him. I've been round his. Nowhere to be seen.

He's probly at the church. Goes Ma. Finally finding her voice. And then she coughs, clearin her throat, like talkin took it out of her.

No he's not. This fella goes. I found a note. I was meant to be going round. Gettin im ready. He'd left a note. Says he can't go threw with it.

Last minute nerves. Goes Margy.

You know his heart was never really in it. This fella goes. Shot gun wedding. Am sure he'll see the baby all right.

Ruby. Shut it. Goes Ma. Coz the baby is getting on her tits.

Ma I'll take her. I go.

Fuck off Darren. She goes.

Am goin the church. This fella goes. Tell everyone.

He might be there now. Ma goes. Sounding just a little bit despret.

Am sorry Frankie. This fella goes. Then this fella really does go.

Ruby. Shut it. Goes Ma. Coz Ruby's really cryin now.

Ma you need to rock her a bit. She'll soon . . .

Darren.

Silence.

Rob stands up. Well. Best get this crappy uniform off. He goes. And he heads off to his bedroom.

Marg looks to Ma. Am gonna go. Am gonna make sure he's not there. You wait here.

And she runs out after that Billy fella.

Ruby's really cryin now. Ma starts pacing the room. Struttin n tuttin n you can tell she's fuming. Really fuming. She starts laughin.

Cheeky fuckin bastard.

And then she's off again. Pacin.

Ma give me the baby.

But she ignores me.

How dare he. How dare he. Each time getting louder, which I think is scaring Ruby.

And then. It was so quick. I would've stopped her if I could but it was that quick.

She goes. Oh SHUT UP RUBY. And she throws the baby across the room. Ruby hits the arm of the settee and falls on the floor.

I freeze in horror. I do. I actchally freeze. And Ma goes into the kitchen. I come to me senses and go and pick her up. Ruby. She's cryin so loud. I hold her to me to try and comfort her. Rock her. Jiggle her. But the cryin gets worse. Our Rob comes through from the bedroom. Stares.

What did she do?

I can't speak.

Darren?

I think she's hurt.

Rob runs to the kitchen. You fucking evil bitch Ma.

But Ma won't answer.

I look at Ruby. And I know what I have to do.

32C Gambier Terrace

15 August 1982

Dear Darren,

I know for a long time we have never seen eye to eye. I know for a long time I have been dismissive towards you. I do not approve of how your mother runs your house. I'm sure we are both clear on that. I remember this street when it was a real destination, a place to be proud of. However, I fear your mother and her ilk have sullied that lately. I naturally assumed I would never be proud of anyone on our terrace again.

I was wrong.

Yesterday I saw you running along Myrtle Street with your beautiful sister in your arms. I saw the state she was in and I saw the panic and care in your eyes. I saw you dash across the street between the oncoming motorcars. I know what you were doing and I am sure in your home you will get no thanks for it. In fact I am under no illusions that you will receive some sort of punishment for it.

I want you to know that you did a very good thing yesterday. I want you to know that what you did was courageous and I am incredibly proud.

For years I have been going to church, professing to be a Christian. I now realize I was most unchristianly in my attitude towards you, and for that I humbly apologize.

There is no need to acknowledge this letter.

Burn it for all you wish. But even though you will never see that little girl again, know you did the good and Christian thing yesterday. You have given that girl the gift of life.

Yours truly,
Helen Chance

HOLLY

THIRTEEN

Irish Alan stood on his doorstep looking slightly bewildered. It was mid-afternoon, but he was still in his dressing gown, unshaven, eyes slightly bloodshot. Maybe he'd had a bad night.

'I'm sorry, Holly, but she's not here.'

'Where is she?'

'Er . . .' Just then a whistling neighbour passed, walking his dog. Both men nodded at each other. Alan then pulled the front door open wider and beckoned me in, clearly embarrassed to be seen looking like a dosser in the middle of the day. We went into the living room and he fanned his hand in the direction of the settee, which I took as an invitation to sit.

Where was she? Where was Rose? Maybe he was going to say, 'She knew you were on to her and has done a midnight flit.'

But how would she have known I was on to her? She didn't know I had the biscuit tin. How would she have known I had worked out her secret? And why had she indeed kept it a secret from me? That is, if I was correct in what I assumed I had deduced. Maybe I was wrong. Should I ask Alan? But then again, if she had kept it a secret from me, maybe she had hidden it from him too. But was that really possible?

Can you keep something like that from the person you love, the person you share your life with, the person who sees you naked? Maybe they never saw each other naked. Maybe they kept the lights off. Or maybe they had a platonic relationship. Questions, questions, so many questions, and not enough courage to ask them.

How I wished I was the yes-woman I had tried to be. A more go-getting woman would have stamped her foot (if that wouldn't be deemed too churlish) and demanded *answers*. A yes-woman would push out her bust and say stuff like 'Come on, buddy, spit it out. I wanna know 'bout my heritage.'

In my head this particular yes-woman looked remarkably like TV cookery presenter Nadia Sawalha. I always thought she looked like she didn't stand for any nonsense. No, sir-ee!

Maybe I could sound like her.

As it was, I trembled a bit and tried to speak, but nothing came out.

Alan was in the kitchen putting on the kettle. He returned and sat on the edge of one of the armchairs.

'She's gone to see her mother for a few days.'

I looked instinctively to the photo in the alcove. Alan followed my eyes.

'Is her name April?' I asked.

Yikes. Jessica Fletcher had nothing on me.

Alan nodded slowly. 'How did you know? Did she tell you?'

'She must've done,' I flustered. 'Where does she live?'

'Greece.'

Greece. Of course she did. Santorini.

'How long's she there for?'

'About a week.'

'You not gone?'

That had to be one of the worst questions I had ever asked. Alan did this little frown thing, then shook his head.

'I prefer my suntans off a neon tube,' he said, then got up and headed back into the kitchen.

So Rose was making out her mother was April. On one level that made sense. She had probably had more support over the years from her than from her natural mother. And besides, what was natural about Frankie? If anything, she was a very unnatural mother.

I had so many questions to ask Rose. I had to see her. I knew if I saw her, I'd find the courage, somewhere, to ask them. I'd have to – no one else could answer the questions apart from her.

But maybe I could ask Alan them. Surely he would know all her secrets and stories and . . .

I saw him looking at me from the kitchen. When my eyes met his, he looked away quickly.

But what if I was wrong? It was completely possible that I was. Maybe Rose really was the daughter of someone called April who lived in Santorini. And the fact that I had 'met' – on the written page at least – someone with that name and that desired place to live in an old diary in an old biscuit tin was merely coincidence.

Merely. Didn't feel there was much 'merely' about any of this.

I couldn't risk too much with Alan. I had to tread carefully.

I also felt that I had to tread carefully with Rose. This is why I had turned up unannounced. Even though my initial reaction had been to phone her and accuse her, or email and pin her down, I had a feeling that if I did that, she might scarper. She had lied to me so much surely she would be embarrassed and angry that I had found her out. So although it had been hard overnight not to just pick up the phone, I had resisted.

But now my efforts had been futile anyway. She wasn't here. In my absence she had gone to Greece. Shirley Valentine, eat your heart out.

'What are you doing on the Wirral, anyway, love?' Alan was asking.

And this was indeed a very good question. Had Rose been here, the answer would have been straightforward, but she wasn't. And I didn't wish to arouse any suspicions. If Alan didn't know, I didn't want to blow Rose's secret.

OK, so that's a lie – maybe part of me did. I was just desperate to talk about it. To someone, anyone. What I had discovered was, frankly, mind-blowing. Well, mind-blowing to me. Mind-blowing and eye-opening and . . .

But then another part of me had to respect her wishes. Even if I was perhaps only imagining what those wishes were.

I was second-guessing everything.

God, I needed to speak to her.

'Oh, I was just in the area.'

He looked most suspicious. As well he might. I had made such a song and dance about leaving to return to London. Rose had even driven me to Lime Street, and yet here I was, back again, a day after my departure. So I lied. So what? Had I not been lied to enough already in this house? Was it not payback time?

Through the back window I saw a butterfly dancing close to the glass.

Ah yes. And Rose had made the ultimate transformation!

'I was meant to be leaving yesterday, but I changed my mind and stayed at my friend Iggy's. He was . . . working round here today . . . so I . . . just thought I'd swing by. I tried her at work and she wasn't there, so . . .'

That bit was true. And amazingly Alan seemed to buy my story. He returned to the kitchen. What did I do now? Now I was stuck here with a man I didn't want to be honest with for fear of upsetting any sort of apple cart?

Just then salvation came in the form of Sylvie. My phone started ringing in my bag. I snapped it up, saw it was Sylvie calling, no doubt having just read the email I'd sent her last night saying I now wasn't coming to Canada. No doubt ringing to scream at me. I killed the call while pretending to answer it. I then spoke to the silent phone, giving the performance of my life.

'Hello? . . . Oh, hi, Iggy! . . . Sorry? What? . . . Of course . . . Sure. No, that's no problem . . . Yes, OK, I'll meet you at the bottom of the road . . . Thanks.'

Alan was coming through with a cup of tea for me as I returned the phone to my bag.

'Sorry, Alan. Iggy's job's been cancelled. He's heading back over the water so I need to jump in and get a lift back with him.'

'Oh right. No worries.'

'I don't suppose you have the address where Rose is staying?'

'In Greece?'

'I'd love to drop her a line. She sent me the sweetest card. I'd love to reply.'

'Oh, just drop her an email. She'll pick them up while she's there.'

'Oh, but I think a card is so much more personal. Please, Alan. She's been so kind to me. I might even send her some flowers.'

Gosh, I was getting quite good at this thinking-on-your-feet stuff. *And lying through your back teeth . . .*

He put down the cup and headed to the sideboard, pulling out a drawer.

Flowers? To Greece? Really?

Five minutes later I left his house with April's address carefully transcribed onto a scrap of paper.

Now I just had to work out what I had done with my passport.

I had never felt more alone. There were no flights to Santorini for another two days and no amount of me groaning with frustration over the phone to various travel agents was going to alter that. Oh, there were flights before then, but they were fully booked. And taking a plane to somewhere incredibly remote like Venus and then scooting back in a dinghy wasn't going to get me there any sooner. Why did April need to live in such a remote place? I looked into so many variations about how to get there my eyes started to blur staring at my laptop screen. There were routes I could take – Athens then a boat – but they wouldn't really be getting me in any quicker than waiting the two days and flying there direct.

I had checked myself into a budget hotel off Tottenham Court Road. Well, I say budget, the cheapest room was over £200, but the interior design certainly smacked of budget. I wasn't sure what I was going to do for the twenty-four hours I would be here before setting off for Gatwick, but suddenly the enormity of what I'd discovered in Darren's diary knocked me for six.

I started to feel exhausted. I lay on the bed, but was unable to sleep. And that is when I started to feel so isolated.

When I was little, my mum had been wonderful when

I was poorly. I would be allowed to stay off school and she would make me a bed up on the sofa in the living room and I would be allowed to watch whatever was on television all day long. She would bring me frequent glasses of water or orange cordial, and lunch would invariably be Heinz tomato soup with plastic cheese grated in and toasted muffins. Heavenly. That is what I wanted now. I checked the room-service menu to discover they only did 'twenty-four-hour sandwiches' and thought better of it.

I had always been so negative about my experience of adoption. I had always maintained my mother had been distant and aloof, more interested in her church and choir than me, but this memory of tomato soup challenged that. Reading about Darren and his relationship with his mother put mine into stark relief. I had been fed, clothed, watered. I had had my fevered brow mopped. We had gone on holidays. I had read books. I had been frowned upon for watching smutty programmes way after my bedtime. I had received an education. I had learned the cello. I had been allowed dreams and aspirations beyond the modest semi where we lived, and I had gone on to achieve some of them. Would I have had that in Gambier Terrace? More than likely not. And whatever Darren had done that day that Helen Chance had seen, wherever he had been taking me, I had to be grateful for it. For what I had ended up with was a damn sight more than what I had started with.

Helen Chance had lied to me. She had made out she couldn't remember me as a baby. And yet she had written a letter to Darren about me.

I wanted to be angry with her, but found it impossible. I realized, rightly or wrongly, that she had wanted to protect me. What had happened that day had been gruesome, and she wanted to shield me from it. Maybe I would have done the same in her position, even if the eventual outcome had been positive.

I had ended up with Tring. And Ted and Jean. And right now, right now I wanted them more than anything else in the world. They were beacons of sanity among the madness I had read about. But of course they were gone.

I knew why I was pursuing what I was pursuing. I knew that for years I had felt like April in the diary, the girl with no history. My life began as a toddler, or at a few months old, or from when I had my first memory. I felt like the girl who just appeared, and I wanted to know from where and from whom.

But why? Why did it matter so much? And why did I suddenly feel so disloyal to the people who were really my mum and dad?

I felt the pain rise through me. I felt my body convulse.

I started to cry. Loud animalistic howls. I turned into my pillow in case I scared the other residents. Surely they could hear me crying in Billingsgate! And once I started spasming and sobbing, I wondered whether I would ever stop.

Finally. Finally it had happened.

'Hello?'

'Jude, it's me. It's Holly.'

'Yes . . . I . . . Your name . . . your name came up.'

He was sounding startled to hear from me. I immediately knew this had been a bad mistake. Never drink and dial!

'How's Henrietta?'

Why? Why was I even doing this?

'Well, at least you're not calling her that . . . name . . . now. Progress, I suppose.'

'I'm sorry,' I offered.

'She's fine. Well, she's had a bit of a cold, but yes. Fine, all things considered.'

'What does that mean, all things considered?'

'It means exactly what it's meant to mean. She's had a cold, but, well, on the whole she's fine,' he said. 'And please don't ask me to interpret "on the whole".'

'No, I won't.'

'Thank you.'

'How's Liverpool?'

'Oh yes. Fine.'

'Good.'

'Although I'm in London again. About to head to Greece.'

'Oh right.'

He sounded hurt. I still had the power to affect his feelings. It felt like a tiny victory, though I wasn't sure why. I suppose the whole reason for calling him was to reach out and find someone who actually cared about me. Job done.

'So, what, are you . . . going on holiday?' he asked.

'No. Still on the search for my family.'

'They're Greek?'

'No. They're there at the moment. On holiday.'

'Whereabouts?'

Why was this important?

'Santorini,' I said, as if it were incredibly important.

'Ah, wonderful. Hen's folks go there all the time.'

Hen's folks. If I went out with someone who forced me to use phrases like that, I think I'd have to top myself. I realized I wasn't saying anything and it was me who had made this call.

'Is she with you now?' I blurted, unable to think of anything else to say.

'No. She's up in Birmingham seeing a pal who's in the Birm Symph.'

And she makes you say that instead of 'Birmingham Symphony Orchestra'? Double suicide points, thank you.

'So what have you found out about your family?'

Oh gosh. Do I tell him? Do I tell him the truth? What do I say? How do I find the words? Even Rose can't bring herself to say it to me, so how can I even dream of saying it myself? What are the words? I know there are words. I know there are proper, appropriate words, but I also know there are those that cause offence.

I found it is easier to respond with 'Oh, just . . . Mum's in a home with Alzheimer's and . . . well, some extended family are in Greece at the moment, so I'm hoping to learn some more from them. Fill in some of the gaps.'

'God, I'm sorry.'

'Not your fault.'

'How old is she?'

'Oh. Only mid-sixties or so?'

'Have you been to see her?'

'Yes.

'How was that?'

'Tough, but OK. It's all made me realize how great Jean and Ted were.'

'Oh well, that's something.'

'And I finally had a cry about Mum today.'

'Jean or . . . ?'

'Yes, Jean. I'm . . . sorry about the funeral.'

'Oh. You know. I've accepted it. Grief and all that.'

'And I'm sorry if I treated you badly. I've been a bit all over the place.'

'Right. Well, thank you.'

'I think I've just buried all my feelings in the quest to find my mother.'

'Well, you have now.'

'Yes,' I lied.

How would Jude react if I told him the truth? His parents were old hippies – he was the least judgemental person I knew. Surely he would be fine about it.

But selfishly, almost fearing it would reflect badly on me, I yet again kept it to myself.

'Sorry to call. Just wanted to hear a familiar voice.'

'Do you . . . want to meet up for coffee sometime?'

'I don't know. What would Henrietta say?'

'Oh, look, Holly, you may as well know. Hen's an absolute control freak. She really does my head in. I don't actually give two flying fucks what she thinks.'

'Oh right.'

'She never used to be like this, but since this drastic fucking weight loss, she thinks she can control every single part of her life. Including me.'

Even though I had no intention of getting back with Jude, I didn't think, this was, for some inexplicable reason, music to my ears.

'I think I went with her on the rebound,' he offered up.

'Yes, but don't beat yourself up about that.'

'Well, you know . . .'

I didn't, but still . . .

'Jude, I'd love to see you sometime, but I'm not sure we should if you think that means there's a possibility of us getting back together again.'

'Your call.'

'Yeah, but I want you to be comfortable with that.'

'It's coffee, Holly. Not a proposal of marriage.'

'Another one,' I pointed out.

'I could feel you distancing yourself from me. I didn't know what to do,' he said like an apology.

'You could?'

'I'm not stupid.'

'I know.'

'Well, let's talk when you're back from Greece or something.'

'Yeah, OK. I can live with that.'

'And if I work things out with Henny, *please* don't tell her I said she was a control freak.'

Henny? *Henny?*

'Guide's honour.'

'It's good to hear your voice, Holly.'

'And yours, Jude.'

'Call me Judith. Please. I tried to get Henny to, but she was like, "That's so childish. No way."'

'Oh, Judith, she sounds like a bitch.'

And we both laughed. For quite some time. And then I could feel the laughter turning to tears. So I quickly made my excuses and hung up.

'Holly? It's Sylvie. Well, I've checked online and you haven't boarded your flight. Call me when you get this. Maybe you've been involved in a fatal road traffic accident. Or maybe you're just a lazy, repugnant loon. Either way, call me.'

Beep.

'OK, so I know you've dropped the dog off at Teddy's and stayed courtesy of *moi* in a rather expensive Thames-side hotel, thank you very much. Where the fuck did you go after that? Hmm? One word, Holly. *Greedy.*'

Beep.

'I've seen your email. Your incompetence knows no bounds. And your ingratitude even less so. And that *does* make sense, but you're probably too stupid to get it.'

Beep.

'I will give you forty-eight hours, Holly. Forty-eight hours. To apologize and get on another flight or you can forget I even existed. Though it rather looks like you already have.'

Beep.

'Rude.'

Beep.

'You have no more messages.'

I had been staring at the ceiling for the past – I checked the bedside clock – forty-three minutes. I felt slightly less alone than I had done a few hours before, partly down to Jude being quite sweet, but also thanks to Sylvie. She might have been vile – she might have been channelling Cruella de Vil – but even so, her rants felt *familiar*.

But still, I knew that I stood on a cusp. I stood teetering at what was hopefully the edge of my journey of discovery. And still, I was facing that journey alone.

I didn't want to go alone.

But who else would go with me?

I sat up and grabbed the remote control. I flicked through the channels till I settled on *Hell Hole*. There she was. Jax, in tears in the toilet, gasping to the camera, 'They all hate me. Please get me out of here. It's not my fault I have a gift. Please.'

I switched off. But knew what I had to do. Knew how to get me some company.

I picked up my phone.

I jabbed in a number. I heard it ring. Just as I thought it was going to answerphone, he picked up.

'Hiya, Pips! How's it going, kid?'

'Good, good. Iggy?'

'Aha.'

'How d'you fancy an all-expenses-paid trip to Greece?'

After being convinced that this wasn't a wind-up, it didn't take me too long to convince him to say yes.

FOURTEEN

Iggy kept giggling that he was a kept man all the way over on the plane. That was, when he wasn't listening to my explanation of why we were heading to the sun. I didn't go into too much detail but just said that Rose had lied to me and I had to confront her. She had said Darren was dead, but I had found out otherwise.

If I'm honest, Iggy did seem to lose interest the more I talked about it, despite making all the appropriate noises and whistles through his teeth that my tale demanded. But they became less keen the longer we were in the air. And by the time we started our descent, he had nodded off and his head had lolled onto my shoulder.

'Madam, can you wake your husband up, please, and tell him to put on his seat belt?' an air steward in an orange jumpsuit with an equally orange face leaned in and hissed at me, while grinning like a constipated Cheshire cat. He had a camp Northern Irish accent. And very high plucked eyebrows. And hair like a toilet brush. And an overpowering smell of Pulse by Beyoncé. Due to the proliferation of orange about him, I assumed he could only be Northern Irish Protestant.

Truth be told, I wasn't that keen on the staff on this plane. They had all developed a fit of the giggles during the safety demonstration, which filled none of the passengers with confidence, it had to be said. And then, to add insult to injury, when Orange Face had distributed the menu cards – which involved him skidding round the plane (no wonder he needed a jumpsuit) and shoving laminated plastic strips in our laps – it was like he was doing it against the clock. I half expected the other staff to be waiting at a finishing line, stopwatches at the ready, showering him with freshly popped champagne. 'Cillian, gurrrl, you *did it*! Twenty-three seconds for eighty passengers! Way to go, babe!'

The menu itself was anorexic. I'm not saying that the food therein would have suited people with eating disorders; it's just that there were only three choices. I plumped for the chilli bean wrap, while Iggy thought he'd try the Tex-Mex wrap.

When Cillian returned brandishing a chip-and-PIN device held aloft in his bright orange fingers, I passed on our orders. He sighed, bored, and said, 'Chilli bean and Tex-Mex wraps are off.'

'Sorry?'

He looked at me like I was an idiot. He leaned in a bit further. This time he said it louder, as if I was foreign or deaf or both. 'Chilli. Bean. And. Tex-Mex. Wraps. Off. You get me?'

And this time he did a slicing action to his neck with his free hand.

'Oh. But there are only three things on the menu.'

'I know.'

'Er . . .'

'Look, do you want the lamb Caesar wrap or what?'

Cillian was becoming impatient now. And I was becoming rattled.

'I'm sorry, it's just . . . well, lamb and Caesar salad don't really go together.'

He was sounding decidedly hacked off this time. 'Oh, really? Forgive me. I didn't know you were a chef, madam.'

'I'm not.'

'Do you want it or not?'

'I just don't see the point of making such a song and dance about giving out the menu cards if there's only one thing available.'

'Really? Well, maybe you should take that up with the airline, madam.'

'I don't know why you didn't just make an announcement over the tannoy.'

Cillian gave me an 'Are you for real?' look and then swiped the menu cards back from me and Iggy and headed further up the plane.

'No food for us, laa,' giggled Iggy. 'We're on the naughty step. Did you see the state of his eyebrows?'

'I know.'

'He looks like a fucking Dolmio puppet.'

The plane seemed to be populated by middle-class types, the sort of people who had only ever eaten brown bread, which made me think Santorini was either going to be as special as April had predicted to Darren or deathly dull. This being June, they were probably all going for pre-summer breaks, whereas I strongly doubted anyone else on board was tracking down a long-lost parent.

Halfway through the flight we saw Cillian leaning against a wall at the front of the plane chatting to one of his colleagues. Well, we could see their legs; the rest of them was hidden by a thin curtain with the airline emblem on it.

'Did you see what happened in *Hell Hole* last night?' Cillian said.

'No, what?'

'Oh, it all kicked off with that one I can't stand.'

'You can't stand any of them.'

'That wee Scouser one now. Argh, she makes my shit itch.'

'Why? What happened?'

'Well, you know they took her out of the Hole and everyone thought she'd been evicted?'

'No! You are joking.'

'Well, she'd been living in her own secret hole watching everything on a screen with headphones on. So she heard them all slagging her off.'

Just then we heard a buzzer.

'Och, it's only the cheap seats. So anyway, they let her back into the real Hole last night and of course she's fuming coz they've all been vile to her, so on my life . . . did it kick off or what?'

'Did you see Madonna's taken her navel piercing out?'

'Stephen, will you put that down? I'm talking. So anyway –' Cillian clearly didn't realize how loud his voice was. In his head a flimsy curtain was the equivalent of a mid-air padded cell '– it ended up with this massive fight. The cops were called and everything, and now they've had to take the show off air.'

'Fuck me, that's terrible.'

'Well, that's what I said to our Claire, so I did.'

The buzzer went again.

'Och, I best go.'

The curtain went back and we saw Cillian slide down the aisle to the seat in front.

'Sorry, madam, I was just serving the pilot his lamb Caesar wrap. What can I get for you, my love?'

I looked to Iggy. He was biting his hand to stop himself from laughing too loudly.

By the time we were stepping off the plane, Cillian was stood at the door with that grin on his face that looked like it had been painted on along with his eight inches of make-up, but his eyes couldn't lie. They were screaming, *Here she comes. Fanny Craddock on crack. And who's that with her? Her dealer?*

'Have a great trip now, you hear?' He grinned, while his eyes said, *Really hope you die a painful death tonight. Or maybe sooner. Careful on those stairs, bitch!*

I returned a similar smile and hurled back, 'Everything you wish for me, I wish for yourself.'

Which foxed him. In fact I heard a whispered 'What was she on about?' as we descended the steps to the runway. I didn't wait for the reply.

The interior of one airport looked very much like the next in my experience: dazzling overhead lighting, chugging conveyor belts, Gestapo-like security observing your every move, strange-smelling toilets, someone crying because they can't find their bubble-wrapped shopping trolley. The exterior wasn't what I expected, though. I'm not sure what I expected a Greek airport to look like, but this appeared to be plonked in the middle of the desert like something out of a Hitchcock film set in the Middle East. I was Doris Day, and Iggy was James Stewart, and we'd come here to find the toddler son we'd lost to international kidnappers. The greying low building with archways all round it spoke to me of countries other than the one famous for olives and grappa. On closer inspection, we weren't in the desert; it was just that the earth surrounding us was baked dry, and actually the building should have been typically Greek – smart white pebbledash reflecting the sun – but had darkened, possibly from the pollution of the planes it welcomed and farewelled. But looking at us, and the way our cab driver from the cacophonous rank viewed us, we were no Doris and James. We were two overdressed loons who looked like they could do with a good wash/rest/holiday. One had enough luggage to fill a small palace; the other clasped a sports bag as if he were off to school for one lesson, then planned to bunk off.

The hotel I had booked us into, Ompreles, was incredibly expensive, but if the website was to be believed, promised laid-back luxury. After a twenty-minute cab drive through narrow streets and then dusty tracks, climbing forever higher, we were deposited at a gap in a very low, pudgy, whitewashed wall that appeared to have nothing beyond it but the sea and sky. The only thing I knew was we were vertiginously high up. As our driver sped off, I was convinced he had left us at the wrong place, but then I noticed a faint 'Ompreles' painted in very pale blue lettering to the right-hand side of the gap. We stepped forward and almost fell into the hotel. The view was breathtaking. We both gasped audibly, then looked to each other in amazement. It was like we were standing at the pinnacle of an amphitheatre, with terraced gardens built on a succession of steps leading down to an infinity pool, which itself seemed to seep into the sea below. I wanted to don a parachute and float down to the bottom. Instead we walked. As we hauled our luggage – I still had my massive rucksack containing all my belongings – down the steps that wound through the terraces, I noticed that the rooms were built into the rock of the hill itself. Each one appeared to be a sort of cave with turquoise shuttered doors. I could see why April had been so drawn to this island. It was like nowhere else on earth. A crescent-shaped volcanic lip protruding from the sea, everything about it was steep, and the villages and towns appeared to cluster at the top of the lip, white buildings with soft edges clinging like lichen to a stone.

As we neared the bottom, a woman magically appeared with a tray holding two glasses of water with lemon in. She greeted us calmly and quietly, informing us she was Petra Boniface, the guest relations manager, and showed us to our own cave.

Petra Boniface. She sounded like a drag queen. What *was* it about this island? I had to stop myself from asking if she had a sister called Bonnie Boniface as we followed her down some steps, and instead I asked her where she was from.

'Chicago. The Windy City,' she said without turning round.

Behind me, I heard Iggy mimic the sound of a fart. And then giggle. If Petra Boniface heard this, she didn't flinch.

'I believe Oprah Winfrey lives in Chicago,' I commented, hoping to convey to Petra in that one small sentence that I was well travelled, well mannered, well-to-do.

'She's stayed here,' said Petra.

'She didn't stay in our room, did she?' called Iggy.

'No. She hired the whole hotel.'

She stopped and then yanked back some turquoise doors. We'd arrived.

The cave/room was simple but clean and elegant. Inside there were more caves hollowed into the rock, like a rabbit warren, all painted white and divided by white lacy curtains. The furniture – beds, chests of drawers – was a dark mahogany, and the sheets on the beds and the throw on the sofa boasted white and lurid lime-green stripes. I had my own little cave bedroom; Iggy had his. Petra looked surprised that I had brought so much luggage for a three-day stay (that is how much time I'd guessed I'd need to find Rose and confront her), but she was too professional to ask questions.

I went in the flap of my rucksack and pulled out a tattered piece of paper. I showed it to her.

'Would you know where this address is, please?'

She glanced at it and nodded.

I couldn't make head nor tail of it. I had transcribed it carefully from what Irish Alan had showed me, but it was all double Dutch to me. Actually, it was all Greek to me, as that is the language I had attempted to replicate.

Petra read it aloud. It sounded like 'Kleftico-mexico-kobodoba-doodiko.'

I felt a wave of relief at that nod and that gobbledegook; the worst thing would have been to discover I'd copied it wrong and it made no sense.

Iggy popped his head out of his cave bedroom. 'I want what she's on,' he said. 'Mental!' Then he disappeared back to unpack.

'That is the post office in Oia,' Petra said coolly.

I didn't know if she had kids, but could just picture her reacting coolly to whatever life threw at her.

Mom, I got a U in my geometry.

[Ice queen voice] Get to your room.

Mom, I pooped myself.

[Ice queen voice] This is ridiculous. You're twenty-three.

Mom, my head fell off.

[Ice queen voice] There's a needle and thread in the third drawer down.

My heart sank. The post office?

But wait. Maybe April was the postmistress in Oia.

I suggested this to the woman. She kindly shook her head.

'No one has an address as such in Oia. Everyone collects their post from the post office.'

'I need to find this woman, you see.'

I pointed to the name at the top of the paper.

'April Hunt,' I said, like she couldn't read.

I heard Iggy calling out from his room, 'We all know what that's cockney rhyming slang for! Don't we, girl?!' and then a fit of the giggles.

I was starting to regret bringing Iggy. Fortunately Petra ignored him.

She smiled, efficiently folded the paper in two and handed it back to me. 'You will have no trouble. The postmistress knows everyone. And if she doesn't, the man in the bakery does.'

How odd.

'And . . . and we are in Oia now, yes?'

I was talking to her as if she was foreign. Well, as if she didn't speak English. She nodded.

'We are on the outskirts of Oia. The town, well . . . village centre is a fifteen-minute walk.'

'Thank you.'

Our guest relations manager proceeded to explain about breakfast by the pool, or in our room if we preferred, but I wasn't listening. I was looking out of the cave door. It was cool and mellow in here, but out there was all bright white light. From here I could see the village of Oia. It was your typical Greek poster view, white dots and blocks with bits of blue and the sun shining like a pink rubber ball behind it. I realized where I had seen it before, on Rose's kitchen wall. And as I stared towards the village, I imagined the walls falling away on all the buildings and seeing a thousand different Roses going about their business like awkward mannequins in doll's houses. I wanted to reach in and pluck one of the dolls out and bring her down into the palm of my hand and say, 'I know.'

I sighed.

Yup, Rose, I did know.

When Petra had left, Iggy said he fancied sitting by the

pool and asked if I was going to the post office. I nodded and said I was. As he disappeared into the Iggycave to change, I noticed he'd not pulled the curtain to as he started to strip. I averted my eyes and headed to my own cave. But not before looking back to see the peachiest of bare bums on display. I could feel myself blush, even though he didn't know I'd seen, then almost fell onto my bed.

And even though he'd had his back to me, I heard him call out, 'Hey! Stop fancying us, Pips!'

I laughed loudly to show I thought that was hilarious. And he echoed the laugh back to me.

I didn't.

I couldn't.

I didn't fancy Iggy, did I?

Oh God. Was this going to be 'a thing'?

(And I loathed that phrase 'a thing', so I really hoped not.)

We go on holiday together and end up sleeping together and falling for each other, like they did in the film of *One Day*? That's what happened, isn't it? Suddenly I was no longer Doris Day; I was Anne Hathaway. And Iggy was . . . was . . . whoever that British bloke was in that film. That, admittedly, quite fit bloke. And we'd cavort semi-clad in the infinity pool after one too many cocktails and then one day we'd be married.

OK, so that's not *quite* what happened in the movie, but . . . you know what I mean.

I didn't want that to happen. I didn't want to suddenly see Iggy in a new setting and suddenly have the hots for him. For God's sake, he only came up to my nipples.

Nipples. Why did I think nipples? Why didn't I say elbows? *Oh God, I fancy Iggy.*

Then I took a deep breath. No, I didn't. He was my friend. *But people sleep with their friends all the time.*

Not necessarily. Heterosexual people of the opposite sex are more than capable of remaining platonic.

I felt better now.

Just then Iggy came bounding into my room and threw himself onto the bed. He seemed to land cross-legged, like a genie in a Disney film. He was wearing a hotel towelling robe and matching white slippers. Underneath, he wore Bermuda-style shorts that had silhouettes of dogs on. Green silhouettes. Bless him, he matched the accessories.

He said, 'Just been reading the blurb in the book thing. These used to be caves what people lived in. Fishermen and farmers. Three hundred years ago. Imagine that, Pips.'

'Wow.' I agreed that was pretty impressive.

'Shame that farmers and fishermen couldn't afford to live here now, like.'

I nodded. And as if for the first time noticed how blue his eyes were.

Oh, Holly, *stop this*.

'You all right, Pips?'

I nodded.

'Worried about Rose and that?'

I nodded.

'Want me to come with you?'

I shook my head.

'Well, I'll keep me phone on. In case you need to call.'

I smiled and mouthed the words 'thank you'.

'Thanks for bringing me, Pips.'

I smiled again. Bless him. He did look adorable in the sunshine. When did runts of the litter get so cute?

'And if there's anything you need me to do, anything, you just holler. Yeah, Pips?'

'Thanks, Iggy.'

Oh, what, like make love to me? Make love to me like I've never been made love to before?

'I might have a cold shower before I head out.'

'OK, babe. I'm gonna head to the pool.'

He hopped off the bed. Just before exiting my cave, he looked back.

'Have you noticed anything weird about here?'

'No. What?'

'There's no tellies. Anywhere. We're cut off from the outside world.'

I chuckled. 'I imagine it's to encourage us to relax.'

'I'm not half gonna miss my Hole.' He winked, then walked out.

The hotel might have been a treat to walk into, but it was a bloody nightmare to walk out of. That hill was a steep climb, and the biscuit tin became sweaty in my hands. Although I'd put on one of my thinnest summer dresses and flip-flops, it clung to me like a wet shower curtain. And who did I see as I neared the top and clung to the wall to drag myself the last couple of steps out of the hotel?

Cillian.

Or whatever his name was. Mr Orange from the flight.

He didn't see me at first. He was walking past the entrance, still in his orange jumpsuit, dragging a matching orange travel trolley with him. He had earphones in and was humming a Gaga tune, shades on. I smiled, even though he didn't see me, and once he'd passed, I followed him and the sign – which wouldn't have looked out of place on a pantomime set – that pointed to Oia. If I just kept a good ten feet behind him all the way, he'd be none the wiser. And that's how it turned out. Until. He obviously wasn't paying much attention to where he was going, too busy staring, as was I, at the magnificent view of the volcanic lip to our left, when he took a tumble and fell flat on his face, emitting a very girly scream.

Instinctively I ran over to him and bleated, 'Oh God, are you all right?'

His sunglasses had flown off his head and he seemed more bothered about them than his own discomfort as I helped him to his feet.

I saw his sunglasses a few feet away and recovered them for him. When I turned to hand them to him, he looked surprised.

'Oh, it's you. The chef.'

'I'm not a chef,' I said softly. My tone was non-confrontational; it was appeasing. I was convinced it was probably the one Mo Mowlam had used at Stormont.

He smiled. 'No, you're just a picky bitch.'

I mock gasped.

'I can say that – I'm not at work now!' he shouted very quickly. And loudly. A passing stray Labrador even looked back to see what the fuss was.

I winked. He laughed. And we walked together.

His name was not Cillian; it was Clifford. Not far wrong, then! And, boy, could he talk. He burbled about seven words a second and I found it impossible to keep up.

'Icomehereallthetimewithwork.Iloveitsomuch.It'samazing. HaveyoutriedtherestaurantsinOia?They'reamazing.What,you've neverbeen?Oh,you'regonnalovetheplace!What'reyoudoinghere? Oh,you'revistingfamily.Oh,that'sbeyond.Itreallyisbeyond.I wishIhad familyhere thatwouldbeamazingonaplate!'

Well, you get the idea.

Though I did clock he used the phrase 'amazing on a plate'.

'Did you just say "amazing on a plate"?' I gasped, slightly rudely.

'I made it up.' He nodded proudly. 'Isn't "amazing on a plate" amazing on a plate?' and then he shrieked.

'Do you know where the post office is?'

'I know where you post letters. It's near where I'm staying. Come on. I'll show you.'

When we eventually arrived at the dusty village square, and what was allegedly the post office, we discovered it was shut.

Oh well. Man in the bakery it was, then.

Clifford/Cillian pointed me down a narrow lane, we bid each other goodbye, and off I went. The bakery and cafe smelt so sweet I thought I might OD on sugar just breathing in. Fans beat down on me, cooling both myself and the shelves upon shelves of cakes and pastries that looked like adornments in a doll's house. Oh well, that fitted my doll's-house imagining from earlier. The rotund man behind the counter smiled and bid me good afternoon in a very convincing English accent. Did I really look *that* English?

I showed him the piece of paper.

'I am looking for a woman called April Hunt.'

His eyes lit up, thrilled to be able to help, and he started ushering me back towards the door.

'I will show you where she live,' he said.

Out on the street, he pointed further down the road.

'Down there, towards the sun. You cannot miss. April live in the little house beside the church with the green windows.'

'That's her address?'

'Yes. Little house beside church with green windows.'

'Thank you very much.'

I walked towards the sun. It seemed to be nestling right at the end of this narrow lane, settling on the ground, about to

346

go to sleep. I'm not sure what I was expecting to find at the end of the lane – possibly a little house beside a church with green windows. And I did indeed find that. But . . . I suppose I didn't expect it to be so easy.

I saw the church. I passed.

I saw a green window. I stopped.

A quaint little white house with green shuttered windows looked out onto the ocean. I could have dived from it into the water. And outside the house, on a patio the size of a wheelbarrow, sat two women in deckchairs. One was an older woman in a massive beekeeper-style sun hat; the other, sporting a cap, was unmistakably her.

It took her a few seconds to register who I was. At first she smiled, the sort of lazy smile you probably give a stranger in a quiet corner of paradise like this. But then the smile relaxed. The face tightened. And she sat bolt upright in her chair.

'Hello, Rose,' I said, and I placed the biscuit tin on the patio wall.

I saw her head lower and she took her sunglasses off to look at it. She stared at it for a long time, her face slowly paling. As if in a series of time-lapse photographs.

'I think we need to talk.'

FIFTEEN

Part of me wanted her to tell me I was wrong. Part of me wanted her to say, 'No, you're mad. You have put two and two together and come up with sixty-five, you silly girl.' Another part wanted confirmation that I wasn't going completely bonkers. As I sat in this room that looked like it had been sculpted from icing on a Christmas cake, a fan whirring so that wisps of Rose's hair kept lapping at her face, the smell of fresh coffee steaming in in waves, I wanted her to tell me the contents of the biscuit tin were just a story, someone's twisted game of let's pretend. But I knew this wasn't going to happen. It would have been hard to put into words how I was feeling, though I did try.

I talked to myself.

How are you feeling?

Because, to be honest, I had never felt like this before in my life.

I tried, but I couldn't.

Sitting before me was Rose. A woman. A rather beautiful woman in her own way but a woman nonetheless. Composed, serene almost, even if her eyes were those of someone standing before a firing squad.

It couldn't be true.

But it was true.

How are you feeling?

I'm feeling I might be wrong. Because this person before me is definitely a woman.

I had been so measured, controlled, on the journey over, but now that I was sat in the little house beside the church with the green windows, anxiety simmered inside me. Soon it would give way to hysteria. The sort that makes you want to do something inappropriate. Like when Michael Jackson died. I had been working late for Sylvie and her wig mistress had called and gasped it to me quite dramatically.

'Jacko's toast.'

'Sorry?'

'Michael Jackson's *dead*.'

I'd left a silence and then couldn't help myself. I had burst out laughing. A real shriek of a laugh. It hadn't lasted long, but it had punctured the silence and caused the wig woman to gasp anew. I had then apologized. It wasn't that I found the death of a celebrity funny particularly; it was just so shocking, something I had never envisaged hearing, that it winded me. And that's how I'd responded. And that's how I felt now, like I could burst into fits of giggles at any second. I couldn't sit still. I played with my dress. I juddered in my seat. A fist of nerves seemed to be squeezing tight on my stomach, my heart, all my major organs, so firm that my eyes might pop out of my head. I had to calm myself. I had to control this. I had heard that deep breathing was good for panic attacks, so I took in big gasps of air and then blew them out. One after the other. And if I had looked frightened, then Rose looked ten times worse. She sat stock still, hands clasped in her lap, a nun in prayer. And all the time she stared at the tin I had placed on the coffee table. April had suggested we move inside to get some privacy. I had hurried in here. Rose had followed slowly, as if on autopilot. What was the privacy needed for? Because I was about to burst into hysterics?

How are you feeling?

Hysterical.

'Where did you get that?' Her voice was a quiet monotone. How did she remain so calm?

'It was under the floorboards. In the airing cupboard. In the flat.'

Rose's eyes widened, then zigzagged round the room. This was quite unnerving, but it looked like she was trying to piece memories together. Memories that might have led to it being put there.

'So how did you find it?'

'The dog knocked the floorboard out, I think. I saw it.'

'You've read it,' Rose added. And although it wasn't a question, I nodded anyway. 'How much is there?'

'It finishes when you take me to Myrtle Street. Then a letter from Helen Chance.'

She nodded.

'What was in Myrtle Street?'

She said something, but it was practically a murmur.

'Sorry?'

'Children's hospital.' She had to force that out. Her eyes were red. One tear fell from her right eye. She immediately wiped it with a now quivering hand.

'I'm so sorry.' She said it like someone was sucking the air from her stomach and it was affecting her speech. Like she was having lipo at the same time as being made to have an important conversation.

'Why did you tell me Darren was dead?'

'Well, he is in a way.'

'But you're Darren.'

'I'm Rose. A very long time ago I was Darren. But I didn't say he was dead. I said he was no more. And that's certainly the truth.'

I was right. She wasn't denying this. I had put two and two together and been correct. I felt the iron fist within start to release its grasp. My breathing became calmer.

'Why didn't you tell me the truth?'

From somewhere a shriek came. Loud. Abrupt. Arresting. It came from Rose. She clutched her stomach as if I'd punched her. I guess it was her Michael Jackson moment.

'Why?' I repeated.

'You don't know how lucky you were getting out of that flat, getting away from her. From all of us. Honest to God, Holly.'

'I know, but why?'

'How? How would I tell you? You come looking for your mother, your past, and you find that . . . that your father's now a woman? There's one for Jeremy Kyle, Jesus.' She was fiery, aggressive, but I would not let her put me in my place. I was angry too.

'You were scared of me rejecting you?'

'Of course I was scared of that, but I was trying to protect you too.'

'Do I seem like the sort of person who'd be that superficial?'

'Oh, you'd be surprised.'

'I know it can't be easy to talk about Darren, but Darren is part of me.'

No response. She seemed frozen. I leaned forward and tapped the tin with my finger.

'So, Frankie was a prostitute.'

'Frankie was a monster,' she barked. 'I was mostly trying

to protect you from that. So it worked out quite well she's doolally tap. You'd think she's a nice, mild-mannered old biddy. You'd think she's your mum. She can't say anything to hurt you. You'd just think maybe the time wasn't right, un-married mum, leave it at that. End of story.'

'But of course it didn't work out like that.'

'No.'

'And the truth was a bit . . . more complicated. Darker.'

'A bit? It was bloody midnight.'

And she shivered. Like a ghost had caressed her shoulder and she had to shake it off.

'What was his name?'

'Who?'

'The man who abused you.'

The eyes flickered. I wondered if she was wearing false eye-lashes. They were certainly lustrous enough.

'You don't use his name in there.'

'It's not me; it was Darren. And it was a lifetime ago.'

'Yes, I know. My lifetime.'

She stood up. She went and stood in front of the fan in the corner, pushing her head down in front of it. Well, if she had been wearing a wig, it would certainly have blown off now. It didn't.

'The man you killed.'

Where was my tenacity coming from? Was I mimicking courtroom dramas I'd seen? Was I the prosecution?

I put it to you, Rose Kirkwood, that on the night of blah, blah, blah you did take a heavy pan, possibly a Le Creuset, though I'm not sure prostitutes in Liverpool had them in the early 1980s, and you did . . .

She didn't reply. She just stood in front of the fan for what seemed like forever.

'Rose, I'm sorry. I want you to know I don't judge you for what you did. You acted in self-defence.'

She chuckled softly. She did – she actually did a sort of laughing noise. Now that was appropriate.

'I also want you to know I won't tell anyone. How can I? I don't even know his name.'

She turned and looked at me.

'What does it matter to you what his name was? He's got nothing to do with you. With your paternity.'

'Because you're my dad and you killed him.'

'Don't call me that.'

'Well, what am I supposed to call you? You're not my mother. You didn't give birth to me. Someone called Samantha did. Where is she?'

'I don't know. And that's the truth. We lost touch.'

I had guessed as much.

'I never thought I'd see you again. You were the only thing that linked us.'

She returned to sit opposite me.

'She didn't seem that bothered about giving me up.'

'I think she only had you because she was too terrified that her parents would find out she'd had an abortion.'

OK, that hurt.

'Sorry.'

'No. The truth is good, no matter how painful.'

'And of course Frankie gave her money. I thought she was a bit greedy about all that if I'm honest.'

'And her parents didn't twig she was pregnant?'

Rose shook her head. I knew I could believe that, even if it was odd. The number of people who'd thought I was pregnant over the years when I wasn't, surely it had to work the other way round as well.

'What happened when you took me to Myrtle Street?'

Questions, questions, questions. When of course what I really wanted to ask was, 'How come you're a bloody *woman*?'

But I felt that was impolite. And Ted and Jean had brought me up to be anything but that. And rightly so.

I also thought that that would come out naturally. At some point. I could wait.

'I took you into their casualty department. I handed you over to a nurse. I gave them your name and address. And told them exactly what had happened. Then I left you there. The next time I saw you was this year. When you walked into the salon.'

'What was wrong with me?'

'I've no idea, but I imagine a broken arm. It was a really odd shape.'

'Then what happened?'

'The police paid a visit. And social services. Frankie denied it. It went to court. Social services kept you. Frankie didn't put up a fight.'

'Well, I'd served my purpose.'

'Exactly. They took her to court. She didn't do any time. All probation. She was fine. But she never forgave me. It was after the police paid their first visit that my diary went missing. I knew what was in it. I knew why she wanted it.'

'Why?'

'So she had something over me.'

'The murder?'

'She used it to blackmail me into sticking up for her buying you off Sammi. And then she used it to punish me with.'

'But she didn't. She left it under the floorboards. All these years.'

Silence. Outside I could hear voices. April chatting to

someone, a passer-by probably. Being so close to the street, it was inevitable, I guessed. Maybe they were discussing the view. Maybe it was someone asking directions.

'Didn't she?'

Rose slowly shook her head. 'For Frankie, revenge was a dish best served lukewarm.'

'I don't understand.'

Suddenly she said, 'Gary. Gary Roberts.'

I didn't know what she meant.

'Such a normal name. For one so unusual.'

Then she looked at me.

'That was his name?'

She nodded.

'Thank you.'

'I thought Frankie was relieved you'd gone somewhere else. One less brat to feed and clothe. Not that she did much of either. And she was. But I'd crossed a line. I'd got her into trouble and she needed payback.'

'What did she do?'

'A month or so later I was arrested.'

I knew what was coming. My heart went icy. It was like my blood froze.

'For . . .'

'For the murder of Gary Roberts. Anonymous tip-off to the police. I was nicked and Woody was nicked. She knew exactly where they'd buried him. We didn't stand a chance.'

'You went to . . . prison?'

She nodded. 'I mean, there wasn't much evidence. I think the coppers thought it was a wind-up at first, but I sang like a fucking canary once they questioned me. Maybe Frankie wasn't expecting that. Maybe she just wanted to put the frighteners on me. I don't know. But I felt so guilty about what I'd done. It didn't take long for it to all come out.'

'But it was self-defence.'

'I still killed him. Manslaughter. My word against a dead man's. A dead policeman's no less. The judge admitted he'd probably fiddled with me. He actually used that word, "fiddled". I don't call habitual rape and abuse "fiddling". But the prosecution made it sound like I was so angry with him, I planned his murder, et cetera.'

Et cetera. It seemed so quaint that she actually said it, even if what she was describing was far from it.

'How long did you get?'

'Six years. Did three.'

'My God, that's terrible, Rose. And . . . presumably you were in a male prison.'

'I was still presenting as male, yes.'

I looked at her, really looked at her, like I was seeing her for the first time. I wanted to immediately see clues I'd not seen before. Big hands, Adam's apple, dodgy wig. I didn't. The woman I had first met in Liverpool had been so heavily made up, disguised, but here in a sunny country she was make-up free, clear-skinned, fresh-faced. She had a natural beauty. I just couldn't see her ever having been a Darren.

'What happened to Woody?'

'Not guilty. No evidence.'

'Robert?' I said, opening up the floor for more discussion.

As soon as I said his name, her body language changed. It was the moment in a Disney film where the cartoon came to life, where black-and-white Kansas turned to technicolor Oz. She talked like a proud parent of how he was now living in America, happily married with three children, doing some job in computers and graphic design that she didn't completely understand. Her joy when talking was that of a proud mother's and I realized with a jolt that I wanted her to talk like this about me. She said things had been fractured for a while, as he hadn't understood Rose's decision to become a woman. He thought that prison had sent her mad, and he had taken a long time to come to terms with what happened to Gary Roberts and how that had been kept from him. But things were getting better year by year, though she admittedly hadn't seen him for five years. She said she would forward me photographs of him once we were back home.

'Though you've already seen him.' She pointed out.

I had? 'Oh. The boy in the photo? By your bedside?'

She nodded.

This promise of future contact made me at once thrilled but also irritated. Did she not have to prove she was worthy of being in my life?

Why was I being so hard on her?

I tried not to think about it. The prosecution returned.

'How did you become Rose?'

She swallowed. 'It's quite hard to talk about.'

Suddenly April breezed through the room. 'I'm sure it's hard for Holly too, Rose. How about I fix you both some drinks? Did you arrive today, Holly? You must be exhausted.'

'I did, yes. I'm OK, but I'd love some water.'

'Coming right up. Rose?'

'Water.'

And with that April breezed out of the room as quickly as she had breezed in, her delicate snow-leopard-print kaftan billowing behind her.

Darren had been right. She was incredibly glamorous. One of those old broads who must have spent hours in the hairdresser's each day having their chignon perfected. I returned my gaze to Rose.

She took a while to start speaking, but once she started, it was like she couldn't stop. Her words were slow and faltering to begin with, but as her confidence grew, and her throat, dry with nerves, was lubricated by April's jug of lemon water, she became more fluent. This was a language she knew, but one she possibly didn't articulate that often out loud.

Prison was the making of me, in many ways. I suddenly had a routine. I was put in a wing for guys who were vulnerable because I obviously seemed so bloody anxious and like I couldn't look after myself. I got quite a bit of respect in there, though – word got round that I'd killed a copper. Routine suited me, and the isolation gave me time to think about what I wanted for the rest of my life. And I knew. I knew I wanted to be Rose. I knew that as Darren I would continue to make poor choices and be a victim because I didn't feel right. The only times I felt right was when I was Lucy. I told the prison chaplain. He'd taken me under his wing. Looking back, I think he fancied me a bit, but probably didn't even realize it himself. So I worked up the courage to tell him. And his response was I was possessed. I wasn't bothered. I thought, Well, I'm happy to be possessed with this strong desire to do something, to be someone, because it felt like the first positive thing that had ever been in my life.

I worked in prison. I worked in the kitchens. I was good, learned to cook. And then they trained me to cut hair in the barber's there. And I found I liked it. Though I would've been more interested in styling women, of course. When my date for release came, I was excited. I knew what was gonna happen next. But I was scared. I knew I wouldn't be seeing Frankie or Rob for some time. And I'd just have to live with that. I had to be prepared for their rejection. God knows why I cared so much about Frankie. She was hardly Mother Earth.

Anyway, I was lucky. When I came out of prison, I went to stay with April. I dread to think where I'd be now if I'd never met her. But these things happen for a reason. And she knew exactly what I had to do. I went to a gender clinic in London. They said I had to pass for a woman for a year before they'd consider surgery. That year was the toughest of my life. Harder than prison, harder than living with Frankie. I hated being seen in public. I was like a vampire – only going out after dark, afraid what people might say when they saw me. When you transition, well, there aren't words to describe it really. I felt ugly. I felt like a freak. Even though I was slender and slight and had quite feminine features, people knew. It only took one bit of name-calling or a laugh from someone on the other side of the street and I'd go to pieces. I'd stay in drinking vodka and pretending it wasn't really happening. I just lay on my bed, counting the days till my surgery. The only person I really had was April.

These days not everyone wants the full surgery, but I did. It was the only way I could properly be Lucy – that's what I was calling myself back then, till one drunken night April said Lucy wasn't pretty enough for me and I was more of an English rose. It kind of stuck. I was impatient. I couldn't wait the year, so April paid for hormone tablets off the black market to kick-start the transition. They were useless, if I'm honest, so I had a boob job in France. Couldn't speak a word of the language. She's been my guardian angel. I had the final operation in 1986 on the NHS in London. Seven hours it lasted. When I woke up, I felt every bad thing that had ever happened to me, or that I'd done, had been washed away. I'd not exactly felt trapped in Darren's body, but I had felt trapped in Darren's head. And now suddenly I was free. I was a woman. I was Rose.

I'd been to visit Frankie and Rob when I was transitioning. It was a bit mad. I didn't warn them what I was doing, just invited them for dinner at this place on Lark Lane that Frankie liked. I turned up late dressed as Rose. They both got the shock of their lives. Rob walked out. Frankie took the free meal, called me a freak, then did what Rob had done. Over the years Rob has got used to it. Frankie was a tougher nut to crack. April thought I was mad even wanting to go there again, but one day, out of the blue, I got a phone call from Rob. Not long after he'd moved to the States. Frankie was in hospital and had given his name as next of kin. She'd been beaten up quite badly. I was staying with April in London. I went back to Liverpool and got her out of hospital and took her home. She didn't like it, but she put up with it and together we established some sort of truce. I visited her every year or so after that. Eventually I moved back up North and . . .

And what? She had run out of words.

'The rest is history?' I offered.

'Everyone wants to know if you've had genital surgery. It's the first thing they ask. Have you had the chop? I find it really rude. Like asking a gay man if he takes it up the arse.'

I was quite shocked at her turn of phrase.

'Do you think you wanted to be Rose so you could forget your past and run away from all the bad things that had happened to you?'

She considered this. 'I don't think so. Though it was an added bonus.'

'But reading your diary, you hardly mention it. I thought transgender people knew from an early age they wanted to be the opposite sex . . . or whatever you're meant to say.'

She smiled. She was the teacher and I was the dunce of the class.

'You seriously think I'd write it all down? What if someone had found the diary and read it? What then?'

I shrugged.

'I talked about Lucy, I think.'

I nodded. 'In the third person.'

'So she was there,' Rose pointed out. 'To be honest, I always knew, but it's that that I ran away from.'

'As opposed to later, me saying you might've run away from Darren and your past?'

She nodded. 'I knew it. In my head. It was my only truth. I knew that so much that was going on around me was wrong. I knew there was something about me that was wrong. But I knew when I played with Frankie's dresses or make-up or played with my hair or . . .'

'Being a woman's about more than that, surely,' I suggested.

'Of course,' she concurred. 'But they seemed to me like little bits of a jigsaw, a passport that would move me somewhere else. To who I wanted to be. Sorry, I mustn't be making much sense. It must be a lot for you to take in.'

I shrugged.

'I always knew I wasn't a boy. No matter what the mirror told me.'

'One must always leave something out of one's diary. Who cares about the truth?' I said in a very posh voice, as if I was quoting Oscar Wilde.

'Who said that?' She sounded keen.

I winced. 'Me, sorry.'

She nodded.

'Actually, it was incredibly brave of you to even write about Lucy, I suppose.'

'I've never felt brave, Holly.'

'I think you're incredibly brave.'

'I was very lucky to meet April. She's been my rock.'

Rose, it would appear, couldn't take praise. I blamed Frankie.

'Well, I do.'

'Irish says I'm brave. I don't see it myself. I'm more confident now, but that's because I'm Rose and not Darren, and it's like everything's slipped into place.'

I realized something. She hadn't said how she had met Irish Alan.

And whatever became of Woody?

As I processed both those thoughts, so close in succession, it hit me.

They were the same person.

Rose's surname was Kirkwood. Alan's was too. Kirkwood. Woody.

Oh, Alan knew her secret all right. He'd been there before it even happened.

He'd been a hardman in the 1980s, but hadn't Rose said he'd had a stroke? Maybe that had softened him? Oh yes. It all made sense now.

'Woody.'

'What about him?'

'Is he Irish Alan?'

Again her eyes widened. I had, I had found her out! But then she gave such a laugh. It was the first time today she had seemed even the slightest bit relaxed.

'No. Woody liked to think he was one of the Krays. Irish is more like one of the Krankies.'

And she laughed. And I laughed. I thought, Father and daughter laughing together. But that didn't feel quite right, of course. As Father was wearing a frock. And had an NHS vagina.

She went on to tell me how she had met Alan when she cut his hair. He fell for her quickly, but she was worried if she told him the truth about her past, he'd reject her, so she batted him away. But he was persistent and eventually she was honest and he'd said it didn't matter at all. I liked Irish Alan even more now. And I was glad I had got the Woody connection wrong. She didn't know where Margy was anymore, or Woody. She said she wouldn't be surprised if Margy had died of AIDS. She said lots of the girls did in the late 1980s and early 1990s. Frankie always felt she was lucky she'd not contracted HIV.

Once Rose'd moved in with Alan on the Wirral, she saw more of an accepting Frankie. And then she had started to lose her memory.

And then really the rest was history.

'As I read the diary, I felt myself growing so close to Darren. I really hoped he was my brother. I really wanted to meet him.'

She looked genuinely touched. 'Well,' she said, 'we're not that different deep down.'

Just then April returned. She stood in the doorway, majestic with the sun behind her.

'Holly, the sun's about to set. If you've not seen it yet, you must.'

I looked back to Rose. She nodded and stood.

We went and sat together on the terrace – that's what April called it, not the patio – and watched an amazing piece of theatre. Every building and wall I could see was covered in people. Like sparrows on a telephone wire they perched to watch the ball of flames fall slowly into the sea. Three women. Three glasses of wine. Three different stories. As the sun neared the waterline, the people on the walls and roofs started applauding. I put my glass down and joined in. I hoped Iggy was watching it too.

April looked to me. 'Isn't it incredible?'

I nodded and looked to Rose. She was looking at me curiously. 'What?' I asked.

'I don't repulse you.'

Again, I couldn't tell whether it was a statement or a question.

I answered it anyway, with a shake of the head, then turned to watch the sunset.

'I'm not quite sure why we're drinking wine,' sighed April. 'I think this calls for something with bubbles.'

'Ooh, pint of cider?' I said with a wink to show I was joking. Both women laughed.

'We'll have to watch you!' April poked me as she returned indoors.

I saw Rose staring at me. 'She's nice, isn't she?' She sounded so desperate for my approval.

I nodded. Then turned to face the sea.

I stayed on the terrace for an hour or so longer. When we said our goodbyes and promises to see each other the following day, we hugged and kissed and the tension between me and Rose had completely vanished. She was less of the ice queen now, and when she hugged me, it was as if it was the first time she'd had permission to do so, as if she never wanted it to end.

As I walked the dusty track back to the hotel, I reflected on the past few hours. The sky was a velvet navy now, glittered with stars. Storm candles flickered outside houses; lanterns hung in tavernas. I heard laughter, music. I heard life.

I turned and looked down to the slick black sea. I had often wondered what I might have inherited from Ted and Jean. Whatever you think of nature and nurture, you can't spend that many years with people and not be influenced by them. A certain stoicism perhaps, an appreciation of manners.

I wasn't sure what I had inherited from Rose, but I knew what I hoped I had. Her courage. Although she had told me so much of her story, I still couldn't honestly begin to imagine how difficult it must have been to go through what she'd been through.

When I arrived back at the hotel and approached our cave, I heard giggles coming from inside. Two people. Two men. Maybe I had got the wrong room?

I checked. No, I hadn't.

I peered inside. The curtain to Iggy's bedroom was drawn open. He was naked. So was another man. They were kissing, then play-slapping each other, giggling. They didn't see me. Iggy's body was so white it was almost blue. The other body was as orange as the fruit. And I'd have recognized those eyebrows anywhere.

Iggy and Clifford/Cillian?

How did that happen?

I decided to go and sit in the bar for an hour. I ordered a gin and tonic. I sipped at it daintily as I observed the stars reflecting in the pool.

People really were full of surprises.

EPILOGUE

London, a year later

I knew what I'd order before I got here: hamburger, a Filet-O-Fish, medium fries and a strawberry milkshake. I know I'll never finish it all, but I don't care. It's a special day – I can have what I like. Rose has a quarter-pounder with cheese, small fries and an orange juice. McDonald's seems to be in a different spot in Leicester Square now, though that could just be my memory playing tricks. I bagsy us a table in the window so I can watch the world going by. Out there, the sky is turquoise and the buildings the colour of gravy; in here is all mahogany wood and Day-Glo art deco lights as we tuck into our fast food.

Rose smiles at something outside. 'State o' that,' she says, and shakes her head.

I turn to see a man dressed in tin foil with his face painted silver pretending to be a statue, some bored Chinese tourists half-heartedly taking photos of him.

'Oh,' says Rose, dabbing her mouth with a napkin, 'before I forget.' She pulls a gift-wrapped parcel from her bag and hands it to me. 'Happy birthday, Holly.'

'Oh, thanks, Rose.'

The paper is white with pink polka dots, very girly, and matches perfectly what Rose is wearing today: a long white PVC rain mac, a pink flower in her hair and pink footless tights. She even has some pink strands of hair.

'Dip-dyed,' she'd explained earlier. 'I could do yours if you like.'

We'll see.

I do what I always do when I receive a present that clearly isn't a jigsaw. I shake it and say, 'Is it a jigsaw?'

She smiles and shakes her head, then carries on eating her burger. In the past year Rose has bought me some awful presents: a ceramic pair of praying hands (even though she isn't religious), a painting of a flamenco dancer and a snow globe with the Liverpool skyline in it.

Actually, I quite like the Liverpool-skyline snow globe. I can shake it from the discomfort of my tiny studio flat in Nunhead and imagine I am back there. I now know where Nunhead is. Which is miles away from anywhere decent.

I rip open the paper and see that Rose has bought me a framed piece of cross stitch. Written in thread in cursive writing, it says:

Daughters hold our hands for a little while, but our hearts forever.

It is completely hideous.

'Oh, Rose, that's gorgeous!'

'Thought you'd like it, hon.'

'Yeah, I do.'

There is no way I am displaying it anywhere.

'Thought it'd go lovely in your little bathroom. Over the loo.'

'Great idea. Yes.'

'Happy birthday.'

'Thanks, Rose.'

I suddenly imagine phoning Rose in the future and saying, 'Rose, hi. It's me. All good here except . . . well, you'll never guess what. My whole flat caught fire. Everything's fine, but what I have lost are the gorgeous embroidered "shit things people say about daughters" picture, the praying hands and Una Paloma Blanca and her castanets. Soz, hon.'

These days I find Rose much more easy-going than when we first met. She reminds me more of thoughtful, caring Darren than the prickly ice queen I first encountered up North. But I can now see that back then she'd been carrying the weight of the world around on her shoulders once I'd reared my ugly head, and was caught in a cat's cradle of lies, desperately trying to create a history for me that sounded presentable, acceptable, nice.

Rose thinks there's a lot to be said for nice.

I don't see lots of her. We speak every week on the phone, and I go and stay in Derwentwater Road with her and Alan once a month or so. Or, like today, she'll come down and stay in a budget hotel and we'll hang out. On my first trip back to the Wirral, I was brave enough to ask why there was a padlock on one of the spare-bedroom doors. Turned out it was the box room in which they kept all their computer and office-type equipment. I was mortified.

'Hey, I seen your friend on telly again the other day.'

'Jax?'

'Yeah. She's on quite a bit now. On *This Morning*. They get her on to do debates. She's dead outspoken. Twitter goes mental about her.'

Rose recently set up a Twitter account when I showed her how it worked. She has thus far written tweets like:

New shoes bit sore lol.
Going london see R Holly. (not the singer lol)

And:

Anyone recomend a good space movie?

As Irish Alan said, she's no Caitlin Moran.

I have a new job. It's only temporary, but I am quite enjoying it. I am working part-time in Frank and Esther's deli round the back of Tooley Street, and as well as serving in the cafe, I'm helping them make sense of their books since their bookkeeper died earlier this year. All the while I continue to weigh up my options to see what I want to do next. Sylvie has been adamant that I will never get a reference from her in the future. In fact her final email to me included the following:

If you dare to offend me by telling future employers to ask for a reference, remember this: I will warn them that you physically attacked me and neglected my dog. And I will send them a photo of the sofa.

Rose's phone makes a loud whistling noise. She checks it. 'It's Irish. He'll meet us at the theatre.'
'Where is he again?'
'Seeing a cousin in Kilburn.'
'Oh yes.'
I knew I would go and see *Miss Saigon* again the minute I heard it was heading back to the West End. The fact that

Rose and Alan were up for it as well was an added bonus. My weekend is going to be very special indeed.

When we finish our food, we walk through the crowds towards Old Compton Street. Rose links my arm and walks proudly at my side. She gets some funny looks, but what do you expect when you're head to toe in pink and white? Rose informs me that she has been to the theatre twice: once to see the ballet, another time to see *Les Mis*. She informs me that she preferred *Les Mis* because 'It was obvious they'd put a lot of work into it.'

I tell her about going to see Miss Saigon as a child, and how Mum told me about the adoption that day. I tell her about Mum making us leave at the interval because there were prostitutes in it. We both stop at that point, look at each other, clasp each other's arms and laugh our heads off.

Rose Kirkwood, it has to be said, has a really dirty laugh.

Alan's waiting for us at the theatre. Bless him, he's got his sheepskin coat on and a flat cap. He smells of Paco Rabanne and cigar smoke. He's already bought three souvenir programmes.

Afterwards we are heading to dinner with Jude. We're not seeing each other, but we do see each other, if that makes sense. He's split with Henny (I still hate that name) and is dying to get back with me, but I am remaining an international woman of mystery and not making my mind up yet. It's been too much of an emotional year. I'm certainly not going to rush back into anything with him. He's not met Rose and Alan before, but he has of course heard all about them.

We take our seats. I sit wedged between them, like I'm eight years old. And sometimes that's what it feels like, being with them. They spoil me and bicker over me. I'm still a novelty to them; they're still only just getting to know me. They both offer me a sweet at the same time and I take one of each at the same time and for some reason this makes them howl with laughter. So loudly the woman in front turns and scowls at Rose.

Rose glares at the woman and rasps, 'What's the matter, love? Have I got a welly on my head?'

We tried to trace Samantha, but as yet have drawn a blank. I'm not so bothered about meeting her now, because Rose feels like . . . well . . . like a mum and dad all rolled into one. There's no word in the English language, as far as I'm aware, that means 'mum and dad all rolled into one'.

'There is,' Alan always says. 'Rose.'

More laughter.

Rob is coming back later this year to show off his new family. He's sent me a couple of polite emails. He seems very bright, and incredibly handsome. He's forty-five now.

'And not a grey hair on his head, the bastard!' Rose always says proudly.

Sometimes when we're out, people – staff in restaurants, say – might refer to Rose as my mum. It was a bit embarrassing the first time, but I think she quite likes it. Maybe I'll be comfortable saying that one day; it's just a word, a name. For now when people ask who she is, I just say, 'My friend Rose.' She seems happy with that too.

A text comes through on my phone. I check the caller ID. It's from Iggy. I open it quickly. It says:

Happy birthday, Pips. Love I and C x

I smile. An usherette is on me like a ton of bricks from the aisle.

''Scuse me? Phones off, please?' she shouts.

'Ooh, which charm school did she go to?' Rose says out of the corner of her mouth.

I smile.

'And did you see the size of her arse?'

I look back to clock it, but just then the lights start to dim and the sound of a helicopter fills the theatre. The orchestra strikes up. The lights dim to nothing.

I feel Rose slipping her arm through mine. We hunker down in our seats.

Another story is about to begin.

extracts reading groups
books new
competitions books
discounts extracts extracts
extracts discounts
competitions extracts events
books new reading groups events
events books reading groups
extracts extracts
new titles reading groups
interviews events
events extracts extracts books
discounts events new
new books events interviews
events new new
discounts extracts discounts interviews books extracts

www.panmacmillan.com

extracts events reading groups
competitions books extracts new books